SUBTLE
FREQUENCY

SUBTLE FREQUENCY

KATHY MORGAN WHYTE

Editors: Deborah Froese, Austin Hatch, Kim O. Morgan
Cover and Interior Design: Emma Elzinga

Indigo River Publishing
3 West Garden Street, Ste. 718
Pensacola, FL 32502

www.indigoriverpublishing.com

Ordering Information:

Quantity Sales: Special discounts are available on quantity purchases by corporations, associations, and others. For details, contact the publisher at the address above.

Orders by US trade bookstores and wholesalers: Please contact the publisher at the address above.

Printed in the United States of America

Library of Congress Control Number: 2025916248
ISBN: 978-1-964686-73-8 (paperback) 978-1-964686-74-5 (ebook)

First Edition

With Indigo River Publishing, you can always expect great books, strong voices, and meaningful messages. Most importantly, you'll always find . . .
words worth reading.

To my remarkable daughter,
whose creative spirit is an inspiration.

ONE

JUST LIKE THAT

"No offense, but—" Click. The phone went dead.

Drake was mid-sentence. "Wait! Don't hang up!" But it was too late.

Through clenched teeth, he mumbled, "Man, if I ever get my hands on him!"

The irritating call focused his mind fully on the investigation again as he rolled into his favorite morning spot. He needed a new clue in the worst way—something, anything—to kickstart the case.

Let today be the day!

By the time the sporty, blue hatchback in front of him pulled away, he was back in the moment. And the doctor's warning about too much caffeine flashed, reminding him that another cup probably wasn't a good idea.

"One black and one with cream," he boldly announced, through Brew Town's aromatic, drive-through window. It's not that he didn't respect the advice, but coffee was one of his guilty pleasures and he would be standing his ground on the matter.

While searching for cash, he heard a flirty musical voice from the other side say, "Morning, Drake."

"Oh, hey, Carri," he said, looking up. "Glad you're back."

"Can't stay away from my favorite detective too long," she teased.

"See, this is why I keep coming here," Drake said in a rugged, morning voice.

Leaning through the driver's side window, he dropped an extra big tip in the jar.

The combination of manly character lines and scruffy stubble-beard was clear evidence that Drake was quite a bit older, but the obvious details didn't seem to dampen her coy playfulness one bit. On the contrary, a beaming smile suggested she didn't mind at all.

Drake gave her a quick wink and drove off.

Within seconds, his expression began to darken as thoughts of the months-old investigation came rushing back. A case involving the kidnapping and potential murder of a child was always emotionally-crushing, and one he wanted to solve quickly, but that kind of luck had not been in the cards this time.

Annoyingly, others at the precinct had already written it off as a cold case, and every one of their icy references stung a little more each time. But Drake had become a master at feigning indifference and letting negativity fuel his determination.

Another cold case? Not on my watch!

The years had challenged him with tough cases and introduced him to the unsettling darkness in human nature, but it also sharpened his skills. Just having to withstand brutal hours and a steady diet of criminality, along with the vile details, had been more than enough to fine-tune his abilities and instincts. And as a natural consequence of the job, he had become the most formidable version of himself.

Being at the top of his game, with a celebrated track record, was a true testament to his success, but even he had suffered a couple of unsolved cases. It was the fate of every detective—and usually just due to lack of evidence—but it still ticked him off.

He thought about how, just recently, he and some of the gang from the precinct had been shooting the breeze at Murph's, the local hangout, when that precise topic reared its annoying head.

Shay Murphy, the longtime owner, kept the lights low and the music faint, so the atmosphere was perfect for captivating conversation. Over the finest stacked subs and cold beer for miles, Drake and the others grumbled about how difficult it was to stomach an offender's guilt when they lacked evidence to charge.

Just having to endure smug looks on guilty faces as suspects walked free was too much, and all the goading most detectives needed to keep after them. Luckily, if they waited patiently, a subsequent arrest would sometimes provide damning evidence. And years of experience had taught them that they probably wouldn't have to wait too long.

Many of the offenders had already secured a place for their infamous names in the archives, which overflowed with files from every imaginable transgression and crime. The records also contained the identities of countless innocent people, who would surely never have imagined their names being memorialized in a police file.

Each case was one of a kind, describing a detailed and sometimes unspeakable event. Drake's own life had been quite remarkable by association but, in his line of work, there was always the possibility that he hadn't seen anything yet.

Fortunately, he was more prepared than most, with an innovative way of using evidence to create a mental storyboard and then bring it to life.

When time permitted, he put his technique to the test by eagerly pulling cold case files, trying to dig up some lead that had been overlooked. Almost without fail, he hit on something new. Although most leads didn't go anywhere, the ones that did gave him the greatest satisfaction. Unexpected justice was always especially sweet.

Those successes led to delivering long-awaited positive news to families and victims who had lost all hope. The opportunity to celebrate their *coup de grâce* was one of the reasons he got up in the morning.

Now, if he could just give the Sweets some good news. Watching another set of grieving parents struggle to hang on in the midst of such a nightmare was almost more than he could bear.

When a child was missing or presumed dead, a case took its toll, and the Sweet case was no exception, stubbornly denying him answers and proper sleep.

He'd been pushing hard, logging extra hours, constantly combing through evidence, and even tolerating a couple of rude, untraceable calls . . . with nothing new to offer. And with each passing day, the chance of finding the six-year-old grew slimmer.

The reality of the stats might be working against him, but he'd made a promise to himself. Even if it took his last breath, he would find Angela.

When Drake came to a stop near the exit of the addictive morning spot, he was enveloped by a crisp current of air that wafted in through the partially open window.

He took a deep breath and focused only on the coolness of the soothing, gentle breeze. Even though there would be a measure of anxiety in the workload ahead, the vibrant, picture-perfect day and a cup of his favorite brew in hand were reason enough to let go of the stress, if only for a moment.

The smell of the fresh, hot coffee drew his attention.

Simply inhaling the aroma made him feel more awake. The prized potion was already stimulating his brain cells and beginning to work its morning magic.

He finally savored the first sip and made a quick right turn onto the familiar street.

To his left, he could see the owner of the quaint breakfast café reversing the 'closed' sign and the neighboring florist filling outside baskets with fresh, cut flowers. They waved and started toward each other as he pulled up to the traffic light. The sixty-second wait gave him time to witness even more of the new day, parading its ebb and flow.

Within minutes, he swung his Jeep into parking space number seventeen, his reserved spot. Time and effort invested in a long career did have a few perks, and he appreciated that one. When the spot was first issued to him, he was struck by how the number had been sort of lucky and seemed to, strangely, follow him throughout life. It was even prominently displayed on his treasured high school football jersey.

When Drake entered the station, the first thing he looked for was the shabby, generic clock on the wall. He couldn't resist a passing sneer because it was way too small for the room, and he, like everyone else, had to squint to check the time.

At eleven past seven, the office was still somewhat quiet and orderly, with desks and computers lined up like dominos before the big chain reaction. Not only was the place softly lit, but it also seemed noticeably refreshed, a pleasant indication that the new cleaning crew was doing a better job than the last.

Within the hour, however, things would be different. Every desktop and workstation would be covered in paperwork, files, food, and other random items strewn about. And by mid-morning a familiar productive hum of activity would simply be background music for justice coming down.

Drake spotted his best friend and partner on the case, Detective John Baxter, filling the break room doorway with his prominence. John's towering height and brawny physique were physical manifestations of his intimidating side, which had effectively put the fear of God into the worst criminal.

He had a warrior's edginess that could surface when he'd been pushed too far. Without a doubt, offenders who were on the wrong side of the law and terrorizing people did not want their impending rendezvous to be with John.

And Drake Harrison did not want anyone but him for a partner.

While Drake was both impressed and amused by John's fierce side, he favored the other, the one where he exuded pure goodness and laughed easily.

"Morning, man," Drake said.

"Hey, what's up?" John thundered.

Drake grinned as he strode in John's direction. "Just the way you like it," he said, handing over the extra Brew Town coffee.

"Thanks. I was just about to settle for whatever's in here today," John said.

"Saved you again," Drake teased. "You know, I have been feeling like something's about to break."

"Hope you're right," John said. "Got anything new? Any of those burner calls again?"

"Well, you're not going to believe it, but I just had one on the way in," Drake replied. "Same rude signoff. Man, I wish we could trace those. If he hangs up on me like that again, I swear I want an airhorn ready."

"What is it he says again?" John asked. "No offense?"

"Yeah, 'no offense, but—' and then click! He hangs up on me. Every time!"

John shook his head. "Jerk."

"Yeah," Drake said. "He's just another one that likes to interfere, probably thinks he's smarter than we are."

"Yeah," John agreed. "But he is paying attention to the case."

"I know, I'm on it," Drake said. "To be safe, we'll keep things on the down-low, out of the press as much as possible. That whole thing is a double-edged sword. We need the media, yet it invites the crazies.

Other than that, I feel like we've gone over everything ad nauseam."

"Yeah, me too," John said, pulling up a chair. "But we do have a couple of call-in leads on the Sweet case. I put them on your desk with that other evidence."

"Okay. Thanks." Drake balanced on the edge of the closest table. "Man, you know this case as well as I do. What are we missing?"

"We need a sighting or a vehicle in the worst way," offered John. "Either would give us a jump start."

Drake nodded. "Yeah. All Trace was left with was a few unidentifiable fibers. You know what we could really use is a little of that Baxter magic, like when you took down the mayor's son-in-law."

John's face lit up, but he shrugged off the compliment. "Hey, I haven't had a chance to tell you yet, but I talked to that sketchy guy again. The one who worked for Chad Sweet. Looks like he's clean for this one, but I'm telling you, Man, that guy's done something. He just rubs me the wrong way!"

Drake's impish grin surfaced and made them both start laughing.

The senior office assistant, Mary, zipped past the doorway just in time to witness their moment of levity. "Morning, guys," she said. "I sure hope my day starts off as well as yours."

"Morning, Mary," came the reply.

John watched her for seconds longer than Drake before springing to his feet. "Hey, can we finish this on my way out?" he asked.

"Yeah, sure," Drake said. "Just one last thing, though. Did you get a chance to look over that Milton County case?"

"Oh, yeah, it doesn't completely line up to me. The victim is about the same age, and the perp was bold but not out of touch like our guy; it's a different psychology. But you should probably still take a look."

"Yeah, I will. We just need that break," Drake said. "That, and more hours in the day."

He grabbed a couple of letters from his inbox as they made their way through the maze of the headquarters.

"I have some free time this afternoon if you need me," offered John. "You know, I want to take this guy down as much as you do. I have a feeling he's a real piece of work."

"Aren't they all?" Drake smirked.

"Good point," John said, stepping through the exit. "Hey, are her parents doing any better?"

"No, not really," Drake said. "Fighting to hang on."

John shook his head. "Hate that part of the job."

"I know, it sucks," Drake agreed. "I'm going to swing by and check on them again soon."

"That's good, man," John said. "Give them my best and just let me know about this afternoon."

"I will," Drake replied. "Where you headed?"

"I'm going to check on a few things I asked the lab to reprocess."

"Anything I need to know about?" Drake asked.

"Only if we get lucky," mused John. "Oh, there's a message from Dr. Brill, but I haven't had a chance to get back to her yet."

"Okay, don't worry about it," Drake said. "I was going to call her anyway."

"Good," John said, hitting the button on the elevator. "On a lighter note, you have a date for this weekend, don't you?"

Drake grinned. "You know that joke's getting old, right? And you should talk."

John struck a power pose and jokingly said, "I don't want to brag, but I have a date with my sister's cat this weekend."

"Let me see . . . D'Artagnan or Mary?" Drake teased, weighing the names with alternating palms. "Are you ever going to ask her out?"

"Told you, I'm looking for the right time," John whispered.

"Yeah, we both need to step up our games," Drake said.

When the elevator opened, John lunged inside and held the door. "I know it's past time, but we'll get to it right after this case."

"Right," Drake said. "Where have I heard that before? Whatever, see you later."

"Yeah, see you," John said, disappearing behind the doors.

After unlocking his office, Drake stepped inside and immediately made his way to the red leather desk chair. It was a special gift from an ex-girlfriend, Sherry Griffin, who had given it to him when he first moved into the new space.

Ever since then, the executive classic had become his favorite, and whenever a little recovery time was needed, it never failed to deliver. As he patted the beautiful leather and sank in, he thought how it was actually looking better with age.

And the same's probably true for Sherry.

She was a spontaneous, sassy brunette who could always entertain him with her unexpected topics of conversation and lofty travel plans. Sherry Griffin, with her smoky eyes and passion for life, was the first to get him thinking about the altar.

But there was never a wedding.

The torturous thoughts came again. *Was it my fault? Was she right?*

But just as his mind stumbled upon the awkward reason for the breakup, he shook his head and quickly dismissed the memories. The parting was really no one's fault, and there wasn't any point in revisiting the issue.

There had always been something holding him back anyway. He couldn't exactly put his finger on it, but it didn't matter. She'd made it clear that she wasn't interested in competing for his time, and that was something he couldn't change. His work was a calling.

He did his best to justify the priority of the job, but she didn't want to hear it. Turns out she'd been down that road before, with a cop named Eddie Driscoll.

The two of them had dealt with a similar issue.

Apparently, Eddie had even moved closer, in a final attempt to improve the dynamic, but despite the extra effort, the relationship never landed on solid ground.

The move, however, did land Eddie in the same precinct as Drake. That turn of events could have been awkward, even a problem, but because they were adults about it, it never was. The guys weren't the best of friends, but they had the demands of the job in common and conducted themselves as professionals.

With victims depending on them, they had no choice but to devote additional hours to their careers rather than their personal lives. It was just part of the process.

Drake solved many cases in those extra hours, especially during the critical ones spent behind his office door.

The closed door might have seemed a dichotomy to some since he was usually so open and approachable otherwise. But when he was working on a case, it was different. His unique crime-solving technique required as much structure and quiet as possible. And that could be a tall order in a busy station.

However, on special occasions, when the stars did align, he was able to summon an almost meditative environment, coercing his subconscious into a more creative and discerning mindset.

And that's when the magic happened.

Drake was shaken from his thoughts by sounds permeating the traditional paneled walls, alerting him as the interior of the office slowly came to life. The familiar rhythms resonating throughout the day were like a quirky melody. With one person after another arriving and adding their own unique sound, it was like one instrument after another joining in to create a full musical piece, eventually reaching a crescendo. And then, finally, the big finish, as they all rushed to leave at the end of the day.

After switching his focus back to the case, Drake was ready to apply the winning visualization technique he had mastered. There would—like always—be missing pieces. But when he encountered absent or sketchy details, to keep continuity, he simply filled in with inspired theory. And by now, his mental movie was getting shockingly close to what really happened.

Drake closed his eyes and let the story born of statements, facts, and imagination fill his mind. As his breathing began to slow and all awareness of his surroundings dissipated, he surrendered to the dreamlike state, and the images began to organize themselves.

It was late, and he could feel the vulnerability of the darkness.

The family had just returned home from the annual community music festival, and in the shadows of the garage, Jacki Sweet rifled through her bag for the right key.

After a brief struggle with the door, they were all safely inside and headed in different directions. Jacki was on her way to remove her makeup and jump into her favorite sweats while Chad made his way to the kitchen. Their six-year-old, Angela, skipped her way to her fairytale bedroom, where she would put on the pajamas she had chosen earlier in the day.

The plan was to meet back in the family room and watch a little TV. Bedtime was going to be later than normal, but it was a special occasion.

Chad was the last to enter, and Angela squealed with delight when she saw him. The king of her world was acting out a royal presentation with an enormous bowl of popcorn. He lightheartedly teased the girls, saying how delicious it was going to be because he, the master chef, had added a new secret ingredient: white cheddar seasoning.

Without awareness, Drake smiled as he pictured the playful family moment.

But the charming scene would last for only minutes before a masked gunman stepped into the family's world. With weapon drawn, he threatened their lives if anyone made a sound, leaving them no choice but to follow instructions.

The parents had prayed he just wanted to rob them and leave, but the intruder had other plans.

Dressed all in black, down to leather gloves and mask, he forced the family into chairs from a nearby game table.

After dipping his shoulder and allowing his backpack to fall heavily to the floor, he reached inside and quickly retrieved some rope and three separate rolls of duct tape. Using the rope to restrain them by size, he bound Chad first, Jacki second, and finally Angela.

Drake's heart was beating faster. He could picture the little girl's face, feel her terror.

For the following step, the invader reversed the order. After cutting a piece of duct tape from each of the three rolls, he stepped close and gagged Angela.

Most likely to scream.

Drake then pictured the parents, silenced and struggling, and could feel their agony.

Donning a roll of duct tape on his wrist, the invader eerily made his way around to the back of the chairs, where he used the remainder to reinforce the bindings.

Statements from the parents explained how he had returned the empty spools to the backpack.

Covering his tracks.

With the family now completely helpless, the gunman began to chastise them for ruining his life. He paced the floor, spewing some diatribe about planning out his whole life and being determined to finally have what he wanted.

Chad was working furiously with the ropes as the sick verbal attack continued, but the more he struggled, the stronger they got.

A clue? Could he be an expert?

While aiming the gun right at Chad, the offender gave another warning not to make a sound and began to untie Angela. But just enough to release her from the chair.

The Sweets were forced to watch helplessly as he continued to terrorize their little girl.

Tears that had been off and on were now pouring down Jacki's face, and Angela's eyes flashed with a fear no child should ever know. Her voice was muted by the duct tape, but Drake could almost hear her screaming. His breath hitched.

The scene was so real that he actually felt for his gun.

If only I could have been there.

When Angela was barely freed, the invader picked her up and callously paraded her around. Chad lurched forward, viciously wrestling with the chair again. There was no warning, when only seconds later, the intruder's gun smashed into his forehead.

The gunman turned and taunted Jacki. "Take a final look."

She fought her own restraints as she watched her sweet girl squirm and kick so fiercely that he almost dropped her before dragging her from the room.

When he returned, Angela was restrained by an unyielding grip, but her whole body shook as she clung tightly to an overstuffed pink backpack.

It surely contained her personal belongings, proof he was really taking her.

With the six-year-old still unable to make a sound and squirming on his hip, the kidnapper walked boldly out of sight.

Sweat began to form on Drake's forehead. He couldn't be sure of what happened next, but his imaginings were close.

As the perpetrator exited, he wrestled with Angela, who was putting up a savage fight, twisting and kicking.

From a nearly undetectable corner of the garage, with a free hand, he picked up what looked like a coffee can. After popping the lid and reaching inside, he located the chloroform and gauze that had been stashed there earlier.

He shifted Angela's weight for the last time and made direct eye contact with her, saying with eerie kindness, "I know you're scared, but everything's fine, and you're going to be okay. But right now, it's past your bedtime, and you need a little nap for the trip."

With that, he placed the saturated gauze over her nose and mouth. When she passed out, his knees buckled slightly from the instant weight shift, but the struggle was over. He knelt down, transferred her to his lap, and opened his backpack. Like every other used item, the can was tossed inside.

Then, for the first time that night, he went off plan. After opening Jacki's SUV parked in the garage and placing Angela inside, he re-entered the home.

Chad was still out, but Jacki was frantically struggling to get free. Her muffled screams were of no help. He came toward her with something in his hand. He held it over her face, and that's all she remembered.

Hardly acknowledging either of them, the kidnapper had chloroformed Jacki and Chad for good measure.

Drake imagined him exiting the house for the second time. It had to be a critical moment. Leaving by way of a noisy garage door was not ideal, and evidence suggested he had chosen a secondary entry point.

With Angela resting over his shoulder, and before taking the first step, he must have cautiously scanned the neighborhood for any activity. The next challenge would have been to make it undetected from the house to his vehicle.

Drake pictured him stepping daringly into the night.

Dressed in black, and barely visible, he probably looked like any parent, simply carrying a sleeping child. Surely, he would have moved quickly to the vehicle and put Angela in first. *In the back seat? In a makeshift bed?* Either way, the evil deed was done, and he disappeared into the night.

The reenactment was over.

Hours had gone by before the Sweets were freed, and they were able to report the abduction to the police.

Drake knew what happened from that point on . . . because he was there.

After arriving with his team, he comforted the frantic parents and took specific note of the disturbing scene. Thankfully, even in their panicky state, the Sweets had known enough from an evidence perspective to leave everything the way it was.

Other investigators gloved up, dusted for prints, took photos, and bagged and recorded every piece of evidence in the house while Drake monitored emergency child alerts and calmed the parents before piecing together their statements.

Jacki was already talking when he pulled a chair up next to the sofa.

"We just kept telling her to be brave and do what he said," she sobbed, rocking back and forth. "We didn't have a choice; he had a gun. And he was talking crazy."

"Can you remember what else he said?" Drake asked.

"Something about not letting a family who has everything destroy his plan," she cried. "It was weird . . . he just went on and on."

"Yeah, he said something about following rules," Chad offered.

"When you don't follow rules, you suffer consequences," Jacki added. "And what else was it?"

"Uh . . . oh, yeah," Chad said. "You're going to pay for your interference. You took my entire life, so I'm taking yours."

"I'm so sorry," Drake comforted. "Was there anything familiar about him at all?"

Chad shook his head. "No, we only heard his voice. His face was covered."

"So, you had just come home from the music festival, right?" Drake probed.

"Yeah, hadn't been home very long," Chad explained. "Do you think someone could have followed us?"

"Anything's possible, especially with a crowd like that," Drake said. "But from what you've said, I think it's more likely that he was already here."

Jacki was nervously wringing her hands.

"Can't we do something, instead of just sitting here talking?" she begged. "I can't stand it. Oh, God . . . my baby! The look on her sweet face ripped my heart out. I tried to show her how much I love her, that everything would be okay, but I'm so afraid she only saw the panic."

Details were coming in random bursts, but Drake was able to organize them in his mind.

"I know how hard it is to try to concentrate," he empathized. "Focusing on anything other than Angela right now is unnatural."

"All I really want to do is lose my mind in private," Jacki cried.

Drake respected that, but if he was going to find Angela, he needed a play-by-play.

"I do understand," he said. "I really do. But to give ourselves the best chance of finding her, we need to collect important information as soon as possible."

That did it.

Despite what appeared to be crippling agony, the Sweets gave a full accounting of—what would later become—their official statement. And once that was complete, they even managed another small assistance by gathering a recent photo and a few other items from Angela's room.

"So, neither of you noticed a strange vehicle or anything like that?" Drake asked.

Chad shook his head. "No, nothing. We didn't see much of anything outside of this room. Is there a way to find his car?"

"Well, every now and then we can capture traffic footage that might match the timeline," Drake explained. "But without knowing the vehicle, it's like looking for a needle in a haystack. Plus, he's already been driving for several hours. But I can still try to map out some possible, directional scenarios."

"Okay," Chad said, pushing away the EMTs, who were moving in to assess his injuries.

After a careful examination, they suggested a trip to the hospital, but he refused, saying he wasn't going anywhere until they found his daughter.

Drake stepped in to try to convince him that he would be a much greater help if his injuries were fully addressed, when a commotion erupted at the front door.

Karen Love, one of the investigators, was holding several people at bay, while asking and answering questions. Turns out, it was a small group of concerned neighbors who, from what Drake could gather, hadn't seen or heard a thing until noticing the emergency vehicles and flashing lights.

Their inability to provide new information was countered by offers of help and an outpouring of love and compassion for the Sweets. Even in the midst of the horrific scene, Drake witnessed the flip side of humanity, the innate goodness in most people.

"Thanks, guys," called Chad from the sofa. "We're grateful for any kind of help." He put his arms around Jacki and held her close as she cried.

She was still there, sobbing into a mound of pillows, when her sister, Ashley Benson, rushed through the door and fell at her feet. The sisters, who were just a few years apart and extremely close, hugged like it was their last breath together.

Jacki choked out whatever details she could while Ashley held her and wept along with every word.

"We'll find her, Sis," she promised. "We're not stopping until we do."

"Ash, I feel like I can't breathe," Jacki said.

Ashley took her hands. "Do you want me to call the doctor? Maybe you should take something. It might help."

"No, I don't want anything," Jacki cried. "I just want my baby. I've never felt so helpless in my life! Is she really gone?"

"Shh . . . we're going to find her, and I'm not leaving your side," Ashley soothed. "Let's pray."

✳

On the way back from the scene, Drake thought about how any kidnapping manifested a parent's worst nightmare. But there was something more here. Something was really off about the abductor and his crazy, threatening rant. And that type of offender could be hard to track, unpredictable.

The eerie details were already gnawing at him. Was there anything he could do that would allow the Sweets to wake up the next morning and have life back to normal? Or would the dark reality be waiting for them again at dawn?

He had to find that little girl. He had to stop their pain.

TWO

NO MORE DISTANCE

"She's a beauty, isn't she?" Clark said to his project manager, Vince Madison, as they admired the finishing touches going on at the newly completed East of Eden office building. Clark Steele had been an architect for almost two decades and yet never tired of that final moment when vision became reality.

The planting of three Japanese red maples and eight burning bushes, along with finishing up the sod on the east side, would be done before noon, and the spectacular new structure would be ready for professional pictures that very day. As the sun reigned majestically overhead, Clark stood motionless, basking in the gilded glow melting over the entire scene.

How many more times will I get to do this?

Clark Steele was a self-made man, and that dignity made every success just a little sweeter. The early days were certainly challenging, but he kept his head down and let his work ethic and determination lead the way. Before he knew it, he'd launched his own construction business and, in the process, made a name for himself.

The unveiling of a new structure was always a great moment to share with the entire crew, who loved working for Clark. He was a perfectionist but still had the warm people skills that sometimes escaped a highly driven personality. And because he showed such great respect for the team, their cooperation knew no bounds. His inspired instructions and timeline promises were always executed flawlessly.

Clark prided himself on hiring the right people in the first place to ensure a certain standard of excellence. But he also supplemented the winning approach with a little custom training that resulted in an exceptionally gifted team. While many referred to the Steele team as the best in the business, they'd been known to affectionately refer to themselves as "Clark's Clones."

And Clark had had to rely on the aptly named team a little more than usual lately. Due to no fault of his own, he'd been unable to be as present as normal during the most recent projects. Luckily, the team was always there to pick up the slack. As a matter of fact, Vince, his right-hand man, would be doing a late fill-in with decorator, Ashley Benson, that very afternoon.

Ashley specialized in residential staging, but her contracts for commercial work were flourishing, along with her glowing endorsements. That made her the perfect choice for Clark's colleagues' current needs and a great addition to his future contact list.

Although he wanted to be part of the meeting, the late change in plans allowed him to leave early and spend some desperately needed time at home.

Thoughts of his wife had been on his mind all day, and he couldn't wait to see her.

From the first time they met in college, he knew Rachel was the one. Her exceptional kindness and profound thinking had been like magnets, drawing him close, and nearly every conversation was deep and charismatic. And then, there was her beauty. Rachel had been blessed with the exquisite looks of a model, and even without make-up, she took his breath away.

He couldn't be happier to be spending the rest of his life with her.

Because she had so much to offer, he was never quite sure what she saw in him—but he loved her playful explanation. "You're a great blend of intellectual and athlete, with an extra dose of 'guy next door' good looks, and I love your hair," she said. His dark blond locks were kept in a ponytail at work but, on her orders, just the opposite at home.

Together, the Steeles made quite the dazzling couple. And it didn't matter whether they arrived at events in jeans or evening wear, everyone noticed.

The two had built an amazing life together and had a lot of fun doing it.

Every now and then, Clark could get off track by overanalyzing or getting lost in projects, but Rachel knew how to bring him back down to earth. She was a master of restoring balance, and her secret weapon was humor.

The common laughter and teasing between them filled their lives with many fun and memorable moments. And for the most part, their marriage had been a blessing.

But Rachel hadn't been herself lately, and when Clark thought about her tears that morning, he felt an ache in his chest that wouldn't go away. In contrast to the great joy they had shared, a current heaviness came from some real struggles for the first time.

One heart-wrenching topic surfaced every year, like clockwork. It came after celebrating the birthday of his niece, Rebecca, who had just turned five. They adored her, but the joyous occasion had become a cruel reminder that they hadn't been blessed with their own child.

"Rach, I've been thinking about you all day," Clark confessed later. "I can't stand it when you cry."

She hung her head. "I know. I'm trying not to, but there's so much pressure right now. And you know Rebecca's birthday is always a trigger for me."

Clark took her hands and pulled her close. "I know, but please don't worry. I promise you; we're going to have a baby."

"I want to believe that," she said. "But look at what we're dealing with right now. How did our lives change so quickly?"

Clark lifted her chin tenderly and looked into her eyes. "Rach, I know the situation's been tough, but maybe we should talk more seriously about adoption."

"We can, but even if that's the answer, you know we still have to tread carefully," she reminded him.

Without a word, he kissed her cheek and held her tighter.

Due to serious health issues, Clark had not been as hands-on at home or at recent job sites. While most people had heard about the virus he was fighting, few knew the complete story.

When he was absent from work for several weeks, everyone thought it was just for some rest and relaxation after another tough bout with the virus. But rather than enjoying some well-earned rest, Clark was spending time at the hospital going through more procedures than he cared to think about. The diagnosis was finally delivered: viral cardiomyopathy. And his heart had been seriously damaged.

His mind raced back to a particularly stressful appointment with Dr. Malloy. "Clark, I'm sorry to tell you," he said, "but things are not improving. And with complications from the condition, other organs are at risk."

"What are you saying, Doc?" he asked.

Dr. Malloy patted his shoulder. "I know we talked about it as a last resort, but I think it's time to consider the transplant. You're still in the prime of your life and, in my opinion, it's your best option."

Clark and Rachel had been blessed with relatively few health concerns over the years, but they were now facing a huge one. The shocking proposal sparked long conversations and many sleepless nights.

The memory led to thoughts of a recent attempt to circumvent some anxiety. He and Rachel had gone on a long-overdue date night that began with dinner by candlelight at Giovanni's, a local trattoria. The charming spot had become a favorite, offering a complete pasta menu, the finest desserts, and a lovely house wine. The staff was wonderfully attentive, and there was always a romantic vibe from start to finish.

"The theater's only two blocks away," Clark said, helping Rachel with her jacket. "Let's walk."

They left arm in arm to catch a nine o'clock rescreening of *Casa Blanca*, and before they knew it, they had tickets in hand.

"It's so much fun becoming classic movie buffs together," Rachel gushed. "While we're waiting for the film to start, we can decide on the next one. I think *Gone with the Wind* would be great."

They had just been seated when Clark felt a slight spasm in the upper left side of his chest. He turned to tell Rachel about it, but she had such a joyful look on her face, he just couldn't do it.

"What?" Rachel asked.

"Nothing. I just love you, that's all," he said.

Almost immediately, Clark found himself captivated by some of the film's early dialogue. So much so that it took a bit for him to realize the feeling had gone away. Now thankful that he didn't have to burden Rachel, he was ready to relax and enjoy the rest of the night.

He put his arm around her shoulder and, before long, Sam began to play, "As Time Goes By." Clark was reveling in the timeless jazz number when, suddenly, he felt another tremor in his chest. He waited for a minute, not sure if he should tell Rachel this time.

But before he could even make a decision, he was hit with a much stronger chest pain. And weirdly, it happened in perfect sync with a dramatic piano chord.

He covered his chest with both hands.

"Clark, what is it?" cried Rachel.

"I'm not sure," he said. "But I think we might need to leave."

Rachel jumped up and led him out into the fresh air.

After a couple of minutes, the feeling passed, but Clark was exhausted and knew he couldn't go on like that. There had been too many incidents, and he couldn't keep disappointing Rachel.

Back in real time, Rachel was still waiting for an answer. "Clark . . . Clark, did you hear me?"

"Oh, sorry, Rach," he said, shaking off the past memory. "I'm trying to tread carefully while we decide what to do. But I am so tired of not being able to live a normal life. You know how active I was, and now I can't even make it through a movie . . . or . . . well, you know."

"What?" she asked. "Please tell me you're not worried about the bedroom again, are you?"

"You don't know how bad I feel about that . . . not being able to love you the right way, without fear of chest pains," he confessed.

She looked up at him and laid her head on his shoulder. "Clark, love is ever-changing, and right now, the most important thing is loving you through this."

"Well, I love you for saying that," he said. "But since we're talking this out, I feel like you're taking good care of me, but you've been a little distant lately."

Rachel quickly shook her head. "No, Clark, I'm just fearful of touching you, hurting you in some way. Ever since you had those chest pains, I've been afraid of causing you a . . . a heart attack."

"Oh, Rachel, I'm tougher than you think," he said. "I can handle whatever life throws at me, but the one thing I can't handle is distance from you."

Her tears began to flow again as she hugged him harder than

she had in a long time. "I'm so sorry. No more distance. We'll just be careful."

"Okay, deal," he said. "Hey, I don't know about you, but I feel like getting out of the house. What do you say?"

Rachel grinned at his unexpected about-face. "Yeah, if you're sure you're up for it."

"Well, let's find out. I'll go get my body armor," he teased.

"You're something else," she said, shaking her head.

✳

After only half a lap around one of their favorite tree-lined paths, Clark and Rachel rested on a massive log next to the lake. Evening was falling over the stillness of the water, but a delicate reflection of the heavens could still be seen.

"Well, we made it halfway," Clark announced.

"Yes, we did, but we also did the right thing by resting," Rachel said. "I could tell you were getting winded."

Clark nodded. "I'll admit it, but I'm still glad we came. And there was no pain this time."

"That's good," smiled Rachel. "Clark, I know we have to make a decision soon, but sometimes, I can't even think about you going through all of that."

"I know," he agreed. "It's like I can accept the transplant in theory, but when I think about the actual surgery, it's terrifying."

"You know, there's really no way of knowing if, or when, a matching donor heart will ever become available," Rachel said. "Maybe some new treatment will be discovered first."

Clark shook his head. "Not likely, Rach. Even though the procedure is scary, I'd be lucky to receive a heart. But if I do the surgery, it could mean a long recovery, another setback in our family plan. And

I feel like I'm letting you down. You've been so patient and support-ive while I've built the business."

"First of all, you're not letting me down," Rachel said sweetly. "Right now, I'm more worried about the procedure than the future."

Clark held her tight. "I know things aren't fair right now, but it's all going to work out," he said. "I promise."

In the next few days, he did some final research, exhausted every alternative, and ultimately, accepted his reality. The idea of transplant surgery, although highly stressful, was the right choice. It was his best chance of survival. If he wanted to live a full life, it was time to add his name to the transplant waiting list.

The doctors were pleased with his decision and immediately started him on a preparatory path. The goal was for him to be as strong as possible if a donor heart was ever located. Even then, there were no guarantees, but at least he would have been given every advantage.

Clark's next order of business was to make tentative arrange-ments with Vince and the team back at Steele Construction. When the normally enthusiastic staff learned the details of Clark's diagno-sis, they were full of questions and concern.

But Vince was able to assure them that a heart transplant was truly the best course of action for Clark. He alleviated many of their fears by reminding them that the procedure was done successfully thousands of times every year.

To lighten their spirits even further, he challenged them to focus on the tenacity and determination of their fearless leader. To a per-son, they agreed that if anyone could face something like that head-on, it would be Clark.

Vince and the crew vowed to create a plan of action for the

business so that when the time came, Clark would have nothing on his mind except his recovery, no matter how long it took.

After reviewing his doctors' directives again, Clark decided to take them very seriously, vowing to do his best. He would take excellent care of his health and live as normally as possible while waiting for the life-saving call.

It was a challenge because he had to fight the daily temptation to dwell on his less-than-ideal reality, but for the most part, he was able to focus on other things. His subconscious, however, was forever preparing for the life-or-death moment.

If only he could be one of the lucky ones.

Until such time, he would await the critical call, always staying prepared to drop everything and make a beeline for the hospital.

He had to survive.

THREE

THE ANOMALY

Drake Harrison took a random call from Willie Tucker, head groundskeeper at Resting Waters Cemetery, and the day turned into one that would stay with him forever. The animated tone in Willie's voice clearly indicated real concern over an anomaly in a less frequented area of the property.

At that point, the location hadn't been designated a crime scene, but Drake instinctively invited a couple of special investigators to meet him there.

As he entered the cemetery's driveway, the blinding reflection from a newly polished hearse made him squint. Trying out a new hands-free trick, he raised his eyebrows, causing his sunglasses to fall from the top of his forehead. The playful but skillful action dropped them perfectly in place.

He had already been briefed on the current situation but was anxious to hear the rest of the story, and he wanted to hear it from Willie.

"I was just starting my daily rounds," Willie said. "Walked right by the site several times before noticing the soil disturbance. The irregularity doesn't make sense because there haven't been any recent services in that section of the property."

"Can you tell by the soil how old the plot might be?" Drake asked.

"It must have been there for a while because of the settling," Willie replied. "But with weather and things, at this point, I'd really just be guessing."

"Well, looks like, we better see what we've got," Drake said. "How many people have access to this area?"

"Basically, everyone who works here," he said. "And, of course, countless friends and family members that visit every day." Willie stopped and shook his head. "The staff and I know this landscape like the back of our hands, and none of us noticed anything abnormal until today, not even our private security."

"Yeah, I know a couple of those guys," Drake said. "I'll talk to them later. Let's take another look."

The mystery was clearly understandable, with the disturbance appearing almost invisible at first glance. In fact, the area in question blended in so well that Drake could easily see how even Willie's highly trained eye would have missed it.

After examining the scene more closely, he figured the lighting was probably why Willie spotted it when he did. Depressing clouds, accompanied by a drizzling but consistent shower, had moved through earlier in the morning. When the dreary mist transformed into a partly sunny day, the filtered light must have hit the spot perfectly, finally revealing the subtle anomaly.

Before upsetting the area and starting the investigation, Drake took quick statements from the manager and the rest of the staff, who appeared to be milling around out of curiosity. None of them, including the boss, could explain the irregularity, and all agreed that something was off.

The entire staff did their best to be helpful but could only offer vague speculation under such mysterious circumstances. Their hushed, theoretical conversations continued as Drake headed over to the arriving investigators to kick around options.

He'd only gone a short distance when Carl Owen, an overeager member of the old-school security detail, chased him down.

"Detective, I'm part of security," Carl said. "I could try to locate any video footage from the area. Maybe cameras captured something. What do you think?"

Drake never broke stride. "Appreciate the offer, but we're on it. Right now, I just need to find out what we're dealing with."

"Okay, let me know if there's anything I can do," Carl called after him.

Once the initial photos were captured, Drake watched the CSI team break ground and very gently dig up the top of the area, where the soil yielded easily. Then they began the careful and methodical work that would, before long, put him in mind of an archaeological dig. He scrutinized and marveled at the skill level of the well-rehearsed actions.

After cautiously working through the first few layers, they had come up empty-handed, but Drake rightly considered every barren shovel a small victory. He was well aware of what might be found in a mysterious grave.

So far, so good.

As the excavation grew, so did his hopes of eliminating the worst-case scenario, even though he'd been fooled before. Before long, he noticed the collective breathing of the team becoming visibly shallow as they continued to dig and examine each new scoop of earth.

"Good work, guys," he said, offering them a bottle of water from a small cooler they'd brought along. They nodded and took a seconds-long break.

Drake was running every scenario in his head as he watched. *What's in there? Don't let it be a body.*

The repeated rise and fall of emotions and passing time only added to his anxiety as he awaited the conclusive answer.

Two excavators in the pit were repeatedly conducting one delicate maneuver after another when, suddenly, the female agent gasped. Her brush stroke had revealed something pink.

Drake's antennae went up.

Pink...pink. And then the light went on. He had committed every minute detail of the Sweet case to memory, and there was a pink connection to the missing evidence. But surely this random incident wasn't related.

Drake watched as the unit continued to painstakingly sift and brush dirt and debris out of the way, completely uncovering what was soon to be identified as a pink nylon canvas backpack—exactly like Angela Sweet's. The scene was connected, and he felt sick.

God, please, don't let her be in there.

There was nothing worse than finding the body of a child. It always felt like evil had increased its footprint in the world, and things would never be the same. His hands were getting sweaty as he paced and willed her to be somewhere else.

The dig team worked as quickly and efficiently as they could, but to Drake, it seemed like an eternity.

"Guys, it's my case," he told them, stepping close. "A little girl is missing."

The one closest to him paused for a second. The disturbed look on his face was proof he understood the gravity. "We got this, Drake."

The weight of Drake's declaration and whispers of concern traveled like the wind through the crowd. Even if fearful of what investigators might find, they were all frozen, seemingly unable to pull themselves away.

Drake's anxiety and the nerve-racking process were unrelenting. He had to endure the slow recovery of additional personal items, including a child's slippers and pajamas. When he made eye contact with Karen Love, one of the CSI team members who had helped with Angela's case on the night of the abduction, he was sure she could read the devastation on his face.

Karen wasn't required to be there but had graciously offered to come along. As the items were being passed up from below, she handled each piece of evidence with almost sacred care.

Even without official identification, Drake knew the items were Angela's and couldn't help feeling the same heartache he had at the initial scene. Being haunted by disturbing crimes, especially ones where children were involved, was part of the job but something he'd never grown used to.

At that moment, he would have taken a lot of other scenarios over finding her in the crude grave.

Oh, God! I have to tell her parents.

He didn't even know if he had it in him to go through the inhumanity of delivering more crushing news to Chad and Jacki.

When he looked up from his thoughts, everyone on the property had moved in closer and positioned themselves around the grave site, as if preparing for a funeral. Their somber faces, whispers, and wringing of hands told Drake they were completely invested in the outcome.

Along with him, they would discover the fate of the precious six-year-old.

Drake purposely distracted himself from the painful moment by trying to get into the perpetrator's head. The subject had oddly, and possibly even cleverly, hidden evidence in such an inconspicuous spot. Or was it? Either way, he had made sure the makeshift plot at Resting Waters had become just another grave among a host of others.

But why bury evidence here? Probably, a question for Dr. Brill.

Even though experience had taught him that guilty parties usually disposed of evidence in more effective ways, there were plenty of offenders with unexplained motivations.

Sadly, law enforcement didn't always find out the reason for their actions. But when they were lucky enough to discover a motive, they had to be prepared for revelations that further expose the troubling complexities of the criminal mind.

Drake couldn't remember investigating a perpetrator who presented quite like this one and found the brazen, hide-it-in-plain-sight mentality troubling. Normally, criminals chose the remotest locations to discard the remains of their evil work.

Even though the evidence had been buried, the unidentified subject had chosen a very open, public location that would be visited frequently. Whoever this was wasn't too worried about someone stumbling upon the gravesite.

Drake's gut told him that this could be one of those times when a perpetrator's strange behavior might make sense to no one but them.

"All clear, nothing else in here!" came a sudden shout from the pit.

Drake's knees nearly buckled as the good news registered, but he managed to remain standing and whispered, "Thank God!"

After making eye contact with the other team members, he said, "Thanks guys. Great work."

The next task would be to share the discovery with the Sweets. He was not looking forward to it, but it had to be done. Every detail provided new pieces to the puzzle, and the parents deserved to hear the update as soon as possible.

In reality, they were all working together. Sometimes, family and friends were able to make connections that investigators couldn't. So, once Drake was back and had gotten confirmation on the new evidence, he made the call.

Chad Sweet answered, and Drake could hear the anticipation in his voice. After mentioning some news in the case, Chad invited him over right away. Drake accepted but would have been more enthused if only he had good news.

*

He hadn't noticed before, having only been to their home at night, but as he got closer, the setting became increasingly idyllic. The smattering of asymmetrical Tudors peppering the streets added an almost storybook spirit to the neighborhood. The enchanted atmosphere made quite an impression because it was so unlike most of his other crime scene destinations.

When the front door opened, the hopeful looks on the faces of the shattered parents tugged at his heart. For a split second, Drake wondered if he'd made the right call. He would like nothing better than to give them some good news, but it just wasn't there yet.

"It's good to see you both," he said. "Sorry we haven't found her yet, but there is something new in the case. Plus, I wanted to come by and check on you anyway."

"Thank you," Jacki said weakly. "May I get you some coffee?"

"I would love that, but only if it's no trouble," Drake said. "Thank you."

"Not at all," she said. "C'mon into the kitchen."

The oppressive silence at the otherwise cheerful dining table was deafening. It had probably been that way most days since Angela's abduction. Drake did his best to get the conversation going, but for a while, it felt one way.

He couldn't help studying Chad, who was displaying almost no appetite, drinking his coffee robotically, and not really engaging with any aspect of the experience. Drake recognized the profound pain.

He finally broke the silence. "Chad, have you been back to work yet?"

"Oh yeah," Chad said. "It was really hard to go back, but it has helped a little. Of course, I worry more about Jacki when I'm not here."

Drake looked across the table where warm afternoon light spilled onto the scene, illuminating the grief and heartache present on Jacki's face. She appeared much older than the last time he had seen her. Her loss of joy had resulted in facial characteristics that might have been a concern to her at one time. But he was sure there was nothing on her mind but her precious girl.

Of course, each passing day without news made it much harder for any parent to stay prayerful and strong. So, Drake's mission was to be as supportive as possible throughout the ordeal—and bring Angela home.

He had previously witnessed both grief and strength in the traumatized mother, and he was certain her defeated outward appearance and inner determination were in direct opposition to one another.

She moved in almost slow motion, buttering a slice of homemade bread, cutting it diagonally, and placing a cotton napkin in her lap. Drake found her slow and methodical movements a contradiction to the churning tornado she had been before.

"Jacki, if there's anything at all we can help you with or do for you when Chad's gone, remember, just give me a call," offered Drake.

"Okay, thanks," she whispered as she smoothed the lap of her floral wrap dress. "But I've kind of gotten into a routine that somehow gets me through the day. It's really nice of you to offer, though."

"Well, I know how tough the waiting can be, but I promise you, we're doing everything we can," Drake said. "We've been looking into a few new leads and a similar case from a couple of counties over. Of course, I'll let you know right away if anything comes of it."

His voice softened. "But I do have something new to share with you. We've actually located some evidence."

"What?" Chad asked. "Where?"

The panicky look on Jacki's face made Drake's heart skip a beat. "Well, it was close," he began softly. He hesitated. "And it was a few of her belongings."

"No!" Jacki cried, clutching her heart. "Where?"

"I'm so sorry," Drake said. "But first, I want you to remember. These are just things. Angela's still out there, and we're going to find her!"

Chad gripped the edge of the table. "What did you find?"

"Her backpack, with slippers and pajamas," Drake said gently.

"Oh my God," Jacki gasped, covering her face. "Please, tell us where."

Drake hesitated. "They were buried in . . . in a cemetery."

"No!" she cried. "Oh my God . . . my baby! Chad!"

"I'm so sorry," comforted Drake. "I was really hoping the scene wouldn't be related. But remember, someone's just hiding evidence. My gut's still telling me she's out there, and like I've always promised you; we're not stopping until we find her."

"I know," Jacki said, shaking. "I . . . I just can't help thinking about what she's going through. It makes me sick. What is wrong with this world?"

"I ask myself that every day," he said. "But, right now, my only focus is on finding Angela."

Drake had been around grief enough to know that Jacki was on the edge and, if his instincts were correct, she was just a wisp away from exploding.

After hanging on every word up to that point, she turned away. Suddenly, along with a piercing cry, came a flood of overwhelming grief as she collapsed forward, covered her face, and sobbed like a baby.

Drake felt the heartbreaking eruption in his bones.

It seemed as if Chad was by her side before the first teardrop hit the table. Drake knew the whole situation had wrung the life out of both of them, but so far, they'd been able to access some hidden measure of strength. It was the mysterious heavenly gift that allowed people to hang on and comfort each other in the most tragic times.

"Where is she?" Jackie choked out in broken sobs. "Please, God, just let her be okay! Chad, I'm trying, but I think I'm losing my mind."

"I've got you," he whispered tenderly. "We've got each other . . . and we're not giving up."

Drake realized the couple had entered a sacred space. He made eye contact with Chad and motioned to indicate that he would see himself out and give them the privacy they needed.

After taking a deep breath, Chad managed to say, "Thanks, Drake. I know you're doing everything you can. Please, just find her."

"You got it," he promised.

After a few more minutes in Chad's arms, Jacki said, "I can't do this another day."

"I've got you. Always," he said.

When he finally started to release her, she clung on even tighter.

Chad tightened his embrace and whispered, "Be strong, Babe. They're going to find her."

After returning from the heartbreaking visit, Drake stepped inside his office and immediately slumped into the cushy desk chair and, out of habit, rested his feet up on the desk.

Updates and wellness runs were extremely important but could sometimes leave him feeling absolutely helpless.

Fortunately, a call to Dr. Brill was next on the list. He always felt better after talking to her. Over the years, he and John sought her counsel on multiple cases, and her insights had been invaluable in understanding the criminal psyche.

Drake really liked her as a person too. She was extremely bright and intuitive but very humble and non-threatening at the same time. Shortly after getting to know her, her clients would literally tell her anything. And, as far as he could tell, she practiced with honor, taking the doctor-patient privilege very seriously. Her patients knew their secrets were safe with her.

It was hard not to marvel at her resilient spirit as well, especially after learning of the personal tragedy she had endured in her own life. She had been happily married in the past but on her own for years now. Her husband, Tony, a park ranger, was doing a walkabout at the state park one day and simply disappeared.

A couple of local detectives were assigned to the case and did a thorough investigation, but it eventually went cold. Drake had even done some work on it from time to time but kept it a secret. He knew it was a long shot and didn't want to encourage false hopes.

The personal anguish Dr. Brill must have suffered during those lonely, confusing years had to be overwhelming, but she continued to see a full calendar of patients. And remarkably, the process of treating their mental health had helped to restore her own.

"Hey, Drake," she said. "It's great to hear from you. How are things going?"

"Well, it's been kind of a rough day so far," he began. "But I get a break at the cabin later."

"Oh, that's good," Dr. Brill said. "Something to look forward to. Hey, I've been going over the Sweet case again."

"That's why I'm calling," Drake said. "Got something to run by you, but you go first."

"Well, I know we've talked about the antisocial behavior—maybe even delusions," she began. "His rant from that night makes me think the lines are blurred in his world. He definitely displays a lot of the signs. Committing an impulsive act, controlling with manipulation and aggression, and using violence against the father are all indicators."

"So, is there any way to get into his head?" Drake asked. "Do you think we should prepare for the worst?"

"He's probably very unpredictable," Dr. Brill explained. "The key is . . . well . . . it's the motivation behind what he's done."

"All we have to go on there is his rant from that night," offered Drake.

"Yeah, it's hard to know what all of that means," she said. "But like we've talked about, he's surely a loner, so he's probably in hiding right now."

"Yeah," agreed Drake. "Well, here's the latest. We found some evidence buried in a cemetery of all places."

She gasped. "You're kidding me."

"No—in a burial plot," he said. "Never seen that one before. Any idea what that could mean?"

"Well, I want to think about it a little more, but off the cuff, I'm wondering if it could be related to some kind of trigger in his life."

"Really?" Drake asked.

"Yeah, triggers can cause very strange behavior," she explained. "Where the subject acts almost involuntarily. On impulse."

"Well, Doc, what's your best assessment right now?" Drake asked.

"After looking at the details from the night of the abduction, I still think he's living out some sort of fantasy or delusion," she said. "And you already know the characteristics of that type of offender."

"Yep, been there before," Drake said.

"Hey, here's a wild thought. With a trigger in mind, he could have literally been 'burying' the evidence," she speculated.

"Wow, that's out there," mused Drake. "But I've heard crazier."

"Yeah, you and me both," she said.

"Well, I better get going," Drake said. "Great insight, as usual. Thanks."

"You bet, always happy to help," she said. "I'll keep working on it. You enjoy your trip."

"Thanks, on both accounts," he said. "You got a busy afternoon?"

"Oh, yeah," she said. "Full calendar, but I'm ready. You know my patients are my world."

"I do," Drake said. "And they're lucky to have you."

"Well, thank you," she said. "We'll talk soon."

"Okay. Thanks, Doc."

Drake began a visual analysis of the crime scene photos and case materials he would need later. For easy retrieval, he placed late photos from the cemetery on top of the other documents inside the file box. The container would be returned to the evidence room until he was ready to formally check it out after dinner.

The text tone on his phone suddenly alerted him to a message from John confirming the last of the new leads had fizzled out. He often thought about how shocked the average person would be to know how many useless leads law enforcement received.

Even so, they had to be fully investigated. The worst part, of course, was the wasted time. But there was a flip side, of which Drake took full advantage. Unhelpful leads, when used in a process of elimination, could actually keep things on the right track.

For example, some of the physical recoveries from the Sweet's home were fairly easy to exclude and, therefore, allowed him to focus most of his attention on the more important evidence and eyewitness accounts.

The family had given him a play-by-play of the abduction and their best description of the intruder, including his build, voice, and demeanor. Every clue was vital, helping him create a mental picture of what happened that night.

Evidence always told a story, but so far, the current collection was still a literary work in progress.

FOUR

A HAUNTED CHAMBER

On his way out, Drake stopped to say goodbye to several coworkers, including a few who were making their way toward the door.

It made sense that Ken Krieger led the group as he was the loudest and most animated. That joyful energy could also be found in his sense of humor, which was a breath of fresh air around the place most of the time.

Morgan Fox followed close behind while still owning her own space. Her independent nature was unmistakable, but her demeanor was unassuming and a bit mysterious.

Drake, like most people, was surprised to learn that she was a martial arts expert. The hidden combat skills were impressive, but he'd even seen her quiet, commanding energy strangely disarm criminals. It was the powerful "I know something you don't know" vibe that seemed to quickly garner respect.

Even though Morgan wasn't much for socializing, and Murphy's—the destination and regular staff hangout—wasn't really her kind of place, she went along occasionally. Most likely, in a diplomatic effort to bond with coworkers.

Bringing up the rear was Nathan Dean, the newbie around the place. Even though he was younger, he was well on his way to becoming a grumpy beat cop who didn't suffer fools gladly. He kept his head down and took care of business. Drake appreciated his work ethic but hadn't fully warmed up to his personality.

As the group departed, they were goofing off and shouting invites, calling for the others to meet up at Murph's when they were done for the day.

Patti Queen, Paul Brady, and Eddie Driscoll, who were still hard at work, hinted that they might stop by, so the animated trio's one last appeal went to Drake. That final bit of playful pressure was the finishing touch on a very noisy exit.

Paul Brady was a seasoned Irish detective with a lightning-fast mind. He was clever, ate up with the job, and was currently helping Drake with an especially complicated cold case.

Eddie, an ambitious cop and Sherry's ex, had transferred to their turf a while back. He had recently passed the detective exam and was still in a state of heightened excitement over the whole thing. But Drake was still waiting for evidence that he had passed the "all hat, no cowboy" test.

Patti Queen—a.k.a. Queenie—was just that, queen of the office and nicknamed appropriately. She was stylishly feminine, sarcastically funny, and one of the best shots in the area. She held her own on the toughest assignments. Over the years, she had saved more than a few male behinds.

After a few laughs with the trio, Drake decided to stick with his original plan and grab some dinner before heading to the cabin. So, after arriving at Rudy's, a smoked barbecue place in town where he knew most of the staff, he enjoyed a leisurely dinner of barbecue chicken and fries.

The night was falling too fast for his liking, but even so, he made a point of staying around long enough to catch up with friends.

"I'll take a piece of that apple pie to go," he said while paying his check.

Now ready for the journey ahead, he just had to stop at the precinct to pick up the case materials.

When he was just about to enter the building, a quick shadow flashed across the basement window, causing him to flinch. He stepped closer and took a good look around but found nothing out of the ordinary.

Eyes must be playing tricks on me.

In the underground workspace, however, a dark silhouette had stealthily crept past the window and into the evidence room. After rifling through images from the Sweet case, a photo was selected and quickly concealed inside a loose jacket.

The figure then drifted across the room and frantically rummaged through video files before randomly tossing something into a very old case box marked *Solved*. After hesitating for a second, the shadowy character raced to the door and exited the chamber, barely missing the next visitor.

Drake, like everyone else, never really liked the basement of the precinct. The building was antiquated, and the lower level gave off an unsettling vibe. Some of the staff even joked about it being haunted. He could deal with it during the day when lots of people were around . . . but going down there, alone, after hours, was something to be avoided.

Pushing the creepy thoughts out of his mind, he started down the stairs with invented confidence. As he reached the bottom level and looked straight ahead, he thought he saw movement again at the very end of the corridor. It was like a dark gust of smoke just rounding the corner at the end of the hall. He could feel a presence. . . and strained to get a better look through the murky lighting.

On instinct, he drew his weapon and cautiously moved down the hallway, pausing to check every possible area of concealment. He slid his back along the wall until he reached the end, where he peeked around the corner . . . and then quickly retreated. He saw nothing but repeated the maneuver to be sure.

The final check was the same, but he lingered a little longer, ultimately scanning the passageway and clearing the area. After convincing himself it was probably just office stories or his mind playing tricks on him, he made his way to the evidence room and hastily signed out the file.

The cabin was only three hours south, and if he got moving, he could still get a good night's sleep and tackle the case bright and early the next morning.

Just as he was hoping, the leisurely drive down was uneventful, and traffic was light. The only thing his trained eye picked up along the way was an expired tag on an older Toyota Camry abandoned on the side of the road. He called it in, knowing the highway patrol would take it from there.

Drake could feel the magical release of physical stress as he reached the last turnoff. At that particular spot, every single time, a peaceful sensation came over him like magic. It was as if his subconscious had registered the peace and tranquility of the vacation spot from previous trips and now, involuntarily, led his descent into chill mode.

As he pulled up to the cabin, he realized it was the only place he could relax to that degree, and he promised himself that he would eliminate future excuses and visit more often.

Once inside, he went through a quick arrival routine and then headed straight to his regular room. After partially unpacking and turning down the bed, he made his way back to check out the kitchen. The cabinets were well stocked with non-perishables, as usual, but he'd brought along some of his favorites to round out the selection.

Off the kitchen was the dining room, with a huge rustic wooden table in the center. Drake could still picture all of the family meals that had been shared around that beauty over the years.

But there wouldn't be a family gathering this time. He would be transforming the focal point of the room into his workstation for the duration of the trip.

When he thought about how he had almost postponed the visit due to the new evidence, he shook his head. Something even more compelling had prevented it. The nagging feeling that he was on the verge of a breakthrough was growing increasingly powerful, and he needed to be alone with his thoughts. And besides, he'd be back in time for the full evidentiary analysis anyway.

Just before heading to bed, he placed the case materials in the center of the table and sat pensively mulling over his mission for the next few days. A child's life was at stake.

After a solid night's sleep, he was awakened by the rhythmic drumming of the woodpeckers. He wondered what time it was but, for once, didn't have to worry about it. The plan was to be off-grid for the time being, and the first order of business would be breakfast and more forbidden coffee. His mom's percolator was an oldie but a goodie, and the coffee it produced surpassed even the fresh brew from his treasured morning spot.

When the scrambled eggs and toast were ready, he tried to stay in the moment and enjoy the most important meal of the day but couldn't resist a peek at photos from the case.

Well, this is what I came here for.

By noon, the massive old farm table was nearly covered with photos, timelines, statements, and more. After a fresh examination, Drake walked through the case moment by moment, questioning everything, and making notes for further analysis.

He'd already done many replications of his movie exercise with some success but would try even harder this time. Due to the absence of distractions, he was able to hit his stride and enter the zone rather quickly. Time flew as he repeatedly relived the case, but sadly, nothing even vaguely resembling a new clue made an appearance.

But Drake knew it was right in front of him. He could feel it. He just couldn't get it to manifest. The odd notion, causing his frustration, became a cue to take a break.

His favorite spot for a comforting escape was the front porch. He loved the Adirondack chairs and how the trees and the two-story overhang shielded the entry completely from the sun and rain. No matter the weather, the covered entrance was perfect any time of year.

Many family conversations had taken place right in that very spot with grandparents, parents, and his sister, Pam, and her family. So many great memories.

His grandfather was his fishing buddy, and the two of them were the first to christen the lake, just down the path out front. After returning from their favorite pastime and storing the catch, they would inevitably meander to the porch. Then, for a good hour or so, they would relax and begin to solve all of the world's problems by way of gripping conversation.

How he missed those talks.

It was past time for lunch, but he would be enjoying it outside, so he really didn't mind. From the simple but bountiful selection in the kitchen, he decided on a canned favorite and whipped up a tuna salad. Unable to suppress a little grin, he thought how the memories of fishing had probably, subconsciously, led to his choice of lunch.

He spent the late afternoon and evening completely absorbed in the case again. After going through a stack of photos and realizing one of the new ones was missing, he tossed the remaining images on the table in frustration. No one was more careful with evidence than he, and he was positive he had placed that photo on top of the other contents in the box.

Thankfully, after doing the exercise hundreds of times, the images were safely stored in his consciousness. He had the ability to conjure up the smallest detail without even looking at physical evidence.

After shifting to interviews with family members and people of interest, everything seemed to check out, just as before. But he closed his eyes and spent the rest of the time moving from beginning to end of the testimony in his mind. The visual pictures created from the crime details flowed one into the other, like a movie.

He took extra time going over the verbal reprimand from the intruder. It suggested familiarity, but the Sweets were positive they didn't know him. Drake had to consider whether the rant came from a demented mind . . . or the family was missing something.

Looking at the whole scenario from a new location and fresh perspective had given him a chance to re-examine every minute detail of the encounter. But even so, the flash of inspiration he needed so badly had chosen to remain elusive.

Time to clear his head again, and he knew exactly what he wanted to do. A few stolen minutes taking in the chatter of the environment had always been therapeutic.

So, newly focused on the varying critter sounds just before dusk, he walked out onto the creaky floors of the front porch and took it all in. As he stood leaning on the handrail, enjoying the tranquility, he looked as if he wanted nothing more than to hang onto that peaceful feeling forever.

The cabin lot was a botanist's dream, offering quite a variety of native trees and plants, and Drake loved how the pines seemed to grow exponentially with each return.

The lake on the property, or Lake Harrison as the family lovingly referred to it, was a bit off in the distance but breathtaking, making it worth the walk. If it was quiet enough, Drake could sometimes even hear the sounds of water life and activities from the porch.

Without realizing it, he'd been focused on impression lines going around an almost perfect geometric clearing that would be the precise location of the family's new picnic table. His eyes followed the lines again and again, and he made a mental note to find out which family member had marked it off so perfectly.

Having already seen the picnic furniture that would adorn the setting in his parents' garage, he couldn't wait for its arrival. The table was designed for outdoor use but had a more refined, indoor appearance. It was the right size for the family and had the same rectangular shape as the clearing.

And then there were the more unexpected high-back, all-weather chairs that his mother said should really add character and create the right atmosphere. Drake thought how perfect the set would look in the idyllic clearing once it was all in place. Maybe they would even hang some twinkling lights for dining under the stars.

He finally gave in and headed to the porch swing, which had become more and more irresistible with each glance in its direction. The darkness seemed to be moving in rather quickly, so he reached behind him to turn on the nearest carriage light.

With eyes tightly closed, he allowed himself to drift into the Sweet's nightmare once again.

The rhythm of his rapid eye movements matched the flashing visuals as he clicked through the scenes from that horrific day.

After a bit, the action suddenly stopped. His face became tense. Clearly, he was laser-focused on something. Something new had captured his attention. Without opening his eyes, he sat forward on the swing, raised clinched hands to his forehead, and summoned the revelation.

"That's freaking it!" he shouted, jumping to his feet and pacing in circles. "It makes perfect sense. And damn, it's been there the whole time."

Finally, something to go on!

The hunch meant new territory to explore and, if he was right about it, could even be the answer to the case. He had to move quickly.

While searching for his phone, he thought about calling John to have him begin working on the new information. John Baxter was such a bulldog; he might even have something by the time he got back.

After a couple of unsuccessful passes through the living area, he went to the bedroom to check the makeshift bookcase.

When he returned, he had the phone in hand, but there was a look of irritation on his face. Service was sketchy, and the battery wasn't even fully charged.

He rolled his eyes. *Not now.*

Drake thought again about calling John—but then quickly changed his mind.

I've got to get out of here.

He was a fast packer, but, at that moment, the handy skill didn't seem good enough. By deviating from the norm and sloppily gathering only essentials, he was able to close up the cabin in record time.

Civilization was just a few hours away, and he couldn't get there fast enough. The breakthrough was energizing, and if the new clue was the key to the case, he couldn't wait to research it.

With the blessing of a little luck, he might finally be able to bring some peace to the Sweet family.

The drive back always felt longer than the drive up, but with the new sense of urgency, Drake was prepared for the feeling to intensify. Oddly, however, the calm country roads and the belief that he may have finally found the answer began to relax him a little.

Once the adrenaline had mostly subsided, he was glad he'd let John sleep. It seemed only fair because if they hit on something while investigating the hunch, they wouldn't be getting much sleep from there on out.

Although the heavy lifting on the case had been done by him, John was his right-hand man all the way. The two of them worked many cases together and knew how to quickly switch from research to tracking.

Drake was excited to be on a new trail and couldn't wait to break the news.

After emerging from the ramp, he thought about how the barren interstate looked cold and unappealing compared to driving the more adventurous, rural roads. But the notion did not dampen his sense of contentment because the highway before him was the road to answers.

The miles rolled by as he mulled over the new hunch, and before he knew it, many familiar sights were coming into view.

He was close now.

Even though he didn't need it just yet, he checked his phone several times. Oddly, the battery was still charging. After laying it aside, he searched the passenger seat for the photos he wanted to show John.

That's when the explosion rang out. And for a moment, time glitched.

A passing semi had crossed the center of the highway and hit his Jeep nearly head-on, spinning it out of control. With no time to respond, Drake had been swallowed up by the grating sound of crushing metal and shattering glass.

The force caused several complete rotations before flipping the vehicle onto the roof and sending it into a shadowy patch of weeds just past the shoulder of the road.

Drake's injuries were fast and severe, his heart pumping the blood of life from every wound. As his heartbeat and breathing dangerously slowed, he could feel himself fading. He no longer had sensory control over his body or the ability to fight for his own life. But mercifully, he was past feeling any pain.

Rather, in the last seconds of awareness, thoughts of his life flickered.

He was eight years old again and could smell the freshly cut grass as his dad tossed him a few pitches in the backyard. The scene shifted, and there was his mom, pinning his badge on his uniform at graduation. Next, a mother in tears appeared and hugged him for saving her daughter from the clutches of a drug dealer. The visions gently faded—just as an indescribable sense of lightness came over him.

He felt himself separate from his body and ascend above the vehicle, where he seemed to hover in place forever. From an unnatural perspective, he saw everything: the Jeep, cars stopping, people running, flashing lights.

And then he saw . . . himself . . . injured and bleeding . . . still inside the Jeep.

No! What's happening?

Calls from the first witnesses on the scene prompted a quick response from the emergency team, who would transport Drake to the nearest and most respected hospital in the county.

Drake continued to watch in awe from above as the attending crew treated his multiple injuries, including a severe head wound, in what looked like a desperate attempt to save his life.

Am I dead? No . . . Angela . . . the case.

He fought but drifted out of consciousness.

Working frantically to stop the blood loss, the crew seemed to be doing everything in their power to sustain his life. They only paused to check the monitor for vital signs and make split-second eye contact.

The ambulance sped toward the destination. Every second counted.

Having already been alerted to as many details as possible, the emergency room staff seemed ready for the hand-off when the ambulance arrived. Drake was rushed into a pre-set operating room, where the final assessment of his condition and life-saving measures could be administered if warranted.

Even with the ER team jumping into action, prioritizing injuries, and connecting him to life support, the head trauma he suffered had caused irreparable damage. The doctors did everything they could, but not much time passed before the local hero, Drake Harrison, was declared officially brain-dead.

Life support systems would be the only thing keeping him alive while the process of notifying his family took place. In catastrophic cases such as Drake's, nothing could be done . . . and doctors would have to explain a zero chance of survival to the family.

It was Drake's father, Richard, who took the call. Like others before them, when he and his wife, Katherine, arrived at the hospital, they were still in their night clothes. Katherine had thrown a floral duster over hers, and Richard wore a lightweight jacket.

Their red eyes and dog-tired faces were proof that this was the worst moment of their lives. The two of them took turns pacing the floor in the ICU waiting area. Little did they know that on top of the tragic news they were about to receive, they would eventually have to endure the gut-wrenching process of removing artificial life support.

Drake's identification had been pulled and attached to a clipboard, which had fallen to the floor, along with the other contents of his pockets, during the flurry of activity in the emergency room. When a nurse picked it up and placed it on the counter, she stopped and studied it for a minute.

"Hey, he's an organ donor," she said to the others. "I'll let Lisa know right away. Timing's everything."

Richard and Katherine Harrison had also learned of their son's donor status shortly after receiving the grave news. They now sat in a quiet corner, comforting each other.

"I'm not surprised, even though he never talked about it," Richard whispered.

"Me either," sobbed Katherine. "It's exactly the kind of thing he would do."

Richard gently took her hands, squeezing them affectionately. "Even now, he's saving someone."

Amid the unspeakable agony, they had to face the harsh reality that their son was already gone. His entire life was now locked into the deepest recesses of his being and functioning only through the miracle of life support.

Without machines, there would be no brain activity, and it was Richard, the patriarch, who finally mustered the strength to do what had to be done. He nodded to the doctor, and the medical staff took it from there. Preparations were now underway for the removal of any vital organs that were undamaged in Drake Harrison's body.

The shattered family was given permission to spend as much time as they wanted by Drake's side before the machines would be disengaged.

His heart beat one last time before he slipped away into the inaccessible void.

The secret to the case went with him.

FIVE

STRANGE OCCURRENCES

The suitability of Drake Harrison's heart was approved and matched to an unsuspecting transplant patient, and the life-saving call went out.

Nearly missing the ring over the volume on the TV, Clark issued a rushed "Hello."

"Hello, Mr. Steele," the voice said. "This is Susan Wright with Lakeside Memorial, and I believe this is the call you've been waiting for."

Clark knew instantly what she meant, and his own weakened heart leaped at the thought. The critical moment had arrived. He would need to leave immediately for evaluation and pre-op procedures.

After managing a polite thank you and assuring her he was on his way, the surreal moment transported him into a trance-like state.

Rachel came rushing to his side. And yet, to Clark, she seemed to be moving in slow motion. When they hugged, he could feel her shaking, but he could also sense her strength. She was his safe haven. Just having her close had restored him to a calm demeanor.

Clark began to supervise the pre-planned routine he'd been instructed to rehearse for timing's sake, ending with the placement of packed bags by the front door. In no time, the physical part was done, but the emotional preparation would continue on the drive over.

✳

Procedures at Lakeside Memorial began smoothly in the hands of seasoned transplant coordinator Lisa Wells. After Clark's evaluation, she reviewed the protocol and took him through processing, including both physical and emotional testing.

"Everything looks good," she said. "They're going to take you to your room now, Clark."

Shortly after, when he was settled in and resting, she reappeared, stepping softly into his room.

"Oh, good, you look comfortable," she said. "Hey, just a reminder. Your most likely scenario is staying at the hospital for a couple of weeks and then some closely monitored recovery time at home."

Clark nodded. "That's what I hear. Thanks."

He was watching Rachel, who was speaking with a nurse just outside the door.

"Of course," Lisa said. "We've already started you on immuno-suppressant medications to prevent rejection. And in the next three months, you can plan on some tests or biopsies to check your progress."

Clark swung his legs over the edge of the hospital bed and stared out the window. "The fun never ends," he said.

Lisa grinned. "You're going to be fine, Clark. Dr. Evans is one of the best, and we have a great match."

Her assurances made him think about his donor. Who was it? What kind of tragedy led to the blessing he was about to receive?

"Do you know who my donor was?" he asked.

"Well, yes, I do have access to that information," Lisa said. "But it's confidential unless involved parties officially agree to disclose."

"How often does that happen?" he asked.

"More often than you'd probably think," she said. "Should be any time now, Clark. Just relax if you can."

He swung back around, rested on the pillows, and studied the private room for a minute.

There was a TV, a recliner, a desk, and everything he needed. It wasn't that bad, except for the walls. For some reason, no matter what hospital he was in, they never got the wall color right. It always felt off. Unfriendly.

All of a sudden, he started shivering. Whether it was a psychological reaction to focusing on the cold, hospital walls, or thoughts of the impending surgery, he couldn't seem to stop.

Rachel snapped to action, covering him with extra blankets and fussing over him until the trembling subsided.

Before long, the final transfer took place. It was just a quick, minutes-long trip. But to Clark, it felt like an eternity.

Doctors and nurses, busy with a flurry of technical sights and sounds, welcomed him to the surgical unit. The critical activity, including monitors, IV units, and even the strange lighting, all played a part in reigniting his profound awareness of the risk.

Dr. Evans, the transplant surgeon, came to Clark's bedside and patted his shoulder. "How you doing, Clark? You ready?"

"Ready as I'm ever going to be, I guess," he said.

The doctor nodded and smiled. "Good. Hey, no worries, we're going to take great care of you, and when you recover, you're going to start feeling a whole lot better."

"Sounds good, Doc," he said. "Thanks."

Dr. Evans gave his shoulder one last pat. "We're about ready to get started." He turned to leave but then stopped. "Oh, look who's here, perfect timing."

"Hi, Clark. I'm Ann Reddick, and I'll be your anesthesiologist today. Let's get you comfortable."

Seconds before drifting out of consciousness, he thought of Rachel.

She's my everything. I can't leave her. Please, God, stay with me and get me through this. I love her so much. Please let us have a family.

✳

Clark's surgery and recovery were extraordinary. A textbook case, from the perfect transplant to his swift recuperation. He was in awe.

He thought back to his first conscious recollection after the surgery and how he was startled by the power of his new heartbeat. It pumped with a force he couldn't even remember experiencing before.

His recovery time in the hospital was a great success but trying at the same time. Staring at the same off-color walls every day was tiresome. He longed for home. There was still some soreness from the procedure but overshadowing everything was the new life energy he felt surging through his body.

Clark didn't mind the testing, physical therapy, and constant monitoring too much. It took up quite a bit of time, and he was learning a great deal, especially about aftercare. And ultimately, the necessary procedures would ensure a timely discharge.

But his long visits with Rachel were the saving grace during his time there. When she showed up, she always had a surprise— some creative way to spend time together. On a couple of visits, she brought a tablet and challenged him to some e-games. Since Clark looked forward to any distraction and never had time for such things at home, he was all in.

Rachel snuggled close to his hospital bed, and the games began. In no time at all, they were lost in competition and laughing loud enough for the nurse to have to quiet them down.

When the day of Clark's release finally came, he listened to his discharge instructions and signed papers. He wasn't thrilled with some of the guidelines and limitations but would follow them carefully. No way did he want to test the orders and earn a repeat stay.

Once he was settled in at home, things only got better, and it seemed to take no time at all for a real sense of vitality to return. From his very first breath with the donor heart, he saw his newfound health as a true blessing. Just the fact that modern medicine was able to offer such a miracle was something he would thank God for every day.

By taking things slowly and diligently following the doctor's orders, he'd even been able to make an earlier-than-expected visit to Steele Construction. Most of the team was on lunch break when he arrived, so he was able to share his good news with nearly everyone. At the end of the update, he was almost brought to tears when an unexpected standing ovation broke out.

Subsequent updates were mainly more of the same, with two minor exceptions: a little anxiety and trouble sleeping. Aside from that, he was feeling great and getting a little more active every day. But he wasn't the only one. Rachel seemed more animated than usual, continually smiling and humming around the house. Nothing seemed to bother her, not even taking care of some of the heavy lifting he would normally attend to.

Clark came up behind her in the kitchen and wrapped his arms around her. "You're happy to have the surgery behind us, aren't you?"

She looked over her shoulder. "Oh my gosh, yes! And I like seeing you doing all the right things."

"Yeah, I'm sure that's why I'm doing so great." He turned her around and gave her a wink.

"And you know me, I like being ahead of schedule."

She grinned. "Yes, yes, you do."

Days went by, and Clark continued to marvel at the astonishing physical healing but was becoming a little troubled by his emotional state. The minor anxiety and trouble sleeping were being overshadowed by more disturbing side effects.

Out of nowhere, a strong sense of foreboding would wash over him, and sometimes it was even accompanied by flashes of strange images that he couldn't explain. Clark was on edge and struggled to make sense of it. After a little brainstorming with Rachel, he wondered if it might have something to do with the lingering effects of anesthesia or possibly new medications.

There were nights when he tossed and turned and others when Rachel found him out of bed in the middle of the night, wandering around the house or reading.

"Clark, what are you doing?" she had cried during the most recent incident.

"Geez, you scared me," he said. "Sorry. I wasn't sleeping again, and I didn't want to wake you."

"Don't worry about me," she said. "This is about making sure you're okay. You know, I haven't even told you yet, but you've been talking in your sleep too."

"You're kidding me," Clark said.

"No," she said. "I can't understand most of what you say, but there were a couple of things I thought I heard pretty clearly."

"Really?" he asked.

"Yeah," Rachel said. "Something about 'took my life' and 'following rules.' I can't remember exactly right now." She scoffed at herself, looking away. "It sounds stupid, I know, but I even wrote it down."

"Geez, can things get any weirder?" Clark asked.

She moved in close for a hug. "It's going to be okay."

As strange as it all was, there were still normal times between the startling incidents, so Clark brushed them off as best he could. But

Rachel was paying attention.

One morning, he almost screamed her name from the direction of the bedroom, causing her to break a glass in the sink. She left it and flew from the kitchen, but the room was empty when she got there. She had to call his name twice before he answered weakly from just inside the master bath.

When she rounded the doorway, he was standing frozen, in front of the mirror, with his head hanging down.

"Clark, you scared me!" she said. "What is going on?"

"Rach, when I looked in the mirror, it wasn't me," he said, reaching for her. "I saw a strange face there for a second."

"Oh my God, Clark," she said, holding him close. "What is happening?"

"I don't know, Babe," he whispered. "This one freaked me out."

"What exactly did you see?" she asked.

He shook his head. "It was like . . . like the ghost of a man staring at me."

"What?" she cried.

"Don't worry, it's probably the medicine," he said. "I think I'm over it. I'll be okay."

"I don't know, Clark," she said. "That's really strange. I think we need to call your doctors again."

"Yeah. Yeah, maybe we should," he agreed.

"Do you want to rest for a while?" Rachel asked.

"No, I'm rested," he said. "I just want a normal day."

"Okay, are you feeling up to breakfast?" she asked as she gently turned him toward the door.

He wrapped her in a hug. "Yeah, sounds good."

Once she had him settled at the counter, she began to flit about, demonstrating a real finesse in the kitchen. While reaching into the fridge for eggs and juice, she said, "I'm so sorry your day started like that, but I'm glad you got to sleep in."

"Yeah, these days, I'm happy to get any sleep at all," Clark said. All the tossing and turning and weird dreams—flashes—or whatever they are."

"Wow, I thought maybe they'd be gone by now," Rachel said, setting out plates. "Can you remember any details? I definitely think we should call the doctors today," she added without waiting for an answer.

"Yeah, but I'm not sure they can handle whatever this is." The comment made Rachel flinch, and Clark realized too late that he had let a bit of panic slip.

"What do you mean?" she asked.

"I don't know," he said. "I think we should run it by them, but the whole thing is just so weird."

"Well, that's for sure," she said. "But I think the side effects are causing you way too much stress. And that can't be good."

"Yeah, okay," Clark agreed. "We'll call after breakfast."

He wasn't getting his hopes up because, every time the doctors had seen him for a recheck, they'd been elated with test results and his overall progress. They'd gone so far as to tease him about Rachel's brilliant home nursing skills.

And, as fate would have it, at that very moment, he was watching her put together a list of medications—in essence—proving them right.

When he finally had the next appointment, he shared the specifics of the weird occurrences—unusual thoughts, flashing images, and talking in his sleep. But the doctors didn't seem fazed and merely suggested that he and Rachel remember what he had been through. They seemed confident that over time, everything, including his sleeping habits, would return to normal.

The reassuring report left Clark feeling some relief, clearly enhanced by the realization that he wouldn't have to go back for a while. In his moment of satisfaction, he offered to take Rachel to dinner, despite it being unusually early. That aside, she was onboard immediately.

"Yeah, any break from cooking is okay by me," she said with a wink.

The open parking spaces were plentiful, inviting them to take their pick, so Rachel suggested a few close to the door. But for some reason, Clark felt compelled to park far away, even though the other spots were much more convenient. He caught Rachel's curious look but said nothing and followed his instincts.

The two of them matched the pace of the leisurely day by making an unhurried walk up to the front door. After stepping inside, Clark noticed only one refined-looking senior couple waiting ahead of them. The place was nearly empty, and the likelihood of being seated quickly looked like a sure thing.

Maybe I can get used to early dining.

"It's like we have our own private booking," he whispered. "I wonder if this is how retired people feel—like they own the joint?"

"Stop!" Rachel said, grinning and shaking her head at his nonsense.

Clark watched as the hostess exchanged pleasantries while seating the couple ahead of them.

"Our hostess is making a valiant effort, but I'll bet she's been on her feet all day," Clark said. "Look how she's leaning on the column next to the table and keeps shifting her weight."

"Yeah, you're right," Rachel said. "When did you get so observant?"

"I don't know," he said. "But let's leave her an extra big tip."

When she returned and escorted them to their table, Clark noticed *Amy* printed on her nametag and tried it out for the first time when he thanked her for the menus. She left them some water, said she would be back in a few minutes to take their order, and hustled off toward the kitchen.

After deciding on prime rib, Clark was taking a thirsty drink of the ice-cold water when he was instantly stricken with a fierce headache. His breath caught, and he was still wincing from the pain when a startling vision caught him by surprise.

His heart rate quickened, and his hands began to shake, even though the unwelcome image had already disappeared.

Rachel took his hands. "Clark, what is it?" Her voice broke the spell, but he could still feel the blood rushing through his veins.

"Another flash. First, the pain in my head—and then an image flickered. But it's gone, just like the others."

"Oh, Clark!" cried Rachel. "What's it this time?"

His mind was still reeling. "It's so . . . so random. But I . . . I saw popcorn."

"What?" she said, looking around. "That's so weird. Do you want to just leave and get some rest?"

"No, I'll be all right," he said. "Let's just finish dinner, and then I can rest when we get home."

"Okay, but only if you're sure," she agreed. "If you need to, we can just take dinner and go."

✳

Later in the evening, soothed by scented candles, Clark and Rachel enjoyed a sweet respite, snuggling in front of the TV. That is, until the episode from earlier in the day came up. Even though it was minor on the list of weird occurrences, it was still concerning.

The strange visions and thoughts were haunting and unexplainable. Clark was secretly starting to doubt his own sanity.

Even though he had just come from a reassuring doctor's appointment, he was no less concerned about what was happening. Maybe it was time to seek a new kind of help. Maybe a neurological or psychological evaluation wouldn't hurt.

But after a short reprieve from any new episodes, he let the idea slip right out of mind.

✳

A number of succeeding days had their challenges, but most were healing, and Clark felt stronger than he had in years. In many ways, it was hard to believe that he'd actually been through major surgery and the strange post-surgery side effects.

It was a humid, sundrenched weekday morning when he made his way over to the window seat facing the front of the house. As he took in the view and his first sip of Columbia's finest, he found himself captivated by the fan of radiant light bathing the flower beds. The almost ethereal scene was hypnotic and summoned him to be a part of it. He rested there for a good while, calmly immersed as if frozen in time, until the alarm in the kitchen broke the enchanted spell.

The jolt back to reality prompted a quick assessment of the remainder of the day. The morning routine had already worn on him, and he could tell he wasn't functioning at a normal energy level. He called work with a few instructions and gave in to the temptation of nature by doing some light gardening.

Because it was so out of the ordinary, the thought took him by surprise. He wasn't usually one for spending much hands-on time with such activities. But his mind whispered, *Today, I feel almost drawn to it.*

It would have been much more in keeping with his character to enjoy the final result of someone else's creative work. But Clark's intuition was telling him that the new longing to be outside with his hands in the soil was somehow connected to his body's own natural recovery plan. If he was right, it was the power of that intrinsic therapy that was luring him into the sunlight and nature.

It was about mid-morning when the iced coffee, which had recently become one of his new favorites, was ready. He grabbed the travel mug and then a pair of gardening gloves from the storage shelf as he exited through the garage.

After taking a few steps, he turned around and, from about six feet, tossed the gloves backward. They landed perfectly on the shelf, almost as if they had never been moved. It was just one of those weird things that happened, and Clark's grin revealed the satisfaction he felt from the perfection of his own aim.

Once the weeding was out of the way, he planted several trays of azaleas as a surprise for Rachel. They were watered well, and he was cleaning up the mess when, suddenly, he flinched, causing him to lose his balance and awkwardly brace himself against the sidewalk.

The startling image of a child flashed. His heart skipped a beat.

In the past, he had instinctively tried to resist the flashes, but not this time. He was determined to hang on to the image. So, despite the panic surging through his body, he kept his eyes closed and tried to stay focused.

Even though the vision lingered for only seconds, he knew what he saw. It was the innocent face of a little girl . . . something about her forsaken expression caused him great anxiety.

With his new heart racing, he headed for the safety of the house. After settling into his favorite spot on the leather sectional, his mind wandered to the peaceful times between past episodes when he had actually convinced himself that he might be able to deal with the strange occurrences. But each time he was faced with a new one, it was becoming more unbearable.

While waiting impatiently for Rachel to get home, he paced back and forth near his computer before finally sitting down. After a few keystrokes, the search bar read *psychologist*.

When Rachel finally entered the room, he was so engrossed in the search that he jumped when she said, "Hey, I'm home!"

Sounding uncharacteristically vulnerable, he whispered, "Rach, I don't think I can go on like this. Something's not right."

SIX

WHEN YOU KISS ME

Clark was making a right into the parking lot when he caught a brief glimpse of the name *Dr. Deanna Brill* on an oversized marquee. The sign marked the frontage of a past-its-prime brick office building, one that perhaps had the ability to dampen the spirits of someone overly sensitive to their surroundings. But luckily, he appreciated such things.

The atmosphere transformed as he passed through the lobby and entered an especially pleasant waiting room. The skillful decorating was casual but elegant. Stylish furnishings, accompanied by soft music and lighting, were an integral part of the warm, inviting ambiance.

After settling into an extremely comfortable upholstered chair, he began his paperwork. The sheer radiance from the table lamp lit the space well, making it easy to complete the documents. And in no time at all, he heard the friendly voice of the office assistant, Becca, calling his name.

Right off the bat, Dr. Brill came across as warm and caring, a true people-person, and he thought she had chosen her profession well. He was also pretty sure he was picking up on a hint of deep discernment. The tell was in her eyes.

As he scanned the room, he found himself taking intricate note of the specifics as if he would be tested later. Eventually, an awareness of his own new observational skills began to register, and he shook his head.

"You probably noticed the older building," Dr. Brill said. "I've been here since early in my practice. Too busy to move, I'd rather spend that time with patients. And, anyway, I love the character of older things."

"Me too," Clark agreed.

"Right, of course, you're an architect," Dr. Brill said. "Well, let's get started. So, Clark, why don't you bring me up to speed with everything that's been going on with you."

Just as he began to share details of the unsettling anomaly in his life, a shadow from a sudden cloud cover moved across the window, casting gloominess over the room. He watched Dr. Brill, who seemed to be listening intently, reach for the remote on her desk and turn up the lights.

"Well, I've been having these strange experiences that are . . . interfering with my life," explained Clark. "Like nightmares, strange preferences—really everything from disturbing thoughts to sudden pictures that flash through my mind. And the weirdest thing is, all of it started after my transplant surgery."

"Heart transplant, right?" she verified. After reaching for her tablet, she made a specific note connecting the start of his distress to the early post-surgery period.

Clark tapped his chest. "Yeah—heart. I've had trouble resting at night, and my wife, Rachel, says I've even been talking in my sleep. I really didn't want to make a big deal about any of this, but things just keep happening. That's why I thought a consultation might be a good idea."

"You did the right thing," assured Dr. Brill.

"The visions seem to come out of nowhere," he added. "And they're so quick, I can't totally grasp them. Some have been mundane, like personal items and things, but the latest ones have been more disturbing."

"Can you tell me about those?" Dr. Brill asked.

"Just the other morning," he said. "I saw the flash of a man's face while I was looking in the mirror. And as if that wasn't weird enough, there was one that was even worse when I was in the garden. The face of a little girl flashed—and I'm not going to lie—it sent chills down my spine. For some reason, I got a real sense of dread with that one."

"Of course," she said. "Normal reaction."

Clark took a deep breath and leaned back in his chair. "Dr. Brill, I have no idea what's happening to me."

"Well, I'm glad you came in," she said. "Let's see if we can figure this out together."

He watched her polish off a few notes before inviting him to tell her more about his general health and, specifically, the heart transplant.

During what would become a lengthy part of the session, she was full of questions, and the exchange got quite spirited.

"Clark, your story is amazing," she said. "I've never worked with a patient who's gone through such an astonishing procedure. Please go on."

When the session resumed, he caught himself closely assessing her character again and wondering where this new obsession had come from. It was like an instinct he couldn't turn off. He really liked Dr. Brill and didn't want to show disrespect by analyzing her the entire time.

Thankfully, she didn't seem to notice.

"Clark, I have to tell you," she said. "Your symptoms are fascinating. Most of my patients come in with issues of a more expected nature—more routine. I don't know if I've ever worked with such an intriguing case, but I really want to help you figure out what's going on."

"Thanks," he said. "I didn't know what else to do."

"Your instincts were right," Dr. Brill said. "Now, let's get you on the books for your next appointment. And, Clark, if you put together a detailed journal of all of the unusual things you've experienced since the surgery and bring it with you next time, that would be a great help. Also, maybe you can find some relaxing activities like meditation, reading, or walks in the park. Good ways to de-stress."

"Okay," he said. "I'll do my best."

"You'll do great," she said. "See you in a few days."

✳

When Clark walked back in for the next appointment just forty-eight hours later, the first thing he did was introduce her to Rachel and present his journal. Dr. Brill seemed to light up as she flipped through the pages and thanked him for doing such a thorough job so quickly.

"This kind of specificity gives me a lot to work with," she said. "Oh, I wanted to ask. Would you mind if we made an audio recording of the session? In case we need to revisit anything in the future?"

Clark grinned. "Other than disliking the sound of my own voice on audio, no objection."

She smiled and pushed the record button. "Whenever you're ready."

"Well, the beginning is probably going to be the hardest to explain because everything was so vague," began Clark. "I just remember tossing and turning at night and feeling a sense of dread. And even though there was no apparent reason for it, I felt like something bad had happened. Since it was at night, of course, I just chalked it up to bad dreams. But deep down, something was telling me it was different."

He looked at Rachel for a quick second before continuing. "And then, I would describe the episodes as split-second images or visions that just come out of nowhere. They scare the hell out of me and then just disappear."

Dr. Brill kept her eyes on Clark while slowly spinning a pen on top of a legal pad. "So, was there anything on those days that upset you or caused you concern . . . anything you can remember?"

"No, it would have, actually, been the opposite," he began. "Physically, I'd been feeling great—so much better than before my transplant.

"Wait, there is something. I've been strangely drawn to things that I never much liked before, like coffee and gardening. That's definitely a weird new thing, but physically speaking, I feel strong, almost like a newer, more invincible me. The success of the surgery has been a complete relief. I . . . I mean it saved my life."

"That's so great, Clark," she said. "Amazing what they can do."

"It really is," he said.

"You know, sometimes I get headaches with the other symptoms," he continued. "And then there's the talking in my sleep, like I mentioned. That's new too. Most of the time, Rachel can't make out what I'm saying, but on one occasion, she's almost positive she heard me say, 'follow the rules' and 'took my life.' She even wrote it down in case it would mean something to me later."

"Hmm . . . well, it's possible you were simply dreaming," proposed Dr. Brill. "But can you remember any more details from those episodes?"

"No," he said, turning to Rachel.

"Well, at first, I thought he was probably just dreaming too," Rachel said. "But now I'm not so sure. Even after long discussions, he could never remember anything more."

"And other than that," Clark added, "I've mostly had weird thoughts and random flashes. The ones I can remember are on the list I gave you. The oddest thing is that some of the images are heavy and negative, while others don't bother me."

"Which ones would you describe as the most negative?" Dr. Brill asked.

After taking a deep breath, Clark said, "Well, definitely the ones where I've seen faces, the man in the mirror . . . and the little girl. The little girl was the most disturbing because I felt like she needed help, like she was in trouble. And it was weird because I felt like I was the one who was supposed to help her. Like all of the episodes, it was fleeting but so real. Even after the vision was gone, I could still feel my heart racing for a while."

Clark shifted in his seat as he recalled the particularly stressful incident—but then shook his head as if trying to erase the memory.

"I know we haven't had a reason to talk about it yet, but Rachel and I really want a family one day," he revealed. "And that little girl looked the way I've imagined our daughter might look."

Rachel took his hand. "Oh, Clark," she said.

"And you feel like this medical situation is a roadblock?" Dr. Brill asked.

Clark glanced at Rachel before answering. "Exactly."

"I'm sure you'll have a family one day," Dr. Brill said. "Let's see if we can get you headed in that direction."

Clark gave her a grateful smile.

"Okay, Clark," she added, "In any of the flashes that you remember, did you ever have a sense of where you were?"

"Hmm . . . maybe." He closed his eyes. "In a few of them, I did feel like . . . like I might be inside a room." And then, as if hypnotized by the memory, he got very still. When he spoke, it was in a weakened voice. "I didn't really feel like me. I wanted to know what happened there. But just like that, it was gone."

Dr. Brill looked at him for the longest time as if lost in thought. Clark wondered if what he said had prompted the reaction.

Speaking very softly, Dr. Brill said, "Clark, you can relax now. I know this isn't easy on you, but you're really doing a great job, and it's giving me a lot to go on. I think from here on out we should plan to meet often, but the sessions don't have to be too long. I do want to revisit that last thought, as well as others, very soon," she added. "There may be more detail there than you realize."

"Does that mean you might already have an opinion?" Clark asked.

"Well, actually, I do have a few things rolling around," she said. "One is the possibility of working with a hypnotherapist. They can be a great help in retrieving memories. Just something to think about."

"A hypnotherapist?" he repeated. "Well, that's something I wouldn't have thought of on my own."

"Well, it wouldn't need to be for a while, if at all," Dr. Brill said. "Just food for thought."

She swiveled her chair to the left. "Rachel, is there anything else you'd like to share before we break for today?"

"Well," she started but then looked at Clark and hesitated.

Clark put his arm around her. "What is it?"

"It's just something I'm not sure I should mention because I don't want to worry you," she whispered.

"Rach, you know you can talk to me about anything," he said. "And we're all about opening up in these sessions—so, please, go ahead."

After pausing for a minute and looking a little flushed, she finally said, "Well, I've noticed that it's a little different when . . . when you . . . kiss me now."

"What?" exclaimed Clark. "Are you kidding me? Why didn't you tell me?"

"I didn't want to worry you," she said. "You have too much on you already."

"Rach, I'm so sorry," Clark said.

"No. No, don't be," she said. "The kisses are great, just a little different. I shouldn't have mentioned it. It's probably just my imagination anyway."

"With everything else that's going on, I'm sure it's not," he said. "Sorry, Babe. We can talk some more about it on the way home."

Rachel rested her head on his shoulder. "Clark, it's really okay."

"Well, Dr. Brill, there's some new information even I didn't know," Clark said.

"Well, that is an interesting new detail," she said. "But you know what, you two, we are going to figure this out. I promise. Oh, and before I forget, Clark, did you remember to bring a list of your current medications? I want to check for side effects."

Now only half-engaged, he fumbled in his pocket for the list. "Uh, yeah . . . yeah, here it is."

"Thanks," Dr. Brill said, walking them to the door.

"You sure look like you're thinking deeply about something," Clark said.

"Well, I wasn't ready to say anything just yet," Dr. Brill confessed. "But I might actually have a hunch about your symptoms. But before I can be less cryptic, I need to convince myself that I'm on the right track. So, I've got some research to do. See you soon."

SEVEN

I'M NOT CRAZY

Clark and Rachel were out of breath when they came racing into the next appointment right on the button.

"Sorry. Traffic," Clark said. "But we made it."

Dr. Brill looked up from her computer with a big smile. Yes, you did. Nice to see you both. Rachel, it's great that you can join us."

"Thank you," she said. "But I don't know that I'm actually of any help."

"Well, I think the last session may have been more productive than any of us thought," Dr. Brill said with a peculiar twinkle in her eye.

"Really," Clark said, giving Rachel a quick glance.

"Yeah, I've got something interesting to share with you, but for now, just grab a chair and make yourselves comfortable," she guided. "And we can just pick up where we left off. But first, tell me how you've been, Clark. Anything new?"

He shook his head. "No, about the same. But there is another episode I haven't had a chance to tell you about."

"Really," Dr. Brill said. "Well, I definitely want to hear about that."

"Well, with all of the medical changes, Rachel and I have been on a health kick, and one of our favorite activities has been walking exercise trails," he began.

Dr. Brill nodded with a physician's approval. "That's great."

"Anyway," he said. "We were both about halfway down this mulched path on one of our regular trails and 'in the zone,' as we like to call it. That's when we rarely talk and just enjoy the fresh air and scenery. No matter where you look on that trail, it's thick with beautiful trees."

"Nice," Dr. Brill said.

"Yeah, well, about that time, Rachel decided to run on ahead to the next exercise spot," added Clark. "She'd been gone for a couple of minutes when I heard a rustling in the woods. I turned toward the sound, and at first, everything seemed hazy. But after my eyes adjusted, there was a flash of an open area that I'd never noticed before. It was fairly big, but what really caught my attention was the perfect, symmetrical shape. In that split second, I remember thinking, 'What is that doing here?' And then, just like that . . . it was gone."

"What happened next?" Dr. Brill almost whispered.

"Well, after the vision," Clark said, "I was just standing there looking at the familiar landscape again. There it was, just as normal as it could be. Once I gained control of my senses, it hit me that I'd probably had another flash, or whatever we've decided to call them."

"And was Rachel still ahead of you while all of this was happening?" Dr. Brill asked.

"Yeah, I could actually see her down the trail," Clark said. "In our regular routine, she runs on ahead to complete the exercise challenge, and then I catch up. But she always looks back to check on me, and in this case, I think she sensed something unusual going on. So, she backtracked."

"If I may interject," Rachel said. "I wasn't right next to Clark when the episode happened, but he's right; I keep a pretty good eye on him. And something didn't seem right, so I went back. When he compared the new episode to the others, there was a difference this time. Apparently, the new vision seemed superimposed over reality."

"Oh, I think I see what you're saying," Dr. Brill said. "In the other incidents, the flashes would entirely replace reality, right?"

"Exactly," Clark confirmed. "But in this case, I was still very aware of my surroundings and that I was still on the trail. What I saw was like a vision layered over the existing scene. Whereas, in the others, everything except the vision seemed to disappear. I wish I could make sense of it. Sometimes, when I haven't had an episode for a while, I think they've gone away. But now, I'm not sure if they ever will. You know, it's really the persistence of the flashes that's brought me here."

"We're going to figure it out, Clark," Dr. Brill said. "Is there anything else from this week or from your journal that you wanted to share?"

"You know, I haven't been able to put my finger on it before now," he said. "But I think I finally have a better sense of what I'm feeling when I'm having an episode. It's almost as if my thoughts are being invaded. Like I'm someone else or seeing images through someone else's eyes. I can feel a presence. How's that for weird?"

Dr. Brill looked stunned. "Well, if that isn't a perfect door being opened, I don't know what is! Clark, I think now is the right time to let you in on a hunch. During our last session, it really struck me that your symptoms showed up only after the heart transplant. And that train of thought took me back to a seminar I attended years ago. Ever since you left, I've been researching the topic, and even though it's a long shot, I think we should, at least, look into it in your case. Are you ready to consider something really off the beaten path?"

"Well, aren't you being mysterious?" quipped Clark.

"Yeah, sorry," she said. "This is definitely something different, though. Our seminar instructor presented us with some compelling research—basically proving the existence of a strange phenomenon. It involved recipients of heart and other organ transplants and specifically touched on psychological changes a patient might go through after receiving the life-saving surgery. So, of course, I couldn't help wondering if your strange encounters could be connected. I'll be the first to admit I'm going on instinct here, but I've learned to trust it over the years. It's always served me well."

"Where is this going exactly?" Clark asked.

She smiled and quickly scanned her prepared notes. "Well, while most people fixate on the physical surgery and recovery, there is, potentially, a more profound process going on."

"And that would be . . .?" coaxed Clark.

Dr. Brill looked him in the eye. "Clark, have you ever heard anything about transplant recipients displaying characteristics of their donors?"

He paused for a second just to process the profound question. "No. What are you suggesting?"

"It's more of a notion than a suggestion at this point," Dr. Brill replied. "But let's start at the beginning. Do you know anything about your donor?"

Clark shook his head. "Nothing. But I've always wondered, even before the transplant."

"Yeah, most people do," she replied. "Let me see if I can explain this a little better. Astonishing evidence exists, confirming the transfer of memories, abilities, characteristics, intelligence, and maybe even spirit, from the physical donor heart to the recipient."

"That's crazy," Clark said. "You've got to be kidding. Never mind. I can tell by your expression you're not."

"No," she said, shaking her head. "Clark, I know every nerve in your body is probably sending out mini shockwaves right now, but just hear me out."

He took a deep breath. "Okay, I'm trying here."

"I know, believe me, I do," Dr. Brill said. "Okay, back to the seminar. As attendees, we already knew that every organ was made up of individual cells, but our challenge was to think beyond biology and ask ourselves if we could believe in the phenomenon proven by the research. Was it possible that every single cell could contain intelligence, memory, feelings, preferences, and potentially much more from the donor? That was the million-dollar question every one of us would have to answer for ourselves."

"It sounds crazy," Clark said. "But you think it could be related to what's going on with me?"

"Well, like I said, it's just a hunch," she said. "But yes, I think it's possible. Some refer to the heart as the center of the soul. Take a look at this brochure. It introduces the phenomenon and talks about a mysterious system of communication between the cells of the donor organ and the recipient. And it suggests that living cells conveyed during an organ transplant, could be thought of as tiny, biological vehicles carrying intelligence, feelings, behaviors, memories, and more."

Clark stared at the pamphlet as if it were the holy grail before he began to read.

There it was in black and white—the suggestion that it was, indeed, possible for the recipient to receive cellular information from the donor. The shocking concept included the transfer of memories, abilities, and characteristics, along with the physical heart.

"As crazy as it seems," Dr. Brill said, "it is a documented phenomenon."

Clark stood and began to pace. "No offense, Doc, but it sounds like science fiction to me. Have you ever worked with a patient who's experienced that?"

"No, I haven't," she said. "And I know it sounds unbelievable, but my research has convinced me that the phenomenon is real. Statistics show that five to ten percent of recipients have reported exhibiting characteristics of their donors. And I'm sure the number is higher because most people don't report. Think of it this way. Every organ is a collection of cells, so when you receive a heart, you can receive billions of cells. And the data suggest that these cells can contain information from the donor. I guess you could think of it as cellular intelligence being transmitted through a quantum energy type of communication. Thoughts, preferences, memories, and more could be transferred. There are other resource books and pamphlets available if you want to read more about it."

Clark reached for Rachel's hand and sat down beside her.

"Actually, if you're okay with it, I'd like to share a few of the documented cases with you right now," Dr. Brill added. "Think you're ready?"

"No idea," he sighed.

"Well, just stop me if anything makes you uncomfortable," Dr. Brill said. "There's one fairly well-known case involving Beth, a forty-one-year-old woman, who received a heart from thirty-three-year-old Kyle Bradford, who died in a helicopter accident. He had gone up in a weather chopper with a friend when conditions deteriorated quickly, causing the pilot to lose control.

"Shortly after Beth's surgery, she began to have almost hypnotic visions of walking through high grass in the countryside. She could actually feel the breeze encircle her, lift her off her feet, and propel her forward, always toward something . . . but she never arrived. Her fierce longing to reach the mystical destination was almost unbearable."

Dr. Brill picked up one of her class handouts. "Here, let me read from her own account. 'When I have the visions, it's like I'm in a trance. And, as if that's not alarming enough, my behavior's been strange and unpredictable. One morning, I got up and repeatedly searched the house, top to bottom, for my riding gear. After I'd literally worn myself out, I collapsed on the bed in total frustration. It was only when I calmed down that I realized I'd had another episode. The whole thing felt so real. But here's the kicker: I don't even own riding gear. I've never been on a horse.

'And besides the visions, I'm also having strange new preferences. After the transplant, all of a sudden, I became an early riser. Up with the sun and ready for a big country breakfast. Prior to the surgery, it was a quick smoothie, and I was on my way.

'Oh, and another thing is my wardrobe. I feel absolutely drawn to very casual wear, like jeans and boots. And every now and then, I throw a flannel shirt in for good measure. That is so weirdly foreign to me because my former wardrobe was much more city chic.

'So, I had to ask myself, *What is happening? Am I going crazy?* The visions, strange food cravings, and now this. I didn't know if I needed a therapist or a vacation.'"

Dr. Brill looked up from the pamphlet. "Beth explains that, during the trances, she could sometimes sense an eerie presence but was surprisingly unafraid. Even though the experience was unsettling, it was familiar somehow. And she could not deny a very personal feeling of connection with the strange energy."

"Yeah," Clark said. "I get that."

"I thought you might," Dr. Brill said. "One beautiful day, well into her recovery, Beth felt compelled to drive into the country to soak up the sunny weather and tranquil farmland. She was almost ready to head home when she came upon a flourishing property where she could see farmhands busy at work. Hypnotically drawn to the scene unfolding, she was compelled to stop the car.

"As she stepped nearer the split rail fence and the vision before her, she could feel her heart beating faster. Strangely, she realized that she could name every piece of equipment within view, recognizing a seed drill, baler, harvester, and others. But it made no sense, and a shudder traveled throughout her body. She had never experienced farms or farm equipment in her real life—only in the visions. But still, somehow, she knew she belonged out there in the middle of the homestead painting come to life.

"Beth offered no resistance as the familiar wind encircled her once more and carried her ethereal body through the moving scene. Off in the distance, she could see an old tractor in front of the barn, with at least a dozen chickens standing guard. The panorama of the rural farmland and all it had to offer gave her a sense of contentment she had never known before. Her heart was overflowing. Here's a little more of her actual account. 'The very moment the breeze set me, ever so gently, on solid ground, I could sense that strange but familiar presence again. And with every footstep toward the barn, the feeling got stronger and stronger.

'Out of nowhere, a small commotion to the right drew my attention—but it was just a couple of the chickens fussing with one another. As I smiled and turned back toward the barn, there he was. A tall, lean cowboy type, in his prime, walking straight toward me. While looking right into my soul, he paused and rested one arm up on the tractor as if ready for a photo shoot. We continued to stare at each other, almost like frozen in time. The exchange of energy was powerful. And I don't know how, but I knew I'd finally reached my destination. I was home.

'As I held his gaze, for just a split second, there was even a name on the tip of my tongue. That's when he pointed to a sign above the barn doors that read *Bradford Farms*. The next thing I knew, I was standing back at the fence again like nothing had ever happened.

'I was still shaking from the experience, so I walked a bit to settle my nerves before driving back. The whole encounter eventually inspired me to search for the identity of my donor. I was astounded to discover that Kyle Bradford had been born and raised on that family farm and was still running it with his dad when the chopper accident took his life.'"

"That's unbelievable," Clark said. "She said so many things that remind me of what I'm going through. The visions, the feeling of a presence—not to mention new preferences. Oh, and how everything felt so real, causing her heart to beat fast. I can't imagine how she felt when she found out the identity of the donor."

"I know," Dr. Brill said. "It had to be an epic moment. You know, even though the cases manifest differently, they certainly seem to have related themes."

"So, you think something like that could be what's happening to me?" Clark asked.

"Well, I definitely think we should explore the possibility," she said.

"Even though I do see similarities, I'm sorry, but it's still hard for me to believe that this is really possible," Clark said.

Dr. Brill nodded. "I know, I get it. However, let's not rule it out just yet."

"Are there more stories like that?" Clark asked.

"Many," Dr. Brill said. She handed him a folder. "This has copies of others I wanted to share with you."

"Wow, thanks," Clark said. "I have to admit, I am curious to see what other people have been through."

"My guess is that you won't be able to put it down," Dr. Brill said. "Before we go on, I have one more story, but it's a little different from the others. This one is a pretty chilling account, so I'll let you decide if you want to hear it or not."

"Yeah, at this point, why not," he said. "I'm already worked up."

"I can save it for later if you want a break," she offered.

"No, I want to hear it," Clark said.

"Well, there was another female recipient, Melanie, who had been having cravings and preferences for things that she had never liked before, such as seafood and the taste of mint," began Dr. Brill. "After her transplant, they had mysteriously become some of her favorites. Her music preferences had even shifted. She couldn't get the strange experiences out of her mind, and in time, decided to inquire about her donor.

"Eventually, she met with the donor family and shared some of the eerie happenings, and they assured her that the new unfamiliar preferences matched the donor's perfectly. Even though the information seemed to help her deal with the anxiety that accompanied the strange new inclinations, sadly, years later, she would jump from a bridge to her death."

Dr. Brill looked up. "Are you sure you're ready for this next part?"

"What happened?" Clark asked.

"Well, the really chilling part of the story was that the organ donor had done the very same thing."

Rachel stirred, scooted a little closer to Clark, and took his hand.

"I'm sorry it's so graphic," Dr. Brill said. "But it's such a powerful example of the phenomenon. I debated whether or not to share that one with you because of its disturbing nature."

"No, it's fine," Clark said. "It's almost as if the donor's spirit was stronger than Melanie's."

Dr. Brill's eyes opened wide, and she hesitated for a couple of seconds, allowing the powerful thought to fully register. She took a deep breath and continued with brief summaries from a few other cases, giving Clark an even better picture of the manifestation in the lives of other recipients.

"So, in short," she said, "there's already been substantial research and documentation on the phenomenon. And, I have to say, my gut is telling me that we should look into it in your case."

"Honestly, Dr. Brill, this is blowing my mind and actually making some sense at the same time!" exclaimed Clark. "One thing's for sure. If that could be what's going on with me, then my donor must have had an intense life. It makes me think it might be risky to dig into. But on the other hand, some validation that I'm not crazy would sure be nice."

"Well, we can dig into it together," she said. "But take all the time you need to consider everything. In many cases, the families and friends of donors and recipients like the idea of meeting and even decide to remain in each other's lives afterward. But you have a lot to think about and certainly don't have to make that decision today."

"No, I really want to," Clark said. "But I'm not going to lie . . . it's a little scary."

"I know it can be, but I'll be with you every step of the way," she promised.

By this time, Clark was on his feet, pacing again. "I appreciate that. I really want answers, but I'm just not sure."

"Clark, here's an idea," she said. "Maybe we could just find out the identity of the donor for now and see if that information alone sheds any light on your case."

Clark took Rachel's hand. "What do you think?"

"Well, I don't see how it could hurt anything," she said. "But, you know, I'll support any decision you make."

He took a deep breath and turned to face Dr. Brill. "I have no idea if I'm ready or not, but let's do it."

"It's going to be okay, Clark," she said calmly. "Always remember, we're in control of each and every step.

"The best approach going forward will be for me to consult with the transplant coordinator and your doctors to share my theory. Then, I think they'll be more likely to provide the identity of the donor and maybe even future contact information."

"Okay," Clark said. "That'll give me time to work on my nerves."

"It's natural to be curious about your donor's identity and still anxious at the same time," Dr. Brill said. "I'm sure it feels more intimidating just knowing it might actually become reality."

"That's for sure," Clark said. "My heart is pounding. And with what it's already been through, I'm starting to wonder just how much it can take."

✳

In the stillness between afternoon appointments, Dr. Brill made her first call to the transplant coordinator, Lisa Wells, who promised to look into it right away.

It didn't take long for the return call, but surprisingly, it came from Dr. Paul Malloy, Clark's cardiologist, as well as an old patient and friend. Dr. Brill had treated Dr. Malloy before on the stresses of the inevitable loss of life witnessed within his profession. Ever since then, they had been good acquaintances.

"Hope you don't mind," he said. Lisa was going to call you back, but when I heard your name, I offered to make the call instead. I hope everything is going well, but I only have a few minutes, so let me get right to it. Dr. Evans and I talked, and I just want to get an update on what's going on with Clark and hear more about this phenomenon." There was an inherent interest in his voice.

"I understand," Dr. Brill said. "Thanks for getting back so quickly."

She gave him the latest on Clark's symptoms and his struggles in recovery, shared her theory, and explained how she thought connecting Clark to the donor family might actually be helpful in his treatment.

"Fascinating," Dr. Malloy said. "But you really believe that's what's going on?"

Dr. Brill took a long, thoughtful pause and said, "What I believe is that we should find out."

"Okay," he said. "This is definitely not the direction I thought the case was going. But I do have a name for you."

When he spoke the name, Dr. Brill suddenly covered her mouth and sank into her office chair. "No!" she stammered. "It can't be."

"Dr. Brill, are you okay?" Dr. Malloy asked.

"Yes. I'm so sorry," she said. "I . . . I knew him."

"Gosh, I'm terribly sorry," Dr. Malloy said.

"Thank you," Dr. Brill said. "Wow, that really caught me off guard. I hope I can focus on the rest of the conversation."

"I understand," he said. "Do you want to talk later?"

She shook her head. "Oh, no, please . . . please go on."

"I was just going to say we've actually had a few other recipients with some unusual side effects," shared Dr. Malloy.

"What—really?" Dr. Brill said. "So, you've heard of the phenomenon?"

"Well, not your phenomenon, per se," he said. "Just of other recipients with . . . let's say . . . issues. Actually, would you consider meeting with a four-year-old heart recipient named Savannah, who's been acting strangely and worrying her parents?"

"Well, yes, of course," she agreed. "I'm open to meeting with her or any other recipient having strange side effects. Maybe I can help them and better understand what Clark is going through at the same time."

"Great," Dr. Malloy said. "Looks like we might be able to help each other with patient treatment."

"It sure does," she agreed. "Thank you, again, for the name of the donor."

"Happy to help," he said. "Best of luck. Hey, my assistant can block another time on the calendar if you want to discuss the specifics of Savannah's case or of working together in the future."

"Sounds good," she said. "If you can transfer me, I'll do that before I hang up. Thanks again."

Shortly after the arrangements were made, Becca, her assistant, tapped on the door.

"C'mon in," Dr. Brill said.

"Thanks," Becca said. "Just wanted to go over a few changes to your schedule for tomorrow."

Dr. Brill nodded but passed right over the topic. "You know, Becca, I'm beginning to think that my connection to these organ recipients is more than random. Something about it is starting to feel like a calling."

"You have another patient?" Becca asked.

"Yes . . . well, maybe," she said. "But I've been thinking. If I can just give them coping skills, and some psychological handholding, maybe I can help right their worlds again."

Becca moved closer and slid into the patient chair next to the desk. "We never know what a day's going to bring, do we?"

"No, Becca, we sure don't," Dr. Brill said. "For just a few minutes, I was imagining a whole new practice. One where I could treat people presenting with more unusual cases."

"Wow, that'd be different," Becca said.

"Yeah, the work would definitely be challenging but exciting at the same time," Dr. Brill said. "Like right now—I can't wait to talk to Clark.

"I think I've awakened a new passion."

EIGHT

PINS AND NEEDLES

The following morning, the radio played softly in the background until the good-natured voice of the weatherman interrupted. The inviting way he said, "clear, with a gentle breeze," inspired Clark to take an unplanned walk. But after switching shoes and gathering a few incidentals, he heard an alert from the video chat room on his computer.

Figuring it was probably Dr. Brill, he looked at Rachel as if to say, "Here we go." Rather than speaking, he had conveyed the thought by matrimonial stealth, a technique he had perfected over the years.

"Good morning, Clark," Dr. Brill said. "I have some information. How are you feeling about things this morning?"

He grinned. "Making sure we're still on the same page?"

"Absolutely," she said.

"I'm ready, Doc," Clark said.

Her delivery was especially gentle when she told him about the forty-five-year-old male who was fatally injured in a traffic accident. Shortly after arriving at the hospital, he was pronounced brain-dead. The huge story was all over the news because the deceased was a very accomplished detective in the area. His name was Drake Harrison.

And he had been a friend of hers.

Even though Clark thought he was ready for the information,

the knot in his stomach implied otherwise. He stayed glued to Dr. Brill's image as he tried to process the story. All of a sudden, he realized there was something hauntingly familiar about it.

"Dr. Brill, did you say you knew the donor?" he asked.

"Yes, and I know how strange that must sound," she said. "But Drake was a local detective that I'd done some work for over the years. Amazing person, super intuitive. He would sometimes give me a call when he needed an assessment on the mental state of a subject."

"Wow, I'm so sorry," Clark said. "Did you know he was an organ donor?"

"No. No idea," she said. "His passing was so sudden. I didn't get many details. I just couldn't believe it when Dr. Malloy gave me his name as your donor."

"That is unbelievable," Clark said. "What are the odds?"

"I know," she said. "It's shocking." The starkness in her face was evidence that the feeling hadn't fully settled in yet.

"You know, something about the story seems familiar," Clark said.

"Oh, had you heard about it?" she asked.

"Maybe," he said. "I think I might have seen it on the news or something. But it just seems so surreal that my life could be connected to such a high-profile incident."

"I know," Dr. Brill said. "But Clark, now we know the identity. And Drake was a really great man."

"Well, I can't tell you how good it is to hear that!" he said. "But I still can't believe I have his heart beating in my chest. Are you absolutely sure?"

"Yes, it's verified," she said.

"So, you think some of the thoughts and flashes could actually be coming from his memories?" Clark asked.

"That's what the evidence suggests," she explained. "And, I was thinking, the life of a detective would certainly have been intense."

Clark paused, almost long enough to make it awkward. "True," he said. "And that could explain some of the strange episodes, but how would we ever really verify any of that?"

"Well, this is a great first step," she said. "But the next step, meeting with family and friends, is where you'll learn more about Drake. And maybe in the process, discover connections that could possibly lead to the answers you need."

"Yeah, maybe," he said. "But, you know, I'm just not sure."

"I know," she said. "Well, look at it this way. A huge door has opened and is summoning you to walk through it, but only if you're ready."

It was a lot to think about, and for the rest of the day, the shocking call dominated Clark's thoughts. Having an actual name and life to research made the whole thing more real. And, if he decided to move forward, he'd have to take part in emotionally challenging meetings with family and friends who were surely still grieving.

Just before hanging up, Dr. Brill added, "You know, you can take whatever time you need to make sure about this. There's no rush."

"Thanks, Doc," he said. "And, again, my condolences."

Clark's life had gone through one exciting phase after another, each one unique, serving a specific purpose on his journey. But as interesting as it had been up to that point, it was nothing compared to his new reality. The phenomenon, along with the donor information, had catapulted his story into another realm.

He'd always thought he would take a long time to decide if the time ever came, but after the call, his mind was already made up. His caution had been overridden by a rush of adrenaline and a desire to know everything as soon as possible. Why was he feeling this way? Why had his heart begun to beat faster just at the thought?

He would call Dr. Brill back first thing the next morning and encourage her to talk to any and all parties that could offer information.

With so much to learn about Drake, he was ready to talk to anyone who was willing to talk to him.

And the sooner, the better.

The stunning revelation was all he could think about. Not only had Drake Harrison saved his life by unselfishly donating his heart, but he might also have—in an almost supernatural sense—downloaded his memories. The thought made him uneasy, yet his heartbeat was just as strong, no matter how much his mind wavered on the idea.

Clark was ready for answers. He had to know more.

If he had actually received memories from a great detective, what information was he carrying around? Was it important? What was he supposed to do with it?

There was certainly a physical component to consider, but now, so much more. Was it truly possible that he was having Drake's thoughts or preferences? Had he taken on any of his characteristics?

Subjects such as cellular communication, or perhaps more precisely, the transfer of an undying intelligent energy, were swirling in his head and being discussed as topics to be explored. Clark understood that no matter what was to come, Drake's heart, now beating in his chest, connected their lives in the most profound way.

"I'm all in," he said, bright and early the next morning. "I want to meet Drake's family and friends."

"That's great, Clark!" Dr. Brill exclaimed. "Just what I wanted to hear." Her own excitement was almost spurring him on.

"I'm guessing those types of meetings have to be handled delicately," Clark said.

"Yes, for sure," Dr. Brill said. "Actually, the compassion shown during the initial approach has everything to do with whether or not meetings actually take place. And I don't want to get your hopes up, but I'm feeling pretty good about our chances. I'll make the appropriate calls. I'm sure we'll hear back right away."

"Good," Clark said. "Something's telling me this could be really important."

With a curious tilt of her head, she said, "Same here. I haven't said anything, but I've been on pins and needles right along with you. My instincts are telling me this could be the key to what's going on with you. I don't know, but I just can't wait for you to explore it further."

"Yeah, me too," he said. "I'm ready."

Clark had hoped the decision would bring some peace, but while he waited, he found himself even more on edge than usual. His visions and sense of foreboding were in full swing, keeping him restless day and night. And not only were recurring visions more active, but a few new ones had joined the fray. Several startling images, where he was looking down on a traffic accident, had appeared.

Did my mind create them because I learned of Drake's accident? Are they really Drake's memories? But how could he witness an accident from above?

Impossible.

But as with other mysterious images, Clark felt certain he was somehow involved, and more than ever, he needed answers.

Thankfully, the wheels were set in motion for the next step: contact.

Dr. Brill was making a list of additional ways to help Clark incorporate the phenomenon into his regular life when the phone rang. Her previous request to contact Drake's family had been approved, and remarkably, she found herself writing down the names of his parents. Without wasting any time, she reached out to Richard and Katherine Harrison.

"Hello," Richard answered.

"Good morning, Mr. Harrison," she said. "This is Doctor Deanna Brill calling. I'm working on an important case that appears to have a connection to your family. It's rather sensitive in nature, so I wondered if now would be a good time for you to talk."

"Yes, of course," Richard said. "How can we help?"

"Well," she said. "I have permission to let you know that my patient was the recipient in a heart transplant case, and we have been given your contact information as the donor family."

Richard stumbled as he reached for an upholstered chair at the dining room table. "So . . . so you're saying . . . your patient is the one who received my son's heart?"

"Yes, sir, according to our records," she said. "Please accept my deepest condolences on your loss. And I must tell you that I actually knew Drake, and I've never known a finer man. I'm a psychologist, and he consulted with me concerning the mindset of criminals from time to time."

"Really," he said. "So, does this have to do with a case?"

"Oh, no, sir," she said. "It's something else. My patient, the recipient, is requesting a meeting with your family. It's actually fairly common for the donor and recipient families to reach out, mostly for healing and supportive reasons. The time together can be emotionally beneficial, and I certainly feel like that would be the case here. The whole experience can be surprisingly therapeutic for everyone."

Richard hesitated, nervously tapping his fingertips on the table. "I'm sorry, but I'm just not sure what to say at the moment."

"I understand," she said. "I know this probably feels a little overwhelming. You and your family may need time to discuss the matter and see if it's something you think you can be comfortable with. I will tell you that, even though one party requests the meeting, both parties tend to benefit."

"So, you think it would help your patient?" Richard asked.

"Yes, sir, I really do," confirmed Dr. Brill. "He's having some symptoms that we might be able to address more fully if we could learn more about Drake. My patient is very anxious to meet you and share his story. And, as his doctor, I think sooner rather than later would be best. But, of course, we want you to be comfortable with the idea."

"Well," Richard said. "I'm still guarded but, I have to admit, curious at the same time. I really need to discuss it with my wife. Once we've decided, I can give you a call."

"That sounds great," Dr. Brill replied. "And, again, my deepest condolences to you and your family."

"Thank you," he said.

"Thank you so much for your kindness and your time, and if you have any questions, please feel free to contact me," Dr. Brill replied. "Goodbye."

✳

Dr. Brill made an impressive attempt at professionalism, but she couldn't totally control the disappointment in her voice when Richard Harrison eventually declined the request. Even though he had delivered the verdict with the utmost compassion, her wounded expression was proof it still stung.

She sat staring into space and began to cry before dialing her sister's number.

"Hello," said Denise.

"Hey, just needed to hear a friendly voice," Dr. Brill said.

"You're crying. What's wrong?" Denise asked.

"Oh, I'm fine. I don't even know," she said. "You know me. I'm usually way more in control of my emotions than this. It's just that a decision didn't go the way I had hoped and may create a setback in the treatment of a special patient. Guess my vicarious empathy has me on edge."

"Or maybe thoughts of Tony are still closer to the surface than you realize?" Denise asked.

Dr. Brill nodded. "Also, possible. You really do know me, don't you?"

"Hey, we're sisters," Denise said. "And I could feel that in our last conversation. Why don't you swing by and have dinner with me?"

"That actually sounds great, but I can't promise just yet," Dr. Brill replied. "Let me call you back. I really need to pull myself together. I have to make an important call. I already feel better just hearing your voice. Thanks."

"Of course, anytime," Denise said. "Hope you can make it later."

"Me too. Love you." Dr. Brill said before hanging up.

✳

While dabbing away the tears and making a cup of hot ginger tea, she began to rehearse the most delicate way of delivering the disheartening news to Clark. After a quick check of her face in a jeweled compact, she reached for the phone.

Clark had just stepped in from checking the mail. "Oh, no," he said. "I was really hoping for good news. But trust me, I do understand how hard the idea of a face-to-face must be for them. I certainly had reservations about even asking, but I just had to."

"Yeah, we had to try," she agreed.

"Did they happen to say why?" Clark asked.

"Apparently, the sister was having an especially hard time with the idea," she said. "And since they couldn't all agree, they just decided to pass."

"Wow, I hate that, but I understand," Clark said.

"Same here," she said. "We just need to move on to the next step."

"You know, Dr. Brill," Clark said. "I think I'm starting to believe in the phenomenon, and my instincts are telling me that something bigger is going on. Can't think of a worse time for a setback, and Rachel's going to be disappointed."

"I know, and I agree with you about something going on," she said. "Even though the Harrisons were our best bet, let's not forget, we still have other options. The new route should only slow us down a little."

"Honestly, Doc, that's what makes me crazy," Clark said. "I can't shake this incredible sense of urgency and maybe even danger."

"Well, we'll move as quickly as we can and try not to let the setback get in our way," she promised. "I'm thinking maybe we can reach out to some of Drake's friends and coworkers. I know his partner, John, personally, so if he's not swamped, setting it up should be easy. Drake's friends won't have the same insight as the family, but if we talk to enough of them, we should be able to piece together a personality and characteristic profile."

"Guess that's our only option," Clark said, sounding more than a little defeated. "I'll share everything with Rachel when she gets home from her fitness class. No need to upset her before then."

"I really hope you two can stay optimistic in spite of the disappointment," Dr. Brill said.

"I'll let you know how it goes," he sighed.

"Hey, I'll be working on some new ideas tonight, and I'll call you tomorrow to fill you in," she added. "Hang in there, Clark."

Throughout the conversation, she had been fighting back the earlier emotions. When she thought about Clark's disappointment and self-doubt, the tears were close to the surface again, and she was reminded of why her practice meant so much to her. She had seen too many people struggling with known and unknown trauma in their lives and even ridiculed. It wasn't fair, and she knew it was her mission in life to do something about it.

In the back of her mind, she was confident that she had Clark on the right track. And with him now fully engaged, she would reach out to John right away. But there were still thoughts of other recipients and what they might be dealing with—possibly even worse things than Clark.

Dr. Brill eased back in her chair and began to study the reproduction of the Mona Lisa on the accent wall directly across from her. She and Denise both loved it and had talked about the determination they perceived in the famous melancholy expression.

Her own face was now mirroring that very determination. She pressed the intercom button. "Hey, Becca, will you come in for a minute?"

When she entered, Dr. Brill smiled at her with a confident twinkle in her eye. "Becca, you know how I feel about my friend, Mona Lisa, don't you?"

Becca grinned. "Of course."

"Well, she's inspired me again," Dr. Brill said. "We're taking this practice in a new direction. I'm going to work with Clark and other recipients and maybe even venture into more mysterious cases."

"Like a specialty practice," Becca said.

Dr. Brill punctuated the air with a flip of her index finger. "Exactly!"

"I love seeing you so excited," Becca said. "And, if you're asking if I'm on board—absolutely!"

"Of course, you're on board," Dr. Brill said. "Couldn't think of doing it without you. You know, Becca, it's weird, but when I think about the new path, I can feel some lost magic returning."

NINE

GRACE UNDER PRESSURE

"Clark, are you sitting down?" Dr. Brill asked. "I've got some news."

"No, but what's up?" he asked.

"You're not going to believe this, but the Harrisons have had second thoughts," she gleefully replied.

"Wow, that's great," Clark said. "What happened?"

"Well, I got a surprise call," began Dr. Brill. "So, apparently, after many hours of deep reflection, Mr. and Mrs. Harrison were feeling less guarded about getting to know the man who received their son's heart. They said they were going to look at the meeting as a way to help you—and honor Drake at the same time."

"Wow, I'm so relieved," he said. "But what about the sister?"

"Apparently, her position hasn't changed, but the parents made the final call."

"Wonder how they got there in the end?" Clark asked.

"Well, the fact that Drake would have insisted on it was, apparently, the deciding factor," explained Dr. Brill.

Clark bowed his head and sighed. "He's saving me again."

"Yep," she agreed, "sure looks that way."

"What do we do next?" Clark asked.

"I have a couple of appointment times for you to choose from," she said.

"I'll take the first one—whenever it is," Clark said.

Dr. Brill smiled. "Already had it circled. I'll set it up right away."

"I can't believe I'm actually going to meet Drake's family," he said.

"I'm excited for you," beamed Dr. Brill. "When you're all together, just relax, get to know each other, and share your story."

✳

The Mediterranean-style home in the Florida Panhandle displayed warm, inviting influences and curb appeal. The blossoming landscape was always immaculate, but even so, the residents had done a little extra fussing over it for the past few days.

From inside, Katherine, who was seemingly completely prepared for the visit, saw Clark's car pull into the driveway and began to pace back and forth.

Richard moved closer and put his arm around her. "Where's that nervous energy coming from?" he teased. "I thought you were all ready."

"I don't know," she said. "It's like a rush of anxiety just hit me."

Pam hurried to her side. "Mom, it's okay. You can still change your mind."

Katherine shook her head. "No. No! I don't want to. I'm fine. But I'm really glad you decided to be here. I know it wasn't an easy decision."

"I'm still not a fan of this," declared Pam. "But I wasn't going to let you and Dad go it alone. If you want me to, I'll go out and talk to them right now."

"Pam, no!" Katherine said. "This is what I want."

Pam took a frustrated inhale and rolled her eyes. "Okay, if you insist. But why don't we at least try to act normal and quit staring out the window." Her sarcastic humor triggered a few grins.

"Dad, maybe you could answer the door while Mom and I bring the food and drinks in from the kitchen," she bossed.

As the Harrisons went about their assignments, Clark and Rachel dallied in the driveway, taking longer than necessary. On the ride over, Clark had been totally at ease, talking continually about how the visit might go, but now that reality was setting in, he too was feeling a bit more hesitant.

"Hopefully, you'll find some answers," Rachel said sweetly. "But, either way, I'm glad we're here."

Clark stared into her eyes. "Me too. I just can't believe I'm about to walk in there and meet my donor's family."

"I know," she said, resting her forehead against his. "I'm sure it's going to be great."

Clark took her hands. "It's great because you're here. What would I do without you?"

Rachel blushed and leaned in for a hug.

"I think I'm ready," sighed Clark.

With that, they collected a few personal items, locked the car, and headed up the walkway. There, they were embraced by a fragrant greeting emanating from scented geraniums, confidently peeping out of a spectacular flower bed.

Frantic nerves kept Clark from saying anything more, but he did exchange one last reassuring smile with Rachel. Primarily, his thoughts were on the fragile reception he was anticipating at the front door.

Before he had even reached the top step, Richard Harrison pushed open the door and issued a hearty welcome. "You must be Clark and Rachel. I'm Richard Harrison. Come on in."

His demeanor was somehow familiar, creating a warm first impression. Without even realizing it, Clark took a deep, relaxing breath.

He stepped forward to shake hands. "Nice to meet you, Mr. Harrison."

"Yes, it's so nice to meet you," echoed Rachel.

"So glad you're here," he replied. "We've been looking forward to your visit. And just call me Richard."

He led them into the living room, where Pam and Katherine had just finished putting out refreshments. The polished cherry table looked very inviting, with a nice variety of cheese, crackers, fruit, and mini muffins beautifully arranged on coordinating dishes. Pam was adding a piping hot carafe of coffee, a full teapot, and colorful mugs to complete the display.

Katherine looked up, and her eyes immediately landed on Clark. She moved gracefully in his direction and presented a delicate hand. "I am so very happy to meet you, Clark. I'm Katherine."

"The pleasure is all mine," he beamed. "Wow, something sure smells good in here."

Katherine smiled. "Oh, that must be the cinnamon in the muffins. They're almost fresh out of the oven. I love baking."

"Really?" Clark said. "So does Rachel."

As he studied Katherine's face, he noticed that her eyes were already a little misty, and it was a quick reminder of the sensitivity he would need to bring to the meeting.

Katherine turned and smiled. "And you must be Rachel."

"Yes, I'm so pleased to meet you," Rachel said. "Thank you for seeing us and for graciously opening your home, which is lovely, by the way."

"Well, thank you," Katherine said. "Let me introduce both of you to our daughter, Pam."

Clark turned to face a slender woman of about forty, who looked less than thrilled about the greeting. She was sunny blonde, around Rachel's height—about five, six—and had a chic, asymmetrical haircut. Her features, like Katherine's, were delicate, but her countenance was tougher. No nonsense.

Pam hesitated but then stepped forward and offered an obligatory "Nice to meet you both."

Clark realized he had not fully anticipated how many family members he would be meeting. He returned the greeting.

"Well, why don't we make our way to the sofas and get comfortable," Katherine directed.

As the others settled in and chatted away with customary small talk, Clark felt Katherine studying him, even glancing at his chest. When their eyes met, she seemed a little startled but managed a quick smile. She immediately turned away, offering to give Pam a hand with hosting duties, making sure everyone had a hot drink and generous plate.

Clark couldn't help wondering if the quick diversion was an attempt to settle her nerves. Now that he was sitting with the Harrisons in their living room, he registered how strange this meeting actually was, despite their best efforts at cordial hospitality.

"Thank you for such a treat," he said. "I hope you haven't gone to too much trouble."

Katherine waved off the concern. "It was no fuss at all but rather a pleasure. I've always loved preparing food for gatherings, no matter the occasion."

"Well, it's a treat," announced Clark. "And this coffee is great. It's so smooth, with almost a hint of chocolate." His puzzled expression implied that he had surprised mostly himself with the description, and for a moment, he swore to himself that he'd tasted this before.

"Oh, you're a coffee fan," Richard said.

"Well, I never was until after the surgery. Now I seem to notice every little subtlety," he explained.

"We have a big variety around here," Richard said. "I think there's some cinnamon and vanilla if you like those. Drake was a fan and insisted we try different flavors from time to time. He loved everything from a regular cup o' joe to the fancy iced coffees and even asked friends to bring new blends back from their travels out of the country. Anyway, this is one of his two favorites—and you're right about the chocolate."

Clark froze. "Really?" The confirmation startled him.

"Yep, sure are," Richard declared.

Strange.

Clark turned to re-engage with the others, but his eyes landed on a photo displayed on the mantel. An icy shiver ran throughout his body. He was staring at the same ghostlike image he had seen flash in the mirror at home. He lost momentary focus. There was no way he could ask, but it had to be Drake.

This is getting to be too much.

"Uh, well . . . we just want to thank you again for seeing us today," he stammered. "Rachel and I want to offer you our most sincere condolences on your loss. I've been hearing the most wonderful things about your son."

"Thank you," Richard said. "He was very special. And we're really anxious to hear more about how the transplant has brought you here."

For Clark, it was a relief to see the family handling the mention of the tragedy with such strength and grace. It would make moving forward a lot less stressful. His plan was to be extremely considerate of their feelings and use their responses as a barometer on how to proceed.

"I'm not exactly sure how to begin," Clark said. "But I'd be happy to start things off if you'd like. The most important thing to me is that all of you feel comfortable. So, please feel free to stop or redirect any line of conversation you need to."

"I'm sure I know exactly what you're thinking and feeling, and I really appreciate it," Katherine said, softening her eye contact. "But, let me put any concerns you may have to rest. Richard and I haven't made this decision lightly.

"On the contrary, we've spent hours deciding what would be best. And we feel good about our decision. The deciding factor was actually Drake. This is what he would have wanted. So, we're here to help in any way we can, and you can ask whatever you'd like."

Clark was heartened by the statement but couldn't help noticing that Richard and Pam looked a little confused.

Katherine cast them a sideways glance. "I know you two think I'm fragile. But I'm actually feeling better, and this is what I want too."

Even though her announcement swung the door wide open for what might be emotionally sensitive discussions, Clark was prepared to tread carefully.

"Well, thank you, Miss Katherine," he said. "But I am having contradictory feelings. When I think of your loss, my heart breaks for your family and what you've endured. And when I think of how Drake's decision blessed me with the gift of life, I am eternally grateful."

Katherine nodded and smiled sweetly. "I understand."

Clark rested his cup on a coaster. "Well, anyway, there are two reasons I've requested the meeting. The first is to say thank you in person. Like I said, I . . . I truly owe my life to your son."

Katherine took a quick breath, closed her eyes, and bowed her head.

"Drake made a noble decision," added Clark. "And I'll never take his act of humanity lightly. I am going to try to live life with a more determined purpose, and I can promise you—I will forever be thankful for the blessing of each new day."

Katherine covered her face and wept softly into Richard's shoulder.

"Thank you, Clark," Richard said. "There is some comfort in knowing that a part of Drake is living on."

"Should we take a break?" Clark asked. "Are you okay, Miss Katherine?"

"I'm fine, really," she said. "I guess emotions are just going to be part of it. Please go on."

Clark proceeded, but with the utmost care, and the Harrisons seemed noticeably touched by his words and truly, grateful spirit, especially Katherine.

"Your grace under pressure, Clark, is admirable," she said. "You're proving yourself to be exactly the kind of man we all hoped for."

"Well, thank you, Miss Katherine," he said. "You're too kind."

Richard interjected, "I have to be honest and tell you that during our grieving, I haven't really spent too much time thinking about recipients or transplants."

His voice was solid, but his eyes were soft.

"And I certainly never considered that we might literally meet one day. And now, here you are, sitting in our living room. I guess it's surreal for everyone, but hopefully, this chance to talk will be a good thing for all of us.

"Oh, sorry," he added. "Hope I didn't interrupt. I think you were about to mention the second reason for the meeting."

Clark stared for a second, seemingly mesmerized by the creamy contents of his half-empty mug. "Oh, no ... no, it's okay."

Columbia? Why am I thinking about Columbia? Not now.

The unfamiliar thoughts were strong and taking over his mind again, but he fought to shake them off.

"Well, actually, the second reason is a little harder to explain," began Clark. "From the time we spend together, I hope to get a deeper understanding of who Drake was as a person. Dr. Brill is convinced that it can be helpful in my case."

After giving a little background on his life and weakened heart, he explained how the doctors had recommended a transplant.

"I agonized over the situation but finally made the tough call," he added. "Surgery and recovery have been textbook perfect, and the doctors have been thrilled."

"Once I was aware of you, I wondered about your health," Katherine said. "Any condition serious enough to require a transplant must have been very scary for you and your family. But looking at you now, no one would ever imagine what you've gone through. You look like the picture of health."

"Well, thank you," Clark said. "I do feel great. But even though the surgery and recovery have gone perfectly well, I've been having some unusual symptoms after the transplant. It's as if I'm not quite myself. I've been having strange dreams, visions, and even preferences that aren't mine."

"Really?" Katherine asked. "Visions?"

"Yeah, it's been pretty unnerving," he said. "But it did lead me to Dr. Brill, and she's been amazing. I'm lucky to have found her."

"Oh, yeah, I talked to her," Richard said. "Very nice. She actually knew Drake."

Clark nodded. "I know, and she said such great things about him."

He hesitated for a moment. "Before I get into the next part, would you be comfortable sharing a little more about Drake with me? I feel like some of your insights might be helpful, maybe even healing, as we go along."

Pam sat up straighter in her seat with her arms folded stiffly and said, "I'll go first if that's okay. But honestly, I should tell you, I haven't really been on board with this whole thing. My family's been through too much already."

"I understand," Clark assured her. "And you just say the word if you feel like we're going into uncomfortable territory. I'm just grateful to be here, and hope this meeting is a positive thing for all of us."

"Well, me too, but I guess that's the big question, isn't it?" snipped Pam. "Is this a good thing or not? I've already watched my parents lose sleep over it."

"Pammy!" Richard interjected. "I thought we agreed."

"I know, but we've been through so much," she said. "We're still healing from losing Drake."

Katherine took her hand. "Pam, what you say is true, and I know you have doubts, but this is what Drake would have wanted. I know it in my heart."

Pam started to respond but then stopped and, with a little melodrama, fell back on the sofa pillows as if she'd completely worn herself out.

The eyes of the whole room were on her, waiting.

"Okay, fine," she said, sitting upright. "You want to know about my brother? He was a role model and best friend. I felt safe when he was around—like there was an invisible shield protecting me. And he was, kind of, like the guardian of my emotional state as well. No matter what I was dealing with, he could help me see it in ways I would never have thought of on my own."

With just a hint of a grin, she added, "He was also funny, and a lot of people didn't know that. I guess his job didn't allow for too much fun, but as far back as I can remember, he could sure make me laugh."

Clark was taking in every word.

"That's so great," he said.

Quickly finishing, Pam added, "Well, he was always there for me, and those are the memories that keep me going. Words could never express how much I miss him."

Even though she seemed to maintain her strength, everyone lifted her up with words of comfort, and Richard placed a fatherly arm around her shoulder.

Katherine patted her hand one last time and said, "Drake was a wonderful son. I wish we could have seen him more often, but his career made incredible demands on his time. As the years went by, we recognized and accepted his work as a calling. That being the case, we treasured every visit.

"He enjoyed the outdoors," she continued, "especially having his bare hands in the soil. Richard and I like our time outdoors too, but nothing like Drake. His love for nature was so organic and contagious.

"And Pam's right. He's always been strong and protective. Even as a child, he seemed to gravitate to situations where people needed help. It was as if he was created to make the world a safer place.

"But he was a contradiction in one way. He was such a charming people-person most of the time, but could also be a bit of a loner, focusing like a laser beam on some task at hand. It's like he just knew what a situation called for and could adapt in the most natural way. He made me so proud. Just watching him become a kind, generous, and accomplished man brought me incredible joy."

"Thank you, Katherine," Clark said. "After listening to you and Pam, I feel even more humbled."

Richard spoke up next. "Drake was at the top of his class at the academy. And as a detective, he worked on many cases over the years. His way of looking at details with such focus and from unusual perspectives solved a lot of cases others had struggled with.

"In those times, he would get quiet and try to create something like a play-by-play in his mind. It could be emotionally and physically exhausting, but the method had proven very successful. With his sharp mind and track record, in very short order, he was at the top of his game."

"He must have helped so many people," Clark said.

"Oh, yeah—many," Richard agreed. "He would sometimes suffer great anxiety trying to break those cases. But his very best moments were when he was able to set things straight. I can't think of anything else that gave him that kind of satisfaction. He lived a life that mattered, and I think he realized how blessed he was to have found his true purpose."

"That is a gift," Clark said. "I'm sure people were honored to know him."

"You'd be right," Richard said.

"Well, maybe now would be a good time to tell you what I've been experiencing," Clark proposed. "I'm not sure how to prepare you for this, so I guess I'll just jump in."

During his talk of visions, strange symptoms, and the path to Dr. Brill to check for a psychological component, the Harrisons had become eerily still. Clark suspected another case of disbelief, but after sharing Dr. Brill's phenomenon theory and stories of recipients, who had taken on or demonstrated characteristics of their donors, he was sure of it.

Are they reconsidering their decision?

Pam was the first to speak. "You've got to be kidding me!" She snapped around to look at her parents. "What did I tell you?"

"Pam, stop," Richard said. "Clark, are you saying you believe you're having some of Drake's thoughts or preferences?"

"Yes, sir. I'm starting to believe that," Clark said. "That's the reason I requested the meeting. These extraordinary thoughts, memories, and visions just come out of nowhere. So, after hearing about Dr. Brill's theory, I'm just trying to find out if any of the flashes of information could be related to Drake in any way, and if they are, confirming that could maybe bring some closure somehow and help my recovery."

"Come on!" Pam exclaimed. "You cannot expect us to believe such a thing."

"Pam, even I don't know what to believe yet," Clark said. I'm just trying to figure it out."

Richard and Katherine seemed guarded but also interested in the phenomenon, and they asked to hear more about any characteristics or preferences Clark was experiencing. But, for the purity of the exchange, Clark knew he needed to hear from them first before giving away too many specifics.

"Maybe, in a way, we could try comparing notes," he suggested. "Richard, you mentioned Drake's love for all things coffee-related earlier, and that caught my attention because, here lately, I can't get enough of it. And, strangely, I seem to be able to recognize many fine points—like the chocolate. But the weirdest part is, my cravings started only after the transplant."

Richard raised his eyebrows. "Really? That's strange."

"Yeah." Clark nodded.

"And, Katherine, you spoke of Drake's love of nature," he added. "That's another new passion of mine. Since recovering from surgery, I've been inexplicably drawn more to the outdoors, specifically gardening. Putting my hands in the dirt. One of my visions even involves a very particular wooded landscape that I feel a strong connection to, that I've never seen before."

He continued with hardly a pause. "I'll share another one with you. I've been watching and recording lots of TV lately, and eventually, it dawned on me that ninety percent of the programs were law enforcement-related. I know it's a small thing, but I almost never took an interest in shows like that."

"What?" Pam said, perking up. "Drake and I used to watch those all the time. He would tell me if they were accurate or not. But just because you like them too doesn't mean anything, probably just coincidence."

Rachel, who had been very quiet, turned and smiled. "That's what we thought at first too, Pam. But the evidence from the actual transplant cases is so overwhelming that we've had to open our minds to the other possibility.

"Believe me, this whole thing still seems unreal, but we just have to find out if Clark's episodes actually make him one of those remarkable cases. When I was listening to your dad, I kept thinking that maybe Clark had been feeling some of Drake's job anxiety. Like you said, his instinct to help. He's had several intense dreams, even one about a fire."

Katherine drew in a quick breath and turned to Clark. "A fire? Please, tell us."

"Well, it was dark, and I was running through a yard," he began. "The flames were already huge near the front left corner of the house. When I reached the window, I was startled by a frantic face inside. It was a young guy, a teenager. I knew him . . . I could feel it.

"He was pounding on the glass with his fists as the flames were getting closer. It was terrifying. I had to do something. I looked around for help, and that's when I saw a huge stone in the garden."

By this time, curiously, tears were streaming down Pam's face.

"I picked it up and motioned for him to stand back from the window," Clark continued. "I smashed into it with all my might, and it broke the first time. All I remember after that is him reaching for me and our hands connecting."

"Oh my God!" cried Pam. "How do you know this?"

"It's just a dream," Clark explained.

"No, it's not!" exclaimed Pam. "That really happened to Drake when he was a teenager. He saved his friend from a house fire."

"What? No!" The flush disappeared from Clark's face as he shook his head. "That actually happened to Drake? No . . . how . . . how could I know?"

"That's what I want to know!" Pam accused. "Because it happened exactly like you said. Who are you?"

"Pam!" scolded Katherine. "He's our guest. And how do we know these things aren't possible? And remember, Clark has your brother's heart!"

Pam softened, but only a little. "Well, if what you say is true, Clark, then I'm sorry. "But where's the proof?"

"That's why I'm here . . . what I'm searching for," he said. "Maybe the dream is proof. If it is a real memory of Drake's, it actually supports Dr. Brill's theory."

"Well, I think something else is going on," huffed Pam. "And I'm sure it's not good for this family!"

"Well, I don't agree!" Katherine said. "I'm glad you came, Clark. And I do sense that there's something to this."

Clark took a deep breath. "Thank you, Miss Katherine. My hope is that over time we'll all understand it better."

After doing a quick reading of the room, Clark decided that everyone had had enough for one day.

"Well, I certainly don't want to overstay our welcome," he said. "Thank you for being so open and generous with your time. What you've shared has convinced me that I do need to pursue this. If I'm truly experiencing some of Drake's memories or characteristics, I need to see where this theory takes me."

"Oh!" gasped Katherine. "Drake used to say that all the time. 'Where this theory takes me.'"

Clark smiled. "See, Miss Katherine. That's the kind of thing I'm talking about. Is it just a coincidence? I don't know, but I need to find out. I'm hoping to have a meeting with one of Drake's coworkers next. Dr. Brill knew his partner, so we feel pretty positive about it."

"Oh, you're going to meet with John Baxter?" guessed Richard. "Yeah, they were great friends and worked a lot of cases together."

If time spent with John could prove to be as helpful as time spent with the Harrisons, Clark felt like he might be on to something. The family had convinced him that his frightening dream and new preferences did line up with Drake's life. The confirmation was already more than expected, and he had only scratched the surface.

Suddenly overcome by a sense of urgency, he needed to know more. He was thinking about the future meeting with John when Katherine begged him to stay a little longer. Since he couldn't bring himself to tell her no, he agreed to stay for just a bit and share a few more episodes.

"In those, I could sense people in trouble," Clark said. "And, weirdly, I felt like I was supposed to help."

"I'm so sorry, Clark," Katherine said. "That must be awful for you."

"Well, it was more unnerving before I met Dr. Brill," he explained. "She's really been able to keep things calm and help me process everything. And now that we have a plan, an actual path of real discovery, I do feel less stressed."

As he stood to leave, the photo on the mantel caught his attention for the second time. He turned away and said, "Anyway, we should be going. And thank you, again, for agreeing to meet with me."

"Please don't feel like you have to run," Katherine said.

The eager plea made Clark wonder if she still had questions running through her mind like he did. "Well, thanks, Miss Katherine. But I don't want to overstay our welcome. Maybe we can get together again if you like."

"I would like that very much. I want to know more about this phenomenon," she replied.

"Wish I could give you proof that it's true," Clark said. "But I'm still figuring that out."

"No, I understand," she said. "And I don't need proof. I know it. I can feel it."

Richard and Pam turned to look at her at the same time.

"Just sitting in the room with you, Clark, is proof that part of my son is still living on—and I'm talking way more than physical. I sure hope you'll come back again. I'd be so disappointed if you didn't," she added. "Please promise me."

Clark took her hands, looked into her eyes, and said, "That is so sweet of you, and I'd like that very much if it's really no trouble."

"None at all," she replied with a wave of her hand. "Don't even mention it."

"Well, I'm just so thankful to you for seeing me," Clark said, almost whispering. "I have new questions now, but I also feel more settled."

Katherine searched his face and smiled. "I'm happy to hear that, Clark. You know, you're a gentler man than Drake, but I see the same unintentional yet confident swagger. I think it's that characteristic that makes people feel secure around you."

Clark could feel her warm, maternal side as she spoke, and he smiled at the flattering comparison.

But in the seconds that followed, his expression transformed into one of compassion. Just before he turned to join the others, he saw the glistening in Katherine's eyes again.

Once more, she quickly turned away, and this time, she started fussing with the table setting. Somehow, he knew she was collecting herself before saying her final goodbyes.

The meeting was a success, and Clark felt proud to share characteristics with Drake, the impressive man the family had described. An undeniable bond was taking shape, and he desperately wanted to continue his search for answers.

Despite longing to stay, he paid homage to the sensitivity of the situation and didn't. There was no reason to risk overwhelming the family. These things took time.

✳

When Katherine recovered, she joined the group and positioned herself close to Clark. She leaned in and spoke softly for only him to hear. "You know, our DNA connects us now. And yes. That photo is of Drake."

TEN

THE SECRET ADMIRER

MONTHS EARLIER

Winston sat on a failing iron bench in front of the local gun store, nervously clutching a package. The hectic construction going on at the fairgrounds across the way was hypnotizing, and he jumped when the shrill pitch of a car horn jolted him back to reality.

Stapled on a telephone pole just a few feet away was a flyer flapping in the wind. When he sauntered over to check it out, he saw that it was promoting an upcoming music festival. After looking around a couple of times, he quickly yanked the notice and stuffed it into his jacket. Maybe he'd find out more about it when he started yet another new job the following morning.

Life hadn't been fair, according to Winston, and he was tired of feeling shunned and excluded. But if he was ever going to have the life he wanted, he had to get past all of that and turn things around. New towns and new faces were part of the plan and had become the norm in his vagabond life.

It had to be that way for now.

He arrived early the next day at Pleasant Springs, an innovative new home community, where he was scheduled as part of the moving crew. Inside a pristine, new double-wide, he located the temporary office, where he had been instructed to check in with his contact, Ashley Benson. She was a specialized home stager, responsible for planning and carrying out the staging of homes once they were completed and ready for sale.

And she was stunning.

Winston couldn't take his eyes off her. From velvety complexion to classic features, she was perfect. Her playful, auburn hair fell just past her shoulders, shimmering with sun-induced highlights that mimicked dazzling copper. He found himself hypnotized and, from that moment on, knew they were meant to be together.

Ashley introduced him to her assistant, Kristen, who answered his last few questions before walking him over to the window. There she concluded the reception by pointing out the location of truck arrivals.

Even though the mini-orientation was clearly over, Winston lingered.

Turning to Ashley, he said, "I noticed preparations going on for a big music festival."

Ashley nodded. "Oh, yeah. I just heard the construction of the stage is almost finished."

"Yeah, that thing is huge," Winston said. "Looks like they're already setting up tents for vendors too. I can't believe how many there are."

"Yeah, it's our biggest event of the year," she explained. "Huge crowd."

"It would be nice to find someone to go with," he said, twirling a roll of box tape.

"Yeah, you'll enjoy it," Ashley said, distracted momentarily by a message Kristen had placed in front of her.

"Sorry, Winston," she said, grabbing a ring binder of multicolored fabric samples and a tote from her desk. "We'll have to get better acquainted tomorrow. I've got to rush. I'm headed to the other side of town for a property tour and estimate."

"Oh, wait. I can help you with all of that," he blurted, stumbling over his own feet as he started toward her.

But she waved him off.

"No. No thanks. I'm used to it. You better go see Arnie before you're late," she directed. "Hope you enjoy working here."

"Thanks. I already do," he said, holding her gaze a little too long.

"Oh, and Kristen," Ashley said, turning. "Remember, I have that meeting with Clark Steele over at Steele Construction at the end of the day. Wish me luck."

With each passing day at Pleasant Springs, Winston was becoming more and more fixated. Not only was he in awe of Ashley's beauty, but he also found her friendlier than most women. She was exactly the type he'd always dreamed of—but could never have.

He vowed to get close to her, even though his track record had been a disaster. In the past, no matter what approach he used, women avoided him. Even if they appeared relaxed at first, it was soon obvious that they were devising getaway strategies.

Every time he thought he might actually have a chance with someone, the encounter ended in a stinging rejection. And the emotional pain of being cast off repeatedly had driven him to a self-imposed abstention—but with Ashley, he was ready to try again.

During each workday, he found creative ways to observe her without being detected. Since the community jobsite had preserved and enhanced as much of the natural landscape as possible, trees and shrubs were plentiful and made for fitting shields.

One morning, shaded under a sycamore, he sat eagerly watching and waiting for her to arrive. When he had built up the nerve and was sure she was settled in, he started toward the office.

There he presented her with a steaming breakfast blend from the local tearoom, exactly the way she liked it.

"Well, thanks, Winston," she said. "That's so sweet of you. It's perfect and from one of my favorite stops. How did you know?"

"Lucky guess?" he teased. But he'd been poking around.

Ashley tilted her head, looking confused. "Wow. Okay. I didn't get a chance to stop this morning, so this is great. Thanks again. Another busy day ahead for me. How about you?"

"Yeah," he said. "We've got an early truck waiting right now and another pulling in at noon. A couple of the other guys should be here any minute."

"Oh, good," she said. "Help is on the way."

Winston leaned in, resting an elbow on her desk. "Yeah, but they can take their time. I don't mind waiting here with you."

Ashley turned to file a couple of documents. "Oh . . . uh . . . well, it's not really all that exciting in here."

"To me, it is," he said, sliding a bit closer.

Ashley leaned back in her chair and announced, "Well, guess it's time for me to get to work."

In spite of the obvious hint and the distance she had created between them, he kept talking.

Ashley maintained a pleasant vibe for a bit longer but finally put on her supervisor hat. "Sorry, Winston, but you're going to have to continue the rest of the conversation outside with the guys. I really have to get to it."

He got the message and left, but worried that he had offended her. *I'm such an idiot. Probably being too much again.*

But after a little time had passed, he let himself off the hook. Surely, she was too busy to analyze his behavior.

When he saw her later, giving instructions to one of the other movers, he quickly made his way over to join them. But just as he got there, she apologized for having to rush off to another task and made a quick exit.

That time, the dismissal was undeniable, and he felt the burn.

In a wounded attempt to take control of the situation, he headed over to an empty box truck to collect his thoughts. The loading ramp was still in place, but he opted for a more challenging entry, and in one motion, he hopped into a seated position just inside the back.

After staring into space for a minute, he pulled a small notebook from his pocket and began to write. The quick entries were notes to himself. He would follow Ashley, continue to study her likes and dislikes, and use the information to his advantage.

She had already mentioned a love for movies, so that, and other personal information, should be perfect for turning things around and endearing himself to her.

Then it would be safe to confess his feelings.

One of his first stakeouts was at the neighborhood florist. When he saw Ashley exit the quaint storefront, she had a big smile on her face and a mixed bouquet in hand.

From there, he followed her home but drove on by so as not to be noticed. It was only when he returned later that he saw the bundle of flowers again, now proudly displayed in the center of the bay window.

That was all the encouragement he needed to schedule an anonymous floral delivery with a note that read: *Can't wait to see you again.*

The bouquet was waiting on Ashley's desk one morning, but no one had witnessed the delivery.

"I can't understand this," she said to Kristen. "This message makes it sound like I have a relationship with this person, but, you know, I'm not dating anyone."

That is weird," Kristen said. "I don't know, maybe we can ask around on break?"

"Yeah, that's a good idea," Ashley said. "Probably just delivered to the wrong person."

Winston kept an eye on her as she went about tracking down the appropriate party all around the job site but never came forward.

Instead, he hung back, secretly enjoying his own handiwork.

At the end of one workday, he had slipped quietly across the freshly laid carpet inside the master bedroom of the newest construction and watched from a veiled upstairs window.

Ashley got into her car, turned over the engine, and then almost immediately shut it down. After shoving the door open and making her way to the front of the car, she pulled an envelope from under the wiper blade.

That was Winston's cue to start making his way outside.

Inside the envelope was a ticket to a new movie release and a second note written in a language that was oddly familiar, just like the first. It read: *I'll meet you there.*

Ashley just stood there for a minute, shaking her head, before getting back into the car. With a curt flick of her wrist, she tossed the items in the front seat, took a deep breath, and began to scan the radio.

By this time, Winston was nonchalantly making his way past the car, secretly taking it all in, when to his surprise, she looked up and waved. The acknowledgment caught him off guard, but he waved back and kept moving.

Maybe she was coming around.

In his mind, Ashley wasn't confused or rattled by the mysterious happenings; she was simply bewitched by the attention.

His next move was to step up his amateur surveillance by following her closely as if she was a cheating girlfriend. The covert tracking would provide him with tasteless entertainment as he surreptitiously monitored her life. And ultimately, he would have the intended treasure in his possession—a complete journal of her movements and activities.

On one occasion, his shadowing put him dangerously close. But, by sporting an oversized sweatshirt, ballcap, and dark sunglasses, he'd created a look very different from any she would have recognized.

The transformation allowed him to sit just a few tables away without being noticed. By keeping his back turned and his face toward his computer, he was in the perfect position to eavesdrop on a conversation between Ashley and a woman named Jacki.

The Parisian Tea Room was one of Ashley's favorites. Winston had picked up an order at the window in the past—but had never been inside. The air smelled of herbal infusions, and the space was perfectly themed, complete with an Eiffel Tower pastry shelf prominently displaying all the classic French desserts.

As he scanned the room, his eyes landed on the woman with Ashley for a brief moment. There was something familiar about her.

"So glad we got to do this, Sis," Ashley said.

Ahh, that's it. Sisters. Was she at the job site?

"I know," Jacki said. "I miss it so much when we can't work it out."

Winston watched as the waitress hurried to their table with menus, two complimentary macarons decorated with images of Paris, and a fresh pot of tea.

Once they had ordered, Jacki asked Ashley how her love life was going, and she responded with an impressive eye roll.

"Ha, ha," Jacki laughed. "Like I always say, no one does a better eye roll than you."

"It's a gift," Ashley giggled.

Even though the question seemed to create a joyful moment for the sisters, it led to a sensitive topic.

Winston's ears perked up when Ashley jokingly brought up "the unusual guy" at work and suggested that he might actually be her only hope for a date. She made light of his attention and the way he seemed to pop up too often and linger without a purpose.

He fidgeted uncomfortably in his seat before leaning back into the conversation again.

"It's no big deal," Ashley shrugged. "It's just that his topics of conversation are awkward, and the rhythm of the exchange is always off. But even though he's different, he's harmless."

"Ash, you should probably be a little more guarded," teased Jacki, folding her arms. "Better yet—just stay away from him."

While Ashley seemed to be considering her sister's advice, the expression on Winston's face changed dramatically, as if a dark cloud had swept over his features. The piercing words had made him furious.

Without drawing any attention to himself, he gathered up his computer and travel cup and exited quietly through the side door. By the time he reached his car, he had convinced himself that he could forgive Ashley of anything—but her sister needed to mind her own business.

Back inside, Jacki asked, "Ash, are you sure you can handle everything you have going on right now? You're so busy and always have to be available when it suits the client."

"Yeah, I know, but I'm fine," she said. "You know I love it. My schedule's crazy, but I manage to squeeze in a few rejuvenating hours. I have to for my sanity."

"You mean like right now?" Jacki said.

"Yes—exactly like right now," Ashley beamed. "My life is going great. It's just not the most conducive to building a romantic relationship at the moment.

"But I do have an exciting afternoon planned," she announced. "I'm in the middle of a master bedroom project at a new Mediterranean villa on the south side of town. That should only take a few hours, and then I have another commercial site to check out.

The commercial side of things is really growing."

Jacki shook her head and laughed. "I get worn out just listening to you."

"I know," Ashley replied. "I just keep pushing forward and don't think too much about it."

"Yeah," Jacki said. "Hey, you don't think it's possible that your coworker could be the person leaving those notes, do you?"

"What? No!" Ashley said, shaking her head. "It's nothing like that. No, he's actually done some really sweet things. He brings me coffee and tea—not the type. He's perfectly harmless."

"Okay, good. Wait . . . you're sure, you're sure?" she asked, grinning.

"Yeah, no way," Ashley said. "I'm positive it's someone else. The notes are just too specific, too personal. You know, as if the recipient would understand them."

"Yeah, I get it. Well, either way, be careful," Jacki lovingly ordered.

With a military flare, Ashley clipped, "Yes, ma'am, I promise!" But then she relaxed, took Jacki's hands, and in a much softer tone, added, "Just kidding. Thanks for looking out for me."

ELEVEN

CONTROLLED REACTION

Despite his personal grief, John Baxter had agreed to shoulder sole responsibility for the Sweet case after Drake's passing. The weight of the task was oppressive, but out of love and respect for his best friend, he wouldn't have had it any other way.

There had been a frustrating delay involving the recovery of the last bit of evidence from Drake's vehicle, but for the most part, he'd been able to work with a nearly complete file. And since the case was already underwater, from that time on, he'd spent every waking hour trying to move things forward without success.

Just when he was about to take another look and really dig in, a call came in from Dr. Brill.

"Hey, John," she said. "How have you been?"

"Well, hey, Doc," John said. "Nice to hear from you. Am I waiting on a report that I've forgotten about?"

"No, it's something else this time," she said. "I need to talk to you, but I'd really like to do it in person."

"Really," John said. "Is everything all right?"

"Yes, it'll make sense when we get together," she explained. "Hey, do you remember that bike path along the lake where we met to talk about the mayor's son-in-law?"

"Yeah, of course," John said. "You want to meet there?"

"Yeah, any chance you could come right away?" she asked.

"Probably," John said. "How soon can you be there?"

She hesitated for a few seconds. "Thirty minutes. Let's meet at that same bench."

"Okay," John said. "Doc, are you sure you're all right?"

"Yeah, I promise," she said. "See you there."

✳

John stayed to the right of the bike path, avoiding traffic as he approached. "Hey, Doc, great to see you."

She stood and extended her hand. "You too, John. It's been a while."

"Sure has. So, what's up?" he asked. "You sounded so serious."

"Well, let's sit down," she said. "You doing okay?"

"Yeah, I'm doing good," John said. "Just anxious to hear what's going on."

"Well, I have something really amazing to share with you," she said. Her eyes were soft, full of compassion.

"Wow, okay," he said.

"John, I'm working with a new patient who was the recipient in a recent heart transplant," she said.

"And . . .?" coaxed John.

She took a slow, deep breath. "And John, Drake was his donor."

John shot up from his laidback position. "What?" he said. "Doc! Are you sure?"

"Yes, it's all verified," Dr. Brill said. "Look, I know how shocking it is to hear this. Believe me, I'm still not over the news."

"Drake was the donor?" he repeated.

"Yes, apparently, he made the decision a long time ago," she said.

"Yeah, I know, I mean . . . about that," John said. "But his heart went to your patient? That's unbelievable."

"I know. I was just as shocked as you when they gave me Drake's name," shared Dr. Brill.

"What brought the patient to your office?" John asked. "Can you say?"

"In this case, yes," she said. "Because I have his permission . . . and he wants to meet you."

"What? Meet me?" John asked. "Why?"

"Well, I'd really like him to tell you his story," she said. "But I will say, I'm all for the meeting. I think it would be a great thing. He's having some strange experiences, and I thought learning more about Drake might be helpful for his recovery."

"Strange experiences?" John asked.

"It'll make more sense when he puts everything into context," Dr. Brill said. "But he's having strange episodes, these visions that are disrupting his life and his emotional health. I do have a hunch about the case if you're ready for another shocker?"

"Go ahead, shoot," John said.

"Well, there is a documented phenomenon that suggests a cellular transfer of information can take place from donor to recipient," she explained.

John leaned back on the bench and folded his arms. "You're kidding me, right? So, are you saying that . . . that your patient could be having Drake's thoughts?"

"Actually, that and maybe more," she said. "I know how crazy it sounds, John, but the phenomenon is a real thing. Of course, we don't know if it is in his case yet, but by comparing notes with people who knew Drake, we're trying to answer that question."

"So, you knew Drake too," John said. "Have you noticed anything weird when you're with the patient?"

"I'm still evaluating," she said. "But I've seen and heard enough to be intrigued, that's for sure. He's already spent some time with Drake's family, and well, there are things that do line up."

"Like what?" he asked.

"Well, like some of the same interests and preferences," explained Dr. Brill. "And a dream that was eerily similar to something that actually happened to Drake."

"Couldn't that just be coincidence?" he asked.

"Yeah, but this is all new to Clark," she said. "These things only showed up after the transplant."

"Well, that's strange but not really proof," John said. "And I'm still not sure how I come into play."

"John, if you would just listen to him and see if anything he says matches what you know about Drake personally or professionally, it would be a bigger help than you know," she implored.

John sat quietly, his eyes following the movement of the feathery clouds reflecting on the lake. He seemed to be contemplating the right decision and possibly considering the anticipation in her voice.

Finally, he said, "Okay, Doc, if you think it's a good idea, I'll meet with him."

She sighed and smiled. "Thank you, John. Hey, I have a patient arriving soon. Can we set a time?"

"Yeah, let me take a look," he said.

After settling on the date, Dr. Brill added, "Thanks again, John. I just have a feeling about this. And besides, you'll really like Clark."

"You know, your visits are always interesting," he said. "But this one is something else."

"Yeah, I know," she agreed. "Hey, just call me later if you want to talk some more, and then definitely after meeting with Clark."

"Thanks," John said. "I will."

✳

Once he was back in the office, the first thing he did was start comb-ing through the case file, which had remained relatively intact during the accident. The exception was a few loose photos, identified as hav-ing been randomly collected from inside the vehicle. The images were taken from diverse angles, and the lighting varied from shot to shot, but all were from the same scene: the cemetery.

John brushed the next few items out of the way, exposing a hand-written note. The scrawl made him gasp. It was Drake's. He would have recognized it anywhere. It read:

Missing: traffic footage and photo. On it.

– D.

He sank into the closest chair and raised his clasped hands to his forehead. The note was another reminder that Drake was really gone. After a deep inhale and slow release, his countenance seemed to improve, as if the cleansing exhale had expelled most of the pain.

"I'm on it too, pal," he whispered.

Not only was the missing evidence frustrating, but it was also a little too coincidental, almost beckoning a probe into incompetence or misconduct. Since the evidence room couldn't be accessed by just anyone, if it was the latter, it might even require an uncomfortable surveilling of coworkers.

John walked across the room and stared through the massive window into the outer office. Queenie, with her magnetic person-ality, had a small group gathered around her desk and appeared to be showing them a few impressive dance moves. Shockingly, even Nathan Dean, the office grump and workhorse, was up on his feet.

Much of Queenie's power was in her persuasive, fun side, but she could be tough as nails on assignment. Other officers considered themselves lucky when they drew her as a partner. Currently, she was paired with and mentoring Eddie Driscoll, the latest cop turned detective.

At that very moment, her newest trainee was trying out one of her party moves and saying something to Ken when the whole group doubled over in laughter.

John, who was nowhere near close enough to hear what was said, started laughing along.

Such moments of levity were rare, but on occasion, the crew did find time for a little fun before gearing up for a day of calls. And from the best seat in the house, John continued to watch until the early morning entertainment began to wind down.

The staff was solid, and no one had ever given any indication that they'd be involved in something like evidence tampering, but anything was possible. The guilty party could be breathing the very same air and, with Drake gone, even thinking the heat was off.

Relationships with the team were good, but John was a detective. And if upcoming clues pointed him in that direction, he'd have no choice but to investigate. The weight of the case was crushing, but his to bear. And he would do his job.

One of the things he'd already done was take up residence in Drake's office. He had confided in a trusted coworker that he was hoping active memories would make him feel closer to answers—and his best friend. A calculation of the hours the two of them had spent in there would have been staggering, an accounting of how they had become like brothers.

"What was it, Drake?" he mumbled. "What'd you find?"

The case was tough but meant everything to Drake. John couldn't let him down.

✳

Days later, Clark pulled into the parking lot at the precinct about thirty minutes early, giving him time to take an unexpected call from Dr. Brill.

"Hey, Doc," he said. "How are you?"

"I think I'm supposed to ask you that," she teased.

Clark grinned. "Yeah, guess so. I'm good. Just a little wound up about meeting Detective Baxter."

"It'll be fine. John's great," she said. "He already knows the gist of what's going on, but you'll have the chance to go into detail. And remember, what do we have to lose?"

"I know, you're right," Clark agreed.

"Hey, I've been thinking about some of what you shared from your visit with the Harrisons," Dr. Brill said. "It's so interesting about the dream and how they were able to match some of the similarities to Drake. And the photo on the mantel . . . well, that's actual evidence in my mind. So, at this point, with nothing eliminating the hunch, we might really be on to something."

"Yeah," Clark agreed. "I just hope I'm up for it."

"If it starts to feel overwhelming, just say the word," reminded Dr. Brill. "We can always take a break for a while."

"No, I'm okay," he said. "It might sound odd, but just knowing that Drake was a great person has given me some relief."

Dr. Brill nodded. "Yeah, I totally get that. And, hey, since it is Drake, don't fight the thoughts or flashes so much. Just try to relax and let them happen. You'll probably remember more that way, and any new detail could help us figure out what's going on. Anything new I should know about?"

"Well, I was talking in my sleep again," he said.

"Yeah?" she asked. "Did Rachel take notes this time?"

"No, but she sure couldn't wait to tell me about this one. Apparently, I said the name Sherry." Clark rolled his eyes lightheartedly.

"Uh oh," Dr. Brill said, grinning. "Any explanation?"

"No, just another weird dream, I guess."

"Okay, that's a good one. I'll add it to my notes," she promised. "Let's keep writing everything down, and we'll talk again soon. Can't wait to hear all about your time with John. Please give him my best."

"Sure will," Clark said. "Thanks for checking on me. Have a great day."

"You too," she said. "Bye."

Clark made his way into the busy precinct, where the environment was almost jarring, especially compared to the mostly peaceful atmosphere at the Harrison's. In contrast, the new surroundings flaunted the high energy and quick, staccato rhythm of business getting done.

As he made his way across the slightly hectic scene, he noticed an ID plaque with the name *Detective Paul Brady* on the closest desk. The officer seemed to be reviewing a statement with an attractive yet forlorn-looking woman with tousled hair.

Detective Brady paused. "Did you need some help?"

"Oh, yeah, I just need to find Detective Baxter's office," Clark said.

"Yeah, no problem," he said. "It's right behind that big window to your left."

"Thanks." Clark nodded and headed in that direction.

He knocked and waited outside, where he was still close enough to hear a bit of Detective Brady's continuing conversation. Apparently, the despondent woman had been through a physical struggle earlier in the day, where her purse and cell phone had been stolen, and she was there to try to identify the offender.

Incidents like that can leave a person's nerves on edge for days. Startled by the thought, Clark looked around. Where had that come from?

Another random bit of information had made itself at home in his head.

As he watched Paul Brady guide the woman through the unpleasant business at hand with an extra dose of kindness, he felt another rush of understanding. Somehow, Clark knew Paul's accent, innate charms, and humanity were gifts that put people at ease. But profound intuition aside, the shaken woman seemed impervious to the special gifts at the moment.

Still contemplating the strange new thoughts, he knocked for the second time. The power of Detective Baxter's muffled, bass tones resonated through the closed door, suggesting he was either in a meeting or on a phone call. So, Clark waited patiently, even though he wasn't sure John had even heard the knock.

After a moment, the door swung open. With phone in hand, John motioned for Clark to enter. As he wrapped up his call, he silently directed him to the only uncluttered chair in the office.

Clark followed the non-verbal cues and made himself comfortable.

"Sorry about that. All clear now," John said, offering his hand. "John Baxter, nice to meet you."

"Nice to meet you too, Detective," Clark said, standing. "Clark Steele."

There was a subtle start as they traded firm handshakes.

"Please, call me John—and excuse the mess. I'm still moving in."

"No, it's fine," Clark said. But the handshake was still on his mind. He had felt a sense of familiarity, as if he had done it hundreds of times.

Did John feel it too?

"Well, tell me, what's going on with you," John said.

"Wow, where to start," Clark began. "Well, a lot of weird things have been going on, and my story's probably going to sound a little crazy. I'm glad you had a chance to talk to Dr. Brill first. Hopefully, she's filled you in a little bit."

"Yeah, she told me that you received Drake's heart in your transplant and, well, some unusual things have been going on," John explained.

"Yeah, that's right," Clark said. "But before we get started, let me just say that I'm really sorry about the loss of your friend."

John bowed his head. "Thank you. He was like a brother."

"I'm so sorry," Clark said.

"Thanks, I really appreciate that," John said. "Uh . . . yeah . . . so, Dr. Brill did give me a quick overview, but I'm still not sure what to make of it or how I can help."

"Well, ever since the transplant, I haven't been myself," Clark said. "I don't mean physically, though. Everything there is great. What's going on is . . . I've been seeing strange things . . . doing things I've never done before. I'm having nightmares, dreams, and even random thoughts that, weirdly, don't seem to be my own."

John reached over and closed his laptop. "Hmm . . . like what?"

"Well, thoughts just flash through my mind, and I don't know where they come from," Clark said. "I seem to know things that I can't explain. I've had these amazing new observational skills and instincts about people. And some of my preferences have even changed."

"Can you be specific?" asked John.

"Well, coffee, for one. That's a new preference, and I seem to know obscure details about it," Clark said. "And even though I've never been much of a fan of gardening, I'm mysteriously drawn to it now. It's like a compulsion that takes over."

"Hmm," John said.

"Yeah, and the Harrison's confirmed those things, among others, as preferences of Drake's," explained Clark. "So, I definitely left there feeling more receptive to Dr. Brill's theory."

"Well, they're similarities, for sure, but not what I would call evidence," John said.

"Yeah, I know," Clark said. "But there's so much more, even a frightening dream that seems to mirror a real event in Drake's life. I was hoping that, by talking to you, I could see if anything else lines up."

He went on to share a careful timeline summary, from his post-surgical experiences to the eye-opening meeting with the Harrisons. The dissertation included his medical diagnosis, the after-effects of the transplant, and his mysterious connection to Drake.

The final point seemed to hit John the hardest. A change of expression created soft shadows that fell over his face, exposing what appeared to be lingering grief.

"I'm sorry, is this too much?" Clark asked.

"No, I'm fine," John said. "I want to hear more."

"Well, it's a lot." Clark sighed. "I'm really sorry to trouble you, but I didn't know where else to turn. If you're sure it's okay to go on, I could tell you more about the episodes."

"Yeah, of course," John nodded.

"Well, one morning, I was looking in the mirror when I saw like . . . like the ghost of a man . . . flash in front of me," Clark began. I'm not going to lie. It freaked me out. I tried my best to forget about it, but I couldn't shake it. And then, framed on the mantel at the Harrison's, was a photo of the very same man. John, it was Drake."

John squinted and shook his head. "You're serious?"

Clark nodded. "Yeah, and that's not all. I've also seen a little girl's face. But that one was more distinct. And weirdly, I felt like I was supposed to help her. You know, like she might be in trouble or something."

John's searching expression made Clark feel a little ill at ease.

Does he think I'm crazy?

"I'm sorry, John. I know I'm rambling, but I'm just trying to get everything out," explained Clark.

"It's okay, don't worry about it," John said.

He continued to make direct eye contact with Clark, but slowly, his countenance changed. The new, measured expression was more like a rehearsed poker face.

If you react too strongly, the subject might shut down. Clark looked around for the source of the strange thought, but it was in his own head again.

"So, you're saying all of this started only after your transplant?" John asked.

"Uh, yeah," Clark said. "At first, I thought it might be medications, but the doctors assured me it wasn't. So, eventually, I had to consider my mental health, and that's when I found Dr. Brill."

"Well, you found a good one there," John said. "When she told me about the phenomenon, I couldn't believe what I was hearing. But I trust her, so I agreed to the meeting."

"Yeah, Dr. Brill's great," Clark agreed. "She has case studies of people with similar experiences to mine. I could share a couple with you."

"Sure," John said. "I've got time."

Clark recounted some of Dr. Brill's research, where the lives of patients had been mysteriously altered by the phenomenon. While the whole concept had been hard for most people to wrap their heads around, John's rapt attention implied an unusual perceptiveness.

"Have you heard of anything like this before?" Clark asked.

"Nope, and I've been around a while," John declared.

Quickly assessing John as a man of compassion, Clark felt like he probably wanted to believe him. But he was a detective, and healthy skepticism was surely a requirement in that line of work.

Clark began to explain the biology behind the phenomenon as best he could. As he rattled off the scientific details, he watched John lean casually but ever more dangerously back in his chair.

"Oops, careful there," he said when it lurched a little too far backward. "Nice chair, though."

John grinned and quickly sat upright. "Oh, thanks. It was a gift to Drake from an old girlfriend, Sherry."

Sherry! The name rang like a bell.

"John, I know I haven't mentioned it yet, but I've also been talking in my sleep," Clark said. "And apparently, one of the things I said was the name Sherry."

"Really? You know anyone by that name?" John asked.

"No," Clark said. "That's just it—no one. And the whole talking in my sleep thing is new."

"You do have some strange things going on, I'll give you that," admitted John.

Clark nodded. "We're just getting started."

"So, this might sound weird to you," John said, "but that biological explanation is actually making some sense to me."

"No. Me too," Clark agreed. "But I'm still processing everything. The phenomenon, Drake's heart, me sitting here."

"Yeah," John said, glancing at Clark's chest. "Drake was all about others."

Clark smiled. "Good man."

"That he was," John said. "And, Clark, I hope I haven't been staring, but the thought of his heart beating in your chest is just unbelievable to me."

"Don't worry about it, I get it," Clark nodded.

While it would have been perfectly reasonable for John to dismiss Dr. Brill's theory as fantasy or science fiction, Clark was hoping the honesty in the details would tempt him to accept that some of Drake's memories and preferences might have actually passed on.

"Clark, the sincerity of what you're saying is hard to deny," John said. "I mean, you seem solid and convincing to me. And if there's one thing I know, it's people.

"But Drake was my best friend, and I need to be extra careful. Right now, I'm torn. You've shared some interesting things, but do you have any actual proof?"

"Well, Dr. Brill could probably provide you with copies of documented cases," proposed Clark. "But my personal story is, obviously, still unfolding. That's why I'm here, trying to find out if any of my experiences are related to Drake in any way.

"Listen, I understand the skepticism," he continued. "In the beginning, it sounded just as crazy to me, but I sensed something real about it at the same time. When Dr. Brill shared actual evidence of the phenomenon, something stirred deep inside. And those sessions are what inspired me to start looking for my donor. It was the only way to test the phenomenon. And truth be told, I didn't have the luxury of rejecting any possibility. I needed answers."

"So, you feel like you've gotten evidence from your time at the Harrison's?" John asked.

"Yeah, I really do," Clark nodded. "After talking with them, I feel more like the phenomenon could be real in my case. It seems like Drake and I share many similarities, and there are coincidences that I just can't explain away. I know how weird that sounds, but I promise you, it's true."

"I'm not doubting you," John said. "In fact, let me tell you straight. At this moment, thoughts of dismissing the whole thing are losing out to my curiosity. If there's even an outside chance you're tapping into Drake in some way, I want to listen."

"Thanks," Clark said. "That's all I can ask."

He picked up the story where he had left off and spoke uninterrupted for a long while. John seemed to be hanging on every word but, again, not saying much.

Clark wondered if he was more convinced or formulating questions.

There's great value in being quiet. Let the subject talk. Don't risk interfering with their train of thought.

The aimless thought made Clark flinch. *Why is an interrogation technique going through my mind? Is John using it on me?*

"Clark, are you okay?" John asked.

"Yeah, sorry," he said, shaking it off. "I just had another one of those flashes."

As Clark shared the details, the color faded from John's face.

"Now that's weird," exclaimed John. "It's like you read my mind."

"I'm sorry, John," he said. "This is just the weird kind of stuff that keeps happening."

"Well, now you have my attention," John said. "Please, go on."

"Well, besides all that, some of the other flashes have been just as strange," Clark said. "Random thoughts and images just pop into my head. I've seen everything from journals, Jeeps, and popcorn to creepy dark figures . . . to name a few."

John seemed transfixed by the disclosure—never breaking eye contact.

Clark shifted in his chair. *Is it my imagination, or is he looking at me differently?*

"This is too weird," John said. "Did you just say popcorn . . . and mention a little girl in distress earlier?"

"Yeah, I guess I did," Clark said.

"Well, I want to tell you something," John said. "But I need to ask you a few questions first."

"Yeah, of course, anything," nodded Clark. "I know this is a lot, John. First, the transplant, and now I'm telling you that I might have received more than Drake's heart. But honestly, I wouldn't be here if I didn't think there was something to this. I'm just trying to find out if it could actually be true."

"No, I get it," John said. "The whole thing is an incredible theory, and you want to know if it's really possible?"

"Yeah, that's it," Clark said.

"Well, here's what I'm thinking. Like Dr. Brill explained, since our bodies are made up of cells, a donor heart would introduce foreign cells," John rationalized. "So, the biological side of things does make some sense. And isn't that why doctors administer anti-rejection medication?"

"Exactly," Clark said.

"So, who's to say that those cells don't transfer life information from donor to recipient?" John posed. "It could conceivably be in any form—intellect, memories, and more."

Clark shook his head. "Yeah, it's mind-blowing. And if information and images from Drake's life have been transferred to me, what does it mean? What do I do now?"

"Well, from a law enforcement perspective, you could even have access to classified details from Drake's cases," John proposed.

Clark felt goosebumps rising, and then the strangest thought went through his mind. He was thankful he had worn the blue, chambray shirt with long sleeves, so the hair standing up on his arms couldn't be seen.

He willed himself to stay calm.

"Clark, I don't want to freak you out," John said. "But a few of your flashes are eerily similar to evidence in a case Drake and I were working on."

"What?" Clark asked. "Are you serious?"

"Yeah, it's probably coincidence, but now I'm curious," confessed John. "Some were closely guarded details never made public."

"Oh my God," Clark blurted. "Some of the flashes could be from a case. Maybe that's why I'm on edge."

"Well, let's not get ahead of ourselves, but something out of the ordinary does seem to be going on," John said. "There are only two ways you could know some of that information. Either what you're saying is true . . . or . . . well, let's start with this. Clark, we're going to need to do a background check on you."

Clark nodded but then froze when the inference registered. He had just implicated himself.

"What?" he shouted, jumping to his feet. "John, you can't believe I had anything to do with a crime. I don't even know what you're talking about."

"Whoa," John said. "Clark, I'm not accusing you. As a matter of fact, my gut instinct is telling me the opposite but, I hope you understand, I have to do my job. The background check is just routine. Painless but required. A couple of our detectives will work with you."

Clark dried the palms of his hands on his jeans as he paced. "Maybe I shouldn't even have come here."

"No, I'm glad you did," John said. "Clark, don't worry, this is just procedure. It sounds worse than it is." He presented him with a clipboard and pen. "I'll need you to fill out this form. It's just information the officers are going to need."

Clark stared at him and hesitated before taking it. "Fine," he said.

His mind was a blur. Was this the right move? Would he be arrested? His heart beat faster as he fought to control his shaky hand. Within seconds, the room went dark, and all awareness was lost. And yet, information continued to appear on the document as if enter-ing itself.

"Clark! Clark, are you all right?" John asked.

John's powerful voice had snapped him out of it. He steadied himself against the desk and handed over the completed document. John took one quick look at it and then took a rocky step backward.

"Clark, you filled out the officer portion, including Drake's badge number," he said. "Where did you get that?"

"What?" Clark was reeling. He reached for the paper. "How . . . how could I . . . know?"

"Good question!" John said.

The two stood face-to-face, enduring an awkward pause.

"Why are you looking at me like that?" Clark asked. He couldn't read John's face.

John shook his head. "Clark, I'm not—" but he was interrupted.

"I think . . . I think I need an attorney," announced Clark. He pivoted and made a beeline for the door.

"Clark, wait!" John said.

Clark never looked back.

TWELVE

OUT OF THE BOX

John was still fidgeting with the clipboard, looking over the unexplainable entries, when Eddie Driscoll walked in.

"What was that all about?" Eddie asked.

John shook his head. "You're not going to believe me."

After a quick rundown, John showed him the eerie document, highlighting the end of the strange encounter.

"That's sketchy," Eddie smirked. "You don't believe that BS, do you?"

"I'm not sure what to believe yet," John said. "I'm going to check him out, but I'll tell you, there are aspects of his story that make me question whether a connection to Drake is really possible."

Eddie sank into the closest chair and planted his crocodile, Tony Lamas, on the desk. "C'mon man, you've got to be kidding me."

"Look, you weren't there," John said. "There was even a weird energy transfer when we shook hands. And get your feet off my desk."

"All right, all right," Eddie said, quickly sitting up straight. "Look, John, I know you miss Drake, but just think about how crazy this sounds."

"I know, but the guy's a patient of Dr. Brill's, and besides, what would it hurt to spend a little time with him?" John asked. "Maybe I'll even recognize some of Drake's habits or characteristics."

"Doubt it," Eddie said. "He might be playing you."

John shook his head. "That's not what my gut's telling me, but you could be right." He handed him the completed form. "Will you and Queenie start a background check?"

Eddie rolled his eyes and shrugged. "Yeah, sure."

"Look, I'm curious from a personal perspective, but mostly for the case," John said.

"I know, I get that," Eddie said. "But think of the risk."

"Well, I think I'm going to meet with him one more time just to see where it goes," John explained.

"What? John, he could be involved in a kidnapping with a deadly weapon!" cautioned Eddie.

"But why would he come here?" John asked. "Look, I hear you, but I've got nothing to lose. If he's involved, I nail him. If not, maybe I discover something that helps the case. Might be worth the risk. I don't know, but I've got to figure it out fast. If he'll even talk to me, that is."

Eddie jumped up and headed out in a huff. "Well, do what you want, but I'm going to be tough on the background check."

John shook his head and shouted through the door, "Easy, cowboy, just do it right."

After rifling through a few desk drawers, John located the pearl-handled magnifying glass used to analyze photos. The ones in question had been examined earlier, but a repeat of the process was never a bad idea.

Even though nothing came of it, he was smiling when he finally pushed the evidence aside. It might have had something to do with the next task, using the visualization technique he had learned from none other than Drake. He closed his eyes and seemed to quickly relax into the exercise. If he could only put himself into Drake's shoes, maybe his imagination would wander into the investigative time spent at the cabin.

John had actually been to the Harrison family retreat many times with Drake, mostly for casework. So, he was very familiar with the layout of the home and the land, but more importantly, Drake's crime-solving routine. The lucky coincidence surely provided him with a privileged perspective into Drake's last visit.

Fresh entries in his open computer file hinted that Drake would probably have been enjoying a morning coffee while reviewing the case. And if answers didn't come without a fight, it would have been just like him to take a break and head for the porch.

That's where the two of them sat, sometimes for hours, discussing tough cases. And since the work was routinely stressful, they also made time for walking the grounds and listening to nature. Really connecting with the tranquility of the property.

Those breaks usually prompted a silly, made-up game. The challenge was to outdo one another by correctly identifying the trees and plants. If they didn't know the real answer, they were required to make something up, and the one who came up with the most ridiculous name was declared the winner. The diversionary foolishness was always followed by an enthusiastic, middle-school laugh.

The cabin wasn't without fun but offered more serious perks. The combination of a relaxed environment and quiet time, with evidence, was ideal for casework—a rare treat, even.

Drake loved the cabin for that and countless other reasons, so it was still a mystery as to why he had packed up and cut his time short. John had even gone to Captain Riley with that concern shortly after the accident.

"What do you think?" he asked.

"I think something happened. He had a reason for coming back," surmised the captain.

John nodded. "Me too. I can't shake that feeling. I've been trying to picture the missing photo from the cemetery series again. Could that have anything to do with it?"

"I don't know, maybe." Captain Riley said. "Good thing you've gotten to the point where you can visualize things almost as well as Drake."

"Well, I don't know about that," John said. "But I know I don't like missing evidence. And even worse is the nagging feeling that someone on the inside could be involved."

Yeah, no one wants to go there," the captain said. "But we do what we have to do. Glad you're the one on it. Keep me posted."

✳

And now, months later, thought John, *things have gotten even more mysterious after the strange meeting with Clark.* "Yeah, wait till the captain hears this," he muttered under his breath.

He had barely gotten the words out when a shout came from Captain Riley's office. "John, get in here!"

"What's up?" John said, reaching the doorway.

"What's this I'm hearing about you sharing classified information with an outsider?" he demanded.

"Where did you hear that?" John asked.

"Never mind," snapped the captain. "Take a seat."

"Sir, I was going to explain," John said. "It's a weird turn of events, but it's also the first hint of anything in the Sweet case in forever."

"What's going on?" Captain Riley said.

"Well, I was going to come to you for permission," he began.

"Look, I'm getting ready to leave for a while," Captain Riley interrupted. "Get to the point."

John sighed and gave a quick rundown of Clark's history, including the phenomenon and his connection to Drake.

With a stern lowering of his eyes, Captain Riley leaned back and folded his arms.

As if indifferent to the action, John went right on, covering Clark's apparent credibility and the weird details seemingly related to the case.

The captain's doubtful expression appeared to soften a bit.

"Sir, I know this is weird," John said. "But the case is going cold, and I've got nothing else to go on. I'm having a background done right now. And if things check out, for the sake of the family, I should probably see where this leads."

The captain rolled his eyes. "And I thought I'd heard everything."

"I get it, I'm still taking it in," agreed John. "But sir . . . the case."

"Listen, I am not a fan of this, but I've seen that look before. So, here's the deal. First, you clear him, and I mean put him through the paces, and then you try to get as many details as you can. If he comes up with information on his own, you can go from there. But for appearances, limit the time spent here at the precinct."

"Done," John said.

Captain Riley pointed and shook his finger. "Look, this is against my better judgment, so I'm trusting you, big time. No deviating from my orders, or I'll shut the whole thing down."

John nodded. "We're on the same page. I was already going to get information from him first."

The captain looked up from packing his laptop and shook his head. "I must be nuts. But I want to be updated on this fantasy case of yours."

"Okay," John said on his way out. "Oh, and since Clark is Dr. Brill's patient, I was thinking about asking her to join us."

The captain shrugged. "Yeah, probably a good idea."

When John was well out of sight, Captain Riley picked up the note that had alerted him to Clark's involvement. Apparently, someone had slipped it into a stack of mail before it reached his desk. After studying the accusatory message for a minute, he tossed it into his briefcase and locked it.

✴

John had barely made his way back to his office when Eddie's head came peeking through the door. "Hey," he said. "Be careful. There's already a connection between Clark Steele and the victim's aunt."

"What?" John exclaimed. "Are you sure?"

"Yeah, man," he said. "Told you I didn't like it. Apparently, they had some business dealings."

"Did you go running to the captain about this?" demanded John.

"What? No," he said. "Queenie and I still have a few more things to check out."

"Well, my gut's telling me Clark's all right, but let me know what else you find," John said.

Eddie rolled his eyes and pivoted out the door. "Yep."

Creating a backdrop to Eddie's dramatic exit was the workspace belonging to Mary Wiggins, the precinct's administrative assistant. As usual, she was busy at work. But if John decided to investigate Clark and his strange phenomenon, Mary was going to get a whole lot busier.

When extra support was needed, Mary found a way, even if she already had a lot on her plate. She seemed to always be there for John, and truth be told, he had a fierce crush on her. But the right time to ask her out never seemed to manifest.

Mary was a slender beauty with natural blonde hair, porcelain skin, and exquisite makeup. The meticulous effort she must have put in every morning resulted in a picture-perfect face that would have been ready for the most discriminating Hollywood headshot.

Even though she turned every head in the room, Mary didn't seem comfortable with a lot of attention. She had the outward appearance of a star but the inner heart of a serious woman. It was as if life had a more meaningful plan for her, and she showed gratitude by making careful choices.

John had once confided in Drake that she had already turned down a couple of proposals and that, to him, showed real character. It meant she wasn't about to settle, and in his admiring mind, those high ideals made her all the more appealing.

After putting a couple of files away, John locked the door and stopped by her desk.

"Hey, Mary," he whispered. "I need your help with something when I get back."

"Okay. Everything all right?" she asked.

"Yeah, probably," John said. "But I might have just gotten permission for something that I'm not even sure I want."

"From the captain?" she asked.

"Yeah," he said. "Hey, I was just going to head out for lunch. You want me to bring you something?"

"Oh, no thanks," said Mary. "I'm good."

"Okay, I'll be back soon." He turned to leave but stopped almost immediately and made an about-face. "You know what? Never mind, this can't wait. Will you get Clark Steele on the phone for me?"

"Of course," she said, dialing the number. A moment passed. "Sorry, John, only getting his voicemail."

"Probably skipped town," teased Eddie, eavesdropping.

John shot him a frosty glance and turned back. "I really need to talk to him. Will you keep trying?"

"Yeah, sure, what's going on?" she asked.

"Long story concerning the case," he replied.

He was just sharing what details he could with Mary when the very loud ringtone on her phone startled them. Without picking it up, she peeked at the screen and then at John. "Clark Steele."

✳

Thirty minutes later, John was headed down a cool dirt road lined with a near-canopy of Southern Live Oaks. He took a right at the end of the bend and immediately shielded his eyes. There, through the shimmering beams of radiant light, sat The Oak Shack, one of his and Drake's favorite burger joints.

Hardly anyone was out on the massive wooden deck that overlooked a charming local fishing hole. The favored spot was one where John and Drake had been able to forget the chaos of the job from time to time and enjoy a great meal. Watching families teach the next generation to fish, with ducks paddling and skimming across the water, was simply an added bonus.

Clark was already there, taking in the view from the hood of his champagne-colored Audi, when he heard a car pull in.

He turned and made eye contact with John, who quickly parked and yanked open his door. "Hey, how'd you get here before me?"

Clark grinned and made his way over to shake hands.

John nodded. "Thanks for coming, Clark. Glad you're still talking to me."

"I was feeling pretty offended when I left," Clark said, "and I'm just here because...because I really don't know what else to do."

"Well, let's go order, and let me tell you what I'm thinking," John said.

Clark followed but kept visual contact with the scenic backdrop. He pulled sunglasses from his pocket and slid them on just before settling into a patio chair. Leaning back, he said, "What a picture. I can see why you and Drake liked this place."

John nodded. "Yeah, loved it. I thought it would be a good place to talk. Clark, I hope you understand why I have to be tough on you right now. If I didn't, I wouldn't be doing my job."

"Yeah, I know. I've been thinking about that, Clark said. "I get it, but it's still frustrating."

"I know, but I have to put your story to the test," John explained. "I'm still waiting for the final verdict on your background check. But is there anything else you want to tell me?"

"No, I had nothing to do with your case or any crime," he said.

"Okay, can you tell me how you know Ashley Benson?" John asked.

"I don't know Ashley Benson," Clark replied.

John folded his arms. "You sure? Interior decorator?"

"Wait a minute . . . Ashley Benson?" Clark asked. "That name does sound familiar. My company had a new decorator in for a meeting a while back, but I wasn't there. Are you telling me that was her?"

"Yeah, the connection showed up during the background check," explained John. "She's the aunt of our victim."

"What?" Clark said. "The aunt? Geez, I came here for help, not to make things worse for myself."

With palms facing the floor, John gestured up and down. "Take it easy."

"John, if it's the same decorator, I wasn't even there," claimed Clark. "I left early that day."

"Okay, investigators are probably already checking it out, but I'll let them know," John promised. "Listen, once you're clear, things should get easier. But for now, I'm just going to be straight with you. The case is already way behind, and every minute wasted means a child's life is still in danger. So, while we wait for clearance, what do you say to testing your flashes? Especially in relation to the case?"

"Yeah, that's fine," Clark said. "But is that possible without making my own situation worse?"

"Yeah, should be a good thing. It might actually help clear you faster," John said. "I've got an exercise in mind where we can analyze your visions and consider if anything really lines up. And we might even get a hypnotherapist involved."

"That's weird. Dr. Brill mentioned the same thing," Clark said.

"Not surprised," John said. "They're great at recovering memories you don't even know you have."

"Little scary to think what else might be in there," fretted Clark.

The screen door from the restaurant flew open, and a fresh-faced waitress in bib overalls headed their way, juggling a full tray.

"Hey, Kid. You need some help?" shouted John.

The wood planks whined with every step as she flashed a big smile. "Thanks, but no, I need the practice."

"You sure?" added Clark.

"Yep, I'm good," she said. "But thanks."

Once everything was on the table and she'd made her way back inside, Clark said, "Well, if that burger tastes half as good as it looks, I'm coming back here."

John grinned. "Oh, you will. I couldn't count the times Drake and I were here. I actually have a picture at home where he and I are sitting in this very spot."

Conversation flowed naturally from there on out, and by the time the meal was over, Clark felt like he had gotten to know John and Drake a little better, especially during talk of more normal things.

After paying the check, they had just turned to leave when a piercing scream rang out from behind.

They spun around just in time to see a boy of about nine fighting a bent fishing rod and yelling from the bank, "I got one!"

It was surely the beginning of another famous fish tale, a story that would be told over and over again.

✳

The next morning, Ken Krieger sauntered past John's open door and blurted, "Hey, do you want to grab lunch today?"

"Oh, thanks," John said. "But I'm going to be tied up with this interview all day."

"Sweet case?" Ken asked, backtracking.

"Yep, and it's turned into something you wouldn't believe," John said. "My meeting is with the transplant recipient who received Drake's heart. He believes he's having some of Drake's thoughts and memories."

"What the hell?" Ken said, stepping inside.

"I know, man, but he seems great, and something about the story rings true," John explained. "I'll have to catch you up later. He's walking this way."

Ken looked over his shoulder. "Wow, okay. Beer at Murph's?"

"See you there," John nodded.

Mary was all smiles as Clark passed her desk. "Good morning, Clark. Sorry, we didn't really get a chance to meet properly yesterday."

He glanced at the nameplate on her desk and grinned. "Well, good morning, Mary Wiggins."

Mary froze for a second, looking puzzled.

What'd I say? Clark wondered. He would later learn that Drake used to pause and use Mary's full name in the same manner. Apparently, even the swagger of his delivery was loosely familiar.

Mary began organizing her desk gratuitously. "I've set up appointments and made some arrangements that should get you guys off to a good start. I'll be here to help if you need me."

"Thanks," Clark said. "Looks like it could be a long day."

The sound of John's footsteps moving in their direction caused them both to turn.

"Oh, looks like he's ready for you," Mary said. "Just let me know if you need anything."

"Clark!" boomed John. "Good morning." He stepped quickly, offered his hand, and then motioned for Clark to follow him down the hall. "Let's get you a cup o' joe, and we'll get started."

"Sounds good," Clark said.

"I know you're a real coffee fan now, so I should warn you," John teased. "This station brew will definitely not make your top ten, but it'll get the job done."

Clark grinned. "Good enough."

Inside the break room, Morgan Fox was sitting behind a stack of files with her morning tea in hand. Clark had noticed her chatting with a coworker the day before and wondered if rumors about his connection to Drake had already made their way around.

"Hey, Morgan," John said. "This is Clark Steele. You've probably already heard; he's going to be helping me on the Sweet case."

After stashing a few photos into a pristine, zippered folder to her right, she confessed, "I've heard a little bit. You know how news travels around here."

John rolled his eyes. "Oh, yeah."

"Well, good luck on the case," she said. "I know it's been frustrating."

"Yeah, thanks," John said. "We better get going."

Although Morgan's interest in his presence to that point had seemed marginal, Clark was sure he could feel her eyes on him as he and John walked to the other side of the room.

"Hey, bagels," announced John. "Help yourself, Clark."

Selections were made, and they were halfway out the door when

John said, "Oh, by the way, Dr. Brill should be here soon. Luckily, she had most of the day free."

"Yeah, she left me a message. I'm really glad she's coming," Clark said.

John nodded and made a quick scan of the room. "Well, look who just walked in."

Dr. Brill looked very put together in a beautifully fitted black pencil skirt, white button-down, and a cropped leather jacket. Basic black pumps completed the outfit, and confidence led the way.

"Hey, Doc," called John. "Over here."

"Morning, guys," she said, picking up her pace. "How are you?"

Clark smiled. "Great. Good to see you."

"Hey, come on in," John said. "Just sit anywhere you want. Oh, wait. On second thought, before we sit, let me show you both this timeline." He was pointing to a poster of the case, taking up most of the wall.

Dr. Brill made her way over to the expansive presentation, posing as wallpaper. "What's this?"

"It's the Sweet case," John said. "Well, in timeline form."

"Oh yeah, of course," she nodded.

"We keep most of this information private so we don't compromise the case. But because of the unusual nature of Clark's story, I've asked permission to share some of it," he said. "And even though the captain wasn't completely on board, he gave limited approval."

Then he leaned in and whispered, "The good thing is, starting tomorrow, he's going to be out of town for a while, so we'll be a little less scrutinized.

"Anyway, the timeline begins with events from before the crime up to the current day. This is a revised version, allowing me to add any of Clark's memories without the risk of influencing him with previous information."

"That makes sense," agreed Dr. Brill. "Well, you guys just go ahead. Pretend I'm not here. I'll only interject if needed."

"Well, as I've already explained to Clark," John said, "I have to do my job, and things might feel a little rough right now."

Dr. Brill gave him a sideways glance. "Hmm . . . sounds like it is a good thing I'm here then."

John grinned. "Okay, let's get to work. Clark, as you can see, the timeline begins with the family being out for the evening, and the abduction happens after they return home. The mother was distracted by a phone call earlier and thinks she might have forgotten to lock a window. Since the perp wore gloves and left no prints, CSI couldn't confirm. But it's still likely that's how he gained access. A lot of charted information is solid theory, and some is actual fact. Notice the color coding. Red is fact; blue is theory. So, if there's anything from your memory that seems relevant, we can just add it."

Clark shook his head, "I just can't believe we're doing this."

John held up three markers. "Pick a color."

"Green signifies life and renewal," interjected Dr. Brill with a wink.

"Let's go with green," Clark said.

"Oh, just one more thing," John announced. "Since Dr. Brill agrees that a hypnotherapist could be helpful, I've had Mary place several appointment times on hold."

Clark turned to Dr. Brill. "Yeah, we were talking about that. And, about how, up until now, my flashes have been spontaneous."

"Yeah, it's a little different when you think about purposely accessing memories, isn't it?" she grinned.

"Yeah, a little weird," Clark agreed.

"Clark, if you'll just take a look at these dates, I'll have Mary call and get you scheduled," John said.

"Hmm . . . the one on Thursday at ten looks good," he said.

Almost before he had gotten the words out, John was headed to Mary's desk. "Be right back."

Although the attention to detail was admirable, Clark wondered if John's sudden mission had more to do with being near Mary. *Another random thought? Or am I just reacting to the obvious: the energy shift in John when he mentions Mary?*

Either way, the thought made him smile.

John bounced back through the doorway. "Appointment's set. Okay, guys, let's do this."

THIRTEEN

UNTOLD POTENTIAL

"So, Clark, this might be the craziest thing I've ever done," John said. "But on the outside chance there's something to this, I don't want to regret it later."

"Well, the whole thing is crazy to me too, but at this point, I'm willing to try almost anything," Clark confessed.

"If I may, John," Dr. Brill said. "Clark started having these strange experiences only after the transplant. And since they don't seem related to anything else in his life, he does fit the profile of a patient presenting with the phenomenon."

"Okay, why don't we just jump in? Clark, go ahead and tell me about anything unusual," John coaxed, "and then we can decide whether or not to make note of it."

"Well, there's this overall sense of dread that I can't explain," Clark began. "And sometimes, when the anxiety hits, I feel like I'm closing in on something. Like a breakthrough of some kind. But I just can't put my finger on it."

"And this is all new to you, right?" John asked.

Clark nodded. "Yeah, after the transplant."

"Okay," John said. "Well, let me bring you up to speed on this end. First of all, Drake was the best detective we've ever had around here. Dr. Brill knows. It's like he had special, intuitive abilities."

"A natural," she agreed. "I'm so glad you got to meet his family."

"Me too, they were great," Clark said. "And I loved hearing them talk about Drake."

"Well, anyway, Drake and I were working on this case and doing everything we could, but we just couldn't nail it," John said. "But Drake felt sure we were close. He actually said something about a breakthrough, like you just did. That was right before he left for the cabin."

"Really?" Clark said. "That's strange. When I get that feeling, it seems related to some kind of trouble, and I feel a strange urge to help."

John stepped up to the timeline. "Okay, let's just stay with that for a minute." In green marker, he started a new column on the bottom left corner labeled *Similarities*. Under the new heading, he listed: *sense of dread*, *close to answer*, and *trouble*.

"If we look at the beginning of the timeline, there are certainly people in trouble, so your thoughts and emotions do mimic what Drake would have been feeling," he added. "But that's such general stuff."

"Well, I'm also having dreams and restless nights, and like I said, Rachel's even heard me talking in my sleep," offered Clark. "And let's see, I've already told you about saying the name Sherry."

"Oh, yeah, Sherry," repeated Dr. Brill.

Clark looked in her direction. "I don't think I've had a chance to tell you, but John said Drake had an old girlfriend named Sherry."

"Well, yes. Yes, he did," she said. "Now that's interesting. Hey, maybe that'll get you out of trouble with Rachel."

Clark grinned. "Oh, sorry, John. Inside joke. Where was I?"

"Talking in your sleep," John said.

"Yeah, there were a couple of other times," Clark began. "Apparently, most of what I said was incoherent, but because of what I'd been going through, Rachel wrote down what little she could make out. She thought she heard me say, 'follow the rules,' and 'took my life.'"

Dr. Brill had learned of the information in a past session and seemed to be calmly reflecting, but John did an unexpected double take. The innocent words had triggered a physical reaction and Clark wanted to know why.

John was already retrieving a document from the beat-up file box on his desk. "I've got to show both of you something. This is a statement from the parents of the abducted child. If you look carefully at the third paragraph, you'll find some of what the abductor said to them that night."

He transferred not only the document to Clark but also the explanation for his strange reaction. As Clark read the parents' account of the intruder's rant, the hair on the back of his neck stood up. There in black and white were the words *you have to follow the rules,* and *you took my life, so now I'm taking yours.*

The flush disappeared from his face as he leaned back in his chair and handed the paper off to Dr. Brill. He had unconsciously repeated the words of the perpetrator.

"Clark, those details from the Sweet case were never made public," John announced.

"Oh my gosh, John," interjected Dr. Brill. "This is real evidence."

"But how . . . how could I know what the intruder said?" gasped Clark. "It has to be Drake. Nothing else makes sense."

"Well, there is the other possibility, but I didn't want to bring it up," John said, taking a seat on the edge of his desk. "Clark, have you ever experienced any kind of lost time or anything?"

"What?" cried Clark. "No. Well, not that I know of. I told you. I didn't have anything to do with this."

"I know," John said. "But you gave almost a word-for-word account of what the kidnapper said. There's either some weird phenomenon going on, as you say, or something more incriminating."

"John, I would never—" Clark began.

"It's fine." John nodded. "Let's just put that aside for now and get back to the statement. What do you think about it?"

"I agree with Dr. Brill," Clark said. "It's finally tangible evidence. Looks like she's right about this."

John shrugged. "Maybe. I almost fell out of my chair when you spoke the same words as the abductor. I've read that account so many times I didn't even need to look it up. You know what? I'm not even going to pretend to understand what's going on here, but if you're for real, we might actually be on to something."

"Clark, you feeling okay?" Dr. Brill asked. "You look a little pale."

"I'm okay," he said. "I think I was in shock for a minute."

"You need a break?" John asked.

Clark took a deep breath. "No, I'm fine. Let's keep going.

"I've had a couple of other pretty weird things happen," he continued. "The first one was over a certain parking space. Rachel and I were out for an early dinner and pulled into a restaurant with a very empty parking lot. Instead of taking a convenient spot, I felt compelled to park in number seventeen, which was much farther away. Rachel couldn't understand why I was so insistent, but she humored me, as she does a lot these days."

"Probably nothing," John said. "But since you brought it up, let me tell you something about number seventeen. It did hold some significance for Drake. His parking spot here at the office was number seventeen, as was his all-star football jersey. How's that for coincidence?

"Let's think. If memories can really be transferred, that number could have been innately familiar. I don't think it has anything to do with the case, but let's, at least, add it to the 'Similarities' column."

New information kept appearing on the poster as the interviewer and subject went back and forth. The whole session was surreal.

Ever since Clark had learned of the strange phenomenon, he'd been vacillating between believing and not quite grasping how it was really possible. But when doubts crept in, Dr. Brill had been his sounding board and encourager. She was the saving grace, always validating his new normal and his continued path of discovery.

In search of healing answers, he was learning to accept his unique reality. He'd been gifted with more than Drake's heart. Clark finally understood that he'd been entrusted with the care and security of memories that had stowed away.

He recounted his many episodes and visions, everything from dark figures to military boots. Items such as clothing, a leather journal, and even a Jeep were part of the growing list of random images. The strange flashes and, of course, his new preferences were still mysteries, unexplained pieces of the new instability in his life.

Out of the blue, John said, "Well, I don't know about journals and things, but Drake did drive a Jeep."

"Clark, maybe you're seeing some of Drake's possessions," offered Dr. Brill.

He shook his head. "I don't know. Yeah, maybe."

"Weird coincidence about the Jeep, though," mused John.

"Yeah, like a lot of things," Clark nodded.

"Clark, you mentioned popcorn in one of your flashes," John said. "Can you tell me a little more about that?"

"Yeah, that's when I was in the restaurant with Rachel," he said. "And the image just came out of nowhere."

"Can you describe what you saw?" John asked.

"It was all over. Like it was spilled," he said, trying to recall the image. "On a sofa maybe, and the floor."

"I don't believe this!" John said, waving around the green marker and searching through the evidence file. "Got something else for you to see."

He handed Clark an eight-by-ten color photo. "What do you think of this one?"

Clark had only held it for a few seconds when he began to feel like he was being pulled into the image. The tight shot revealed what appeared to be the edges of a sofa and table, with popcorn scattered about. Exactly like his vision. As he studied it, his memory took him deeper until the eerie familiarity of the scene began to fully register.

When he could speak without trembling, he said, "John, it's so real. It feels like I was there. Is this part of the case?"

"Oh, yeah," John said. "On the night of the abduction, the intruder interrupted the family watching a movie. The conflict sent popcorn flying, and what you're looking at is an actual crime scene photo from that night."

"Oh my God," Clark whispered. "But why do I feel like I was there?"

"That's what we need to find out," John said.

"It's okay, Clark," soothed Dr. Brill. "Remember, feeling emotionally connected to the memories is normal."

"We're close to finishing," John said. "Are you okay to go on?"

Clark handed him the photo. "Yeah, I have to."

"This is actually a good thing, Clark," Dr. Brill said. "All of it will help us understand and give us more control."

"It's okay, I'm fine," he said. "Just on edge."

"Well, if you're okay to go on, we should really put this popcorn reference and the words you spoke in your sleep in a different place on the timeline," John said. "The new section is only for facts, and your details match existing evidence.

"I keep thinking about how many times Drake must have looked at that photo," he added. "And, assuming you weren't there, his photographic mind must have captured the image which then, somehow, astonishingly made its way to you."

"I don't know what to say," Clark said.

"This is where hypnosis could help," Dr. Brill advised. "There might be more detail than you're able to remember right now."

After adding the new information, John declared, "How about a break?"

Clark shook his head. "How can you switch gears so quickly?"

"Lots of practice," John said. "We'll be sharper when we come back. I've got to say, Clark, you've given me a lot to think about. And, as strange as it seems, I'm not ready to dismiss Dr. Brill's theory just yet."

"Clark, everything does seem to be pointing to the phenomenon," she said. "But remember, you're not alone. We're in this together."

"Thanks, Doc," he said. "Right now, the case seems like the most important thing, so I'm just going to try to stay focused on that."

"I think that's wise," she praised. "My instincts are telling me that, somehow, this path is connected to your recovery."

"Come on, guys. A little downtime?" begged John, leading the exit.

After stretching their legs and making a few calls, they discovered the last of some homemade chocolate chip cookies in the break room. Friendly conversation and the unexpected treat did much to dissipate the intensity of the morning.

"Hey, I'll be right back," John said, jumping up.

He stepped out and made his way to the far side of the room, where he met with Queenie about the status of the background check.

"John, we can't confirm Clark's alibi on the night of the abduction," she said. "According to his statement, he drove to a park, where he sat by a lake contemplating his upcoming transplant."

"Thanks, Queenie," he said. "Nice work."

"You bet," she replied. "But John, be careful. I have some doubts."

John nodded. "I'm on it."

When he peeked his head back inside the break room, he said, "Hey, guys, we still have a few minutes. I think I'm going to step outside for some fresh air. Anyone want to join me?"

"If you don't mind, I'm going to stay here and make a couple of calls," Dr. Brill said.

But Clark jumped up. "I'm in."

John led the way to a family-owned café just a couple of doors down, where they found some shade under an umbrella at a nearby bistro table.

"We can sit here," he said. "I'm in here all the time; they don't mind."

"Hey, I know we're on a break right now, but being outside makes me think of another episode," Clark said. "I'll tell you about it when we're back inside."

"Nope. Against the rules," John teased. "Now you have to tell me."

Clark grinned. "Well, remember how I was saying that gardening—being outdoors—has become a new passion? When I say that, it's not lightly. I mean, I feel irresistibly drawn to it, like I need to have my hands in the dirt."

"Hmm . . . curious, but I don't think it's related to the case," John replied.

"Yeah, I'm just trying to remember everything," shrugged Clark.

"That's good," John said. "You know, Drake did love nature.

That's one of the reasons he loved the cabin so much. Maybe we should, at least, chart that under 'Similarities.'"

He looked around as if just discovering the brilliance of the day. "You know, when it's like this, even I could handle a little more of getting back to nature."

Clark grinned.

"Clark, I have to ask you something," John said. "It's about your alibi. When you were at the park and sitting by the lake, did you interact with anyone?"

After a slight pause, Clark said, "No, I don't think so. Saw a few familiar faces and waved, but I don't remember speaking to anyone. I was so in my own head at that moment, thinking about the transplant."

John nodded and quickly glanced at Clark's chest.

"I can't imagine what it's been like for you on a day-to-day basis," he said. "Especially never knowing when the next episode is coming."

"That's why I'm here," Clark said.

"Yeah. Well, I think we've gotten our daily dose of Vitamin D," John playfully announced. "Let's head back inside and take another look at what we've got."

Following his lead, Clark headed for the entrance and, in just that split second, felt deep in his gut that there was nothing more natural in the world than entering that building.

Once inside, John said, "Hey, I know, I'm always jumping from one place to another. But I need to grab Eddie while he's here. I'll join you and Dr. Brill in just a few."

"Yeah, no problem," Clark said.

John hustled over to Eddie's desk. "Hey, you got a minute?" he asked.

"Sure, what's up?" Eddie replied.

"I talked to Queenie, and I know the background check isn't

perfect, but ease up, will you?" John said. "I have what I need for now."

"John, are you sure?" Eddie said. "I mean, how well do we know this guy? It's possible to get too close, you know."

"Yeah, I know. But he was preparing for transplant surgery and recovering during that time period," John replied. "No way."

"I get it, but weirder things have happened," reminded Eddie. "He could have an accomplice. John, maybe you just want to solve this one so badly because of Drake."

"Yeah, I do," John retorted. "But that's not all of it."

"Well, things aren't really stacking up exactly the way we like," Eddie warned. I know it's not my case but I really think every stone should be overturned."

"Yeah, but you're right. It's not your case!" snipped John. "It's uncharted territory, and I'm walking a fine line here. Just back off, man."

"Hey, I didn't mean anything by it," Eddie said. "I just want to make sure I'm doing my due diligence."

"Look, I've got a specific plan in mind, and I don't need someone working against me," John said. "I know you're trying to make a name for yourself, but I'll let you know if I need your help again."

Eddie shrugged. "Okay, fine."

John turned and, with a heavier stride, marched back to his office.

"Sorry about that, guys," he said. "It took a little longer than I thought."

"It's fine," Dr. Brill said. "We were just going over a few things."

"Well, Clark," he said. "I guess you're on again."

"Okay, we were just talking about the episode out in the garden," began Clark. "I was planting some flowers for Rachel when that weird sense of uneasiness came over me. I felt dizzy.

"The next thing I knew, the face of a little girl flashed and took my breath away. In the past, my instinct had been to resist images, but that time, I tried to hang on. And something gave me the feeling she was in danger and needed my help. Then, just like other flashes, it was gone. My heart was racing, so I headed back inside. At first, I was a little worried about the whole thing causing a setback, but after relaxing for about an hour, I felt back to normal. Ever since that day, though, I haven't been able to get her out of my mind."

"Can you describe her?" John asked.

Clark wasn't sure why John wanted the description but didn't ask for clarification. Somehow, he felt sure that if he just went with it, the answer would reveal itself.

"It's not easy to focus on that particular vision," Clark said. "Because that one's hard to separate from the anxiety. But, if you think it's important, I'll do it."

"Clark, remember, if you get uncomfortable, we can always stop and talk about it," reminded Dr. Brill.

"Absolutely," John agreed.

"I'm okay," Clark said.

"Well, I'm strictly going on instinct here, but I really need that description before I can share more," John coaxed.

Clark took a cleansing breath and began, "She looked to be about six or maybe seven years old with sandy blonde hair, fair skin, and bluish-green eyes."

His eyes slowly closed. The image was almost clear. "I could only see her from her shoulders up, but I definitely felt she was of slight build, smaller-framed. Her face was oval with small, almost fragile features. Except for her eyes, which were big and round. And I felt a sense of panic, a powerful urge to help her."

Clark stopped for a few seconds and shifted in his chair.

"I know it might be uncomfortable, Clark, but you're doing great," encouraged Dr. Brill.

"Whenever you feel ready, Clark," John prompted.

"I noticed her hair," he almost whispered. "It was past her

shoulders, soft and wispy with that childlike messy look. I couldn't see her hands, but something about the way her shoulders were positioned made me think she might be reaching for something or just leaning forward."

Clark's shoulders dropped as he suddenly sat back in the chair, took another deep breath, and rested. "Sorry, that's all I can remember," he said.

"Clark, that's amazing recall from such a quick vision," John praised. "Like, detective good. Very impressive.

"Let me ask you something," he added. "Can you remember seeing anything around, or behind, the little girl?"

"No, just darkness," Clark replied.

"Okay," John said. "Well, I was just about to show you something, but my gut is hinting at an even better idea."

Clark made eye contact with Dr. Brill just before John began to patrol the room.

"We need to respect a certain order to keep the credibility of the investigation intact," John lectured, almost as if talking to himself.

Finally, he said, "Okay, you guys. There might be something interesting happening here, but I'll need to check on a couple of things. Just relax or even catch a few more minutes of sun if you want. Meet me back here in fifteen?"

"Yeah, sure," sighed Clark. His energy had waned a bit from earlier in the day, and he was hopeful that a brief walk in the sunshine would help him recapture the momentary loss of vitality. "I think I will step outside for some more air. You know, doctor's orders." He grinned at Dr. Brill. "You want to join me?"

"Someone actually listens to me," she joked. "Sure, I'm in this time. But then, sorry to say, I'll have to get going to make my afternoon appointment."

John motioned for the two of them to go first, and then he split off to carry out a separate mission.

By the time Clark and Dr. Brill had exited the building, John had already retrieved a couple of messages, visited Mary's empty desk, and searched half the office looking for her.

When she finally stepped out of the supply room, she almost bumped right into him lingering in the area.

"Oh my gosh, John," she blurted. "You scared the daylights out of me."

"Sorry, Mary, but I need you to do something for me right away," he said, almost stepping on her words. "Can you please have our best sketch artist come in immediately? I think we might be on to something, and I really need this to happen now, if not sooner. You can drop everything else and make this top priority."

"Wow, okay," she said, looking puzzled. "I do have some other things to discuss with you, but I'll give Georgia a call first."

"Thanks, it's important," nodded John. "We'll get to those other things after."

"Okay," she said, picking up the phone.

John made his way over to Paul Brady's desk, where Paul was working on another cold case of Drake's. Out of necessity, he had become the lone investigator.

"Hey, Paul," John said. "How's the case going?"

"Taking forever," he said. "There's an important traffic component to this one, and I feel like I've been living in the viewing room."

"Been there, done that," John said. "Actually, I should be spending time in there now, but my case is missing some footage."

"That sucks," Paul said. "Sorry, man. Hope it turns up."

"Yeah, thanks," nodded John. "Hey, if you get a break later, join me and Ken at Murph's for a beer."

Paul grinned. "Sounds good."

FOURTEEN

SKETCHY BUSINESS

O utside, Clark and Dr. Brill just turned the corner after finishing their first lap around the block.

"Doc, I just realized we're always focused on me, and I haven't had a chance to ask you about yourself," Clark said. "Do you have a family? Married?"

"Well, that subject gets right to the heart of my story," she said. "I was happily married, but my husband went to work one day . . . and . . . and never came back."

"What?" he cried. "What happened?"

"We still don't know," she said. "He was a park ranger and out on rounds one day and just disappeared. It's been years ago now."

"So, you've been waiting all this time, and you've never heard anything?" Clark asked.

"No, and that's the hardest part," she said. "The not knowing makes it almost impossible to move on."

"Oh my God. I'm so sorry," Clark said. "I didn't mean to bring up anything that would upset you."

"Oh, I know," she said. "Don't worry. I'm not upset at all. Like everyone else in the world with issues, I've had to fight my way back. I'm still fighting. But even during the worst period, my work has been my saving grace. And when I look back, I think I was actually treating my patients and myself at the same time."

"You've had all of that to deal with," Clark said, "and then I come in and dump my issues on you."

"Clark, first of all, it's my job. That's what I'm here for," she said. "But let me tell you a secret. I did find healing through acceptance and therapy, but besides the obvious, there was still something missing. And it's not even the magic of a relationship that I'm talking about. It's more like that ethereal spark of life. And that's where you come in."

"Me?" he asked. "What do you mean?"

"Well, I've always loved my practice, but over the years, it had become pretty routine," she confessed. "But something about your case lit a fire in me again. Maybe it's the intrigue of exploring the more mysterious elements of the human experience. Whatever it is, I feel almost reborn."

"Wow," Clark said. "So that's why you're redirecting your practice."

"Exactly, and I have you to thank. Now, enough about me. Let's talk about this morning," she said.

After one final, brisk lap, enjoying the fresh air and mild temperatures, the two of them rested on the tumbled stone seating wall near the front door.

"Can you believe our sessions have led us here, Clark?" Dr. Brill asked.

"No, it's surreal," he said. "I mean, Drake Harrison's heart, my memories, the case . . . are all things I would never have dreamed of." He glanced at the upstairs window. "So, what do you think's going on up there?"

"Well, since it's the last thing we talked about, I'm guessing it has something to do with the little girl," offered Dr. Brill.

"Exactly what I was thinking," he said. "But I can't imagine what."

"Me either," Dr. Brill said. "But I trust John. Isn't it about time to go back up?"

Clark checked his watch. "Yep, sure is. Guess we're about to find out."

When they entered the office, Clark could see Mary across the room, picture-perfectly framed within the door casing. She and John appeared to be engaged in lively conversation, and oddly, he found himself imagining them as a couple.

"They look nice together," he said. "Wonder if they've ever thought about dating?"

"I don't know," whispered Dr. Brill. "But I think Drake used to tease John about that."

As they walked closer, Mary turned in their direction and smiled. "Oh, hey there. We've got some appointments ready for you, Clark, but I'll let John tell you about it while I get back to work."

"Appointments?" he asked, glancing at John.

Clark stepped aside, allowing Mary to pass, while John took a couple of steps backward and lightly perched on the front of his desk. Sporting a new expression, he watched Mary almost all the way back to her desk. If Clark wasn't mistaken, it was close to a 'cat that ate the canary' look.

"Glad you guys are back," he grinned. "It's been a very productive fifteen minutes. "Oh, Dr. Brill, didn't you say you have to leave?"

"Yeah, I do, but not until I hear what's going on," she half-teased.

"Well, first of all, the appointment with the hypnotherapist is a go for Thursday at ten," he said. "Second, I wanted to reconfirm that the victim in this case is, in fact, a six-year-old girl. Clark, when you were able to give such an intricate description of the girl in your vision, I wanted to show you some evidence.

"But then, a better idea came to mind. Hopefully, a sketch artist is on the way up here as we speak. With your high ability to recall details, I'm pretty confident the artist can produce a likeness to the little girl you saw. Hope you're okay with that, Dr. Brill."

"Yeah, sounds like a great idea," she said.

"So, that's what's been going on," Clark said before turning to Dr. Brill. "What am I about to get myself into here?"

"Would you like me to explain it, John?" she asked.

"Sure, you know the drill," he said.

"Well, most of the time, the session only takes a couple of hours. The sketch artist applies your description, asking questions along the way for fine-tuning purposes," she explained. "Sometimes they're able to show you a variety of random photos that can help trigger similarities to the subject. If a witness is struggling to provide the best descriptive details, the photos can be a tremendous help."

"And when the composite artist combines those techniques," interjected John, "it can be amazing to see what they come up with."

"Okay," Clark exhaled. "How much longer before the artist arrives?"

"Only another twenty minutes or so," John said. "She was very close. And while we're waiting, we can look at that timeline again and make sure we have everything charted.

"Since we already know what happened during the abduction, what we're going to do is sort of like reverse engineering. We'll work backward to see if any of these clues or circumstances fit the known outcome.

"At the same time, we can pray for inspiration. And if we get lucky enough to wander onto Drake's path, we might even be able to save a little girl."

The talk about the missing girl made Clark think about Rachel and how badly they wanted a family. He had no idea how their story would end, but if he could help another family find their child, he was ready to do whatever it took.

"Guys, I hate to run, but I'd better get going," announced Dr. Brill. "Clark, you're in great hands. And I can't wait to hear how the rest of the session goes."

"Thanks for being here, Doc," Clark said. "I really appreciate it."

"Wouldn't have missed it," she said. "Bye, John. We'll talk soon?"

"Yeah, I'll fill you in as soon as I can," he said. "Thanks for coming in."

Clark immediately made his way over to the timeline, where he stood frozen, still not believing his own eyes. Some of the flashes of information from visions and dreams that had been tormenting him were now represented as actual facts on a police timeline, perfectly in sync with the details of an open case.

"You know, if the thoughts and visions I'm having could really help find that little girl, this whole thing would be worth it," he announced.

Just like Dr. Brill had predicted, his quest to learn more about the donor's life, and even his subsequent involvement in the case, had been the best thing for him. In a weird way, the whole experience was masquerading as an unusual form of therapy.

It was definitely healing to receive validation that he wasn't crazy and to know that the information he was providing might actually be helpful in solving a crime. Especially one involving a missing child.

For the life of him, Clark couldn't imagine why he'd been chosen as a player in the manifestation of such a phenomenon, but he was actually starting to feel privileged.

When Georgia arrived, she headed straight for John's office, toting her drawing paraphernalia, but began to tiptoe when she got close to Mary's desk.

Before she could reach it, Mary suddenly looked up and squealed, "Georgia! Wow, that was fast."

Georgia placed her hands on her hips and laughed. "I was trying to surprise you."

"Aww, too late," Mary said, heading around the desk for a hug. "So great to see you."

"You too," Georgia gushed. "It's been too long."

Mary nodded. "Yeah, I know. We need to do something about that."

"So, tell me, how's John?" crooned Georgia, dragging out his name.

"Georgia!" Mary scolded before laughing and shushing her.

"Hey, I'm rushing in for the appointment, but do you think you could take a quick break to catch up when we're finished?" Georgia asked.

"Of course!" Mary said. "Can't wait to hear about what you've been up to. And really, thanks again for coming in on embarrassingly short notice."

"No problem, happy to do it," Georgia said. "John must be anxious, so I'm going to head on in, but I'll find you when I'm finished."

"Perfect," Mary said.

When Georgia turned, John was already standing in the doorway. "Well, hey, John," she said sweetly.

"Hey, Georgia. Thanks for rushing in like this," he said. "You know I wouldn't even ask at the last minute unless it was critically important."

"Yeah, no worries," she said. "I was open."

Once in the room and freed of essential baggage, she turned in Clark's direction.

"Georgia, this is Clark Steele, who is assisting me on an open case," John said.

Clark made his way closer and offered his hand. "Nice to meet you."

"Same here," she said. "Just give me another quick minute, and we'll be all set."

While she finished arranging her drawing tools, John double-checked the security of an overlay used to conceal the timeline.

He explained that the three of them would spend the next couple of hours combing over the particulars of the child Clark had seen in his garden image.

Just the mention of the little girl, and there it was again, the uncomfortable knot in Clark's stomach. He wondered if anyone else was feeling it. Georgia's face didn't give anything away, but maybe she'd learned to ignore such feelings and focus only on the art.

When she gave him the go-ahead, Clark began a thorough description. It included all the features he had shared with John, but as a result of Georgia's clever questions and guidance, even more detail.

"Clark, your descriptive skills are great," she said. "The fine details make my work much easier."

"Seems like we've gone over a lot already," Clark said. "So, do you think we're getting somewhere?"

Georgia smiled. "Oh, yeah."

The intricacies of the creative back-and-forth took time, but there was finally a brief lull in the process. Clark glanced over at John, who was seated on the opposite side of the room, next to a vintage accent table. Under the soft light of a simple brass lamp, he appeared to be making furious notes.

He's probably working on a list of things we still need to do.

But Clark was sure John was listening, taking in the important work going on in the room.

"Hey, just let me know if you guys need anything," John said, looking up. "Coffee?"

Georgia smiled. "Gosh, if you're sure you don't mind, I would love one with a little cream."

"Sounds good to me too. Just like that," added Clark. "I can give you a hand, John."

"No, I'm good," he waved. "You guys keep going."

Clark watched him exit the room and pass by Mary's desk, where she and Paul appeared to be in deep conversation. He grinned as he thought how John would probably have been tempted to interrupt the cozy visit if he wasn't right in the middle of a critical sketch artist session.

John did a double take at first but then picked up his pace and shook his head with a discerning grin as if he had a secret.

Clark and Georgia had settled back into the rhythm of their task when Georgia leaned over and pulled a few books out of her shoulder bag.

"We're moving right along, and I think we might be ready for these pretty soon," she said. "I'll explain in just a bit."

"Oh, okay," Clark said. "Where were we?"

"Just finishing up with her features," Georgia said as she added a few pencil strokes. "Can you tell me more about her expression?"

"Hmm . . . yeah. It was different," he said softly. "I felt like she was almost looking right through me. Or maybe it was more a look of melancholy. Yeah, I think that's it."

"Really good, Clark," Georgia said. "It's going to take me a few minutes to finish, and then we can take a quick look. You and I should be able to tweak the drawing and then go from there. For now, you can just relax for a little bit."

Clark didn't let on, but he was dying to see the image. He had only seen the work of great sketch artists on TV and couldn't wait to witness it for himself.

Since it seemed like the perfect moment to give Georgia some space, he decided to do a quick check-in with Rachel. After heading toward the exit and acknowledging a few of the staff along the way, he stepped just outside the door to make the call.

"How's it going?" Rachel asked.

"Great, I think," he said. "John brought in a sketch artist to try to capture the image of the little girl. She seems really pleased so far and doesn't think it will be too much longer."

"Oh, wow, can't wait to see that," she said. "Anything else going on?"

"Well, I had an interesting conversation with . . . with Dr. Brill, but . . . I'll have to fill you in . . . later," stuttered Clark, slowly looking over his shoulder.

"Everything okay?" Rachel asked. "Clark. Clark?"

"Yeah, sorry, Babe," he finally answered. "I just got the weirdest feeling that I was being watched."

✳

Still a little edgy from the weird vibes, Clark cautiously scanned the room as he headed back. When he finally reached the doorway and looked up, he almost couldn't breathe. There, on top of John's desk, sat the easel with Georgia's sketch directly facing him. A shudder literally ran through his entire body.

"Oh, my God, Georgia," he declared. "I don't know how you did it, but that is so close to the little girl I saw."

Clark looked to John for a reaction. John seemed strangely startled by the image at first but then broke into a relaxed grin.

"Great," Georgia said. "Clark, let's take a few minutes to discuss any changes and then see what we get."

The two of them were able to enhance the image by making a few minor changes here and there, but Clark got to witness the process this time. He watched Georgia make the nose a tiny bit fuller and alter the shape of the bottom lip, lifting it just slightly at the corners. When they were happy with those features, they moved on.

Clark studied the image. "There is something else, but I can't put my finger on it. It's driving me crazy. Something about her eyes, I think."

"The color?" Georgia asked.

"Hmm . . . no." And then, all of a sudden, he blurted, "Oh, it's her eyelashes. They were darker. Thicker."

"Okay, let's try that," Georgia said, making the adjustments.

Clark couldn't believe how quickly and accurately she was able to incorporate the additional details. And in no time at all, the three of them were staring at the final image.

"That's her!" Clark erupted.

He stood motionless, in absolute awe. And Georgia's face was a beaming reflection of his reaction.

"Well, I was going to refer to my features book for some fine-tuning, but it looks like we've managed just fine without it," she said.

Apparently, unable to wait another minute, John rushed to the easel and placed a photo right next to Georgia's rendering. "Guys," he said, "Angela Sweet, our missing child."

There, in the picture, was the face Clark had seen in the garden and in every other place he had tried to recall the image. While artist works were never perfect, Georgia's drawing was astonishingly close and left absolutely no doubt that it was the same little girl.

Clark couldn't stop staring. "This is unbelievable, Georgia. You really captured her. But seeing how the image matches the photo takes it to another level."

"Thank you, Clark," she said. "That's always nice to hear. It was a complete pleasure to work with you. And now, I just pray that you guys are able to use this in some way to help find that precious girl."

"That's the plan," promised John. "Thanks again for coming in so quickly and for such a great sketch. The resemblance is amazing, Georgia. And it really strengthens our evidence."

"That's great," she said. "I sure hope you find her. Just let me know if there's anything else I can do. I'm going to spend some time with Mary before I head home. Good luck to you both."

Clark and John had begun to help her reorganize her materials when John said, "Hey, it's all right if you just want to leave your gear in here until you girls are done. Clark and I will probably be gone, but Mary can let you back in."

"Yeah, that'd be great," she said. "Thanks, John."

Once Georgia was on her way, Clark and John sat down for a recap. They went over the new information but spent most of the time on the sketch. John explained how he could have just shown the photo to Clark, when his suspicions were awakened, but the sketch artist route had been much more effective. By requiring Clark to produce the image first, they now had legitimate corroboration of evidence.

"I'm wondering about one thing," Clark said. "If Drake only saw Angela's picture, how was that a real memory to pass on? And, come to think of it, some of the other flashes are like that too."

"Yeah, I've noticed how you seem to have some firsthand flashes and, let's say, secondary images," John surmised. "I've been trying to figure that one out for myself. The only theory I have is from information I've read about how the brain works. It's like a supercomputer taking in everything and creating a record. All information is just there, and the brain doesn't necessarily make distinctions."

"Dr. Brill said something like that too," Clark replied. "So, you think Drake must have looked at that photo over and over, committing it to memory."

"Yeah, he looked at all the evidence that way," John added. "He would meditate on a case and create something like a movie. If details were unconfirmed but solid, they got treated like real evidence in his mental exercise. That's how he solved a lot of cases."

"And here I am right in the middle of one," Clark said.

"Yeah, and we just need to find out how you got here," declared John.

Is he having doubts again? Does he still not believe?

Clark sighed. "All of a sudden, I'm feeling exhausted."

John smiled. "Well, my friend, it's time to wrap for today anyway. You've passed the first test, so, if you have the energy for it, what do you say we keep going?"

"Yeah, fine," he agreed. "What's next?"

"Well, unless anything more important comes up, let's plan on meeting at the hypnotherapist's office on Thursday," John said. "And I think it would be a good idea to visit the cabin after that. Maybe Saturday. If Drake did discover something there, we really should check it out."

Clark stepped toward the door. "Works for me. Plus, it'll give me time to update Dr. Brill. Oh, hey, I want to talk to you about my background check. The interview was a little rough. Apparently, my company did have a meeting and some business discussions with Ashley Benson. But I wasn't even there, John. And I guess you know they weren't happy with my alibi. Looks like I picked a bad night to take some off-the-grid, personal time."

"Those guys are just a little gung-ho about doing their jobs. I told them to lay off for now," John said. "Don't worry about it."

"Well, I appreciate that, but if this is causing problems, maybe I can try something else," Clark offered. "I already feel like I understand more about what's happening to me. And I don't want you taking heat for having me around. Who knows if this can really work anyway? Maybe now is a good time to walk away."

"Clark, you don't have to worry about any of that," promised John. "Remember, this process can help clear you. And just so you know, I could tell what kind of person you were the minute you first stepped into my office. If I can't read people by now, I should probably consider another line of work."

"Thanks," Clark said. "I appreciate that, but let me think about it."

Before making his way out of the room, he turned and took one last look at the precious face staring back at him from the easel.

"Don't think too long," John said, giving him a quick pat on the back.

He followed Clark out and made his way over to Mary's desk, where he very artfully asked about her conversation with Paul. The approach was strong, but not perfect, as it hadn't entirely hidden his jealousy.

Mary's face flushed. "John, Paul was just being friendly. He mentioned the case but only about the background check and how the others were saying they couldn't rule Clark out. I reminded him that the investigation was in the best hands possible. And after that, he was just telling me one of Ken's crazy jokes and making a little small talk. That's all."

They were abruptly interrupted by John's phone. "Baxter," he said.

"Did I not make myself clear?" snapped the captain.

"Sir, I don't know what you think is going on, but I've been following your instructions," John said firmly, heading for his office.

"Why am I getting calls about you and Clark practically living at the station?" he asked.

"Not true," explained John. "We haven't been here that much, and we're making some headway. I think we might be onto something, and I'd like to brief you on it, but I'd also like to know who the snitch is."

"Well, the call was untraceable," Captain Riley said.

"How convenient," John said with a little snark. "Sir, I promise you, we're doing everything above board. A lot of time has passed, but as you know, Drake and I had a pact. It's not over till it's over. This is the first time the Sweet case has seen life in a while, and the last thing we need is a distraction. I hate to say it, but it has to be an insider."

"Well, you know, I hate snitching even more than insubordination," the captain replied. "But a cowardly snitch is the worst. I've got to run, but I have an idea. I'm coming back early, but don't mention it to anyone."

"You got it," John promised.

Mary peeped her head in the doorway. "Everything okay?"

"Yeah," John said. "With a little luck, I might have just bought some more time. Now I need to talk to Clark. If my instincts are right about him, he's not going anywhere. No way would a man with Drake's heart keep the investigation from moving forward. Not when he's a six-year-old's only hope."

FIFTEEN

DADDY DEAREST

Down a barely visible driveway, the concealed home stood in a clearing, surrounded by acres of conifers. In contrast to the more unruly, natural surroundings, the place was freshly painted and adorned with perfectly manicured landscaping.

The arched front door was a highlight, along with a small round window just above it. Together, they complimented the home's other charming features and conveyed a welcoming ambiance.

But the home's inviting presentation was in stark contrast to signals projected by the homeowner, who clearly wanted to be left alone and made sure the word was out.

A few false rumors were circulating concerning the matter, but most locals had simply accepted him as a typical recluse. So, with neighbors either obliging or being too scattered, he had the freedom to do as he pleased.

The eccentric loner had chosen his family's secluded property precisely because of its obscure advantage. An expanse of trees added to the privacy he found essential, making it easier to go undetected. Staying to himself and cultivating a quiet persona was the perfect way for Winston, the owner, to safeguard his anonymity.

The property had once belonged to his parents, who had held onto it for a while after retiring to Hawaii. When the number of trips back and forth began to wane, they passed it on, giving him a real place of his own for the first time.

Such a gift was a real surprise because he'd been a handful, causing his parents a lot of undue stress, apparently since the beginning. On more than one occasion, he'd heard them reminisce of the shocking pregnancy and how they'd never planned on starting a family.

But as nature would have it, their pragmatic acceptance of the new reality led to an innate love for their son. They did their best, and by middle school, he showed some promise in the arts as a budding painter and pianist. His creative skills and hard work were to be celebrated.

His behavior, on the other hand, was not. He had become a loner who wandered into unhealthy territory, mastering conflict, fantasies, lies, and deceit, keeping his parents constantly on guard.

Although Winston loved and appreciated his parents and their efforts, the family bonds had become strained and superficial in important ways. So, as the years passed, he became increasingly isolated and protective of his private thoughts. He found it excruciating to open up when his beliefs seemed to act only as magnets for everyone's judgment.

But apparently, despite everything, his parents wanted to see him safe and sheltered.

Winston eagerly accepted the home, and within its walls, he was determined to finally make his forbidden dreams a reality. He had convinced himself that, up to that point, life had denied him every relationship he ever wanted, and he was tired of waiting.

His first bold move had gone off without a hitch, so he was carefully planning the next. And the special, pint-sized human he now had for leverage would be his bridge to the one he really wanted.

From the first time he laid eyes on Ashley, he knew she was the one. And even at that very moment, almost every obsessive instinct in his body urged him to go back to see her. But for now, it was too risky.

In the interim, he would keep busy planning the best way to proceed. One option would be to take her against her will, either personally or by hire. He knew some shady characters who would do almost anything for money, but if he chose that route, his identity could be compromised.

If he did the job himself, she might hold it against him, and that was a thought he couldn't bear.

The better option would be to use her niece as a bargaining tool. But with the lingering commotion still centered around Angela's abduction, he thought it best to lay low for a long while. Staying away from Ashley was torture, but eventually, it would all be worth it.

Until then, he would prepare for her arrival. The house needed to be perfect, so she would love it. Once she got over the initial shock, she would come to love him too. His secluded childhood home would be their perfect refuge.

Just past the foyer on the right were French doors leading into his office. Even though he'd spent a lot of time getting the workspace just right, he was perpetually reorganizing, never completely satisfied.

He had even changed his mind several times on the location before finally settling on the front room, where he could place his desk in the velvety lighting of the bay window.

The windows were adorned with plantation shutters, which were beautiful to look at but also provided an additional benefit. By constantly adjusting the slats to the perfect angle, Winston was able to keep a watchful eye on the driveway and on any intruders who might come near.

In a direct line of sight from his desk were stairs leading to the finished basement. If the door on the lower level were open, a sense of wonder and magic would envelop the entire staircase. The vivid colors and beautiful light emanating from a sparkling chandelier were like magnets beckoning entry into the room.

Once inside, it was like stepping into a different world. That entire part of the home had been decorated like a castle fit for a little princess. The walls appeared to be covered in a light-colored stone, but upon close examination, it was apparent that a decorating product had been applied to create the stone-like texture. Enhanced by a little artistic painting, the make-believe adornment had come to life.

Rolling clothes racks sat diagonally in the far corners and brimmed with frilly dress-up clothes. An assortment of fancy shoes including heels, glittery boots, and even ballet slippers, lined the bottom shelf, while a hatbox, pink boa, and tiara were prominently displayed on top. One could easily imagine the hours of fun a little girl would have with such precious things.

But on most days, at a child-sized vanity table, there sat a sweet little girl who appeared withdrawn.

Normally, she loved to play, especially with makeup, and could sit for hours, trying her hand. But at times, even her very own assortment of colorful beauty palettes failed to serve as a healing distraction. On the contrary, the activity would, sometimes, take a strange turn, where she would go to extremes, aggressively applying too much, almost as if creating a mask.

Opposite her vanity, on the outside wall, was a luxurious, four-poster bed with a white canopy of mosquito netting tied back at each corner. In any other situation, it would have been the kind of bed that would have produced night after night of beautiful, childlike dreams.

But those didn't exist for her anymore. And she wore despair on her sleeve.

"Why are you always moping around?" demanded Winston, barging into her room.

She cringed but continued to stare into the mirror. "I want to go home."

"Well, I've done everything to make this room look like home for a princess. Like a dream," he said. "And you're still pouting all the time."

She hung her head and whispered, "I just want my mom and dad."

"I told you, you're getting a new family," he drilled.

Ever since he'd hung the photos of himself and Ashley on the textured walls beside the bed, her programming had begun.

"It's hard for me to believe you forgot again," he scolded. "I'm starting to think you're doing it on purpose. Remember, I'm your dad now, and Ashley's your mom."

Even though he expected more back talk, she remained silent. But the look she gave him in retaliation said, "You're nothing like my dad."

He pointed at her and ordered, "Follow the rules, keep the peace."

Indoctrinating her to accept a new life was proving to be a little more difficult than he had imagined. For the most part, she sidestepped trouble by following orders and staying out of the way, but when it came to old memories, her deep attachment was an ongoing problem.

As recently as the day before, he had noticed her defensively snuggled into her glittery comforter, surely dreaming of her family.

How could she, after all the time I spent decorating the room and stenciling "Angela"?

✴

From early on, Winston promised never to hurt Angela, and so far, he'd kept his word. There were conditions, however. Follow his instructions carefully, and she and her family would be safe.

After watching him bring a load of firewood into the library one day, she looked up from her book and cautiously asked, "Why do you have pictures of my Aunt Ashley?"

"I told you, that's your mother," he corrected. "And she's going to be here soon."

Angela brightened. "When?"

"That's not for you to know," snapped Winston. He continued to organize the wood in the bin next to the fireplace. "Remember what I told you about asking too many questions?"

Angela started to cry. "I know . . . but I miss my mom and dad."

"Well, we're going to be a new family soon, and I've got to get this place ready," he mumbled. "That includes hanging pictures."

"I want to go home," Angela whimpered.

"Angela, that's enough!" barked Winston.

She hung her head and whispered, "Sorry."

After a few poignant tears fell onto her book, she seemed to gather herself. She began to study him closely as if trying to understand what he was up to and why it made him happy. When he caught her staring, he glared back in a twitchy response and quickly ordered her off to her room.

It irritated him to use the beautiful princess chamber he'd created as punishment, so he made sure the penance never lasted too long.

✳

It was seven thirty when the alarm went off the next morning.

"Let's go," Winston shouted downstairs. "You awake?"

"Yeah, I'm awake," came the sleepy reply.

"Well, get dressed and get up here," he ordered. "Breakfast at eight. And you know you have to set the table."

Angela rolled her eyes. "Okay, I'm coming."

"Morning, sleepyhead," he announced as she shuffled into the kitchen. "Put out three place settings."

"Three?" she asked.

"You need practice for when Ashley gets here," Winston explained.

The look on her face said it all. Her nightmare was real.

"We'll start your lessons at exactly eight-thirty," he said.

When she didn't answer, he snapped, "Did you hear me?"

"Yes," she said softly.

He grabbed a skillet from the stove and spun around in a threatening manner. "Okay, then. As soon as you're done, go get your books."

After doing more pushing food around on the plate than eating, Angela headed back to her room to collect her bookbag.

Winston's paranoia meant schoolwork and extracurricular activities had to be conducted inside the house. He had risked taking her out a couple of times, under an anxious and watchful eye, but a few close calls convinced him it would be less stressful to remove her from all contact with the outside world.

So, she stayed within those walls, where drama was a daily occurrence. Her fate appeared more and more hopeless, as if her own life was on track to one day mimic the strange and secretive life of her captor.

Later that morning, she sat staring at her schoolwork. "Can you show me the math one more time?" she asked.

"What?" demanded Winston. "You know how to do that. Are you stalling again?" He was convinced she'd been wasting time, pretending to have trouble with subjects she clearly understood.

"No, I really need help," she whimpered.

He came to her aid but was still suspicious that the stunt was some kind of childish diversion.

"Okay, put everything away," he said. "After lunch, you can choose art or music."

Most afternoons consisted of enrichment classes followed by free time. Winston didn't mind teaching her to paint or play the piano because she really tried hard. And when the lessons were over, she even used her free time to practice. The creative arts seemed to be one of the very few things that lifted her spirits.

Too often, he would find her moping on the cushioned window seat in an anteroom just down from her bedroom. It was positioned just below the only window she was allowed to go near, because it faced the back of the property, where everything was most veiled.

One day, he demanded, "Why are you always staring out that window?"

Angela hung her head and sighed. "I miss playing outside with my friends."

Winston glanced at the level backyard, which was enormous and completely bordered by majestic evergreens. It would have been the perfect place to run in the grass and feel a sense of freedom, but he had trained her not to even ask for such things.

Something else she was forbidden to ask about was the green door with the digital lock that was just down the hall from her bedroom. Winston made it very clear that it was his private room, and she was to never go near it. Of course, making it off-limits only made it all the more irresistible.

One day, she had gotten too close and tried to peek through the bottom of the door frame just as he happened to come downstairs.

"What are you doing?" he shouted. "I told you, never go near that door!"

The heated screams caused her to jolt and quickly move away from him, tripping over her own feet. The landing was awkward, but she managed to push herself up and crawl backward.

Winston couldn't control his rage. It was fully blown. He became red, his face twisted, and veins swelled in his neck, a frightening image. Angela bolted up and went running to her room.

"Get back here!" he shouted down the hall.

His anger was at a new level.

Angela was cowering in the corner, still shaking, when he stomped into the room. He stood glaring over her for a few seconds before taking a couple of hostile heavy steps in her direction.

Her piercing scream stopped him dead in his tracks.

And then, as if coming out of a trance, he shook his head, stumbled backward, and turned away. As he staggered across the room and up the stairs, Angela sat trembling with the sound of each and every footstep.

It was a long while before he came back down, but the time upstairs had been good. He calmly offered her a heartfelt apology.

He explained that their new life on family property was unique and that there would always be people who wouldn't understand. There might even come a day when dangerous people came looking for them. And, because of that, he had to make sure they were protected. So, for her own safety, he hadn't allowed her near the room with the electronic lock because it held his personal business and, more importantly, his weapons.

"But I've been thinking about it, and I've decided it's time," he said, "It's time to show you what to do if anyone comes on our property."

Angela was clutching her comforter like a shield. "I . . . I don't want to know what to do."

"Well, I get that, but this is important," he said. "We both have to know how to protect ourselves."

"Well, I'm only a kid," she said.

"Yes, but you're a very smart kid," he countered. "Now, follow me."

Angela moved in slow motion, taking her time to get up and follow him to the hallway. Learning the secret to the mysterious room she'd always been curious about now appeared to be the last thing on her mind.

She had almost reached Winston when she turned and raced back for Ursy, her stuffed unicorn. As she held on tightly, she took the final hesitant steps toward the unknown.

Once they were standing guard in front of the strange door, Winston ordered, "Turn around and face the wall."

Her small body was shaking, but she obeyed, slowly turning her back to him.

Strange buzzing sounds and a slight creaking rang out as the door opened.

It was the perfect moment to lock her inside, where no one would ever find her. But with no apparent malice at all, he said, "Okay, you can turn around now."

Winston had a lot of strange quirks, and the creation of the room had been no exception. At first, looking inside was like looking at Christmas. Shelves on three sides were full of colorfully wrapped packages and mysterious boxes, arranged so perfectly that it would have been wrong to even touch them.

Flawlessly displayed on top of a desk, facing the final wall and in perfect alignment, were three computers, six mobile phones, and several arts and crafts items. Above the desktop, papering the entire space was a collage of photos and newspaper clippings from the abduction and Drake Harrison's death.

Angela stared, wide-eyed. "What is this?"

"Mostly my personal business and no concern of yours," Winston snapped. "But it's also where I keep some of my guns, and I want to show you one."

With that, he reached to his right and slowly drew a handgun from the shelf. As he admired it, a strange smile crossed his face.

Angela gasped and backed away.

"It's okay. Guns are only scary when you don't know how to use them," he said, almost caressing the weapon. "Even though you're little, you've got to understand that people who intend to hurt us and our families could show up here at any time. So, we both need to know exactly what to do."

Winston thought for a second about how that must sound. He, the one who had taken her from her family, was now talking about other bad people coming to hurt them.

He glanced at Angela, who was looking very pale like she was about to cry. But the tears never came. She was surely fighting them back as she had been trained to do.

"This is the gun you'll bring me if I can't get to it myself," he explained. "There's a code for the digital lock, but I'm not going to give it to you now. If the time ever comes, all you have to do is enter the code, and the lock will pop open.

"Do you understand me?" he demanded.

"Yes," she winced.

"Okay, that's enough for today," he said.

Even the words of release weren't enough to bring the color back to her face.

"What's going on with you?" Winston asked.

"I think something's wrong with my heart," she said. "It's so loud."

With a dismissive wave of his hand, he said, "That's normal, you'll be fine."

Then, brandishing the gun like an expert, he took aim at different points in the room and pretended to shoot.

Angela trembled and held tightly to Ursy in front of the strange room.

It was obvious that the gunplay made her even more nervous, but Winston did nothing to ease her anxiety. In fact, in his mind, she would just have to deal with it. He had to be prepared for anything.

When he finally placed the gun back on the shelf, he bumped one of the packages, causing a tag to dangle. It read, *Ashley*.

Angela gasped, placing her hands over her mouth.

"What's with you?" demanded Winston.

"Nothing," she whispered.

"Well, mind your business," he ordered.

And he knew she would.

Under his charge, her behavior had morphed into a type of robotic obedience, just the way he liked it. He had convinced her that following orders and being cooperative were the very things that would keep her safe.

While he appreciated that she hadn't given him any real trouble up to that point, he was always suspicious of what she was thinking. She never revealed too much. And to him, that meant she was hanging on to her memories for dear life.

As much as he hated it, her mind was her sanctuary, and he didn't have access. There, he was sure she was still dreaming of her mom and dad.

And it had to stop.

SIXTEEN

WHEN I SNAP MY FINGERS

The calm environment and comfortable chair were like unexpected gifts for Clark since he'd had very little sleep the night before. He figured Serena Storm and other therapists must take the preparation of their rooms very seriously, making sure conditions contribute to a successful session. Quiet celestial music even played in the background.

John and Dr. Brill, who had joined him for the appointment, were chatting quietly in an outer room where they would be observing. They'd been briefed on the significance of the huge two-way mirror and the four speakers in the corners of the space.

For the rest of the morning, they would be able to see and hear everything without actually being in the room. Apparently, that arrangement had proven best because when others were present, they sometimes became unintentional distractions.

Prior to getting started, Clark and the others spent a brief time reviewing his symptoms and the particulars of hypnotherapy. And while he learned that sessions come with no guarantees, Serena seemed positive about her ability to help enhance his memory recall.

"Clark, I really think I can help," she said. "And I see this as an epic sort of case, a chance to investigate a powerful phenomenon and maybe even help solve a crime. With that in mind, I might ask questions and give guidance based on your memories and Drake's."

She confidently began the session with a short preliminary discussion about what to expect. From there, she explained that her goal would be to provide instructional relaxation techniques to help him achieve deep concentration and focus.

"Once we reach that state, we become more open to discussion and suggestion," she said. "The relaxed state is precisely what helps us remember events and details that we didn't even realize we had stored away. It's sort of like you can see things and answer questions without your conscious mind interfering. We'll be making a video recording that you're welcome to watch later if you like."

"Well, probably like most people, I've only seen hypnosis on TV," Clark said. "I've always been a little skeptical and pretty convinced I'd be a terrible subject. But, if it can help with the case or my issues, I'm willing to give it a shot."

Serena smiled. "You know, there's really no way of knowing how a session is going to go or how you'll respond as a subject. The funny thing is—most of us have experienced a form of self-hypnosis without even knowing it. Think about how you might have been watching a movie or driving when, at some point, you realized you weren't consciously engaged in the activity," she explained. "Your mind had simply relaxed and wandered off in another direction. That's a very basic example of what it's like."

"Yeah, I know what you're saying," nodded Clark. "I've had that happen."

"Well, then, I have a perfectly normal client to work with this morning," she teased.

Clark grinned. "At least relatively speaking."

Serena made sure Clark was feeling comfortable before sliding the light switch slowly downward, causing a twilight to fall over the room. Then she suggested that he relax, close his eyes, and focus only on the music and the softness of the chair.

"We'll sit quietly for a bit while you settle in, relax, and just enjoy the restful environment," she explained softly. "Just let yourself exist, Clark. Focus on how you're feeling completely safe, comfortable, and content."

She had no way of knowing, but she had perfectly described how he was feeling. As opposed to the considerable amount of stress he'd been under, the tranquil vibe was nice, and he found himself enjoying the beginning of the session.

His relaxed body language must have been a signal because Serena confidently eased into the first exercise.

In a very smooth, monotone delivery, she said, "Just listen to the sound of my voice, Clark. You can keep your eyes closed if it's comfortable for you. When you hear the snap of my fingers, you're going to be in a deep sleep. We're going to talk about how you've been feeling. Can you tell me anything about your dreams or how you've been sleeping lately?"

"I haven't been sleeping well," he whispered. "Nights are restless, and my wife hears me talking in my sleep."

Serena snapped her fingers and waited for a few seconds. "What does she hear you say?"

"Something about 'following rules' and 'took my life,'" he said.

"Just relax and focus deeply on only that dream, Clark," she prompted. "What can you remember about it?"

His breathing was nice and steady, but he gave no response.

"What's happening, Clark?" Serena asked softly.

He hesitated. "I don't remember. I only know because of Rachel."

Serena leaned in. She kept her voice steady and comforting. "It's okay, Clark. We're moving on. Can you remember another dream?"

"Yes," he said faintly. "In a hallway."

"Picture the hallway now," she whispered.

"It's dark, hazy . . . I see a shadow," Clark said. "No . . . it's gone."
He rubbed his arms. "It's cold. I'm following it . . . nothing there. I
can't remember."

"Are you getting closer to the shadow, Clark?" Serena asked.

"I don't know," he said. "I can't remember anymore."

"Okay, it's fine. But now you're back in the hallway," she directed.
"I want you to remember what it felt like standing there, seeing the
shadow. You take the first step and then another. Look around and
tell me what you see."

"I'm against the wall . . . sliding," Clark said. "I feel a door . . . and
turn. It says 'Evidence.' It's getting dark. Blurry."

"Okay, Clark," Serena said calmly. "Just take a few more steps."

He shook his head. "No. It's dangerous."

"You are completely safe, Clark," she promised.

"No. It doesn't feel safe." His voice sounded strained. "I can't see.
It's too dark."

"Okay, you don't have to go any further," Serena said. "For now,
just concentrate on relaxing again. We'll continue in just a minute."

After the brief respite, she said, "Now, let me ask you about one
of your flashes. You said earlier that you were gardening when you saw
a little girl's face. Clark, I want you to picture her again. Really study
her face. Focus on nothing else. Can you tell me what you're feeling?"

"I'm afraid for her," he said.

"I understand, and we're going to try to help her," Serena said.
"Just relax and meditate on her face, her name, her essence."

As some of the tranquil sensations returned, Clark's heart rate
began to drop, and he reclined a little more in the chair. He could
feel himself sinking into a deep zone of relaxation and, for just a split
second, thought he might be dreaming.

Once he redirected his mind to the surrounding comforts again,
he began to feel completely liberated from any physical tension and

fought the urge to doze off.

Sleep had almost overtaken him when he jolted upright.

A new flash had caught him off guard, and even though it was just a spark, he had seen the vision clearly. He kept his eyes closed and tried to hang on, but it flickered and vanished.

Serena studied him and added a phrase next to a time stamp on her screen. "Synapses firing."

"Clark, I'm always listening if you want to share," she almost whispered.

"So tired," he said. "I saw a tiara."

The seemingly innocent words caused John to jump from the collapsible director's chair he'd been sitting in and move as close as possible to the glass. "What did he just say?"

"John, what is it?" Dr. Brill asked.

"I've got something to show you and Clark," he said. "But let's listen."

The soothing sound of Serena's voice was like butter emanating from the speakers. "It's okay, Clark. I know you're tired, but would you please describe it to me?"

"Old gold... spikes," he began, "... little spheres. Not real... like a toy. Band on the bottom with colored stones."

"Hmm," Serena said. "What are the colors?"

Clark searched for details. "Red, in the center, and I think... blue and green. I feel like I've seen it before. But where?"

"It'll come to you, Clark," lulled Serena.

She turned and gave a thumbs-up to John and Dr. Brill, who were still watching and listening intently to every word exchanged between therapist and subject.

John turned to Dr. Brill. "How do you think he's doing in there?"

"I think he's doing great," she replied. "And, you know, including this session, none of the research we've done has eliminated the phenomenon. So, I still think we're on the right track."

John nodded and turned back toward the inner room.

"Okay, Clark, now just let your mind drift back to that peaceful place again," Serena said. After a couple of minutes, she added softly, "Take yourself back to the walking path. Feel the breeze and sunshine on your face. Watch Rachel turn and smile as she runs on ahead. Now, leisurely, look to the left of the quiet path. What do you see?"

"Trees . . . so green. I love it here." Suddenly, Clark grabbed the armrest and gasped. "There it is again."

"What do you see?" prompted Serena.

"That perfect area, in the middle of the clearing," he said, sounding confused. "I should know why it's here. Can't remember. I want to stay, but I've got to sit down."

"Remember, you're completely safe, Clark," promised Serena. "Can you still see into the clearing?"

"No, it's gone," he said. "Rachel's coming back."

Serena whispered, "It's okay, Clark. Accept her help, and rest as long as you want."

Just then, a silent alarm sounded, an electronic reminder that it was time to start wrapping things up for the day.

Serena had explained earlier that with hypnotherapy, it was always best not to press too hard the first time around.

"Clark, just one last thing," she resumed. "I want you to remember the popcorn. Think about what it sounds like when it's popping. Can you smell it? Really focus on the smell and try to recall the image you told me about earlier."

He could hear her words, but it took a minute for the reference to fully register.

"It was everywhere," he said.

"What else can you see?" coaxed Serena.

"Too close," he said. "I don't know. A sofa, maybe. There's a bowl on the floor . . . popcorn everywhere."

"Good, Clark," she praised. "Just relax. Let your mind feel at rest as it remembers. Hold on to the popcorn image. Don't let it go. But now, feel yourself moving away from it, and tell me about anything else you see."

"Nothing. No . . . wait," he said, gripping the chair again. I'm moving."

"Good, Clark," calmed Serena. "That's perfect."

"Popcorn on the sofa and table," he offered, with no prompting. "A blue bowl on the floor."

Serena asked nonchalantly, "What color is the sofa?"

"Dark brown. Leather," Clark replied immediately.

"Good," she added in a hushed tone. "Keep zooming out and watching, zooming, and watching. What else can you see, Clark?"

"Chairs. Wooden chairs," he almost whispered. "Three near the sofa. I'm in a room. It doesn't feel right."

"What are you feeling, Clark?" piloted Serena.

He shook his head from side to side. "Something bad happened."

"Don't worry, we're going to fix it," she promised. "You're doing great. Look around again. What else do you see?"

"The room . . . chairs," he said, sitting up very abruptly. "What's that? Rope . . . and something shiny. Like duct tape."

The negative energy was overwhelming and made him squirm.

"You're doing great, Clark," Serena repeated. "What are you feeling?"

"Something terrible happened. I need to help," he said, breathing faster. "It's my duty."

"Clark, just take a couple of deep breaths," Serena said. "How are you supposed to help?"

"I don't know," he said. "Something's wrong. I don't feel like me."

"Who do you feel like?" Serena asked.

"Someone else," whispered Clark.

"What are they thinking?" she coaxed.

Clark's voice became dreamlike. "He's worried, but he knows what to do."

"Yes, he does, and we're going to help him," she assured. "Remember, we're all on the same team. You've done so well, Clark. You can just relax now. You don't have to think about or feel a thing."

In the outer room, John and Dr. Brill received a wave from Serena and began to hastily gather their belongings. The signal meant the session was winding down, and she had invited them to be there for Clark the moment he was finished.

"Thank you for listening and following the sound of my voice today, Clark," came her soft tone through the speakers. "I am going to count to five and when I get there, I'll snap my fingers. You'll be wide awake, relaxed, and refreshed. One, two, three, four, five."

At the sound of the snap, Clark began to move around a bit, raised his arms, and stretched. Feeling a little confused, he said, "Are we done?"

Serena smiled. "For today. How are you feeling?"

"I don't think I know yet. But I guess I feel pretty good," he said.

"Well, you should," she praised. "You were a great subject and settled right into the suggestions. You did recall more detail, so, we have some new information."

"It's weird, but I think I remember some of it," he mused.

Serena noticed Dr. Brill and John standing at the door and motioned them in. "Glad you're back," she said. "We should have just enough time to go over the session before I have to break for my next appointment.

"As we went along, I was going to try to figure out whether the flashes had been coming from Clark or Drake," she added. "But the nature of the session made it impossible in real time. It was way more important to stay connected to Clark and keep him focused and comfortable with the process.

"And he did great," she announced. "As I'm sure you both heard, some new information came forward, details from the room, the tiara, and more. Once I review the video and organize my notes, I should be able to extract everything of value from the session."

"Don't mean to rush you, Serena, but do you have a timeline on that?" Dr. Brill asked.

"Should just be a day or two," she said.

"Great," John said. "We already have some good stuff. But we can't wait to hear your final thoughts."

Serena turned to Clark. "In the meantime, Clark, it was a pleasure to work with you. Your case is so intriguing that almost any therapist would want to be involved in it. The opportunity to help someone explore an obscure phenomenon doesn't come along every day."

"Yeah, it's a life changer, that's for sure," he agreed.

"Well, fingers crossed that the new information becomes part of your understanding and healing," Serena said.

Clark couldn't get over how she'd been able to keep him completely comfortable during the process. Her easy guidance enabled him to explore his experiences in a subtle way and, admittedly, had been liberating. Weirdly, though, continuing the discussion in a present, fully conscious state was also cathartic.

While he was reconnecting with the normal state of being, his analytical mind was considering every additional bit of information. The new details, he had to admit, were surprising. Everything from vivid colors to chairs, rope, and duct tape, added specifics he hadn't been able to recall before. Dr. Brill's instincts about hypnotherapy had proven very productive.

It was a great step forward, but there was something more.

Even though he couldn't completely wrap his head around it, there was one thing that would stay with him forever: feeling like he was someone else. When he connected to the memory flashes, it was as if he were experiencing everything through the senses of another person.

Clark had felt the haunting grief from the one sharing his memories. It was as if he were on a mission to find out who was responsible for the tragedy that took place in that room. And at last, Clark had no doubts.

It was Drake Harrison.

SEVENTEEN

FRIENDLY FIRE

It was still early Saturday morning when Clark and John drew near the end of their three-hour journey south to the Harrison family cabin. And the pre-dawn departure came with a special gift: a chance to witness the shadow of night transforming into a dazzling sunrise.

The glory of the event seemed to energize their conversation, which mainly focused on Clark's session with Serena. The unique form of therapy had been fascinating for all of them, although in different ways.

John said he had observed his share of hypnosis appointments over the years but was still amazed every time a therapist piloted a subject to new discoveries. The eye-opening sessions provided proof that a wealth of information, reticently burrowed in inaccessible memory banks, can remain secret until the right stimuli coax it to the surface.

Apparently, in the past, law enforcement had been more skeptical about using therapists. But times had changed. Cases had been solved with information retrieved through the process, and outcomes like that speak for themselves.

Clark couldn't believe the details that had come to light that morning in Serena's office. But as impressive as they were, they hadn't yet led them in a new direction. What they had done, however, was enhance and reinforce growing evidence insinuating that Clark might truly have been touched by the phenomenon.

The specifics that came to mind during the zooming exercise added to the verifiable details. He'd been able to recall clear physical facts about the contents of the room, but also finer points, like specific colors and even the existence of rope and duct tape.

And under Serena's expert guidance, he remembered more specifics from his shadow dream, obscurities that had been locked away without conscious awareness.

Then, there was the surprising flash memory of the tiara. He hadn't had an episode for a while and had certainly never expected one live in the middle of the session. But now, with the benefit of hindsight, it seemed perfectly logical, due to the tranquil, hypnotic environment.

Following the session with Serena that day, Clark, Dr. Brill, and John went to lunch and then returned to the office. There, John rifled through several files before finally producing new photo evidence to show Clark.

After taking the prints, Clark watched John slide a clear plastic bag under the document organizer on his desk. He was too far away to identify the contents and didn't want to ask, so he focused on the evidence at hand.

Among the items were actual photos from the crime scene. Images of the sofa and popcorn spill matched so perfectly to the description he had given. They were like looking at screenshots from his mind.

He was holding physical copies of images he had seen so clearly in flashes and under hypnosis. The photos revealed the same furniture, bowl, rope, and duct tape, and they were more than mental pictures. They were the real deal, from the actual crime scene. The nightmare really happened, and his new heart connected him to the mystery.

His emotions were stirred to the point that he didn't feel like himself again but rather like Drake standing in that room. Not only could he feel the lingering, negative energy, but he could also feel Drake's resolve, his innate sense of duty.

And for Clark, just sharing a connection to such a great man helped to ease a lot of anxiety associated with the phenomenon. Dr. Brill had called it. She had anticipated that very outcome. Another of her theories had proven correct.

"You know, Drake was at the crime scene," John said. "He actually stood in that room and must have studied the photos hundreds of times. It's no wonder those images surfaced."

"Yeah, it's almost like he's directing me from the grave," whispered Clark.

John froze for a second, but then he reached for the sealed plastic bag he had set aside earlier.

"I wanted to save this for last. Since it's not a photo, but a tangible piece of evidence, we have to be especially careful. All the necessary tests have been done, but to ensure integrity, we still handle it with great care.

"The new memory flash you had in the session with Serena sent chills down my spine, and I couldn't wait to show you this," he added.

He secured the item and handed the transparent bag over to Clark, watching as if waiting for some significance to register. Clark found himself looking at a small piece of cream-colored cotton fabric imprinted with tiaras. The tiaras matched the one he had seen under hypnosis and sent a familiar shiver through his body.

Somewhere deep inside, he sensed what it might be, and his hands began to tremble.

"It's the same tiara," he said, trying to keep his voice steady. "John, is this Angela's?"

"Yes, and it's another item Drake must have looked at dozens of times," explained John. "I'm sorry I have to show it to you like this, but I do think it's important. That piece of fabric came from the clothing she was wearing when she was abducted. And out of nowhere, you were able to describe that tiara."

Clark's knees felt weak, and he slowly collapsed into the nearest chair. The fabric sample had cast another powerful reminder that the whole thing was more about finding a little girl than about his psychological turmoil. When her parents came to mind, he could almost feel their pain.

"I'm sorry about this part of it, Clark," soothed Dr. Brill. "Are you okay?"

"Yeah," he said. "But how do people do these things?"

She shook her head. "I know, it's the worst. And holding a piece of tangible evidence makes it all the more real. But you'll be okay. You're strong, Clark. You've proven that."

"I'm okay," he said. "I guess I just had a . . . a moment."

"I get it," Dr. Brill said. "I'd wonder about you if you didn't. You know, just like you, every recipient is dealing with something unusual. Your situation just happens to involve a crime, and you're handling it as well as anyone could. Remember, the three of us are a team, so if we keep pushing forward, maybe we can find that little girl."

Clark turned the fabric over and over before handing it back. "What do you think, John?"

"Well, you know I want that more than anything," he said. "And you two have convinced me of way more than I expected. But I can feel it. I'm on thin ice around here."

"What are you saying?" Clark asked.

John hesitated. "I'm saying I'm not sure."

"John, don't leave me hanging now," begged Clark. "If I don't have you on my side, I don't like where this is going."

Dr. Brill quickly stood up. "John, Clark had nothing to do with this!"

"Hold it. Hold it, you two," John said. "I'm not ready to throw in the towel, but we have to produce some kind of proof."

Clark was up and pacing. "Maybe it's at the cabin."

John shrugged. "Maybe."

"Remember what you told me?" Clark said. "Drake had great luck there, so maybe we'll find something."

John shook his head. "I know, but I don't know how much time we have before the captain pulls the plug."

"John, let's just go then!" begged Clark. "The cabin might hold the answers."

After a very deep breath and an uncomfortably long pause, John finally said, "Okay, let's do it!"

Plans to visit the cabin were finalized right then and there. They would pack, pick up provisions, and meet back at the office first thing on Saturday.

After Clark and Dr. Brill had gone, John went to check his mail and was met with an unusual sight. Nearly everyone was there. Sometimes, during lunch hour, the others would pop in and eat while they were working, but it was rare to see almost all of them at the same time.

"Hey, John," Ken shouted. "We left some extra burgers in the break room. Grab one and come join us. You blew my mind with that case, man. You've got to update us."

"There in a minute," John said.

When he got close, he boomed, "Hey guys. What are you ya-hoos up to?"

"We've been sitting here talking about your mysterious case," started Ken.

John raised an eyebrow. "Is that right? What about it?"

"Well, it's pretty weird," Ken said. "You freaked us all out, you know. We hope you're right about it, but it's not looking good. Queenie was just telling us that the ropes used on the family were tied with constrictor knots, you know, used in sailing. And the background check revealed that Clark did some boating and water sports."

John shot a critical glance in Queenie's direction. "That's pretty flimsy. You guys don't have anything better to do?"

"John, you know we're on your side," she explained. "But we can't just ignore what we found. Plus, the case is strange. It's making everyone suspicious."

"Yeah, it's strange," muttered Nathan, rubbing his chin. "But I'd just follow the facts."

John smirked. "Well, thanks for the tip, Nathan."

Paul, who was seated at the next desk over, whirled his chair around. "Hey, John, I heard they located your traffic footage."

"Yeah, finally," John said. "After I threatened to tear this place apart, somehow, it just mysteriously reappeared. Anybody know anything about that?"

Breaking an uncomfortable silence, Paul finally said, "Not me, man. Just trying to lighten the mood."

"Me either," echoed Eddie. "But John, there's growing evidence that points to another version of the case. Other issues."

John bristled. "What are you talking about?"

"Well, I've already told you about Clark's lack of a solid alibi and about his connection to the little girl's aunt," Eddie said. "And I'm not buying that phenomenon. It's just too weird."

"Clark has already explained the alibi and the connection," John shot back. "There's nothing on his record. Not even a traffic ticket.

And you guys really don't know what you're talking about concerning the phenomenon. He's under Dr. Brill's care, and there's medical proof that recipients can actually receive cellular information from their organ donors."

"Remember, John, we also found out that Clark's uncle is buried in Resting Waters Cemetery, where Angela's belongings were found," added Queenie, brushing right past his attempt to enlighten them.

"Coincidental, I'm sure," John countered. "He did live in the area."

"Maybe too coincidental?" probed Ken. "Circumstantial evidence is definitely taking shape."

"If Clark had any involvement in the abduction, why on earth would he be here trying to help us?" John demanded.

"Psychopath?" laughed Eddie, looking to the others for a reaction.

"Maybe it's some kind of weird diversion," Nathan said, offering his untrained two cents worth.

"The guy was ill and waiting for transplant surgery at the time of the kidnapping," John said.

Eddie stood and faced him. "John, it's not going to hurt anything if we keep digging. You gave us the background check, and I just want to do my job. I even got the captain's approval."

John gave Eddie a long, dagger-filled stare before abruptly turning his back on the conversation.

"Fine, do your job!" he called over his shoulder. "But don't get in my way. And good luck with a motive!"

"John, wait," Eddie said. "John!"

John never looked back. Instead, he locked up and, without saying a word, left early. Normally, he would have done his best to leave the job behind, but with the day's friendly fire, it was especially tough.

Negative vibes were the last thing any detective needed. If others really wanted to help, they should be supportive and come up with solid evidence rather than intrusive speculation. Until then, their theories didn't merit attention.

The weight of the case was on John, and he had to follow his own instincts. Clark's story was off the beaten path, but John had been given no reason to doubt him. On the contrary, Clark had become more believable and was actually proving to be a potential asset in the case. That said, his involvement was still strange—a mystery—and one John was committed to solving.

But for now, work was work, and home was home, and his freshly painted Craftsman was coming into view. When he was off duty, it was his sanctuary, the one place he could truly be himself.

"Just John," as his sister, Grace, liked to say. "Our rock."

He would do anything for his family, and their assorted requests included everything from driver's training to cat sitting. Whenever Grace and his nephew, Adam, went out of town, they wouldn't think of leaving their precious, persnickety cat, D'Artagnan, with anyone else.

With each stay, it usually took the feline guest a day or so to warm up, but once he did, he was all over John and everything else in the house. He pranced around like he owned the place and was merely, charitably, allowing John to visit.

It was not uncommon for the two of them to spend a lot of time in the kitchen. Unlike some men, John enjoyed the cooking process and, over time, had become pretty good at it. One of his favorites was chicken with a creamy herb sauce that was ready in about twenty minutes. He simply put it over wild rice and voilà. Delicious and fast.

The macho detective probably wouldn't want anyone to know, but he'd developed a habit of letting D'Artagnan sit in the dining room chairs with his food dish. Over time, the circumstantial acquaintances had become genuine friends and enjoyed many great meals together. To top off the friendship, they even paid homage to a common preference: keeping conversation to a minimum.

Later in the evening, John was watching TV from his favorite recliner when D'Artagnan jumped on his lap. The less-than-graceful action caused him to juggle a tiny leather notebook he had just removed from the end table.

Listed on the left side, page one, were evidentiary notes from the Sweet case, some of his own as well as weaker points brought up by coworkers. On the opposing page, the text read, *They don't know everything* and *Strange things going on.*

Odd messages to the captain, along with evidence tampering, could alter one's perspective. The disturbing facts were pointing to an inside saboteur. And while the behavior of some had already raised concerns, potentially, it could be anyone.

John laid the book down and dialed the captain's number.

"Riley here," he answered.

"You back yet?" John asked.

"Yep, got in last night," Captain Riley said. "Anything new?"

"Well, my case seems to be the talk of the town," John grumbled.

"That right?" the captain asked.

"Yep, getting some pushback, and Eddie says he talked to you," John said.

"Yeah, he did," confirmed the captain. "He and some of the others have another theory they want to follow involving Clark. John, I gave a soft go-ahead but told him to stay out of your way."

"That's funny," John said. "I told him the same thing."

"Well, he's got some good points, but he better be following my orders!" snapped the captain.

"Captain, I get all this, but my gut's telling me I might be on to something, and I want to see it through," John explained. "The revolving evidence and interference means someone's playing games. Right now, the issues are minor, but I'd really like to put a stop to them so they don't spiral out of control. And I'm working against time here."

"Well, it's not going to hurt to have the others chase a different theory," Captain Riley asserted, "and besides, I want to know more about this Clark Steele, myself. But I hear you, and I'm going to share something with you in the strictest confidence. Here's what I've been thinking. As much as I hate it, we're going to have to look at some of our own."

"Totally agree, sir," John said. "I know we haven't had a bad cop in a long while, and I hate it too, but I've been thinking the very same thing. Something's up."

"You know, there's one person, in particular, I want to clear first for covert reasons, but I'll fill you in later," Captain Riley said.

"Okay, let me know if I can help," offered John.

"I'm going to need your help sooner than you think," Captain Riley advised. "And to quote Muhammad Ali, we're about to 'float like a butterfly, sting like a bee.' But for now, you don't know anything about this."

John grinned. "About what, sir? Goodnight."

After opening a recent document on his tablet and settling back in with D'Artagnan, John began to create private profiles for each of his colleagues. Even though he had affection for each one, he'd been forced to consider them in relation to the usual motivations for misconduct. Love, hate, jealousy, revenge, greed, and even glory were normally at the top of the list.

Detective Paul Brady, a rising star, was about forty, single, a big-picture guy, and as sharp as they come. Paul was married to the job and logged in way more hours than necessary. John had never had a single issue with him and always admired his ambition. So, unless ambition had become an obsession, Paul couldn't be tied to a motive.

Officer Ken Krieger, the department comedian, was in his fifties and had never been married. He dated often but seemed to have impossibly high standards. A joke making its way through the office hinted that he had actually put a date right out of his car because she didn't like The Rolling Stones. John had always admired Ken's dedication to the job and the humor he brought to the squad room, but one thing had been bugging him lately: Ken seemed overly interested in the case.

Eddie Driscoll, the newest detective and a transfer from another precinct, was single and in his late thirties. He had dated Sherry Griffin for a while, just like Drake, but there was no issue there as far as anyone knew. Eddie could be overly eager, as with the current case, but with new investigators, that wasn't unusual. Other than that, nothing stood out.

Morgan Fox was a thirty-something officer, an aspiring detective, and the most mysterious. She was married but private, especially about her personal life. Interestingly, even though she projected the persona of a loner, it didn't keep people away. Her charisma seemed to radiate from a calm, powerful energy. If John was forced to play devil's advocate, he might question whether the energy was clever or sneaky.

Nathan Dean, the newest officer, was in his thirties and a little testy. Not easy to warm up to. He was married to a demure little wife that John had seen only a couple of times. Nathan was a hard worker but not an out-of-the-box thinker, so he would probably be the most resistant to the idea of the phenomenon.

Detective Patti Queen—a.k.a. Queenie—was in her late forties with fun and contagious energy that filled the room, and her sarcastic wit could take down anyone. Her Cosmo style was always front and center, but she was a weapons expert and a force to be reckoned with. Queenie claimed to be happily divorced, but that's pretty much the extent of what she had revealed about her personal life. No red flags.

John looked up at the chiming mantel clock. Another thirty minutes had ticked away. Even though he'd made a vow to leave work at the office, some cases were relentless.

He placed the tablet on the end table and dimmed a nearby candlestick lamp before making a quick adjustment to the recliner's handle. The sudden action forced him and D'Artagnan to hang on as the back of the chair abruptly lurched toward the floor. Once they had recovered, he pulled a Tartan throw blanket from above his head and covered himself and part of the cat.

At about the same time, and under the cover of night, the captain entered the precinct carrying only a duffel bag. Once inside, he made his way to his office, where he worked on four tiny speakers in the upper corners of the room. He had installed them many years ago when he first arrived. When the work was finished, he reversed his watchful steps, keeping his head on a swivel and slipping away into the darkness.

EIGHTEEN

DÉJÀ VU

Clark frantically searched the cluttered bed for his ringing phone before finally locating it under a stack of clothes next to a half-packed suitcase. "Hello," he said.

"Hey, just checking on you before you leave for the cabin," Dr. Brill said. "I know the other day was kind of rough on you."

"Yeah, but I'm doing better," he said. "This trip is giving me something new to focus on."

"Just what I wanted to hear," Dr. Brill said. "I must tell you, Clark, I'm just so impressed with how you're handling everything."

"Thanks, Doc," he said. "But that's thanks to you. And speaking of that, how are you doing?"

At that very moment, she was staring at a picture of Tony on her desk. "Better than in a long time," she said wistfully.

Clark smiled. "Good to hear."

"You know, Clark, you've made it through the initial shock and conquered a lot of anxiety already," Dr. Brill said. "And I think the work with John, although intense, has really been great therapy for you."

"Yeah, me too," he agreed. "Being able to analyze the flashes in relation to the case has helped me sort some things out."

"That's the idea," Dr. Brill said. "So, I guess you and John are working on the information from the session with Serena?"

"Oh, yeah, it's already plugged into the timeline," Clark explained. "I'm glad you thought of hypnosis."

"Me too," Dr. Brill said. "Can you believe how comfortable you were during the session?"

Clark grinned. "I know, maybe too comfortable. Remember, I almost fell asleep."

"Well, you wouldn't be the first," laughed Dr. Brill.

"Yeah, probably," he said. "Hey, Doc, I'm starting to get a little worried here. Some of the other officers are acting suspiciously, even targeting me, and I'm not sure John's totally on board, either. How do I protect myself?"

"John's a good man," she said. "Give him time."

"I know," Clark said. "I just don't want him to have any doubts."

"He'll get there," she said. "What's the plan at the cabin?"

"We're going to work as fast as we can because the little girl's already been missing for a while. If we could just hit on something, maybe there's still a chance of finding her."

"That's your answer, right there," she said. "If you can prove what happened, the others will have to back off."

"Right," nodded Clark. "Well, we're just searching for anything new and hoping Drake might have discovered something out there."

"Well, good luck," she said. "And my best advice to you is just let the flashes come, and your instincts be your guide. They've served you well so far."

"True," Clark said. "Thanks, I'll do my best."

"Just think, if you could find her, what an ending that would be to your story!" she offered.

"If we could just be that lucky," Clark said. "Well, hey, I'd better get moving. I've got a lot to do to get ready on time."

"Okay," she said. "I have another transplant recipient arriving in a few minutes, anyway. Safe trip, and remember, I'm just a call away."

"I know. I appreciate it," Clark replied.

"Oh, hey, my patient is ringing the buzzer," Dr. Brill said. "You take care of yourself."

"You too, Doc," Clark said. "Bye."

"Bye," she said, heading to the door to welcome four-year-old Savannah and her mother inside.

✳

Before Clark knew it, the cabin was rolling into view at the end of a very long driveway. Almost immediately, the significance of the location hit him hard, lulling him into a quiet, pensive state.

Rather than feeling awkward, the prolonged silence felt more like a gift. Not only did it give him time to get his bearings, but it also elevated the sound of the birds chirping a daybreak welcome.

John stopped unloading the car for a second to take a deep breath of the fresh air. "Ahh," he exhaled. "It's been a while since I've been out here. But I can still remember Drake's routine like it was yesterday. The first thing he did was get organized, and he was very particular about it. If you were within earshot, you might even get a few tips on how order produces more free time."

Clark grinned as he admired the casual architectural simplicity and appeal of the vast log cabin. "Wow, what a place. It really is beautiful here. Peaceful. If you wanted to work without distraction, this would be the place. No wonder it was Drake's hideaway. Maybe the relaxing vibe and change in scenery will bring us some good luck."

"Let's hope so," John called from the porch as he unlocked the sturdy timber door. "It can be a little musty in here when it's been vacant for a while, but we can just air it out while we get settled."

Clark dropped his gear just inside the doorway and took his first look around. A strange sense of déjà vu flooded his consciousness almost immediately. He'd had no memory flashes from the location, and yet, strangely, the familiar ambiance felt like home.

John had turned on a few lights and made his way to the kitchen to put away provisions. When he finished, he stopped and took a good long look all around.

"Man, the memories are rushing back," he said. "Drake and his family loved it here."

"Well, I can see why," nodded Clark. "It's the perfect retreat."

"Yeah, and weirdly, it's the perfect office too," John added. "We were pretty productive out here."

"Hope some of that rubs off," Clark said.

Even though he was dealing with new pressure, Clark was energized and fully committed to navigating the experiment they were about to undertake. And just knowing that Drake and the gods of righteousness might be riding shotgun reinforced his resolve.

"Just pick a room, Clark," John directed. "Wherever you're most comfortable."

"Okay, thanks," he said, heading down the hallway and stopping at the first bedroom. "This one will work, John. Are you sure it's okay?"

"Yeah, absolutely," called John. "I always sleep in the one at the end of the hall, so that's my pick. As soon as we're settled in, we can organize the case and get to work."

"Great, I'll be ready in a few," called Clark as he crossed the threshold of his cozy, new quarters.

Minutes later, they were both standing over the massive dining table, coffee cups in hand, organizing evidence. The main attraction was the timeline, extending down the entire length of the center, giving the appearance of a table runner. All related materials were displayed around the premier centerpiece in an orderly fashion.

Clark grinned when he noticed that, just like other occasions, John had separated a few things, most likely for presentation at a specific time.

"Okay, let's see if we can figure out what we've missed," John announced. "The timeline takes us from before the abduction all the way to Drake's possible epiphany prior to the accident. We have photos, interviews, and physical evidence from the original crime scene and from the cemetery. The perpetrator wore gloves and was especially thorough at covering his tracks. Our Trace Evidence Unit examined a series of samples, but we got next to nothing, just a few unidentifiable fibers."

"What did they find at the cemetery?" Clark asked.

"Her backpack, slippers, and pajamas, with the tiaras. That little piece of fabric I showed you was from the collar," John explained. "Here, let me grab those photos for you."

"Why in the world would someone bury evidence?" Clark wondered aloud. "And why in a cemetery?"

John handed him the photos. "Motivations can be a horror show and complex. Hard to break down. Dr. Brill wondered if choosing a cemetery might indicate some type of psychological trigger or twisted way of literally burying the evidence."

Clark shook his head. "Man, that's nuts."

"Yep," agreed John. "You know, choosing a cemetery could be seen as bold in one way because it's so public, but also shrewd because the disturbance would be hard to detect among acres of graves. Either way, Dr. Brill was sure the perpetrator would present with an odd psychological history."

"Kind of creeps me out," Clark said, returning the photos.

Yeah, you wouldn't believe the stuff we deal with," John said before turning his attention back to the timeline. "Let's see . . . we have the actual evidence, interview files, and now, your visions on the board. Even though they haven't provided solid clues, they have corroborated existing evidence, giving the phenomenon theory more credibility.

"There must be something to it," he added. "Along with Drake's heart, it does seem like you've received some of his characteristics and memories."

"Some of the others don't think so," probed Clark.

"You let me worry about them," asserted John. "They're not read-in, and they're certainly not in charge of this case."

"I don't really care what they think, John," Clark confessed. "But I do care what you think. And for some reason, I feel like I'm speaking for Drake too."

John froze in place before turning to face him. A few seconds ticked off. When John looked away, he reached for the nearest chair and awkwardly took a seat.

"John, I . . . I'm sorry," Clark said. "I didn't mean to upset you."

"No, it's not you," John said. "It's just that I could feel Drake's energy there for a second."

He felt it! A shudder ran through Clark's body. "No, I know, John. I felt it too when I said, 'I care what you think.'"

"Well, if you're trying to convince me, it's working," declared John. "Wow. Okay. Well, let's see if we can get back on track and tap into that gift of yours."

"Are you sure you're ready?" Clark asked.

"Yeah, you?" John countered.

"I'll be fine," Clark said.

John stood and waved his hand over the massive display of evidence. "I think our best approach is to try to mimic the way Drake would have done things. He always started with a review of the material, making sure it was fresh in his mind. Then he would close his eyes, meditate, and create a mental movie of the crime."

"Okay," Clark said, already reviewing the transcript from the abductor's tirade.

"That speech was weird," John said. "He told Angela's parents they had ruined his life with their selfishness and interference and took away what he cared for most. He also said that because they didn't follow rules, they had to suffer consequences."

Clark frowned. "Yeah. Strange."

"And then his final comment was, 'You took my entire life, so I'm taking yours,'" John added.

"Well, I'm not a detective, but all of that seems like a big deal to me," Clark said.

"You sound like Drake," John said, shaking his head.

Clark smiled. "Well, at least it gives us a window into his mind. And the family didn't have any enemies or conflict in their lives?"

"No. Nothing," John confirmed. "They were completely baffled. We wondered if it might be a case of mistaken identity, where the perpetrator was taking revenge on the wrong people. We're not sure about much, except that he did seem out of touch with reality."

"Yeah, but what he said to the family was so specific," Clark said. If we just knew what he meant by it."

"Drake thought the same thing, but if the answer's hidden in that tirade, we haven't figured it out," John confessed.

"So, the parents have provided the only information we have on the kidnapper," stated Clark. What did they remember?"

"Well, they gave a physical description of a muscular, medium-built man, about five ten to six feet tall with light to medium complexion," began John. "He was wearing a mask, but they could clearly see the skin color around, what they described as fierce, blue eyes. They said he seemed strong physically, but something was off about his demeanor. His behavior was erratic. Angela's mother even wondered if he was on drugs."

John searched for a report on the table. "Let's see . . . he was dressed in all black, including gloves, boots—about a size ten—and a backpack. They described his voice as thin and shaky, one they would never forget."

"That's a lot of information too," Clark said.

"Yeah, I know," John nodded. "We feel like we have plenty of evidence to convict when we actually find him."

"We've had no sightings reported, so, assuming she's still safe, he must have her in a secluded location," he added. "We're still trying to figure out how he disposed of the evidence. It's very unlikely that he would have done it the same night. So, either he came back or had help."

"How did Drake find out about the cemetery?" Clark asked.

"The head groundskeeper alerted police," John said. "And Drake took the call. The cemetery staff was questioning a makeshift grave that shouldn't have been there. It had been excavated and camouflaged so perfectly that no one noticed, even the most expert among them."

"I'm guessing all of the cemetery staff checked out?" Clark asked.

"Yeah, but we still don't know how someone gained access without anyone noticing," explained John. "There was one kind of sketchy guy working there, but he was cleared."

Clark shook his head. "I have so many questions."

"Drake and I have probably discussed them all," John said. "What are you thinking?"

"Mostly about what went on at the scene," Clark said. "But right now, we're here to find something new that could lead us to a suspect, right?"

"You're on it, Detective Steele," John teased.

Clark laughed it off but felt a distinct sense of satisfaction.

"Hey, there is one more thing," John said. "Drake had some threatening calls from burner phones."

"Burner phones?" Clark asked.

"Yeah, throwaways. Hard to trace," John explained. "Extremely brief calls, altered voice, mostly warning Drake to back off. He also told him, 'No more media.'"

Clark shook his head. "And nothing ever came of that?"

"No, couldn't be traced," John said. "And he just seemed to be playing a game. The last thing he'd always say to Drake was, 'No offense, but'—and click—he'd hang up on him every single time. Used to make Drake so mad. Haven't heard from him for a long while, but if he calls again, it gets patched straight through to me now."

"Do you think he's really the guy?" Clark probed.

"No, not really," John said. "He's never said anything specific about the case. Seems more like an attention hound to me. But, if it is him, he'll trip up eventually."

Clark nodded. "Yeah."

"Hey, I don't know about you," John said, "but that muffin didn't fill me up. I think some bacon and eggs are in order. Let's fix a real breakfast and take our meeting to the porch."

"You don't have to twist my arm," Clark said. "I'm always hungry, and I have been looking forward to getting back outside."

The weathered door let out a familiar creak as John pushed it open and held it with his foot, allowing Clark to pass him on his way out. With breakfast in hand, they made their way to the first couple of chairs in the shade, where the perfect mid-morning temperatures were simply pleading with them to stay a while.

The two could not have looked more content within the fortress of trees, dotingly guarding them under its canopy.

John scanned the scene. "This is what I'm talking about. It really is the perfect place to clear your head and center yourself."

Clark took a deep breath. "Yeah, there's something really pure about it."

"Okay, let's go over the whole scenario, just like Drake would have done," suggested John. "We'll meditate on all of the information, from beginning to end, and try to create a running movie. If we get lucky, maybe a new detail shows up."

The only conversation for the next twenty minutes was the repartee of nature and the sound of the wind exhaling gracefully. It was obvious that both men respected the exercise and were practicing with the utmost seriousness. Looking at either of them was like looking at one of Serena's clients in a totally tranquil state, either meditating or under self-induced hypnosis.

Off in the distance, gravel flew like shrapnel as the Four Runner took the turn onto the property much too quickly. The hostile racket jolted them back to reality, interrupting their silent movie activity midstream.

"Inside!" shouted John. His voice had taken on a powerfully animated tone that Clark hadn't heard before.

The two moved like lightning, adopting defensive postures just inside the front door as the out-of-control vehicle raced closer and closer.

John drew his weapon.

✳

"Hello, hey there. Sorry about the dramatic entrance," called the unexpected visitor, looking a little harried and breathless with amusement. "I almost passed the driveway."

Clark and John remained protectively behind the doorway, where John was keeping his right hand hidden, not revealing the gun.

"Yep, you sure did," he countered. "What can we help you with?"

"Well, I live just down the road and try to keep an eye on the cabin when the Harrisons are away," the caller said. "I noticed your car at the last minute and decided to swing in and check on things. Are you a friend of the family?"

"Yeah, I've been here many times," nodded John. "What's your name?"

"Oh, sorry, Perry Redmond," he said. "I've lived out here about fifteen years. My wife and I sure have been thinking a lot about the Harrisons since the loss of Drake. So tragic. What a great man."

Seemingly satisfied that Perry wasn't a threat, John signaled Clark "all clear," and stepped into full view, exposing the firearm.

"Yeah, Drake was the best," John said. "We worked together for many years. I'm Detective John Baxter and this is my . . . my assistant, Clark Steele."

Perry tipped a weathered ballcap. "Nice to meet you both.

"So, you're a detective too," he said, eyeing the gun. "Hope I didn't startle you guys. You know, I think, I've heard Drake mention you a few times."

"Probably. We worked a lot of cases together," John said, holstering the weapon.

Perry looked around as if reminiscing. "Yep, the Harrisons sure had great family times out here. I've witnessed some and heard about others. They were all looking forward to spending time together in the new picnic area, but Drake never got to see it finished."

"What do you do, Clark?" he asked abruptly.

"Architect, what about you?" returned Clark.

"I actually have a farm that's been in my family for generations," Perry said, standing taller as if unable to resist showing a little pride. "It's a lot of work, but I have good help, and I love it. Can't imagine doing anything else. I was actually on my way down to the feed store when I stopped, so I better get moving. You guys enjoy your stay.

Please give the family my best, and we're just right down the road if you need anything."

"Thanks, good to meet you, Perry," Clark and John replied in nearly perfect sync.

"Hey, take it a little slower this time," directed John.

Perry grinned. "You got it." He hopped into the Four Runner and headed back down the driveway at a snail's pace.

Clark noticed John grinning from ear to ear as he watched Perry drive until he was completely out of sight. When he turned and made eye contact, they both started laughing.

Something about the exchange felt familiar to Clark as if it were an inside joke. But he just shrugged it off and asked, "What do you make of all that?"

"Well, with that aggressive entrance, I wasn't sure what was going down," John replied.

Clark shook his head. "Me either, but he seems okay."

"Well, you noticed I wasn't taking any chances, right?" John added, patting the gun.

"Seemed like a good idea to me at the time," Clark said. "But man, what a sudden jolt from our movie. He does seem like a decent guy though. Everyone loved Drake, didn't they?"

"Everyone," John declared. "He always went out of his way for people. I've never told anyone this before, but I have a nephew, Adam, who's being raised by a single mom. Unfortunately, his dad was a classic cheater who didn't give much time or respect to his family.

"When he finally left for good, it was so hard on Adam. I tried to spend as much time with him as I could, showing up at games and school events, but there were still times I couldn't be there. It broke my heart, but as you're witnessing, the schedule of a detective is all over the place.

"Drake and I were talking about it one day, and he offered to help out. And from that time on, he became like a big brother, filling in at events I couldn't make. The two of us were already the best of friends, but that personal situation bonded us like brothers. Anyway, we were able to spend a lot of quality time with Adam when he needed it most.

"And one of the things I'd always appreciated about Drake was his discretion," John added. "He never told anyone about my personal business. He was completely humble about his involvement, and every detail of the situation stayed between us. That's a true friend."

"Yes, sir," agreed Clark. "You guys did a great thing."

"Well, he's a great young man," John nodded. "Hey, we better get back to it before the weekend gets away from us."

"Yeah," agreed Clark. "Well, sorry to say, nothing new grabbed me during the movie exercise. And I ran the whole thing through my mind several times. I guess I need more practice."

"You and me both," John nodded. "Hey, there is one thing I wanted to mention again. Drake only had a couple of photos out when the accident happened. And I've always thought they might mean something, especially since everything else was tightly packed away."

"What were they?" Clark asked.

"A few from the cemetery, but just the ones from before the dig. I've always wondered if he attached some significance to them," mused John.

"Well, photos of the site don't seem as important as the actual physical evidence to me, but hey, what do I know?" Clark said. "Can we take a look?"

"Yeah, sure," John said, leading the way inside.

The photos in question were just where he'd left them earlier, separated, at the very end of the table. After handing a few to Clark, he continued to study them over his shoulder, even though he had seen them dozens of times.

At first, Clark hardly noticed anything unusual. To him, it just looked like a well-manicured section of the property. But the groundskeeper had identified the area as suspicious, so he began to study it more closely.

"Oh, I see it now," he muttered. "There's like a barely recognizable border there. No wonder they all missed that."

"Yeah," John said. "Well, my gut could be wrong but knowing Drake the way I do makes me think there could be something to it."

"Yeah, I see what you mean," nodded Clark. "You know, I was just thinking. If Drake was here at the cabin when he stumbled onto something, I sure wish we knew what he was doing."

"I know," John said. "Well, he did have a couple of favorite spots. Let's see, he was probably either on the porch or walking the property. He loved that and said he did some of his best thinking 'immersed in the serenity of nature.'"

Clark grinned. "I like the way he thinks. Since nothing else has worked, do you think we should walk the property?"

"It's not a bad idea," John said.

"Hey, I'd love to give Rachel a quick call and then grab a cup o' joe for the walk, if you don't mind."

"Wouldn't mind a cup myself," agreed John. "Let's take ten, and then I'll show you the rest."

In the kitchen, Clark found the stash of flavors the Harrisons had been kind enough to offer for their enjoyment. He would never have considered trying most of them before his odd conversion, but the power of the new preference was strong, steering him toward something more adventurous.

When John walked in, he was deciding between cinnamon and caramel delight.

"Have you ever tried either of these?" Clark asked.

John smiled. "I was always a regular coffee guy, but Drake almost had me converted too. I do like the caramel."

"Caramel it is," proclaimed Clark, firing up the pot before drifting off toward his cozy room.

"Hello," Rachel answered in an easy, smoky voice.

Clark smiled and rested on the log-framed bed. "Hey, I miss you already."

"Miss you too," she said. "How's it going?"

"Well, everything's okay, but we had an unexpected visitor and John had to draw his gun."

"What?" she cried. "Clark!"

"Everything's fine!" he assured her. "It ended up just being a neighbor speeding into the driveway. But until we knew what was going on, John wasn't taking any chances. Turned out he was actually a decent guy. I'll tell you more about it when I get back."

"You sure you guys are all right?" she asked.

"Yeah, Babe, we're fine," Clark said. "Hey, I only have a few minutes right now, so are you okay?"

"Yeah, perfect, other than being apart," she said. "I hope this is all worth it."

"My gut's telling me it is," Clark said. "If my flashes can help John find that little girl, it will be. Look, I miss you like crazy, but something just feels right about what we're doing. But I've been thinking, and I promise you, as soon as this is over, we're going to start our family."

"Clark!" she gasped. "Are you sure you're ready?"

The expectation in her voice made him smile. "Never been more ready for anything!"

"Oh, Clark," she said. "I love you so much."

"Love you too," Clark said. "We'll talk all about it when I get home. So, is everything else good on your end?"

"Yeah, no excitement like you and John," she declared. "But I talked to Dr. Brill, and you should hear about her new transplant patient. I only know about it because they're going to be part of an open support group."

"They?" he asked.

"A little girl and her mom," Rachel said.

"Oh, okay," he said. "Can you tell me about it quickly?"

"Well, let's see. She's a four-year-old," Rachel said, "who received her heart from another little girl. And when she heard the name of her donor, she told Dr. Brill that she knew her. And when Dr. Brill asked her how, she said, 'She lives in my heart.'"

"Wow, what a way to explain it," Clark said, rubbing his arms. "Goosebumps."

"I know, right?" agreed Rachel.

Clark shook his head. "Such an innocent way to describe the connection. And yet, the weird thing is, I know what she means. Hey, I want to hear more about it, Babe, but I'd better head back out, so John and I can make good use of our time. Just wanted to hear your voice. Love you."

"Love you too," she said. "Please don't overdo it while you're there."

"I won't," promised Clark. "I'm doing great. I'll be home before you know it."

It only took a few quick steps before he was back in the dining room, where John was towering over the near end of the table, studying evidence.

"What are we looking at?" Clark asked.

"Testimony," John said, handing over statements from the family, including the highlighted speech from the abductor.

"This rant is haunting," Clark said. "I feel like there has to be a connection, even if it's remote."

"I know. I've been beating my head against the wall trying to figure it out," John replied. "There are different ways to look at it. Just like you said, there could be a one-sided connection. Or the kidnapper could have completely disconnected from reality and taken revenge on the wrong people."

"If theories overlap, what do you do?" Clark asked.

"Investigate all angles," John said. "Sometimes it's the most benign clue that gets the ball rolling."

"The abductor could have known about the family without their knowledge," Clark proposed. "And, for some reason, that makes the most sense to me, but I see what you're saying. Theories could be linked."

"Drake and I felt the same way but checked out everyone on our very weak suspect list," explained John. "Honestly, we had only a few people of interest, and from the beginning, our guts told us they didn't have anything to do with it."

"Hmm. . . oh, looks like coffee's ready." Clark made his way to the kitchen where he filled and presented two large mugs. "Ready to head out?"

"Let's do it." John wrapped his hands around the mug and smiled as if reveling in its warmth.

The tour began, and the steam rising from the caramel delight led the way. The first stop was a treasured spot behind the cabin, where an erratic border of shrubs created a natural enclosure.

"The extra privacy back here draws wildlife like magnets," explained John. "There were times we got to watch deer and other animals romp around for hours."

"Maybe we'll see some," Clark said.

John walked to the center of the trees, facing the back, and summoned Clark to a perfect vantage point. "Look from right here," he directed.

Clark took a few quick steps, turned, and gasped. Straight ahead through the trees lay one of the most spectacular views he'd ever seen. The panorama of dense forest and vivid colors seemed to go for miles, ending with a faint glimpse of a small, alluring village.

"Wow, I wasn't expecting that," he exclaimed. "What an awesome view."

"Love doing that to people," John laughed. "This is one of my favorite spots. Let's head around to the left side of the house, and I'll show you the stream."

Clark nodded. "Hey, John, I've been wanting to ask you something. It's about Dr. Brill. Do you know anything about the story of her marriage?"

John gave him a sideways glance. "Would you be talking about the disappearance of her husband?"

"Exactly!" Clark said. "So, you do know. I just feel so bad for her and wish there was something I could do."

"I know what you mean," John said. "Some other guys were assigned that case years ago. It's a tough one, and it's been cold for a long while. Drake worked on it from time to time but kept it a secret. He didn't want to get her hopes up."

"Really?" Clark said. "Well, I know she's strong, and she'll be fine, but if anyone deserves a happy ending, it's her."

"Yeah. Maybe when I get time, I'll dig that file out again," John offered.

"That'd be great," Clark said. "And if there's anything I can do to help, just say the word."

"You got it," John promised.

As they continued exploring the property, Clark's mind wandered back to the case. The peace and quiet did seem to be working to his advantage, allowing him time to mull over important evidence and unanswered questions without distraction.

When they came upon the brook, John said, "You know, being here brings back memories of the Harrison kids playing in the stream. And, of course, it makes me think about the Sweets. How many special family moments have they missed already?"

"Yeah, I know," nodded Clark. "And there's never been a single sighting?"

"None," John said.

"So, did any of the people of interest have ties to remote properties?" probed Clark.

"No, not one," John said. "But I like that you're thinking like a detective again."

When the stroll brought them around to the front of the cabin, Clark said, "I still think the abductor could have known about the family in some way."

"Yeah, that's definitely one of the angles," agreed John.

The tour continued around the perimeter of the property, and Clark could feel the slightly cooler temperatures moving in, hinting at the sun's imminent departure. Before long, it would be setting just beyond the trees.

"Drake loved it when the daylight shifted like this," John said. "He said it brought with it a purer, softer light that made everything look airbrushed."

"He's right," Clark said.

"Let's head over to the left, and I'll show you the path to the lake," offered John. "We don't have to walk all the way down unless you want to. We'll still get a great view."

They had only taken a few steps when John's text alert went off and stopped him dead in his tracks. Within seconds, Clark picked up on his worried expression and the tiny tremor in his hands. John seemed hesitant and looked at Clark a couple of times before reading the message out loud. "John, it's him! Patching the call through."

Clark gasped. "Drake's caller?"

"Yep," John said. But his answer was slightly obscured by the ringtone. "Baxter," he said.

"Let me talk to Clark," came the distorted voice over the speaker.

Clark looked at John, stunned.

John took charge. "You can talk to me."

"Look, I'm going to make this short, Detective," the caller said. "Either you put Clark on the line, or this call is over."

"How do you know Clark?" John asked.

"Last chance," came the reply.

Clark stepped forward and said, "This is Clark."

"Clark Steele, to be exact," corrected the caller. "Look, I'm going to tell you the same thing I told Drake Harrison. Back off!"

"How do you know me?" Clark asked.

"You guys should know by now that I have my ways," he said. "By the way, how's your heart?"

How does he know about that?

The comment was not only disturbing but irritating, and Clark could actually feel the color draining from his face. He knew he had to fight the sensation and go on the offensive.

"My heart's fine," he declared. "How's your conscience?"

"Don't go there," the caller warned.

"Little touchy?" Clark asked. You invaded my privacy. How do you like it?"

"No offense, but– " Click. He hung up.

"And the famous signoff!" announced John. "You okay?"

Clark shook his head. "Yeah, but how does he know me?"

"Well, if he has any tech ability at all, he can find anything these days," offered John. "See what I'm saying, though? He never reveals anything that would connect him to the case. His behavior is vaguer. Annoying. Like someone playing the big man. Seeking attention. But we're keeping him on the radar."

"Man, that was out of the blue," Clark said. "I wasn't even sure what to say."

"Well, I liked it when you called him touchy," chuckled John. "He just wastes our time, so we've mostly been tolerating him, hoping he trips up. It's about time someone new challenges him."

Clark couldn't resist a grin.

"If you're okay, we should probably get back to it," John said.

"Yeah, sure," Clark sighed. "I was thinking the kidnapper said the Sweets destroyed his plan and took his entire life. That's a huge statement, but also personal. Did you get to interview many friends and family members of the Sweets?"

"Oh, yeah, but no one had much to offer," John said. "They couldn't come up with a single person who had even said anything negative about the Sweets."

When they came to a stop, the walk had landed them about a hundred yards short of the lake. The panorama of the sun sparkling on the water, surrounded by a bastion of trees, was so peaceful that for a few blissful minutes, time was suspended. They stood silently, honoring a classic moment of perfection that should never be spoiled by conversation.

Without even discussing it, they headed on down to the water's edge. To the left, and far down on the opposite bank, Clark could see two teenagers —a boy and a girl —with fishing poles in the water. Just a few feet away was a quilted blanket and a brimming picnic basket, all set for open-air dining at dusk.

"I sure wish more kids had days like that." The sound of John's voice had broken the silence.

"Yeah," Clark agreed. "Nowadays they just stay inside and connect through devices. They have no idea what they're missing."

"Yep, and look at those two, out in the sunshine, fishing, laughing, picnics," observed John.

"Hey, speaking of that, where's the picnic area Perry mentioned?" Clark asked.

"Oh, yeah, I'll show you on the way back," John said. "Let's walk the rest of the perimeter, and we'll get a better view from the other side."

As they crossed over the driveway opening, where Perry made his NASCAR entrance, John said, "Clark, I hate to bring it up, but it looks like our trip out here hasn't been what we'd hoped for. I'm feeling like we'd better head back in the morning and see what's happening at the office. Things were getting a little out of hand back there."

Clark stopped. "That's exactly why I don't want to go back. They're making me feel like a suspect."

"I'll handle them," John promised. "But if we've hit a dead end, we don't want to waste any more time."

"I know, but my gut's telling me we should stay," Clark said. "I'm not ready to give up."

"Me either," John agreed. "But we've tried everything, sketch artist, hypnotherapist, movie technique, even retracing Drake's steps. We've got new information, but not what I need to help the case or prove your innocence."

"Well, we have a little more time, right?" Clark implored.

John nodded. "Yeah, but I just wanted to prepare you."

"For what?" he said. "What am I facing when I get back there?"

John studied him for a long time before answering. "I don't know."

Clark hung his head and marched forward, separating himself.

"Clark," called John.

In the quiet of the afternoon, the soothing sounds of nature serenaded them as they followed the tree line back toward the cabin, single file. Every once in a while, John stopped and looked around, seemingly still checking for the best vantage point.

"Hey Clark," he finally called. "You can see the picnic area pretty well from here." He was facing in the direction of the lake but from a new angle."

Clark kept walking. "I don't care."

"Clark, what was it you said just a minute ago?" John asked. "We still have a little more time, right?"

After a few more steps, Clark stopped and turned around. "Where is it?"

"It's right there about midway in the clearing," guided John.

Clark followed the bearing of John's extended arm, but it took a minute to zero in on the spot. As the image came into focus, he began to feel lightheaded and reached for a nearby boulder to steady himself.

The coffee mug slipped from his hand and shattered.

"Clark, are you okay?" gasped John.

Clark stood frozen in place. "John, I've seen this! On the walking path with Rachel."

"What?" John said.

But Clark stayed silent, taking in the vision matching the past episode. He kept constant eye contact as he slowly moved a couple of steps to the left and supported himself on the nearest tree.

He was drinking in the familiar scene when a mental flash from the cemetery caught him off guard. Within seconds, images of the picnic area and cemetery began to overlap.

John raced to his side. "Clark, are you all right?"

"I . . . I think I just need a minute," he said.

Being careful not to take his eyes off the picnic area, Clark walked backward in search of the perfect spot. Once he was happy with the location, he was able to superimpose his vision from the nature walk over the picnic area. A perfect match.

John stayed close as Clark went through the strange process.

"This means something," whispered Clark. He closed his eyes and tried to relax, but he could still feel the goose bumps.

After a ragged breath, he said, "I'm sure of it, John. As soon as I looked at the picnic site, I felt strange, and then my mind started to flash back and forth from there to the cemetery. Both sites are almost the same size and shape. So perfect. And, somehow, I knew Drake was thinking the same thing. The images started to overlap in my mind. I could see the gravesite, and I . . . I could hear thoughts," he whispered eerily, as if in some sort of trance. "It's perfect . . . too perfect."

And then, suddenly, in an altered voice, he shouted, "That's freaking it. It's got to be!"

The unnatural comment caught John so off guard that he stumbled backward as if he'd seen a ghost.

"Drake?"

NINETEEN

STILL ON THE CASE

Clark and John were still reeling from the unnatural outburst when they pulled out of the driveway the next morning.

"I'm telling you, Clark," John said. "I know Drake's voice. And I don't want to freak you out, but when you yelled, you sounded just like him."

Clark shook his head as a new shiver ran down his spine. "Now I have his voice? How is that possible?"

"I . . . I don't know, but it was dead on," John whispered.

"Something felt different this time, John, but I'm not sure I want to talk about it," Clark admitted.

"Talking has gotten us this far," John said. "Might be a good idea."

"Yeah, you're right," agreed Clark. "I can't believe I said that out loud. It felt so involuntary like I wasn't in control. Maybe Drake was really trying to tell us something."

"Well, I'm sensing more and more of Drake in you every time something new pops up," John confessed. "And I'll tell you one more thing. You certainly didn't get that voice by being involved in the crime. You are now officially critical to the case and have my full attention!"

"Finally," Clark sighed. "Thanks, John."

"No, I mean it, no more doubts!" he promised. "They're going to have to go through me to get to you."

Although Clark was still feeling unsettled, the words he'd been waiting to hear fully registered, and he breathed a deep sigh of relief. At last, John believed.

"Are you okay, Clark?" John asked.

Clark nodded, "Yeah, I think so. But, John, there's definitely something to all of this. I just know it. I felt like I was seeing through Drake's eyes again, and he was on to something. I could feel his breakthrough. And that's the most powerful episode I've had. When I was looking at the picnic area, the cemetery kept flashing in and out. The images were so similar, so precise. The next thing I knew, I was focused on the burial site and wondering who could have created it so perfectly."

"Maybe Drake thought the perpetrator had to be a professional or something, like a groundskeeper or landscaper," John said. "And you know what, shots of the gravesite were out in the Jeep. That's a theory we hadn't talked about before, but it does make some sense.

"The average person wouldn't have been able to camouflage the area so well. They would have needed special skills and maybe even tools to pull that off. Yeah, it's a long shot, but we should probably look into it."

Clark nodded. "It feels big to me. The connection was so strong. And then, the voice."

"The voice," whispered John. "I don't know any more whether I'm talking to you or Drake, but I need both of you on this case. And we need to get on it."

Time and leisurely miles raced by as they shared ideas and planned the next move. The landscaping revelation had produced new possibilities and new energy. Even though the lead was iffy, at least it was something to go on, something that might help determine whether Drake had uncovered evidence.

Clark could tell that John was invigorated by the idea of digging a little deeper into the contact list and conducting second interviews.

"It should be eye-opening to see if anyone of interest has a groundskeeping or landscaping background," Clark said.

"Definitely!" John agreed. "You know, I'm already missing the cabin, but I'm glad to be heading back. Now that we have a potential lead, I don't want to waste any time. I'll have Mary arrange the Sweet interview first thing."

"Think we can make it by three?" Clark asked.

"Yeah," John said. "After that, we'll set tentative times for Jacki's sister, Ashley, and a roofer named Carson Peak. He did a repair for the Sweets about five months before the kidnapping."

Clark sat back and folded his arms. "Really!"

"I know what you're thinking, but he easily cleared the initial interview," John said.

Before Clark knew it, the drive was over, and John was pulling up next to his car.

"Looks like we made it," John announced.

"Yeah," Clark said. "Well, I can't wait to fill Rachel in on the latest, so I'm going to take off. See you at the Sweet's."

Clark arrived first and was admiring the beauty of the neighborhood when John pulled up. After discussing the delicate handling of the impending conversation with the heartbroken parents, the two investigators started up the circular driveway.

The white French Provincial, waiting at the end, was something to be admired. In Clark's mind, the elegant brick home would always be a favorite, timeless in its traditional styling. From the carved front doorway and shuttered windows to the high roofline, he found the home stunning. But as solid and picturesque as it was, it hadn't been able to spare the residents a terrible tragedy.

The walnut front door swung open, slowly revealing Chad Sweet on the other side. He smiled and extended his hand. "Hey, John, nice to see you again."

"You too, Chad," John said. "You look good."

"Well, thanks. A little thinner, about ten pounds. You must be Clark," he said, leaning around John.

"Yes, very nice to meet you," returned Clark.

"Well, please, come on in, I'll get Jacki."

"You can just make yourselves comfortable in the family room," he said. He led them straight ahead into a casual but elegant space, with one exception.

Taking up a good portion of one corner was a mini trampoline with random toys scattered about. It looked as if a child had been playing. Had Angela left it that way? Could the parents not bring themselves to disturb anything?

Clark had barely gotten settled when Jacki Sweet walked quietly into the room. He stood immediately, along with John, showing her due respect.

She looked lovely, even though the inevitable expression of anguish was looming.

John spoke with a high level of kindness. "Hey Jacki, it's good to see you. This is Clark."

With a half-smile, she said, "Hi, nice to see you both."

"Would you guys like something to drink?" Chad asked.

Clark smiled. "No, thank you."

"Oh, no thanks," echoed John. "We shouldn't be long. I don't want to get your hopes up, but we've stumbled onto something in a very unusual way. It's not exactly a clue. We're calling it a hunch instead."

Chad looked at Jacki and took her hand. "We'll take any kind of news. Please sit down."

"Thanks," John said. "Well, Clark is involved in the case through a fascinating phenomenon we'd like to tell you about if you think you're up for an amazing story."

"Yeah, anything," Chad said. "But John, before we get started, I should tell you something. We got a strange voicemail, but the caller didn't leave a name. It was just a weird-sounding voice telling us to be wary of new case information."

"What?" John exclaimed. "Did you get any other details from the call?"

"No, nothing registered on the display," Chad said.

"Well, I hope you can put that right out of your mind," coaxed John. "I don't know what that's about, but I would never subject you to anything questionable."

Chad nodded. "We know, John, that's why we're still having this meeting."

"Well, thank you," John said. "And I can assure you, I'll do everything I can to find out what that was all about!"

John's body language appeared relaxed, but Clark was sure he was steaming inside. He'd been fed up and very vocal about someone messing with the case.

"Well, Clark, it looks like you're on," John said.

Shortly into Clark's story, the Sweets were wringing their hands and shifting in their seats. But before long, the excess energy subsided.

Jacki, in particular, seemed to have become quietly captivated, absolutely lost in the moment.

Clark studied her. *Is this her first respite from thoughts of the abduction?*

"So, let me get this straight," Chad said. "You think some of your visions may be from Drake and related to the case?"

Clark nodded. "Yeah, we do. We've been able to match some of them to actual evidence. John and I have been through timelines, evidence, a sketch artist, and even a hypnotherapist for confirmation. The hunch we're working on happened just yesterday. It was a mental flash that was like another split-second window into Drake's mind."

"The new hunch involves a landscaping vision," John interjected. "But first, since the abductor thinks he knows your family, we want to go over the specifics of what he said again and see if anything new comes to mind."

Jacki took a soft, deep breath and nodded.

"Remember, he rambled on about 'ruining his life' and 'destroying his plan,'" John said. "And then he said something like, 'You took my entire life.' So, in his unstable mind, he believes that he's been offended in some way. Have you noticed or heard of anyone showing signs of mental instability?"

"No," Chad said. "We've been over this so many times and just can't think of anyone like that."

"Well, since we're trying to follow up on the landscaping idea, can you think of any neighbor, friend, or family member who would have worked in that field or knows someone who did?" probed John.

"An unhappy coworker? Changes in anyone's behavior? Any past landscapers you may have forgotten? Sorry to throw so many questions at you, but something might trigger a new thought."

"Well, Chad had one coworker who was upset about his hours, but that turned out to be nothing," Jacki said.

John nodded. "Yeah, we have several people like that who were cleared in the beginning, but we're going to do new interviews."

"As far as past landscapers go, there was only the one," Chad said. "Before and after him, I did it. And I can't think of anyone else in that field."

"You asked about changes in behavior," Jacki whispered. "The only thing I've noticed from people is more love and kindness." She rested her hand over her heart. "And I don't know what we would have done without that support, especially from my sister."

"Yeah, Ashley seems great," agreed John. "We're actually going to talk to her next."

"Yeah, she mentioned that," Jacki said.

"So, as far as you know, none of what we're discussing today would apply to Ashley's life either?" John asked.

"No, I can't imagine what," Jacki said. "We've literally talked about everything. She's been working harder than anyone to help us think through every possibility."

"As a home stager, her job would put her in contact with landscapers," John proposed.

Jacki folded her hands in her lap. "That's true. When do you talk to her?"

"Five o'clock," John said. "If we can get a list of the landscapers she knows, we'll pay special attention to anyone who might have displayed any weird behavior."

Jacki tilted her head and took in a tiny, startled breath.

Clark had been watching her carefully and caught the spark in her eyes.

Why was that a trigger?

"Jacki is everything all right?" John asked.

She answered slowly. "Probably, but when you said, 'weird behavior,' it made me think of something." Then she waved her hand, dismissing the comment. "Oh, never mind, I'm sure it's nothing."

"No," John said. "Everything's important."

"Well, I probably shouldn't bring it up," she said. "But I guess you're going to talk to Ashley, anyway. It was a long time ago, but there was a weird guy who worked around some of the homes she was staging. We talked about it a couple of times, and I advised her to stay away from him."

"What?" John exclaimed.

"Yeah, but it was so trivial," reflected Jacki. "He almost immediately moved on, and I don't think she ever saw him again. I'm sure it's nothing. Ashley wasn't concerned at all."

"Well, maybe so, but I definitely want to ask her about it," John said. "We want to cover all bases."

Clark was getting good at reading John's energy by then and was pretty sure he was ready to rush out the door. But to his credit, he took a deep breath and spent a few extra minutes reassuring Chad and Jacki that Angela was still top priority.

"Because of Clark, we finally have something to go on, and we're not going to rest until we find her," he promised.

"Thank you, John," Chad said. "And you too, Clark."

"We're always here for you," John reminded. "If you come up with anything new, no matter how small, just give me a call."

"Thanks, we will," Chad said before turning to Clark. "I have to be honest with you, Clark, your doctor's theory is hard to believe. But we're desperate, and that means we're open to any kind of evidence. We were crushed by the loss of Drake, so even the slightest possibility that any of his thoughts might be channeled through you actually brings new hope."

"Well, I'm humbled to help in any way I can," Clark said. "And I do feel like Drake is guiding me. So, in essence, still on the case."

"What a wonderful thing to say," cried Jacki softly. "Please find our baby."

*

"Come on in, guys," Ashley said, opening the door to her condo. "Nice to see you again, Detective. And Clark, is it?"

"Yes, Clark Steele," he said. "Very nice to meet you. Actually, I hear our paths almost crossed recently."

"Really?" she asked. "How's that?"

"Well, I own Steele Construction, where apparently, you had a meeting with some of my associates."

"Oh, my goodness," she exclaimed. "I certainly did. Clark Steele. Yeah, I remember. You had to leave early that day. And now you're here. I'm absolutely confused, but I can't wait to hear what this is all about."

"It's good to see you again, Ashley," interjected John. "We won't take much of your time, but something interesting has come up in the case. It's related to Clark, and we'd like to talk to you about it."

"Absolutely!" she said. "I'm riveted already. And don't worry about the time. I'm actually finished for the day."

After John's warm introduction, Clark began to retell the same remarkable story he'd shared with her sister and brother-in-law. Unlike others who heard of the phenomenon for the first time, Ashley seemed more comfortable with it, even intrigued. She silenced her phone, placed it face down on the end table and listened as if spellbound from beginning to end.

"Astonishing," she said. "I've never heard of such a thing."

"Yeah, most people haven't," Clark said. "I can tell you, no one was more shocked than me. Trust me, it's real."

She nodded and sat back in silence.

"We've all been there, Ashley," John added. "And one by one, we've had to accept the phenomenon. The proof seems undeniable."

"So, a lot of the mental flashes and visions have been confirmed by actual evidence?" she asked.

"That's right," John said, "repeatedly."

She turned to Clark. "Wow, I can't even imagine how you're dealing with such a thing."

"It's completely taken over my life, that's for sure," he explained. "But the psychologist I mentioned, Dr. Brill, has been a godsend. Her instincts concerning the phenomenon were spot on, and she's been instrumental in my search for answers. Because of her, I think I'm finally getting more in touch with not only the phenomenon but related feelings."

"That's good," she said. "Wow, Dr. Brill's cases must be interesting. I'm kind of intrigued by anything mysterious or unexplainable. Stories like 'The Telltale Heart.' Stuff like that."

"Yeah, well, I wasn't so much in the past, but this situation has changed everything," admitted Clark. "The phenomenon is unnerving, but it can also irresistibly draw you in. And, you know, I've gotten to a place where I'm starting to see the whole thing as a miracle. Not only did Drake's heart save my life, but I also believe it transferred information and intelligence that was stored in every cell."

"But how do you cope?" she asked. "Never knowing what's coming next."

"Well, the way some of the flashes manifest is stressful," he began. "But in this case, the information is so important; the discomfort is a small price to pay."

"Wait," she said. "So, are you guys saying that the phenomenon has produced something new concerning our case?"

"Well, Ashley, it's not exactly a clue," clarified John. "But just yesterday, Clark had some new flashes, and he could sense Drake's intuition concerning a landscaping connection. It's an angle we hadn't considered before, so we're taking a new look at the case with that hunch in mind."

She shifted eye contact from one to the other. "Landscaping?"

"Yeah, well, at this point, we'd just like to ask who you might know in that field," explained John.

"Well, I've been around quite a few landscapers in my line of work," she said.

"Can you think of any that you might have had negative feelings around?" queried John.

Ashley sat back and folded her arms. "No, not off the top of my head. But I'd really have to think about it."

"It could be important," John explained. "As a matter of fact, if you'd be willing to make a list, that would really be helpful. And I don't mean to pressure you, but the sooner, the better. We feel like we might be on to something and don't want to waste any time."

She nodded. "Yeah, I totally understand. I'll do it right away."

"Oh, I wanted to ask you one more thing," John said.

The obvious setup put Clark on alert. *Here it comes. The question John has been waiting to ask.*

"One of the possibilities has always been that the kidnapper is mentally unstable," explained John. "And when I was talking with Jacki earlier, she remembered a weird guy that worked around you for a while. Do you know who she's talking about?"

"What?" Ashley exclaimed. "Oh, my gosh. She didn't. Wow, I had totally forgotten about that guy. Look, I'm sure that's nothing. He was just a day worker with Miracle Movers—the moving crew, not the landscapers. Anyway, we worked in the same community for maybe a couple of weeks while I was staging properties for the builder.

"His name was Winston, but he never really did anything. He was just one of those people who seemed to overstep social boundaries. You know, asking too many questions, overly eager, bringing me coffee. See, even now, I feel ridiculous saying that."

"No, it makes sense. That's how your instincts work," praised John. "But I see what you're saying. When was the last time you saw him?"

"Gosh, I'd have to look up the dates from the job, but it's been a long time," she said. "And I don't even remember seeing him on site for the last few days of the move-in."

"Do you remember the timing in relation to the abduction?" John asked gently.

"I think it had to be weeks before, maybe," she shrugged. "After the kidnapping, we couldn't think of anything else, of course. And I never thought of him again."

"Do you know his last name?" John asked.

"No, I don't remember, but maybe some of the crew might," she offered.

"Can you describe him?" probed John.

"Hmm ... about six feet tall, I guess, average size, kind of muscular, fair skin, and brown hair."

"What about his voice?" John said.

"Ugh, I didn't like it," she said. "There was something pathetic about it."

"Well, this could be a long shot, but we definitely want to talk to him," John said. "When you make your list, please include contacts from that particular job site, if you will."

Ashley nodded but seemed lost in thought.

"What is it?" John asked.

"Well, there's probably one other thing I should tell you," she confessed. "I'm sure it's nothing either, but you might as well know the whole story."

"Yes, any detail is worth hearing," John said.

"Well, another sort of weird thing happened at that same job site," she began. "Flowers and gifts were delivered to me with unsigned, personal notes. At that point, I just thought someone had the wrong party, so I asked around, but no one knew anything about it. Eventually, I just gave up trying to figure it out, and then all of a sudden, it stopped. And I haven't thought about it since."

"So, this admirer and the weird guy both disappeared at about the same time?" asked John.

"Yeah, I guess so. Pretty close," she said. "And I probably know what you're thinking. Could they be the same person? No, John, I'm sure that's just a coincidence. I was very busy at the time, and in the scheme of things, both situations seemed insignificant."

"Do you have any of the notes or gifts?" John asked.

"Oh, gosh no," she said, "I threw those away a long time ago. But I'll get you the contacts from the site as soon as possible."

"Thanks," John said. "Now, back to Winston for a minute. Do you remember talking about your family around him?"

"That was something I did find a little strange," she said. "He asked about my family. When I responded, I was purposely vague but might have mentioned having a sister in town. And now that I'm thinking about it, Jacki and Angela came by and picked me up for lunch once or twice, but I have no idea if he would have noticed.

"Oh, no . . . oh my God, John!" she cried. "I can't believe that never hit me. Are you thinking there's a connection, that he could have been involved?"

"Well, excuse my language, but you can damn sure bet we're going to find out," he announced.

Ashley wrung her hands. "John, I'm so sorry. I feel so stupid. Please let me know if there's anything else I can do."

"We will," he promised. "And Ashley, don't worry. Clark and I don't even know if we're on the right track yet. So, hang in there."

He jumped to his feet, and Clark followed suit.

"Thanks for everything, but we better get going," he said. "We've got to track this guy."

"John, I wish I could do something," fretted Ashley as she escorted them out.

"Just send the list, and please, don't worry," he said. "We'll be in touch."

By the time the door closed, John was talking fast but in a whisper. "Well, that's the first clear connection we've had to anyone. We should have Mary reschedule our last interview, so we can get on it."

"What do you need me to do?" Clark asked.

"Oh, sorry, Clark," John said. "I didn't mean to assume or get pushy. I guess the new hunch just has me a little fired up."

"No, it's fine," Clark said.

"Well, you've done more than you know already," praised John. "In a cold case, any new lead is a big deal. And we have you to thank for that. You know, we've been spending so much time together, I guess I'm starting to feel like you're actually my partner. Look, if my gut is right, I think things are about to get a little crazy, so if you're not feeling up to it, or just need a break from all of this, it's okay."

"No way!" insisted Clark. "I'm fine, and I'm in this to the end, whatever that means. You're not getting rid of me that easily."

"Well, okay then, let's do this!" John said. "So, according to Ashley, Winston's behavior was unusual. That's already suspicious, but if he was also the secret admirer, it becomes an even bigger red flag."

Clark nodded. "Yeah, for sure. Remember, the abductor did seem delusional about a connection to the Sweets."

"Right," John said. "And Dr. Brill was pretty sure there would be a disturbing history, maybe even from a young age. She also mentioned tendencies such as obsessive-compulsive disorder and antisocial behavior."

"Yeah, he's definitely worth checking out," Clark said. "Do experts have any idea how someone with those tendencies might behave in a situation like a kidnapping?"

"Just educated opinions," shrugged John. "Our best bet is to track the new lead as fast as we can and keep praying she's alive. Are you okay if we leave your car here and I'll bring you back later?"

Clark nodded. "Yeah, sure."

"Then we can head back to the office," proposed John. "We'll get the wheels turning by making some calls, and then, once Ashley's list gets there, we can really dig in. The moving company from the job site was Miracle Movers, so we can start with the supervisor on that project."

John tossed Clark the keys. "If you'll drive, I'll make some calls right now. I'll have Mary look up full contact information on Miracle Movers, so we'll be ready to roll when we get there."

"You got it," Clark said, catching the keys perfectly, even though the toss had been unexpected.

He hadn't gone far before pulling into a drive-thru for cold drinks when he heard Mary's voice on the speaker. Apparently, she was just about to leave for the day.

"You want anything?" he whispered to John.

John covered the phone. "Just a drink. We'll order some take-out when we get to the office. We're probably going to be there for a while."

Clark heard him pleading sweetly, "Mary, I know you're about to leave, but this is urgent."

"Where have I heard that before?" she teased.

"I know, I know," he said. "Sorry."

"No, it's okay," Mary said. "It's been a long day, but what's up?"

"Okay, I need you to find out as much detail as you can about the staff at Miracle Movers, especially the supervisor," he said. "Clark and I need to do some phone interviews as soon as we get there."

"Everything I can find will be on your desk before I leave," she promised. "Hey, the captain was looking for you and wondering if you had time to meet with him this evening."

"Yeah, sure," John said. "Just tell him I'm on my way in. Hey, thanks, Mary. See you tomorrow?"

"Yeah, see you then." She smiled and stared dreamily off into the distance.

When Clark and John finally reached the lot, John began to scan the area, and in a matter of seconds, his eyes became fixed on a shiny, black SUV heading east, about half a block away.

"Mary's car," he sighed.

Clark grinned. "Yeah, just missed her."

Once inside, they were met with an uncommon stillness. As John unlocked his office, he said, "Hmm . . . where is everyone? And what time is it?"

"Uh, I'm not sure, but it must be around six," Clark said. During a quick scan of the room, his eyes landed on the tattered old clock.

He gasped. "John, that clock. It was in one of my flashes."

"What clock?" John said.

"Right there on the wall." Clark pointed and closed his eyes. "Yeah, I remember feeling annoyed."

"Hmm. Weird," John said. "That clock used to aggravate the heck out of Drake."

"Another memory?" Clark mused. "I'm telling you, it's never-ending."

"I'll bet before long, the memories will blend right into your normal life," John said. "Probably seem very natural. Look how much better you're already doing."

"Yeah, but they still catch me off guard," Clark confessed.

"I know, but what a gift," John said. "If you really think about it, my friend, you're a walking miracle."

Now standing behind his desk, John picked up a neatly prepared folder from the uppermost tray of a mesh organizer. After tapping it on the desktop a couple of times, he said, "Looks like Mary came through again. Here we go."

"It's good to have something new to focus on," sighed Clark.

John nodded, then slid a couple of takeout menus across the desk. "If you see anything that looks good, just order two. While you do that, I'm going to step out here to find the captain and call that moving company. Be right back."

Clark had barely gotten the order placed before John was back at the doorway, whispering,

"Hey, Clark. The captain has a plan and thinks you might be able to help us out. How do you feel about that?"

"Yeah, whatever you need," he said.

"Come with me," waved John.

Clark followed him through the main office to the captain's door. At first, he thought no one was there because the lights were so low. But then he heard soft music. As they entered the room, he could see someone relaxing in an old standard-issue chair in a dark corner.

Once they were close enough to see, and before anyone could speak, Captain Riley put his finger to his lips and shushed them.

He waved them closer, inviting them to sit.

Strangely, Morgan Fox entered quietly from a separate door and pulled up a chair.

"Morgan is the first one I cleared because we need her specific skills," whispered Captain Riley. "She's been doing surveillance on the others, with a little help from a couple of agents who owe me favors. Some questionable issues have come up, so we're moving to the next phase of the plan. Remember when I mentioned a sting?"

John leaned in. "Yeah, of course."

"Well, it's a go," the captain said. "And we could use your help, Clark, if you're okay with it."

"Yeah, sure!" he said. "Whatever I can do."

"Good," Captain Riley said. "But first, there's a lot going on around here, as you probably know. And I have to tell you, some of the others are pushing a theory involving you. They're fighting hard to have you detained."

Clark flinched. "You mean arrested?"

"Not exactly," the captain said. "Different standards, but it doesn't matter. I'll be making the decision. And I'm going to be honest with you, I'm not sure where it's going to fall yet. So, with that in mind, do you still feel the same about helping us out?"

"I think so," Clark said, turning to John. "What do you think?"

"Captain, I can guarantee you, Clark had nothing to do with this," pledged John. "Who came to you this time?"

"Several others, but they came with evidence, John, and it wasn't without merit. So, I allowed it but reminded them, in no uncertain terms, to stay out of your way. I'd like to know if my orders are being followed, but I'll get to that later. Right now, we need to focus on this evidence thing."

"And you think Clark can help?" John asked.

"Yes," the captain said. "And maybe even prove his innocence in the process."

"He's already proved it to me," bristled John. "I just haven't had time to fill you in."

"John, it's okay," Clark said. "Captain, I'm in!"

Captain Riley took them through the timing and every minute detail of the secret mission. The setup made perfect sense to Clark, and he understood the role he would play in it. If everything went according to plan, they should know very soon if anyone took the bait.

The unlikely partners sealed the deal with high fives and headed back to their previous locations.

✳

"Miracle Movers. Arnie Swift. How can I help you?"

"Arnie, this is Detective John Baxter, and I need to ask you a few questions about an employee who worked with you months ago." John began.

"And who would that be?" Arnie asked.

"His name was Winston, and he worked with your crew at the Pleasant Springs Community project," John said. "What can you tell me about him?"

"Oh, yeah. Winston," Arnie began. "Well, we were short-handed, and he answered an ad. He said he'd worked with another mover a few counties over, but since we needed someone right away, we didn't really check it out. It all worked out okay, though. He insisted on being paid in cash daily, which I don't like to do, but I was desperate for help. So, am I in trouble for that?"

"We don't care about that," John said. "We just want to find him. What kind of a guy was he?"

"In my opinion, unusual, but a decent worker. He left early, though, with no notice. Didn't finish the last couple of days. That was a headache I didn't need."

"Yeah. So, would you know where to find him?" John asked.

"Nope, vanished without a word," Arnie said. "One of the other guys on the crew, Scott Sweeney, probably knew him a little better than the others. But when he disappeared, even Scott didn't know where he went."

"If you could give me Scott's number, I'd like to call him," John said. "And you have my number if you think of anything else."

"What kind of trouble is he in?" Arnie asked.

"Well, right now, we're just acting on a hunch, so I have to keep it close to the vest," John explained. "I'm sure you understand. Anyway, thanks for your time."

"Happy to help," Arnie said.

Just as John hung up, Clark announced, "Indian takeout for dinner."

"Sounds good," John said. "How long?"

"About forty minutes," Clark replied.

"Okay, good. The supervisor over at Miracle told me Winston demanded daily cash payment," explained John. "Good way to make sure no paper trail exists."

Clark nodded. "Yeah, a little suspicious."

"Well, while we're waiting, I'm going to call another guy, Scott Sweeney," John said. "Clark, I'm breaking rules here, but I trust you, and we have to move fast. Would you mind calling the next one on the list and asking some of the same questions? Just tell them that you're calling on my behalf, and if you want a little more privacy, you can use Mary's desk. And then, hopefully, dinner will be here, and we can compare notes."

"Sure," Clark said. He grabbed a fresh legal pad and made his way to the new workspace. Even from there, he could hear John's booming radio voice clearly, "Scott Sweeney?"

"Yeah, who's this?" came a spry, cordial voice over the speaker.

"Detective John Baxter and I'd like to ask you a few questions about a coworker from a few months back."

"Really?" Scott said, sounding surprised. "How can I help?"

"You were on a Miracle Movers project at the Pleasant Springs Community for a few weeks," began John. "And there was a guy there by the name of Winston, who was also working with the moving crew. What can you tell me about him?"

"Oh, Winston Stanley," Scott said. "I remember that guy. No one liked him much, so I talked to him, mostly because I felt a little sorry for him. He didn't even finish that job."

"Yeah, that's what I hear," John said. "What'd you guys talk about?"

"Hmm . . . I don't know. Job, weather. He brought up women once, but that seemed to be a touchy subject," Scott said. "He was a pretty uptight guy."

"Can you remember if he ever said anything about landscaping?" John asked.

"Uh . . . yeah, he did, actually, but only to me, I think," mused Scott. "As far as I know, he never said anything directly to the landscaping crew, but he liked to critique their work. One day, he told me they needed a sod leveler. I think I looked at him like he was crazy. Never heard of it. So, I asked if he'd done that kind of work before, and he just said he'd done a little bit of everything. Even though he was vague, he did seem to know what he was talking about. But with his demeanor, I didn't press."

Scott had just confirmed the first reference to the landscaping hunch. It was a small link, but it was a lifeline.

John had been writing furiously but stopped to take a long drink of soda. "Did he mention where he was from or where he was living?"

"Not to me, but one of the other guys said he mentioned something about doing a big painting project at that new mall just across the state line," Scott offered. "I think it's called Brook Gate Mall. He might live over there."

"Okay, thanks, that could be helpful," John said. "Did you ever notice the kind of car he drove?"

"Hmm . . . well, I saw a guy drop him off in a silver Accord a couple of times," he began. "And one time, he showed up in an ugly old gray van with Utah tags and parked it way out of the way. I only know the tag details because I had to head down that way on my break and passed right by it."

"Do you remember any numbers from the tag?" probed John.

"Oh, geez. I might have back then, but not now," Scott said. "Guess I've forgotten. Sorry."

John wrote down Serena's name next to Scott's on his notepad.

"Anything else you can think of before I go?" he asked. "Did Winston mention family?"

"No, I don't remember anything like that," Scott said.

"Well, if you do, please give me a call," John directed.

"Of course," Scott promised.

"Thanks," John said. "I might be back in touch."

As he disconnected, he made eye contact with Clark, who was holding up two takeout bags. "Supper's on," he announced.

John waved him in. "I'm starving. How'd your call go?"

"He couldn't really offer much," Clark explained. "Basically, he didn't like the guy and made a point of avoiding him."

John nodded. "Well, my guy gave me a little more to go on. We just hit on a landscaping connection. Let's get a plate, and I'll fill you in."

TWENTY

SHOW TIME

"Man, I didn't get enough sleep last night," Clark said the next morning. "Only a couple of hours. I kept thinking about what Scott said."

John nodded. "Yeah, me too. Well, sleep or no sleep, we're on."

"Guts and caffeine," Clark said, raising his mug.

John grinned and led their exit from the break room.

"Wow, it's so noisy," Clark said. "What's going on again?"

"Oh, everyone's here for mandatory sensitivity training, and meetings around here come with a lot of grumbling," explained John.

He shot a couple of quick glances Mary's way, but she was on the phone and didn't even look up. Reading John's downcast expression, Clark said, "I'll bet she's just deep in those calls from Ashley's list."

John smiled. "Yeah, you're right."

"So, what do we do first?" Clark asked.

"Would you call the Brook Gate Mall and get in touch with the supervisor from that painting project?" John asked. "It should have been booked just before their grand opening."

"Sure," Clark said. "Got a number for that one?"

"Oh, sorry," John said, handing him a copy of the contact list. "Hey, I'm going to see if I can locate some early traffic footage. We didn't have anything specific to go on back then, but with an old van and Utah tags, I want to revisit it. You good?"

"Yeah, man," Clark said, waving him off and taking a seat just outside the office.

When John passed Paul Brady's desk on the way out, Clark heard Paul say, "Hey, how's the case going?"

John kept moving but looked over his shoulder. "Well, we're on a fresh track. And it looks like the captain may have some new evidence for us that could help."

"Awesome, maybe it's your big break," Paul called after him.

"Man, I hope so! See you at the meeting," he said, just before disappearing around the doorway.

Only minutes later, John was watching traffic footage from the night of the abduction. The video evidence that was originally unavailable due to mishandling or tampering had mysteriously reappeared recently in the actual case file box. And it was up to him to determine whether it was just a weird coincidence or the result of nefarious activity.

The entire viewing process was a crucial step, but extremely tedious. Detectives dealt with it because it lowered the risk of a target or something unexpected falling through the cracks.

John was slowly shuffling through footage in search of the van in question when he found a potential match. As he zoomed in on the clip, a hazy Alabama tag and plate number came into focus. The vehicle was much newer than the one they were looking for, but he still made note of it and went back to the seemingly endless task.

After a while, he'd been reviewing from the same position for so long that he almost fell asleep. His eyes were half-closed when not one but two vans suddenly appeared near the end of a new section of footage. Startled from his near slumber, he shook himself fully awake and leaned in closer.

The two vehicles stayed close together and then quickly merged onto the interstate at precisely the same ramp. The unlikely scenario had him almost hypnotized when the video abruptly clipped off.

"Argh, not now," he grumbled.

Besides dealing with the frustration of a very untimely interruption, he now had to initiate a search for the next video in the sequence. And locating footage from another camera location generally took a little luck.

If the box was organized and the videos labeled properly, it shouldn't take too long. But with projects such as that, there was always the possibility of camera malfunction, weather obstruction, vandals, or dozens of other problems. Detectives just kept their fingers crossed that the clip they needed wouldn't fall into any of those categories.

The next scene covered a section of the highway about five miles down from the last. Although anything could have happened during a blackout of that many miles, at least the traffic flow was light, making for stress-free viewing. John watched as several eighteen-wheelers and a modest number of family sedans went by, but no van.

Those who had been to the video rodeo enough times knew to prepare for a dead end but still longed for a spark, any spark that meant they were on the right track. One lead could give a case new life.

John was still fighting to stay awake but surrendered to a long yawn and nearly missed it. Just coming into view on the screen was the older looking of the two vans.

He jumped from his chair and congratulated himself with a fist of solidarity. After pausing the playback and zooming, the tag was displayed more prominently. The first letter at the top appeared to be a "U." If correct, there was only one state that started with that letter.

There also appeared to be an "R," and maybe the numbers four and five at the beginning of the tag number, but the details were distorted. The icon in the middle resembled a mountain, but he would need to compare it with Utah tag images to be sure.

The first digit on the right side of the plate might have been a "one" or a "seven," but that was also in doubt. The entire image suggested that the camera lens had been scratched or obscured in some way.

John watched for a bit longer, but when the second van failed to appear, he began to wrap things up. Even though there was still a lot of viewing time left, it was more important to start the tracking process on the existing plate.

So, after capturing the image, he left everything just as it was with a note containing instructions forbidding anyone to touch anything without contacting him first.

✳

Clark had been shuffled from person to person by the Brook Gate Mall receptionist, apparently in an attempt to locate someone with the authority to disturb the manager. He was beginning to think John should have made the call. When John identified himself as a detective in his authoritative voice, people sat up and took notice.

After one last hold, Clark was finally connected and provided with contact information for the crew chief.

"Leo Martin, Prestige Painting, how can I help you?"

"Hey, Leo, I'm Clark Steele, assistant to Detective John Baxter, and I'd like to ask you a few questions about a painting project from a while back."

"What's this about?" Leo asked.

"We're looking for information on a guy named Winston who worked on that project," Clark said.

"Oh, you mean Stan Winston?" he asked.

Clark hesitated. "We're actually looking for a guy who went by Winston Stanley. But the names are obviously similar. So, your Stan could be our Winston, playing loose with his name. What can you tell me about him? Do you know where he was from?"

Why does questioning feel so natural?

"I don't really know much firsthand, but I did hear some of the crew talking," Leo began. "The guy seemed like a loner and apparently didn't have a great relationship with his family. Word was that he went back and forth quite a bit, so that's why he looked for flexible work. The story was that his parents retired, moved away, and left him their property in Utah."

The Utah connection hit Clark like a ton of bricks. First, the van with Utah plates, and now this home state link. *Is it possible we're on the right track?*

Leo's response to his request for a quick physical description was familiar, a very close match to the others. Everything was pointing them in Winston's direction, and nothing was eliminating him. He couldn't wait to get off the phone and share the news with John.

"Thanks, Leo," he said. "You've been a big help. We might need to call again."

"Yeah, no problem," Leo replied. "Good luck."

When Clark caught sight of John entering the main office, he hung up quickly and hustled in his direction. It was time to deliver an important message. In the center of the main room, he announced, "John, the captain had to head out."

"What?" John said. "Did he mention the evidence?"

"He left a folder in the top right drawer," Clark said, playing his part perfectly. "He said it could be big. The keys are on top of his desk. We just need to lock it when we leave and give Mary the keys."

"Okay, let's finish this Utah thing, and we'll check it out."

There were discerning glances and curious shrugs from Ken and the others, but no one said a word. Although they appeared to be minding their own business, Clark suspected he wasn't the only one acting.

"Queenie, what time does that meeting start again?" Morgan asked, breaking the awkward silence.

"About an hour, I think. "It's sensitivity training . . . again," she joked. "And I'm starting to feel a little insensitive! So, they better get on with it."

"Morgan laughed. "Hey, I've got some stuff to do. Will you text me if they happen to start early?"

"Yeah, girl," Queenie said. "I got you."

"Thanks," smiled Morgan. "See you in a bit."

Within minutes, she had covertly entered the captain's office by way of a secondary door and flexibly twisted her small frame into the only closet in the room. The outer office was still buzzing, but the soft music playing close by was masking most of the ambient noise. She silenced her phone and settled in for what could be a lengthy surveillance.

In a secure location, Captain Riley sat watching a video feed from the hidden cameras he had recently installed in the speakers. With the announcement of valuable new evidence in the case, the trap was set.

"John, do you really think someone will bite?" Clark whispered.

"I don't know. Let's hope so. Right now, we just wait for any alert from the captain," he advised.

"He's watching on a monitor, right?" Clark asked.

"Yep," John said. "If he sees any sign of movement, we'll know immediately."

Clark shared the latest information from Prestige Painting, and although John hadn't verified it yet, he countered with details on the Utah plate description.

"We should know something soon because I placed top priority on running the incomplete tag number," he explained.

"Is it just me, or is the hunch looking a little more credible?" Clark asked.

"No, you're right," John nodded. "Hey, there was some kind of image on the plate that looked sort of like a mountain. Let's look up the Utah plate designs and see what we find."

"Okay, maybe it'll take my mind off . . . well, you know," Clark said, glancing toward the outer office.

There were several options on the tags, and one was a great match for John's image. But contrary to their best guess, it wasn't a mountain at all. It was a natural arch, officially called Delicate Arch, located in Arches National Park near Moab, in Grand County, Utah.

Clark smiled. "Well, now that I've seen it, I know why it looked like a mountain in that blurry image. The shape is similar, and we couldn't see the cutout in the center."

"Yeah, you're right," John said. "And it's definitely a Utah tag. Let's pray they match up those numbers."

The words were barely out of his mouth when the analyst, nicknamed Codeman, called with a quick update. "John, I haven't matched anything yet, but the "R," as the first letter, doesn't work with the other numbers."

"I was afraid of that," John said. "Well, we just confirmed the image as Delicate Arch in Grand County, Utah."

"That might help," Codeman said. "I'm going to try some other combos."

"Okay, call me back as soon as you have something," instructed John. He turned to Clark. "Okay, where were we?"

"While you were watching the traffic footage, I was going over everything that points to this Winston guy," explained Clark.

"Well, now we can add the two Utah connections—the tags on the van and Winston's own words," John added.

"Yeah," Clark said. "We have at least one mention of his land-scaping knowledge, and the timing is suspicious too. It looks like he dropped out of sight right around the time of the abduction. I know it's all circumstantial and non-conclusive, but it must carry weight when there's a lot of it."

"That's how it works," John confirmed.

Secretly tucked away in another room, Captain Riley continued his e-stakeout in front of a sizable monitor. Things had been un-eventful to that point, but it wasn't long before a hooded figure came skulking into the frame on the right side of the main screen.

Morgan's phone was silenced when the captain's alert went out, but John's issued a low, grating sound. He fumbled to shut it off as he and Clark raced for the door.

In the captain's office, Morgan was poised to pounce, but she stealthily waited until the subject was caught red-handed with the fake evidence folder. Then, moving in relative silence, she opened the closet and stepped out behind the offender.

After an apparent scan for weapons and repositioning to strike, she piercingly ordered, "Drop it!"

The hooded figure froze with stolen evidence in hand and began a slow, cagey turn toward her. Then, in a sudden flash, the folder full of loose paper was thrown, like confetti, into Morgan's face.

As if her mind had converted the spray into a solid object, she blocked the bouquet of papers in a sweeping motion with her left hand and brought her right down in a knife strike to the neck.

The blow drove the intruder's upper body into the desk and slammed their knees into what had to be excruciating contact with the floor. With the offender stunned and writhing in pain, Morgan moved in and swiftly placed the cuffs. After turning them over, she leveled a look of disgust at one of her respected coworkers.

John, Clark, and Captain Riley reached separate entry doors just in time to witness the high point of the short melee. The rest of the staff, who were on their feet by then, were waved off by John while Clark blocked the entrance.

But the situation had been neutralized, and Morgan had everything under control. The captain had chosen her for her specific abilities and panther-like skills, and she did not disappoint.

"Great work, Morgan!" he said.

"Thank you, sir," she replied.

"You!" John thundered, glaring at the perpetrator.

"Get him up off the floor," barked the captain. "What the hell is wrong with you?"

"It's not what it looks like," gasped the offender as he fell into the chair, clutching his ribs.

"Oh, really," mocked John. "You're going with that? I think it's exactly what it looks like. Stealing evidence. And you, of all people. Who do you think you are messing with my case?"

"Well, someone had to do it," Eddie shot back. "I'm sorry, but I can't believe you bought that guy's bullshit story."

Clark flinched. The comment stung a little.

"Are you possessed?" demanded John. His voice was resonating with anger. "Clark is legit! He knows things he couldn't possibly know."

"Well, I think he could be involved in the abduction," returned Eddie with almost smug conviction. "There is a lot of circumstantial evidence, John. He even fits the description."

Clark started to speak, but John beat him to it.

"News flash, it's not your case!" he shouted, standing over Eddie.

Clark could feel the pervading tension but, for some reason, wasn't that bothered by it. In fact, he felt the urge to step in. But the intense expression on John's face caused him to respectfully stay out of it.

"Why, Eddie?" demanded the captain. "I warned you to stay out of the way."

"I know, but—" Eddie said.

"But nothing!" shouted Captain Riley. "Who else is involved?"

"No one. Just me," he offered.

"We'll see about that," the captain said. "How long have you been tampering with the case?"

Eddie sat silently.

"Why screw up your career now?" pressed Captain Riley. "And right after a promotion!"

"I wasn't trying to screw it up," Eddie said. "I was trying to help my career. All I did was borrow a little evidence. The case looked like it was off the rails to me, so I thought if I proved another theory, I might get a little respect around here."

"There is a little girl's life at stake, and you're worried about respect," roared John. His already intimidating voice cast a rare, unpredictable quality. "I've got to get back to my case, but I am not finished with you yet."

John's statement would have been the perfect cue for Clark to remove himself from the scene and find a less heated environment, but he still couldn't pull himself away.

"We've been doing surveillance on you, Eddie. You've got more explaining to do," the captain said. "You've been at this way longer than you're admitting. Let's show John what you've been up to."

John looked almost as surprised as Eddie.

"Word on the street is you've been taking payoffs," continued the captain. "And we have the video evidence from some of your package exchanges, so you might as well come clean."

"I don't know what you're talking about," he protested.

Clark studied him. *Buying time.*

"The hell you don't," challenged the captain, booting up the computer. "We can take a look at the footage right now."

"You must be mistaking me for someone else," Eddie said.

"Well, who does that look like to you?" the captain asked, pointing to the video, paused on an unmistakable image.

"Captain, that's not me," he said.

Clark shook his head along with John and Captain Riley, who were clearly not buying a word of it. They looked at the footage again and then shot daggers at Eddie.

After the long stare down, Eddie finally took a deep breath and shook his head. "Never mind, just shut it off. Okay, fine. I screwed up!"

"You think?" the captain asked. "Start talking. And you can start with the bank account in California."

"I'm probably going to move there one day," he blurted while rubbing his right knee. "Not that it's anyone's business."

"Oh, it's our business now," Captain Riley said.

Eddie sat stubbornly, not offering another word.

"So, you want to continue, or would you like me to do it?" the captain asked.

"I just wanted out of here," Eddie finally admitted. "That's why I've been living small and taking every dollar."

"John, close the door," the captain said. "You need to see something. He's been on the take and sending cash to a friend in California."

"Nice," John said, his voice dripping with sarcasm.

"He's been looking the other way instead of bringing drug charges," the captain said. "He's in deep."

"Interfering with witnesses, tampering with evidence, taking payoffs . . . what haven't you done?" John seethed.

He yanked a moaning Eddie up by the lapels. "You don't know how hard it is not to blast you right now. The crap you pulled could have derailed this whole case. And your big theory is to reject a phenomenon you know nothing about and go after an innocent man." John shoved him hard back into the chair.

"John, knock it off," Captain Riley ordered. "Let me show you something. When we saw this bank footage from California, our mouths literally fell open. After making a withdrawal, Eddie's friend strolled out of the bank and graced us with a look right into the camera."

Captain Riley froze the footage.

"Oh my God. Are you kidding me?" John said, taking a closer look. "Sherry Griffin?"

"Yep, Sherry Lynn Griffin, to be exact," explained the captain. "She disappeared after dating Eddie and Drake. Hadn't been seen by anyone until she secretly showed up at Drake's funeral. It seems Eddie was the only one to notice, and the discreet reunion led to dinner afterward, followed by a plan. The faster Eddie could make money, the faster their new life could begin."

"What the hell, Eddie," John said, finally taking a seat. "What is wrong with you?"

Eddie dropped his head and clasped his hands. "The whole thing just got out of hand," he said. "During the entire time she was with Drake, I tried to handle it, but I'm not going to lie. I still had feelings for her."

He looked up again. "And, of course, Drake was the main topic of conversation over dinner. It was a natural thing, and she couldn't help reminiscing about their time together. But after she spoke so highly of him, how could I compete? So, I exaggerated my new position and told her I was involved in one of Drake's big cases. That's what started the whole charade, and before I knew it, I was in over my head. But I had her respect and didn't want to lose it."

"Wow, that's pathetic," John said. "If I didn't want to blast you, I'd feel sorry for you." He turned in a huff and made his way toward the door. "Boss, I'm not done here. I've got to get back to the case. He's not going anywhere, is he?"

"No way!" Captain Riley said. "Go ahead, take off."

That final exchange was an undeniable cue that caused Clark to back away and head to John's office.

John faced Eddie one last time and warned him, "You better hope your actions don't prevent us from finding that little girl. Or all of this is going to be the least of your worries."

✳

The ringing of his phone caused him to take a deep breath before backing out of the interrogation room. Even through the walls, Clark was pretty sure he heard him say, "Leo."

Once John was back in the office, Clark asked, "Leo with Prestige?"

"Yeah, he was just saying that Winston's property is in a remote location," John said. "Good to know."

"If he's the guy we're looking for, that could explain how he's gotten away with this," Clark offered. "Easy to disappear in a place like that."

"Yeah, but we have some highly skilled people in the game," John stated confidently. "Hopefully, you'll get a chance to see an entire team come together and execute a pre-planned mission. It's pretty remarkable if I do say so myself."

"I'm going to head back down to the viewing room," he said.

"Hey, I know we need to talk some more about Eddie, but we have to work these new leads right now. So, if you wouldn't mind checking with Mary to see what's left on the list, that'd be great."

"Yeah, sure," Clark said, following him out. But before they'd even reached Mary's desk, John's phone went off.

"Baxter," he answered.

"We've got a hit!" Codeman said. "John, the first letter wasn't an 'R,' it was a 'K.' When we combined it with numbers four and five, we came up with a few possibilities. The Delicate Arch helped narrow things down, and the first number on the right side of the plate was a seven. When we got everything entered, there was only one possibility. Your Utah plate number is K45 7RF."

"Great work!" John praised. "Who's it registered to?"

"Winston Chambers II," announced Codeman. "Your text should be dinging any second with the address. We're going to keep running a complete search on Mr. Chambers and should have more details for you shortly."

"Awesome work!" John said. "Thanks, man.

"You bet. Later," he replied.

John turned to Clark. "I've been doing this a long time, and I can be wrong every once in a while, but you usually get a gut feeling when you're on the right track. And I am feeling it right now. Codeman figured out the plate number, and guess who owns the vehicle?"

"Not Winston," Clark said.

"It's registered to a Winston Chambers II. It's a little different, but is it just a coincidence that the name, Winston, is on that registration?" John asked. "I don't think so. And if it is him, he's probably been using aliases all over the place. While Codeman is working on the details, we need to get a team ready to move and we need to do it now.

"It's show time!"

TWENTY-ONE

WAR ROOM

The briefing John gave Mary was short and sweet, but she'd been around the block a few times, and it was all she needed. Without delay, she assumed the role of supervisor, kicking off administrative operations.

Her personal workspace was quickly transformed into the hub, from where she would oversee others. By placing calls, while rearranging the area, no time was wasted, and a competent support team was quickly assembled. Her prompt actions were proof that she understood procedure and the urgency at hand.

"Hey, Mary," John said. "Here's the address. We're going to need immediate flights to Utah and connections to the local guys with vehicles and weapons ready to go. And fully charged phones, backups, maps—you know the routine."

"I've got it, John," she promised. "No worries."

The captain's door flew open. "What's going on?"

"We got a hit, sir," announced John. "We're going to Utah."

"Who's going to Utah?" demanded the captain.

"Me and Clark. Right away," John replied.

"Not so fast. In my office!" Captain Riley ordered.

After listening to John's update, Captain Riley said, "Look, you can go, but Clark stays here for questioning. It's time for me to make a call on this."

"Captain, he's telling the truth," John countered. "He's innocent. There's more to tell you, but there's no time. We have to go, or we're going to lose this lead."

Captain Riley shook his head. "You can handle it on your own. Now that Clark knows he's under suspicion, we can't risk losing him out of state."

"Sir, this whole case has new life because of Clark. We need him," argued John. "I'm telling you; he knows things. His voice even sounded like Drake's the other day."

Captain Riley rolled his eyes. "John, c'mon! Don't make me worry about you too."

"Captain, just trust me this one last time," he begged. I'll explain it all to you later. This is our only chance, and we have to move now!"

They stared hard at each other without saying a word as the precious seconds ticked by.

Finally, John slammed both hands down on the desk. "Captain?"

Captain Riley stood, pointed his finger, and started to speak.

But John cut him off. "Captain, I've got this, I swear! If I'm wrong about it, I'll bring Clark in myself!"

Without lowering the intensity, or his finger, the captain commanded, "Don't make me regret this! Go on. Get out of here."

✳

John made his way straight to Clark, who was pacing, just outside the office.

"Was that about me?" Clark asked.

"Yeah, but we're good. Let's not worry about that right now," whispered John. "I want to get back to the logistics of the mission.

The captain's threat—I mean order—was the permission we needed to start coordinating with the FBI on the location of the property and the safest rescue strategy.

"A secluded site can be a little tricky and adds to the level of difficulty. But the good news is, it also provides excellent cover for the team. Depending on the degree of seclusion, and on the outside chance we might need it, we should probably put in a request for helicopter or drone surveillance."

Clark perked up. "Yeah, makes sense," he agreed, following John into the office.

"You can probably tell that things are starting to get a little crazy," John said. "And maybe I've asked too much of you already, but you and Drake's memories could be a real asset in Utah."

"I want to go!" Clark said.

John grinned. "Okay, good. Right now, Mary's getting contact info for the local authorities, who can recommend detectives, resources, and also special agents in the area."

"So, the war room will be on their turf," stated Clark.

John gave him a quick side-eye.

"Listen to you!" he said, shaking his head. "Yeah, we're going to need an immediate briefing with local guys, FBI, and others, who can have a meeting place ready for the minute we land."

After checking an alert on his phone, he added, "Looks like we're on the next flight to Salt Lake. If you're sure you're up for this."

"Yes!" Clark said, releasing a deep sigh. "You want me to grab a bag and meet you at the airport?"

"No time, you better stay here," advised John. "There's so much going on, I don't want to get separated. If we have to jump and run, bag, or no bag, we'll figure it out."

"Okay," Clark said. "Maybe Rachel could drop a bag at the airport."

"That might work!" John said. "I'll have Mary email the flight info."

His phone interrupted the planning. "Baxter."

"You sitting down?" came Codeman's voice over the speaker.

"Not a chance," John countered. "But let me have it."

"Okay, turns out there's more than one Winston Chambers," he began. "The van is registered to a Winston Chambers II, who is now residing in Hawaii."

"What?" John said, pulling up the closest seat.

"He has a son, Winston Chambers III," added Codeman. "His age and description fit your guy. I'm sending photos your way.

"And the preliminary digging shows that he did have psychological issues. Didn't really get along with people and was kind of an outcast. Apparently, he lied to his parents constantly and lived in a fantasy world. By the time the parents became aware of more serious problems, he was of age and limiting his contact with them."

"Man, we need to talk to those parents, but not right now!" John said. "Too great a risk they could alert him. But their help could be invaluable at the right moment."

"I'll send everything over, so you'll have it when the time is right," promised Codeman.

"Thanks," John said. "That profile fits."

"Sure does," agreed Codeman. "We'll keep working on this end, and you guys be careful out there."

"You got it," John said. "Thanks, man."

Both Clark's phone and John's had been pinging throughout the conversation, and every subject line specified details of the operation, including flight info.

"Hey, I'm going to go call Rachel for a second and confirm all this," Clark said.

John nodded. "Okay, just meet me back here."

After gathering a few essentials, John turned to retrieve a pre-packed bag he kept at the ready. The useful practice had come in handy more times than he could count. By the time he was locking up the lower cabinet that had been safeguarding the duffle bag, Clark was back.

"Ready," announced Clark.

John looked up. "Yep, me too. Let's do this."

They passed right by Mary's reimagined workspace on their way out. "Thanks, everyone," John said. "We appreciate your help.

"Mary, I have both of my phones," he added, "so let's stay connected."

"Absolutely," she agreed. "I sure hope you guys find her, John. And be safe! You know, I'll be praying for her and the team!"

"I know," he nodded. "We're going to do what we do, but we'll take all the prayers we can get. Better run if we're going to make the airport."

When they deboarded the turbulent flight, John was grinning. "Did you hear those sighs of relief?" he asked.

"I think everyone is thankful to be on the ground," Clark said.

"Yeah, me too," John agreed. "Our instructions are to head toward baggage claim, even though we're all self-contained. Our contact person and a few others should be there waiting."

As they approached, Clark could see a slightly disheveled surfer holding a sign that read *Harrison*. He turned to John, who confirmed the identity with a nod.

"Some undercover guys take casual to a whole new level," John teased. "Our arrangement is for him to greet us and give us a secret operation name. It's a safeguard to protect those involved and put everyone at ease."

"John Baxter, I'm Scooby," the undercover cop said faintly when they got within earshot. "I believe 'Subtle Frequency' is our magic phrase. And I have to ask, what in the world does that mean?"

"We'll explain it to everyone at the same time," John said. "It's quite the story!"

Scooby introduced the others as they all headed out and piled into an awaiting van.

"It's only a ten-minute drive to our meeting place, and everyone should be there working already," he explained.

"Great," John said. "How in the world did you get the name Scooby?"

"Well, I love scuba diving," he said. "So, as soon as the guys heard that, it was Scuba, Scoobs, and finally, Scooby."

"Well, Scooby, we don't know what we're getting into here. You got an oxygen tank handy?" teased John.

For the rest of the drive, the vehicle was animated with conversation as the team got to know each other. And in no time, they were pulling into the parking lot of a massive, new office complex that almost looked abandoned without lights or other vehicles in the lot.

They drove around back, where one of the office spaces finally stood out, even though the blinds were closed. Random light peeked out around the perimeter of the windows and through barely open slats on the blinds.

Throwing the van into park, Scooby announced, "This is the place. The captain knows the owner of the complex, and he lets us use the space for meetings when we have a big team. It's perfect because no one else is here after six."

Wasting no time, John and Clark grabbed their gear, walked on ahead, and waited by the entry door. When the others caught up,

Scooby stepped to the intercom and let the awaiting team know they had arrived. The sound of the buzzer immediately welcomed them inside. After clearing the lobby and turning left, they followed Scooby to a conference room just down the hall.

As Clark and John entered the elegant meeting room, the smell of fresh pizza was deliciously overpowering. An impressive cherry-wood conference table with leather-bound chairs took up the entire center of the space. Computers, notebooks, and other paraphernalia were scattered about, a clear indication that work had already begun.

John continued to look the place over and rested on a new focal point for a moment. At the front of the room stood a matching podium along with a massive dry-erase board, creating a backdrop on the wall behind it.

His attention quickly shifted to the agents, who were busy at work and seemingly unaware of the fine accommodation. Rather, they appeared to be blocking everything out and concentrating solely on the case.

"Hey guys," announced Scooby. "Meet the original team."

The first agent to step forward introduced himself in a perfect baritone. "Special Agent, Dan Jordan, FBI." With Hollywood good looks and strong frame, he was the epitome of a classic-looking hero and might as well have been chiseled from granite.

"John Baxter," John replied. "Good to meet you. This is my team: Clark Steele and detectives Rory Smith and Duke Lawson."

"Hey guys," Dan said. "Nice to meet you. These are two of my best."

Flanking him on one side was a lovely, seemingly eager agent in her late thirties, and on the other, a stocky sidekick that Clark assessed as a Bureau veteran.

"Jaye Ryker," said the female agent. "Nice to meet you guys."

"Ted Graham," followed the other. "Good to be working with you."

Out of nowhere, the slamming of a door caused everyone to jump. "Oh, sorry, wind must have caught it!" a stately, serious-looking man said. "I'm Captain Williams. And on the local side, these are three of our detectives, hand-selected by me: Miles Watson, Tom Ratcliff, and I think everyone already knows Scooby."

"Hey guys, we have pizza, lasagna, drinks, and it looks like even some salad and dessert," Agent Jordan announced. "In order to save time, let's all get to know each other and start the briefing while we eat. John, why don't you go on to the head of the line since you'll be talking first?"

He swept his arms toward the buffet. "And just so everyone knows, this spread is not the norm around here. The captain's buddy ordered catering for a meeting earlier in the day and remembered that we'd be here tonight. He was kind enough to ask the caterer to cover us as well, so we can all thank Tom."

"Thanks, Tom," they all said in clumsy unison.

John made his way to one end of the food table to start the line. But in very short order, the line had transformed into a jumble of hungry agents swarming the food.

The entire team was busy eating and getting acquainted when Agent Jordan leaned over to John. "John, I'm not rushing you at all, but whenever you're ready, you can make your way up front and get things started. We're all anxious to hear from you. Oh, and I wanted to let you know that we have transportation set up for Dr. Brill. She'll be with us in the morning."

"Thanks, good to know," John said. "I knew she'd come through."

Agent Jordan nodded. "Looks like we pulled a good team together."

"Yeah, and now we're about to find out if we're on the right track," John said. He pushed his plate forward, stood up, and made his way to the podium.

His mighty voice quieted the noisy room within seconds. After properly introducing himself and thanking everyone for jumping on board so quickly, he painstakingly covered the details of the case and the suspect, including Dr. Brill's psychological profile. He had debated over an interactive briefing format, but it proved to be the right call, allowing for input and questions throughout.

The participation of the new team members revealed a respectable grasp of the case, suggesting they had taken the time to do their homework before the out-of-towners arrived. And that kind of dedication usually positioned a team way ahead of the game.

When John got to the part about Clark's involvement, the room got extremely quiet.

"I know, I know," he said. It's highly unusual for non-law enforcement to be included in a mission, but hear me out."

Many questioning glances were exchanged as he shared the story of Drake's accident and Clark's phenomenon. No doubt, skepticism filled the room, but to the agents' credit, they maintained a quiet and respectful tone.

Eventually, however, a perfect opening presented itself, and a barrage of questions concerning the phenomenon broke the silence. At that point, John reintroduced Clark and handed the meeting off to his honorary partner.

The magic of Clark's persuasive countenance and personality was a marvel to behold. He dealt with their legitimate concerns like a pro, dispelling most of their doubts, just as he had with others. Clark Steele came across as authentic and credible to a room full of experts trained to spot the contrary.

Some members of the team were sitting back in their chairs, listening intently, while others leaned in as if being closer to the information would help them understand it better. As Clark added detail to the unbelievable journey he'd been on, a measure of respect seemed to be mounting.

The ability to analyze the situation through a law enforcement lens surely offered a unique perspective. Since most people would have wanted nothing to do with a potentially dangerous mission, the team could probably appreciate a willing layman. Especially one who had devoted himself to hours upon hours of doctors, hypnotherapy, and investigative work to help with a random case.

Clark went on to explain how the mental flashes, characteristics, instincts, and maybe even courage he had received from Drake were now part of him. And he assured the room, he felt compelled to do whatever he could, no matter the danger.

The group seemed to perk up even more when he got to the part about Dr. Brill and what she had to say about the phenomenon. Even with the time constraints of the moment, Clark managed to disclose enough history to give the seasoned pros plenty to think about.

"As I've learned from Dr. Brill, there are lots of documented cases, and one is more mind-blowing than the next," he said. "Wish I had time to share some of them with you. But you can find articles and books if you want to read more about it. For now, I'll do my best to explain my understanding.

"Organs are made up of cells, and it's believed that those cells store all kinds of life information, such as intelligence, memories, and preferences. So, by way of the transplant, those foreign living cells and all their information are placed inside the recipient's body.

"As the donor cells begin to communicate with the recipient cells, on some subtle frequency, if you will, information that was previously housed in the donor's body may now reside in the recipient's," he added. "And in this case, that would be me."

"Crazy," blurted Scooby.

"I know, man," Clark nodded. "I thought the same thing. But all the episodes and assessments I've been through have changed my mind. Not only do I believe in the phenomenon, but I believe in my own case. There's so much more to tell you, but for time's sake, I better hand things back to John."

"I have to admit, guys, I'd never heard of the phenomenon before either," John said. "But there's no other way to explain some of what Clark knows. Several of his mental flashes included important case details that hadn't been released. So, he was able to confirm facts we already knew to be true. Plus, the hunch from his epiphany at the cabin is what led us here.

"And this might sound crazy, but I actually think some detective instincts might have made their way to Clark," grinned John. "That's why he's here. He's been essential. The break we've been waiting for.

"That being said, he's aware of the danger and knows he's free to walk away at any time. But I think I know him well enough, by now, to know he's not going anywhere," he added, glancing at Clark.

With that, he invited Special Agent Jordan to the front to review personnel and mission preparation. Dan spent the first part of the brief covering what they had learned while researching the addresses and names of residents, past and present. The property was, in fact, located in a very remote area surrounded by a dense forest of trees, and they had already deployed a drone for a flyover.

As video and still images began to pop up on screens, Agent Jordan used them to explain how the team could best get their bearings. The house was defended by trees on all sides and sat in a clearing. The only break in the natural wall was a nearly hidden gate at the southern entrance to a long driveway.

To prepare for security cameras and maybe a remote entry

system, the captain promised to add his best tech to the surveillance van. Every detail was critical to the safety of the team, including those who would approach from other directions or use tree cover for their surveillance locations.

A considerable amount of time was spent determining optimal offensive positions for team members who would physically occupy the property. Their positions would be set far enough back to avoid notice but forward enough to be effective when the critical time came.

From his team, John and Rory Smith would cover the western side of the property, while Special Agents Jordan and Ryker would cover the eastern side. Special Agent Ted Graham would cover the northern end of the estate, while the captain, Duke Lawson, Clark, and Dr. Brill would be out of camera range in the surveillance van hidden near the entry to the property.

Detective Miles Watson would be in a backup position behind the agents on the east side. And Tom Ratcliff, a local detective, would mirror that position on the west by placing himself behind John, Rory, and Scooby.

In a forward position, Scooby would act as a decoy by entering the property and creating a distraction that would, hopefully, lure Winston outside. So, they needed to come up with a convincing reason for him to be wandering the property. Suggestions included straying off course while hunting, keeping an eye on wandering kids or pets, or even surveying the surrounding area.

Apparently, Scooby would be the perfect bait due to his non-threatening persona and his ability to create innocent scenarios that rarely aroused suspicion. His goal would be to draw Winston as far away from the house as possible. If successful, John's team would enter the home while the others prevented Winston from reentering.

The instincts of most people would send them frantically racing in to save a victim, but real pros knew better. Every move of a mission had to be carefully planned. It was the only way to prevent dangerous reactions from the suspect or other unknowns. And with Winston, perhaps not solidly connected to reality, the accepted theory would be especially true in his case.

Special Agent Jordan explained that they should be in place before dawn to minimize the chance of anyone seeing them take their positions. He relayed the weather forecast, which showed some possible fog in the early hours, which would fortunately work in their favor.

They discussed weaponry and gear, transportation to the location, and their state of readiness from the moment of arrival. Even though the entire team would be linked up with headsets, they would still need to be deathly quiet during the surveillance period.

Critical agreements were made. Special Agents Dan and Jaye would handle the arrest of Winston along with Scooby so that John, Ted, and Rory could enter the house to search for Angela. Tom and Miles would offer backup wherever needed. If the team could secure Winston, everyone in the surveillance van would be free to enter the property, offering additional assistance.

Special Agent Jordan went over the plan one last time, covering positions, roles, and timing. He briefed the room on the outlying backup, who would be working behind the scenes, double-checking to make sure all technology was functioning perfectly. They would also clear entry through other properties to establish a secure perimeter and manage the numerous other details supporting a complex mission.

"Okay, Scooby," Agent Jordan said. "What's the verdict on your character?"

"Hmm," he murmured. "Well, I really like the surveyor angle because it just seems the most believable to me. But I'll need to get up to speed on a little lingo."

Duke Lawson, the quietest member of John's team, spoke up. "Well, I can help you there. I was a surveyor for nine years before joining the force."

"Facts?" Scooby asked. "Man, that's great."

"Yeah, I still have all of my equipment," Duke said. "Too bad it's not here in Utah."

"Oh yeah, but maybe we can locate some gear around here," Scooby suggested.

"I can help make calls," Duke said. "Hey, maybe I should play a second surveyor since I already know the job and the lingo. They do work in teams."

"It would leave us with one less person in the van, but that's fine. We've got it covered," interjected Captain Williams.

"Sir, you know that Dr. Brill will be joining you, right?" John asked.

"Yeah, plenty of room," he said.

After a brief discussion with Agent Jordan, John called for everyone's attention. "Look, neither of us is a fan of changing up details late in the game. But everything about this operation has been last minute, so what's one more thing? And the kicker is, we actually both like the idea.

"It will look legit and give us two guys in a forward position to deal with Winston from the get-go. Plus, Dan, our trained sniper, and others can have their sights locked on him from the moment he steps foot outside."

He turned to Scooby and Duke. "Okay, you two, we like it, but you've got some homework to do. Scooby, just make sure you enter the property alone at first so our target isn't too spooked."

Agent Jordan spoke up. "After you quickly explain your mistaken intrusion, you can introduce your partner, Duke, who is just a few steps behind. Be apologetic and say things like 'sorry,' 'we'll get out of here,' or 'didn't mean to intrude.' But to delay him, ask questions too, such as 'Have you ever had your property surveyed?' You know, stuff like that. You guys know the drill."

John went back to the images up front and did one last play-by-play of the action for the following morning. The only change indicated was the addition of Duke as the second surveyor on the west side. As he spoke, every eye was glued to the screen as if committing each move to memory.

On instinct, he took a moment to give the team a little more information about Angela and her family. While most in the room had worked on child abduction cases and already knew the awful feeling in the pit of their stomachs, the extra detail seemed to cause a stirring.

John had inadvertently charged up the room.

"We finally have a good lead, and after meeting all of you, I feel like we have the right team," he announced. "The plan is solid, so let's get out there and do what we do. Dan, any last-minute notes?"

"For the guys who are entering the house, just remember we don't know what we might find in there," Agent Jordan said. "And depending on this guy's mental state, there could even be traps. Gear up, stay alert, and prepare for anything. We've got a lot of ground to cover, so let's head out."

The gang was piling back into the shuttle when John leaned over and whispered to Clark. "After everything we've been through, can you believe we are actually standing here, right in the middle of an active mission?"

Clark grinned. "It's like a strange dream but somehow familiar at the same time. Kind of like the rest of my life, I guess. It's weird, but I can feel Drake's presence, his fire for the case. It's almost as if his spirit won't rest until we find her."

"Wow!" John said, shaking his head. "Well, you keep tapping in. And God, I hope we're right about this."

John offered his fist. "Let's do it for Drake!"

"For Drake," echoed Clark.

TWENTY-TWO

PROVIDENCE

The weatherman was right. An oppressive fog blanketed the entire area as the team moved into position. Hazy conditions made the undertaking more challenging, but everyone arrived on time and eventually settled in according to plan.

Clark and Dr. Brill had front-row seats in the surveillance van stationed at a nearby, predetermined location.

"Is it my imagination, or is the fog starting to lift?" Dr. Brill asked.

"No, I think you're right," Clark said. "I'm not sure how much longer we can count on the extra atmospheric cover."

Dr. Brill spun around to look at him, but he just shook his head and grinned. "I don't know. Don't ask."

Captain Williams was up front, glued to his phone, while Ryan performed a thorough check of all communication devices and monitored equipment.

When Scooby and Duke appeared on one of the screens, Clark said, "Wonder how those two are feeling this morning?"

"Apparently, they spent most of the night going over surveying procedure and vernacular," Ryan interjected. "But they seem good. I heard them say they were ahead of schedule and using the extra time to double-check protective gear."

Dr. Brill smiled. "They look very authentic."

"Yeah, that's good," Clark said. "For the mission to go according to plan, they're going to have to pull off an innocent but believable intrusion. Being undercover requires a certain plausibility and composure, along with a natural aptitude for improvisation at a moment's notice."

When Clark stopped and stared at Dr. Brill, she gave him another one of her knowing smiles.

"Did I just say that?" he asked.

She shook her head. "Just go with it, Clark."

In the background, Clark heard Ryan mention that he and the captain had gone out earlier and placed a few reconnaissance drones in the outlying regions of the property.

"Oh, yeah?" Clark said. "Think you'll need 'em?"

"Yeah, maybe," Ryan said. "While we were out, we discovered a security camera we missed. Had to update the team with avoidance instructions."

"Oh, wow," Clark said. "That was lucky."

After fiddling around for a while longer, Ryan sat back and put his feet up. He finally seemed satisfied that everything was synchronized and working perfectly. The support van with video, audio, phones, maps, and screens lit up everywhere was truly a rolling, technical marvel. With all of the tools and the best agents at their disposal, Clark knew the mission was ready.

He checked on Scooby again and could see that he seemed confidently settled into his forward position.

Clearly displayed on the next screen over was the same van that had been in the driveway the day before. He'd overheard the captain giving the surveyors a brief on the vehicle, explaining that its very presence was the strongest indication that Winston was there.

As the minutes ticked off and the fog continued its climb, Clark could feel the day bringing them closer and closer to the risky encounter. If they could just see some sign that the suspect was awake, things would, hopefully, kick off and go according to plan.

Scooby and Duke seemed to be following instructions to a tee, waiting patiently for the go-ahead from Special Agent Jordan. That would be their cue to begin the well-rehearsed ruse, and the operation would be underway.

On another monitor, Agent Jordan stood frozen, seemingly awaiting any sign of life in the house, when suddenly he flinched. Startled, Clark followed the direction of his gaze to an adjacent screen, where a shadowy image flashed past the front window.

"What is it?" Dr. Brill asked.

"Movement," he whispered.

"What?" Captain Williams said, stepping quickly to the screens.

The development seemed to have hypnotized Agent Jordan, who, without taking his eyes off the scene, alerted the team, placing them on standby.

Clark did a quick scan of each monitor and could see that everyone's eyes, like laser beams, were suddenly locked on the front of the house.

There it was again. The vague figure, who had stopped this time and seemed to be adjusting the blinds.

"Hold your positions!" whispered Agent Jordan.

That's when the entire front room suddenly lit up, causing Dr. Brill to jump.

"Oh, geez. Sorry," she sighed.

They all stood motionless as if a spell had fallen over the van.

The light seemed to be coming from a large TV screen, suggesting the tenant might be going through some sort of morning routine. And since the process could potentially involve Angela, Clark knew they would want to get him outside before that could happen.

The agents seemed to be assessing the situation when the outline of a man approached the window. This time, the man boldly stepped forward, stood in clear view, and looked out over the property, gazing in their very direction.

The disturbing action made Clark shiver.

Even though the team members were safe and couldn't be seen, he noticed the uncomfortable eye contact between them. Watching the target had to be like watching a suspect through a secret mirror. You know they can't see through it but sometimes it feels like they're staring right at you.

However, this was a little different. The sensation was unnerving, but almost irrelevant by then, as the time was so close. Serious tension arose from trying to anticipate the critical moment.

Faintly, through their devices came Agent Jordan's voice. "Stand by."

"John, are we good?" he asked.

"We're good," whispered John.

"Scooby, Duke . . . on my cue," Dan primed.

"Move in!"

Scooby was fumbling with equipment when he stepped out of the trees on the western side of the property. He looked back and forth from the drawings in his hand to the actual property several times, intentionally projecting a state of confusion. He seemed to be scanning the property, paying special attention to the front window, but the man who had been standing there had disappeared.

Clark's instincts were telling him that Winston had already gotten a glimpse of Scooby.

"They're here!" came a wild shout from inside. "Get up! It's time. You know what to do. The code. The code is 8-1-1-8. That's 8-1-1-8. Go, now!"

When the front door crashed open, Clark got his first look at a man fitting the perfect description of Winston. The subject came charging out, confronting the stranger on his property, with a rifle pointed right in Scooby's direction.

"What the hell are you doing on my property?" he demanded.

"Oh man, I'm so sorry," began Scooby in his casual, charming way. "My buddy and I were surveying some adjacent land over here, and I guess we got off track."

He was still doing his creative best to explain the mistake when Duke stepped out of the woods. Winston looked shocked and immediately took an awkward step backward. Once he regained his footing, he began to move the rifle back and forth between the two of them.

"Hey man, we don't want any trouble," Duke said coolly. He put his hands up in front of him, keeping them low, near his concealed weapon. "It's an innocent mistake. We just got a little off course."

"Yeah, I'd say you did," accused Winston. "If you're surveyors, you two aren't very good at what you do, are you?"

"Well, we like to think so, but we did kind of mess up this morning," Scooby admitted. "Sorry."

After the apology, Clark was sure he'd seen the suspicion level on Winston's face diminish. Scooby's famous ability to put people at ease truly was a gift.

"We were having trouble finding the main marker on the next lot over, and I guess we just didn't realize how far we'd strayed," added Scooby. "Man, I know this is our fault, but I'd sure feel a whole lot better if you would put that gun away."

Agent Jordan's team was silently moving forward, using the vehicle and house as fresh cover, placing them nearer the action.

At the same time but seemingly unaware, Winston had been stepping backward. Reacting to his shift in position, Agent Jordan and the team halted their own progress. Within seconds, they stood motionless and perfectly silent as the target drew closer and closer.

Clark watched as the fake surveyors kept Winston distracted while John and his team stealthily made their way into the home. Their body cameras allowed him to feel like he was right there with them as they slowly and methodically cleared the upstairs rooms.

No sign of Angela.

It was frustrating to watch, but there was still a lot of ground to cover. So, he stayed glued to the monitors as John and the others carefully continued to inspect every threatening inch.

Silent instructions were signaled as they headed toward the lower level, where a glow emanated from an open door. With every step closer, the glittery light reflected on John's face, illuminating his piercing, fixed expression.

Clark was almost positive he'd seen the room from the outside only minutes earlier. He was sure it was dark. His first instinct was to warn them, but then a sudden sense of calm descended. Somehow, he knew John would take every precaution.

His eyes darted to another screen, where Winston was throwing around his imposing voice again, declaring, "No, I won't be putting this gun down, and you two can just go right back the way you came."

"Freeze!" came Agent Jordan's startling command from the right, just behind Winston.

On instinct, the subject turned in that direction, where Special Agents Jordan and Ryker were planted close-range, with sights aimed directly on him.

In that split second, Scooby stepped forward, blocked the rifle, and gave him a powerful elbow to the chest. Winston dropped the gun as he fell backward, but Duke was there to secure it immediately. Swarming agents encircled the scene, and within seconds, every gun was trained dead on Winston.

The surveillance van received an immediate all-clear from Tom Ratcliff, who was now holding a new position on the western side of the property.

"If Tom knows me like I think he does, he's expecting me to come racing into the action any second," Ryan said, sporting a big grin and already driving too fast. As if he'd anticipated the prediction, Ryan Gear had already disengaged the electronic gate and was tearing through it on his way to the scene.

Clark, Dr. Brill, and the captain held on for dear life.

When they came to a stop, Captain Williams glaringly rolled his eyes at Ryan and then cautioned everyone to stay in their current positions until he was positive things were under control.

Clark saw that the other law enforcement vehicles, which had been stationed around the area to secure the perimeter, had followed them in.

Agents Ryker and Jordan dragged Winston to his feet, searched him for weapons, and placed him in handcuffs. Once he was no longer in control, his countenance changed dramatically. To Clark, he was behaving more like a victim, with his head hanging down and his body collapsing.

"Where's Angela?" demanded Agent Jordan.

Winston smiled defiantly. "She won't go with you. She knows what to do."

Not so hidden in the menacing comment was an admission that Angela was there. But even if the statement was true, there was no way of knowing what condition they might find her in. Every part of Clark's being was praying for the best-case scenario, where she would be unharmed. But at that point, if they could just find her alive, he'd take it.

John, Ted, and Rory were making their way down the stairs to the lower level when a call from Agent Jordan stopped them cold.

He relayed Winston's ominous comments and recommended extra caution.

"I'm still going in," announced John. "Backup's close behind."

Clark watched as John quietly continued down the wooden steps until he reached the second one from the bottom. As soon as his foot landed, the plank moaned like an old screen door. If anyone was in that room, Clark knew he'd been compromised.

"Angela?" John called. Nothing. "Angela, are you in there?" Not a sound.

"I'm with the police, sweetie, and we want to help you," he added softly.

After a few seconds, he took the final step onto the landing. Just as he leaned forward, an ominous sound rang out—the unmistakable rack of a semiautomatic. The frightening reality was that it hadn't come from the team. It had come from the strange room.

John quickly motioned for the agents to retreat up the stairs, where he had them wait safely on the first floor. He hustled outside and straight to Agent Jordan, where Clark was sure they were about to reassess the plan.

"John, was that what I think?" asked Dan.

"Someone racked a semi," John said.

"Damn! And no sign of the girl?" Dan asked.

"No," John sighed. "If we could just get a look in that room without going inside."

"Hey, we could use one of the drones," Ryan said, standing close by. "I'm already bringing them in, so I could try to position one at the basement window."

"Do it," clipped Agent Jordan.

"How soon will it be here?" John asked.

"Thirty seconds," Ryan promised.

John nodded and raced back inside.

With Winston in handcuffs and held securely in one of the police vehicles, everyone else was cleared and stationed around the property. Clark, on the other hand, was just about to leave the van when Agents Jordan and Ryker rushed in. They were discussing monitoring the footage from the drone, and a sudden impulse compelled him to stay a while longer.

Another nudge from Drake?

Whatever it was, he was going with it. There wasn't enough time to analyze why he was feeling perfectly at home in the middle of a dangerous operation.

John and several others were linked to the drone footage from their devices. Everyone with a view of a screen could watch as Ryan expertly guided the drone to the basement window on the west side of the property. He moved it all around, apparently searching for the best vantage point, but was unable to locate Angela or anyone else in the room. He repeated the scan, continually making adjustments.

After a number of passes, Clark called out, "Wait, Ryan. Go back."

"What?" Agent Jordan asked.

"Hang on. I think I saw something," Clark said, carefully watching Ryan back up the scan. "There! Stop! Look . . . in the mirror."

The goosebumps must have traveled like a virus.

An audible gasp came from the team as they studied the image coming into view. Angela's little vanity mirror was reflecting a new nightmare. Just under the window, where the drone was hovering, sat a little girl at the head of the bed, with a loaded gun pointed right at the doorway.

"Dr. Brill exhaled, "Oh, God . . . it's Angela! She's alive!"

"Yeah, thank God!" Clark said. "But she has to be so scared. We've got to get that gun out of her hands."

He turned to Agent Jordan. "You know, I was just thinking with all she's been through, maybe she'd be more likely to talk to a woman.

And since we have Dr. Brill and Agent Ryker here, do you think one of them should try?"

"Do you read minds too?" Dan asked. "That's exactly what I was thinking."

"Sorry. I shouldn't have spoken up," Clark said. "I don't know where that came from."

"No, it's a good idea," Dan said, offering a high five. "You sure you're not a detective?"

Clark grinned, and Agent Jordan turned his attention to Dr. Brill. "You okay with this, Doc?"

"Of course," she said. "Most of the cases I've helped with have involved parental abductions, where the child is rarely hurt, but reasoning with a child is still reasoning with a child. This is all about being gentle and reassuring her that we're here to help her and get her back to her family."

"Right, but there's a weapon," he reminded her. "You just need to get her to put it down safely, and Jaye can take it from there. She'll be right with you."

"Okay," she said. "I've done these intercessions before. I'm ready."

Agent Jordan whispered hasty instructions to Jaye Ryker as they all followed him outside. She grabbed a Kevlar vest and helped Dr. Brill into it as they ran toward the house.

"Be careful, Clark," shouted Dr. Brill over her shoulder.

"You be careful, Doc," he called. "I'm going to get as close as I can." He hurried across the lawn and settled near the window, where Ryan was keeping the drone in position.

Agent Jordan updated John and released the first backups, allowing Jaye and Dr. Brill to take their places. The fresh team quickly exchanged a few whispers and hand signals before starting quietly down the stairs. When they reached the bottom step, Dr. Brill made final eye contact with Jaye, took a deep breath, and then exhaled slowly.

"Angela," she said in a soothing voice.

No answer.

"Angela, my name's Dr. Brill," she said softly. "And I'm here to help you. I'm so sorry you've had to go through all of this. But you're safe now, and I want to help you get home to your mom and dad."

Nothing.

"There are lots of people with me who are worried about you too, and they want to make sure you get home," she said. "We'd all feel so much better if we could hear your voice. Would you please say something—anything—so we know you're okay?"

It was clear from the drone footage that Angela had dropped her head at that moment. Clark could see her shoulders trembling and realized she must be crying. Tears could sometimes be a good sign, but Angela seemed to lose momentary awareness of the gun and let it fall to her side.

Clark flinched. *We've got to secure that weapon.*

Just then, an unexpected sound caused the whole team to jump. Through sobs came the first, sweet sound of Angela's voice, "I . . . I don't know if I'm okay."

"It's okay, honey. You're probably just scared," lulled Dr. Brill.

"I . . . I don't know what to do," Angela cried.

"I know. I'd be confused too," comforted Dr. Brill. "But I promise you, you can trust us."

Angela shook her head. "Winston said don't trust anyone. He said you're here to hurt us."

"That is not true, sweetie. There are a lot of great people out here that just want to help get you home," Dr. Brill promised.

"Who else is here?" she asked through ragged breaths

"Oh, some detectives and FBI agents, and even the guy who helped us find you," announced Dr. Brill.

"Is he the police?" Angela whimpered.

Dr. Brill shook her head. "No, but he helped the police find you."

"Why?" she asked.

"Well," Dr. Brill said. "He's a really good person who likes kids a lot and thought it was the right thing to do."

"But how did he know I was here?" Angela asked without tears this time.

"He has a very special way of figuring things out. Maybe he can tell you about it after we get you home," Dr. Brill said.

"What's his name?" Angela asked softly.

"It's Clark. But for right now, honey, we've got to get the gun put away and make sure you're safe," redirected Dr. Brill.

"No, don't come in!" cried Angela, raising the gun.

"Okay, sweetie," Dr. Brill comforted while looking to Jaye for any help. "I'm still right here."

"I want my dad," Angela cried.

Dr. Brill took a deep breath and tried again. "I know, honey. Angela, your mom and dad miss you so much. We're going to get you back to them, but I need you to help me do it."

Nothing.

"Angela?" called Dr. Brill.

After a long pause, she answered, sniffling, "Can Clark come in too?"

"Oh, honey, that's probably not a good idea," Dr. Brill said.

"You said he cares about kids," Angela said.

"Yes, he does, sweetie. Okay, let me check," Dr. Brill said, anxiously looking over at Jaye again.

After exchanging a few whispers and hand signals, she said, "Angela, I'm going to try to find Clark. My sweet friend, Jaye, with the FBI, will wait right here until I get back."

She raced quietly outside, where she ran the innocent request by John and Agent Jordan. "No. That's not happening," Dan said.

Before John could interject, Clark came racing to within earshot and pressed hard for it. "John, there's always risk, but I'm not worried. Who knows what she's thinking? But if my presence makes her feel safer, I want to do it."

John was a little caught off guard by the level of passion in Clark's voice. Something about it was giving him powerful Drake vibes again.

"Dan, I know it doesn't make sense. It's just a childish request. But we're out of time. And maybe it could help," John said.

Agent Jordan shook his head. "No, we can't put him in an armed situation."

Clark spoke up. "Look, knowing I like kids probably makes her feel safe, and she wants me to come in, right? What if we make it conditional? We can work with that. Angela has to put the gun down safely for me to enter."

John and Agent Jordan both looked stunned.

"John, I want to go in," begged Clark. "I need to go in!"

Something in that final plea caused the hair to stand up on the back of John's neck.

"Dan, I'd normally be right there with you," John said. "But trust me, part of Drake is living on in Clark. With Clark, we get Drake, and I'd trust him with my life. He wanted to rescue Angela more than anything in the world. His heart and Clark's phenomenon have gotten us this far. Let's trust them this one last time."

The seconds were ticking.

"Dan!" barked John.

Dan paced and mumbled under his breath, "They're going to have our badges."

"It could work!" urged John. "And there's no time left."

Agent Jordan tossed his vest to Clark. "Do it."

✳

Dr. Brill raced back into position and sweetly said, "Okay, honey. Clark's on his way."

"Hi, Angela," he said just a few seconds later. "I'm Clark. I am so glad you're okay!"

"Me too," she sniffled. "Are you coming in?"

"I want to, but they'll only let me come in if the room is safe," he explained. "So, we need you to, very carefully, lay the gun down on the floor."

"Wait, but you really like kids, right?" she asked.

"I sure do," Clark said. "My wife and I want to have a little girl just like you one day."

"You do?"

"Yeah. And once you're safe, I can tell you all about it," Clark said. "But the first thing we have to do is put the gun away so no one gets hurt, especially you."

"Winston said I'm only supposed to give it to him," she said.

"Well, he's in the police car and can't hurt you or keep you here anymore," explained Clark. "We have a big team, and we're going to make sure you get home safely."

"I know how to put the gun away," she said. "Winston taught me."

"No!" Clark said, flinching, "My friend Jaye, with the FBI, needs to do it, sweetie."

"Why?" she asked.

"Because even though you know how to do it, Jaye's had a lot more experience, so everyone will be safer that way," explained Clark.

"Okay," she whispered.

"Thanks for trusting me," Clark said. "Now I'm going to have to trust you too, right?"

"Yeah," she said.

"Good," Clark praised. "Can you lay the gun on the floor very softly and then get in the middle of the bed?"

Angela looked at the gun one last time before slowly and delicately placing it on the lush area rug at her feet. "Okay," she said.

"Good, sweetie. Now listen carefully," he began. "When we come into the room, you have to stay completely still. Can you tell me where the gun is right now?"

"On my rug. On the floor," she replied.

"You're all by yourself, right?" Clark asked.

"Yes," she said.

"Okay, that's good, don't move at all," instructed Clark. "My friend Jaye is coming in first, and she's going to walk over and safely put the gun away. But don't worry, I'll be right with her."

While he was negotiating, John and Agent Jordan were moving into closer positions, passing Dr. Brill, who was still waiting on the stairs. Even though backup would only be a few steps behind, Clark knew things could still go wrong. But after one final look at the drone footage to confirm that Angela was centered safely on her bed, he signaled Jaye.

She cautiously peeked to her left and then stepped just inside the doorway. Clark followed and got his first glimpse of the beautiful, desperate little girl. There she was—real—the same girl he had seen in his visions. He wanted to cry.

"Hi, sweetie," he said. "Please don't move, okay?"

Angela just shook her head up and down and started to cry as Jaye stepped softly but with purpose toward the firearm. To Clark, it looked like her eyes were locked on Angela and the gun almost simultaneously. She reached out, covered the gun with her hand, and slid it even farther away from Angela. Within seconds, she had skillfully taken possession of the weapon.

"Guys," she called. But John and Agent Jordan were already in the room.

"Hot," she said, handing it over.

"Hi, Angela," Clark said, smiling and moving closer. "These are all my friends. And just to be safe, they have to make sure no one else is down here, okay?"

"Okay," she whimpered.

John and Dan secured her room and then continued down the hallway.

That's when Clark fell to his knees and reached out his arms. "I am so, so sorry, sweetie, for everything you've been through. But I promise you're safe now. We're not going to let anything happen to you."

Angela seemed to study his face for a minute and then, while sobbing with her whole body, raced into his arms and collapsed. "Thank you for finding me," she cried.

The terrified little girl seemed to trust him completely and, for the first time, he knew what it felt like to be a protective parent. If the feeling foreshadowed his role as a father, he knew his very best days lay ahead.

After waiting safely on the sidelines for her call to enter, Dr. Brill walked into the room, beaming.

"This is Dr. Brill," Clark said. "She's a great friend who helped us find you."

"Hi, Angela," Dr. Brill said. "We're all so happy you're okay."

Angela dropped her head and smiled. "Me too."

"You did a great job, sweetie," Clark said. "So proud of you."

Angela hadn't heard words like that in a long time, and the sparkle in her eyes said it felt good.

"Come on, let's get you home to your mom and dad," Dr. Brill proclaimed, reaching out her hand.

But Angela hesitated. "What about Clark?"

"I'll be right behind you, I promise," he said. "I just need to contact a friend for a second."

After they left the room, he heard loud footsteps just before John and Agent Jordan reappeared.

"All clear," John said as they quickly passed through. "It's our caller. We've got a room full of evidence."

Within seconds, the room was quiet again.

Clark stayed on his knees and closed his eyes. "Rest easy, my friend. Angela's safe. We got him."

TWENTY-THREE

SWORN TO SECRECY

When Clark stepped outside, he found himself immersed in a brand-new flurry of activity. No matter where he looked, he could see individual team members tying up various aspects of the mission.

Since it was still early, John had been working with Mary to see if she could finagle quick flights home. If things worked out, Chad and Jacki Sweet would be invited to the office for the breathtaking news later that day. But for the moment, everyone on the team was sworn to secrecy.

"Sorry to make you guys withhold the good news," John said. "But I really want to break it to the Sweets the right way, not over the phone. It's always better in person.

"And, Dr. Brill, that's where you come in," he added. "Having you there will provide additional support for the family."

"Of course," she said with a bright smile.

Clark thought about how her hunch had led them to the extraordinary outcome they were all witnessing. *No wonder she can barely contain her joy.*

And he felt the same way. While struggling to incorporate the phenomenon into his own life, he'd been able to help navigate the rescue of a missing child. The whole thing was surreal.

John's phone rang out. "Hey, how's it looking?" he answered.

Mary's voice came over the speaker. "Well, I placed the calls, and everyone will be here, even Ashley Benson. I just told them you had some new information to share."

"Perfect," John said.

"And I can't believe it, but you're all on the same flight back," she added.

"That's great. Thanks, Mary!" gushed John. "You're amazing. Just send the details and remind me to take you to dinner."

"Yeah . . . uh, okay," she laughed. "See you when you get back."

John ended the call and turned to Clark. "Did I just say that?"

"Maybe your exhaustion is acting as truth serum," Clark teased.

"Funny," John said. "Well, whatever it is, it's time to get a handle on that part of my life anyway."

They crossed the driveway to discuss the wrap-up with the others and stopped near the unmarked car holding their perpetrator.

"Clark. Clark!" bellowed Winston through a partially open window. "Hey . . . I want to talk to Clark!"

"You're done talking!" barked John.

"Clark. Hey, Clark!" he shouted.

Clark grinned at John. "Trust me, I got this." He took a few steps forward and opened the rear door. Winston froze but then sat back with a self-satisfied grin on his face. "Clark Steele, with Drake Harrison's heart."

But before he could speak another word, Clark said, "No offense, but—" and slammed the door in his face.

"Nice!" John said, hitting him with a high five. "Drake would approve."

Once they joined the others, the discussion centered on the Utah team that would oversee the collection and processing of evidence in the days ahead. But the ultimate goal was to continue state-to-state

collaboration until Winston was charged with every provable offense, and the Sweet family could begin to feel the onset of justice.

When Clark looked up, he noticed Angela standing with Dr.
Brill and a few others. "There she is," he told John. "I'll be right back."
But on his way over, Agent Jordan intercepted him to offer compli-
ments on the mission.

While they spoke, he could see Angela tugging on Dr. Brill's arm
and whispering in her ear. At the perfect moment, Dr. Brill gave her a
warm smile, took her hand, and led her straight to him.

"Hey, Kiddo!" he said.

She marched right up and took his hand. "Can you stay
with me now?"

"Yep, I think we're stuck with each other until we get you home,"
he teased.

She actually giggled, and it melted his heart.

"I'll see you two in a few minutes," Dr. Brill said. "I'm going to
find John."

"Hey, let's see if we can find a place to sit down," Clark said.

They landed on the steps of the tech van, where he began to tell
her a little about the other members of the rescue team.

"You can meet them if you want," he offered.

"No," she said, squeezing his hand tighter.

"It's okay. You don't have to," he promised. "We can think about
it later."

John's famous voice came booming around the van before he did.
"Okay, you two. Our ride's here."

Angela took cover behind Clark's shoulder until he reminded
her that John had never stopped looking for her. After cautiously
reappearing, she coyly played around on the steps for a bit, slowly
moving in John's direction. Once she settled, she was sandwiched

perfectly between the two of them. Her sweet act of faith was subtle but encouraging.

The three of them walked toward the awaiting car where Clark could see Dr. Brill beaming from the rear seat. He and Angela piled in the back, and John rode shotgun.

"Hey, sweet girl," gushed Dr. Brill. "So glad we get to ride together."

"Hey, what about us guys?" teased Clark.

Dr. Brill grinned. "Oh, yeah. You guys too."

Angela giggled for the second time and, again, the sound was like therapy to Clark.

The ensuing conversation between the doctor and her tiny patient was a warm, back-and-forth exchange that flowed easily, laying the groundwork for a relationship based on trust.

Suddenly, Dr. Brill said, "Oh my gosh, honey! Are you hungry?"

"Yeah," she said. "I . . . I forgot to eat."

"Well, we'll fix that as soon as we stop," promised Clark.

But Dr. Brill was already holding up a snack bar she had retrieved from her bag. "No worries, this ought to do it until we can get you a proper meal."

✳

Just before boarding the plane, a revision of seating assignments was approved. Clark and Dr. Brill, who were not originally booked in the adjoining seats, would now be next to Angela. Apparently, she had begged them not to leave her side, and after a few quick adjustments, the sweet request was granted.

"This is good," Dr. Brill said. "The extra time will help me prepare her for the reunion with her family. Seeing each other for the first time can be very emotional and it's important not to overwhelm her in her fragile state."

"Yeah, makes sense," Clark said.

He watched with great reverence as the same strong, brilliant doctor who had changed his life displayed a gentler, more youthful side.

"Your mom and dad are going to be so happy to see you," she cooed.

Angela smiled. "They probably won't believe you found me."

"Well, we were never going to give up," interjected John from across the aisle. "But that guy right there, sitting next to you, he's the one who helped us find you."

She turned to Clark. "Are you going to tell me now?"

"I promise to share the whole story with you soon," he said. "But, for now, I don't want you to think about anything but feeling safe and happy and being on your way home!"

Now securely snuggled between Clark and Dr. Brill, Angela smiled, closed her eyes, and drifted off.

Since the mission in Utah had called for only restricted communication, Clark and John used the quiet time for a more open analysis. During the rescue, a pre-planned separation had been in place to ensure Clark's safety, and he understood completely. But when details began to change on the fly, fortunately, he'd gone with his instincts and exceeded all expectations.

"Well, you were really something back there," John said, leaning across the aisle with a fist bump.

Clark grinned, responded in kind, and asked, "What do you mean? And by the way, thanks again for bringing me along. I know you didn't have to."

"I wasn't leaving my partner behind," John teased. "And don't think I didn't notice your contribution . . . even discovering the reflection in the mirror."

Clark just shrugged it off. "I don't really know what made me stay in the van and watch the video. It's like I couldn't pull myself away."

"Well, I get it," John said. "So much of what we do is based on gut feelings. Agent Jordan told me that you also mentioned bringing in a woman to help put Angela at ease. Drake vibes again?"

"Probably," Clark smiled. "I hope I didn't step out of line. It just came out. Instead of fighting the inclinations, I'm trying to let them guide me. And I did feel a little more in control this time. Maybe I'm finally getting the hang of it.

"Hey, there's something I wanted to ask you," he added. "The second Angela ran to me, and I knew she was safe, was one of the greatest moments of my life. I've never felt anything like it. And I think it was a . . . a dad thing. Does it always feel euphoric when you rescue people?"

John grinned. "Why do you think we do this? Seriously, there's nothing better! We get the chance to rescue people from unspeakable situations. And, when it works out, it's the greatest feeling in the world. Drake used to be on a high for weeks after a mission like that."

"Well, I can believe it," Clark said. "But right now, it's almost like a dream."

"Yeah, I know," mused John. "Just think of all the time we spent trying to find a clue, and now she's sitting right there next to you on her way home."

"A miracle," Clark said.

John nodded. "Yep, but we did it! Well, with a little help from Drake."

"You think?" teased Clark.

"What I think is that I smell dinner," John said, inhaling the new aroma wafting through the cabin. "Once we're finished, let's try to squeeze in a nap. You're going to want to rest up for what you're about to witness next."

"I don't know, the day's already been one for the books," Clark said. "Angela's safe, and I'm no longer a suspect. Doesn't get any better than that."

John grinned. "That's a good day!"

The remainder of the journey was peaceful, with virtually no turbulence, and in the stillness of the flight, Clark got a quick rundown on Eddie's interference. But rather than spend a lot of time on it, John seemed more focused on preserving the good vibes from the rescue.

Once their caravan arrived back at the station, Clark helped Dr. Brill get her bearings. They found an isolated banquet table in a quiet corner of the conference room, where she could hold the final, in-depth chat with Angela before she was reunited with her parents.

Since both of them had already gained her trust, they agreed that one of them should stay close by at all times.

"Angela's case is a little different for me since we don't know all she's been through," explained Dr. Brill. "But sometimes, I'm a fan of just letting nature take its course when the family first sees each other. If they're a strong, loving family, that dynamic should see them through. But, with one caveat. I think we should caution the parents not to overwhelm her with too many questions too soon. All of that will come later in her sessions."

Clark completely understood the strategic approach and knew for certain that his new, little friend couldn't be in better hands. He stayed close and listened as Dr. Brill began to work her magic, chatting with Angela about her parents and the reunion that was only moments away.

The most heartwarming air of respect shone on his face throughout the conversation.

"I'm so glad we're back home," began Dr. Brill. "Aren't you?"

"Yeah," Angela whispered.

"And I'm really glad you got to know Clark," Dr. Brill added. "He's a good friend of mine. And John too. They're both very nice."

"Yeah," said Angela. "They never stopped looking for me."

"I know! And they found you and got you home on the very same day. How do you feel about that?" Dr. Brill asked.

"Happy," she said, wringing her hands. "But I'm kind of nervous."

"Well, you know what?" Dr. Brill replied. "That's a very normal feeling."

"Are my mom and dad here?" Angela asked.

"I'll have to check with John, but they should be here any minute," Dr. Brill said warmly. "Are you anxious to see them?"

Angela began to fidget with her hair. "Yeah, but I don't know what to do."

"Oh, don't worry, sweetie, you will," Dr. Brill promised. "It's something you never forget. Did you ever learn to ride a bike?"

"Yeah, I can ride by myself," she said proudly.

"Well, even though you haven't done it for a while, I'll bet you haven't forgotten," began Dr. Brill. "I think seeing your parents is going to be kind of like that. Your love for them is natural, and you'll just know what to do."

A bright smile lit up Angela's sweet face just before she said, "Can we see if they're here?"

"Sure, let me check," Dr. Brill said. "It'll just take a minute. You and Clark can visit while I'm gone."

Clark watched Dr. Brill stroll casually toward the exit but then quicken her pace after checking her phone.

Maybe they're here.

He could only imagine what it would be like in that room when they realized their prayers had been answered.

✳

Jacki burst into tears, and her whole body collapsed as she fell into her husband's arms.

"She's safe!" Chad cried, holding her tightly. The long embrace hinted at a necessary connection, where it took both of them to function as one.

John was beaming from the delivery of the overwhelmingly joyful news.

"John, please tell me this isn't a dream," Jacki pleaded.

"No, it's not a dream," he said. "She's safe, but I do need to share one thing with you before you see her."

"What?" she demanded. "Whatever it is, please tell me. I just want to see her."

With a wave, John handed it off to Dr. Brill.

"Mr. and Mrs. Sweet, we don't know all that Angela's been through yet, so in her best interest, we need to be as normal as possible while she acclimates," she began. "Her initial psychological evaluation is good, and she appears to be in great physical health. We still have a million questions, of course, but the best plan is to save them for her counseling sessions. It's imperative that we don't overstimulate her right now. In the beginning, her most urgent needs are love and normalcy, and the rest will come with time."

Chad and Jacki stood trembling, looking into each other's eyes. The awaiting reunion would be the first test, among many, to see if they could keep things positive and normal for their precious girl.

John nodded. "Okay. It's time."

Dr. Brill raced for the door. "Oh, wait, can you give me just a second to get back with Angela? I promised her I'd be right back."

Jacki whirled around to face John with a wounded look on her face. "More waiting?" But before John could react, Chad stepped in.

"I know the seconds feel like hours, Babe, but it's okay," he said. "She's here. She's safe."

Jacki squeezed his hand. "I know . . . I know . . . I just want to hold her."

"Me too," he whispered. "We're going to be a family again."

The flush on Chad's face made him look like a new man. After the abduction, he'd been forced to find a level of strength he'd never known and maintain it for the entire time Angela was gone. If he wanted to keep his wife and her sanity integrated, that was his only choice. And unfairly, he'd been living in that amplified state for way too long.

But from the moment John gave them the good news, his face seemed to shed traces of the long-held tension and take on a new vitality. He and his family were going to start life over again.

Finally, on John's cue, the Sweets followed him out the door and turned to look down the corridor to the right. Coming from the conference room, just past the break area, was their baby, with Clark and Dr. Brill on either side, all holding hands.

When Angela made eye contact with her mom and dad for the first time, Clark and Dr. Brill both flinched as if they'd felt a tiny shudder of static electricity.

Clark looked at Dr. Brill. "What was that?"

"Later," she whispered.

They knelt down, gently squeezed Angela's hands, and released her.

Jacki was already sobbing and running wildly in her direction but only made it a few steps before stumbling to the floor. Chad, who was right behind her, managed to only partially break her fall. But they both recovered quickly, landing on their knees with outstretched arms.

Jacki cried from deep inside, "Oh my God . . . my baby!"

"Mommy, Daddy!" sobbed Angela, racing into their arms.

"We've missed you so much," wept Jacki. "I love you. Are you okay?"

"Yeah," she cried. "I love you too."

The Sweets wrapped Angela up so tightly that she almost disappeared.

John gave Clark a knowing look. "What'd I tell you?"

"Yep, you were right," Clark said.

Chad and Jacki had their little girl safely in their arms, hugging her, kissing her, touching her hair, and checking her over as if praying she wasn't a dream.

Not only was she real, but she truly seemed okay. The nightmare was over.

From across the room, Mary was escorting Ashley into the touching scene. Even though she'd been briefed, she looked mystified, as if her mind still couldn't process the evolving miracle. From a distance, she stood frozen and seemingly unaware of the tears falling tenderly down her face.

While watching the magic unfold, her instinct must have been to rush in, but she resisted. And the self-control gave her sister and brother-in-law a great gift, more private time to revel in the magnitude of the precious moment.

But before long, Jacki looked her way and cried out, "Ash!" And in an instant, she was on the floor celebrating with her family.

"Ashley!" Angela screamed, jumping in her lap.

"Hey, sweet girl," Ashley said. "I've missed you so much."

The heartwarming reunion continued to unfold with family and witnesses rejoicing together.

When emotions began to settle down, Chad took Angela's small hands and softly said, "I love you, baby girl, and I'm so sorry I couldn't protect you."

She reached up and patted his face. "It's going to be okay now, Daddy."

The sweet, innocent gesture broke everyone. Even exhausted team members, who had been trained to control their emotions, were no longer able to fight it. Tears flowed, and an atmosphere of pure bliss overtook the room.

✳

"Thanks for everything, Doc," John said a bit later.

"You too," she said. "The work you did with Clark has been the best part of his therapy."

"Yeah," agreed Clark. "Once I realized that the memories could be related to a case, things started to make sense. And I'd always had the feeling that I was supposed to help."

"Well, you were a natural," Dr. Brill said. "I felt like I was working with John and Drake again. And I don't say that lightly. Drake was very special."

John nodded. "You got that right! And Clark's not half-bad either. He'd actually make a good detective."

"That, I can believe," she said. "But having him change careers wasn't part of our therapy plan."

"Well, you never know," John teased. "I'll be around, Clark, if you two want to reconsider. Anyway, thanks for everything, Doc."

"You too," she said. "I'm going to check on the Sweets. Clark, you good?"

"Yeah, Doc," he sighed. "More than good."

As she headed off, Ashley came rushing up to take her place. "Thank you so much for not giving up!" she gushed.

"Never an option," John said.

"I'm so happy for you and your family," added Clark.

"Thank you too, Clark, for everything," she said. "You know, it's just so painful to know that I didn't read Winston better from the beginning. If I had, I could have saved Angela . . . my family . . . everything they've been through. I wish he'd taken me instead."

"Well, you're all safe now, and that's what matters," John said. "But it's odd you should say that because it's possible you were his true target. Angela might have just been a bargaining tool. But, hey, please promise me you won't beat yourself up with all of this. Good people are fooled by predators all the time. They don't suspect devious behavior because their own minds are pure, the way it should be."

She smiled. "Thanks, John. And Clark, we sure wish you all the best with everything. You've been an absolute blessing to our family."

"It was my honor," he said.

"Well, we'll never forget what you did or about your incredible story!" Ashley said, turning to leave. "Remember how I like that stuff."

"I do," Clark said. "Maybe I can share a few more of the cases with you."

"Oooh . . . yes, please," she called over her shoulder.

TWENTY-FOUR

IN THE ZONE

Clark arrived early at the coffee shop and ordered the first round of java and a couple of breakfast croissants.

While looking out the window, he noticed a group of kids playing in the park across the street, with most parents keeping a close watch. However, there were a few spending a little too much time on their phones. With the kidnapping still top of mind, he wanted so badly to remind them that it only takes a second.

"Hey, it's kind of early for daydreaming, isn't it?" teased John after making the long trek over to the table.

Clark spun around at the resonant sound of his voice. "Oh, hey, Partner."

John was standing there with outstretched arms. "Baxter and Steele, together again."

"Dynamic duo," kidded Clark. "Hey, coffee and breakfast are already here."

"Looks good," John said, pulling up a chair.

"Man, have you been replaying everything, non-stop, like I have?" Clark asked.

"Oh, yeah," John said staccato style. "Nerve-racking and thrilling at the same time, isn't it?"

"You can say that again!" agreed Clark. "The highlight of a months-long roller coaster for me. And I'm still feeling the effects."

"Me too," John said. "You know, when I think about the time Drake and I spent on the investigation, it seems like years ago now instead of months.

"And after the accident, when the weight of the case shifted to me, honestly, it looked pretty hopeless. Then one day, like magic, you walked into my office and laid this unbelievable story on me. Who would have dreamed that you and your phenomenon would lead us to Angela?"

"Yeah, but Dr. Brill's intuition really launched the whole thing," Clark said. "All credit to her."

"Credit to me?" said a familiar face, approaching the table.

"Doc!" exclaimed Clark. "What are you doing here?"

"Well, John mentioned that you guys were meeting today and invited me to join you," she explained. "I really can't stay. I only have a few minutes, but I just had to stop by."

"Glad you could make it. Have a seat," John said. "Hey, how's your new specialty practice coming along?"

"Well, I can't talk about current patients without permission, of course," she explained. "But I can tell you they're extraordinary."

"I'm sure you'll get them on the right path like you did, Clark," John praised. "You know, when he showed up, it was hard to accept the phenomenon, but I'm glad I trusted you. And then, when he brought up images and facts that matched details in the case, I'll admit, I was hooked."

"Me too," Clark said. "When I started to accept that my visions might contain information from a case, my mind really began to open. But even though the revelation was validating and healing, I still had concerns. I wasn't sure where it would lead or if I was up for it."

"A first for all of us," Dr. Brill said, smiling. "But I knew you were up for it."

"Well, thanks," Clark said. "But I almost didn't have a choice—the flashes were too persistent."

Dr. Brill's eyes were soft, full of compassion. "Remember how we thought that Drake's characteristics and influence might have manifested more powerfully because of his intense desire to find Angela?"

Clark grinned. "Yeah, well, it still makes sense to me. Hey, and speaking of powerful, what was that surge I felt when Angela saw her parents?"

"You know what?" she said. "Because we were holding her hands, I think the love she felt for her mom and dad might have passed through us too. Guess that's another mystery we're going to have to investigate," she added with a wink.

"Hey, John," she said, "not to change the subject, but did Clark tell you I'm starting a support group for recipients, and invited him to be part of it?"

"Really?" John asked. "Clark, you'd be great at that. You really connect with people, and I'm sure they'll relate to what you've been through."

"Thanks," Clark said. "Yeah, I'm thinking about it."

"You have a lot to offer, Clark," praised Dr. Brill. "It wouldn't be the same without you."

"Well, thanks," he said. "I do feel like I've had endless experiences through all of this, so maybe there is something that would be helpful to someone. But it was really through spending time with you and John that I learned to relax and engage . . . trust the connection to Drake. And that was a game-changer—a complete change of heart if you will. It was like summoning him to guide my steps. But that part is so personal."

"I understand what you're saying," Dr. Brill said. "But there are still plenty of commonalities. And you might be surprised by how others relate to the even more unique aspects of your experience."

"Well, I hope you do it," John interjected. "Seriously, Clark, you do have a lot to offer. Drake would have been so impressed with you. Your instincts and willingness to get involved were inspiring and very much like . . . like Drake's energy."

"I could feel that!" beamed Clark. "The force of his cellular memories definitely led me in the right direction. And most of the time, it was like he was right there with me."

John nodded. "Yep, even I felt it. If it wasn't for the phenomenon connecting the two of you, who knows if we would ever have found Angela. And the way you handled the critical moments during the rescue, it's like you were in the zone. Going on instinct."

"Yeah, I don't know what came over me, but I'm glad it worked out the way it did," Clark said.

"I remember you telling me how natural it felt, Clark, like you just knew what to do," shared Dr. Brill.

"That's why I went to bat for him," John interjected. "I was feeling Drake vibes again."

"I know," Clark said, shaking his head. "It was strong, so I just went with it."

"And now Angela's back home, and here we are," grinned Dr. Brill. "I think we can all safely say we've shared a life-altering experience. But even though we've changed forever, it feels like it's time to find a new normal."

"Well, I'm ready for that," Clark said, smiling. "Oh, I meant to tell you guys, I got a nice call from Mr. Harrison the other day. They'd really like to stay in touch. Apparently, Mrs. Harrison insisted on it. She's so sweet.

"They were thrilled to hear that we found Angela and sent along congratulations. You know, I was just thinking they're among a very few people who could appreciate Drake's paranormal involvement as much as we do."

Dr. Brill nodded. "True! And I think staying connected is going to be a good thing for all of you."

"And as far as the details," John said, "you guys will figure it out."

"Speaking of figuring things out, what's up with you and Mary?" teased Clark.

John gave him a sideways glance. "What do you mean?"

Clark broke into a broad grin. "You know exactly what I mean. I'm not blind."

"Is Drake putting you up to this?" John asked. "He used to tease me about Mary all the time."

"Nope, just me. I think," laughed Clark.

Dr. Brill sat back, smiling, as if she were just a fly on the wall, observing their friendly banter.

"Okay, so I've always wanted to ask her out, but I wasn't sure how she'd feel about it," John said. "Plus, I've been a little hesitant to mix personal life with work. But I've come to my senses, and we're actually having dinner this weekend."

"Well, there's some more good news," Clark cheered. "Happy for you, man. I think you guys might be meant for each other. And you know it was past time for you to ask her out."

"Well . . . actually . . . she, sort of . . . asked me," stammered John.

Clark shook his head. "What? Okay, well, either way, it's great."

"I'm just hoping we can find something to talk about besides work," John said.

"You will. You guys get along great," Clark reminded him. "Just be yourselves."

"Yep, old rules are usually true," declared John.

"Now you sound like Dr. Brill," Clark said.

She smiled. "Just like me."

"Hey, you know what she told me the other day?" Clark said. "It was the coolest thing. Now that I have someone else's cells, preferences, and memories incorporated into my own, I asked her if I was still really me. Or if I'd lost some of myself."

"Well, there's a deep question," mused John.

"Right," Clark said. "Doc, since you're here, I'll let you tell him."

Dr. Brill looked off into the distance as if trying to recall the conversation. "Oh, I just told him, let's not think of it as subtraction, but rather addition. You are totally you but with additional gifts."

"I like it!" John said.

"You know, sometimes, I think about other recipients," Clark said, taking on a more serious tone. "What secrets are they carrying around? Would a person who couldn't sing or play music be able to after a transplant? Could someone else expand their intellect? We already know, firsthand, what a role it can play in crime-solving."

Dr. Brill nodded. "True. It's definitely powerful and, as I'm finding, sometimes even scary. You wouldn't believe how strangely it's manifesting in a current case. Don't be surprised if I call you guys for backup on this one."

"Always here for you, Doc," promised John.

"Always!" Clark agreed. "You know, some recipients even tell of eerie transformations, such as mannerisms...like the way they walk. And if you really dig deep, just imagine the other implications. Would medical conditions, age-related differences, or even cultural characteristics transfer?

"What if a doctor who found the cure to some deadly disease lost their life and donated organs? Could the secret to their medical breakthrough be transferred to a recipient? From personal experience, my answer would be a resounding 'yes.' And a case like that would change lives. The possibilities are endless if you ask me."

"They really are," agreed John. "I'm sure we'll all be following transplant stories more closely from now on."

Clark nodded in agreement. "I know. At this point, I just want to continue working the phenomenon into my own life and move forward. Rachel and I are ready for a family. You know, I wasn't going to say anything just yet, but we have an appointment to look into adoption."

"What?" exclaimed Dr. Brill. "Clark, that's awesome. I'm so happy for you guys!"

"That's great, Clark" added John.

"Thanks!" Clark said. "Yeah, we're ready! I feel more settled now. More in control."

Dr. Brill was glowing. "You're ready, Clark!"

"Even I can see that," John said. "Watching you with Angela was all I needed to see."

"Thanks," Clark said. "I'd already made a decision, but the feelings I felt during the rescue added something new. It was a heart thing. Again, a dad thing. I couldn't wait to tell Rachel about it. Anyway, I'll let you guys know when we hear something."

Dr. Brill smiled. "Great! I just can't wait."

John took a quick call while Clark and Dr. Brill continued to chat.

"Everything okay?" Clark asked a few minutes later.

"Yeah, just a quick update from Mary," John explained.

Clark nodded. "Hey, have they learned any more about Winston?"

"Yeah, a little more," offered John. "I still can't believe he was the caller. Did not fit the profile. Anyway, his parents were pretty helpful in getting him to talk. He's got multiple charges, so he'll be going away for a long while and getting the psychological help he needs."

"Thank God he wasn't a more violent person," Dr. Brill added. "But that said, he still terrorized a child and did who knows how much psychological damage."

"Right," John said.

"Did they ever figure out why he buried the evidence?" Clark asked.

"That one is weird," John said. "Remember, he was an expert landscaper, but we're still working on how he accessed the cemetery. Some of our own staff worked security over there, including Eddie, but none seemed to know anything. The captain, however, has an informant who claims Eddie sometimes took payoffs to disappear during his shift. He's denying it, of course, but we'll get it out of him.

"You know, Dr. Brill you were right on target about the psychology of what Winston did. So, apparently, throughout his life, whenever he had a problem, his dad gave him the same advice. He'd say, 'Son, deal with it. Then bury it.'"

"You've got to be kidding," Clark said.

John shook his head. "Nope. Obviously, Winston took the quip literally. See, you just never know how an unhealthy mind is going to process things."

"Psychological triggers," Dr. Brill said, shaking her head. "Well, my friends, I'm so sad to miss the rest of the visit, but some of us have to work."

Clark and John stood.

"Thanks for coming by, Doc," Clark said. "It was so great to see you. And count me in on the support group."

Dr. Brill's face lit up. "Clark, you made my day!"

"Good to see you, Doc," John said. "We'll talk soon."

They watched her until she was halfway across the room. "Take care, guys," she called over her shoulder.

"Man, there goes a bright light in the world," Clark said.

"No arguments from me," John replied.

"So, where were we?" Clark asked. "Winston's trigger?"

"Yeah, but it was his obsession with Ashley that really started the whole thing," John explained. "He showed up at a tearoom in disguise, where the sisters were together. That's when he overheard Jacki advise Ashley to stay away from the weird guy at work. So, he got angry and left.

"Apparently, that's when the scheming started. In his warped mind, Jacki had interfered with his plan to be with Ashley, and she had to pay. That was the catalyst for the abduction and the devious new pathway to Ashley. Can you believe an innocent comment like that started the whole thing?"

"Wow," Clark said. "What a nightmare for the family. I sure hope they're making up for lost time."

"I'm sure they are," John nodded. "They've been through hell, but they have Angela back, and she's doing great. Some families aren't so lucky."

"Anything new on Eddie?" Clark asked.

"Well, I hear, he might be facing some felonies," John explained. "All I know is, he'd better have a good attorney. And even if they give him any benefit of the doubt, his big theory was totally unfounded, not to mention unfair to you. His actions probably caused delays in the case. That thought still makes me crazy and I resent every wasted second, but mostly how he may have extended the family's grief."

"Yeah, I know," Clark nodded. "I didn't really understand exactly what was happening when he was questioning my alibi and other details, but I could feel the tension. That's when I thought about walking away."

"Thank God you didn't," John said. "I might still have an unsolved case on my hands."

Clark nodded. "Well, that was just it. I couldn't stop thinking about the family or that little girl."

"That's what keeps us around," John said.

"Oh, hey, Eddie did officially admit to taking the photo and misfiling the video footage," he continued. "He took the Resting Waters photo because he knew it was important to Drake. And he wanted to scan those video records to make sure there was no recorded evidence that identified him or any of his shady deals going down near the cemetery. We didn't have proof in our files, but thankfully the captain was able to secure incriminating footage through another channel."

"Still can't believe it was him," Clark said.

"I know," agreed John. "Makes me furious. Hey, remember your dream, the one where you saw an evidence room in the basement?"

Clark nodded. "Yeah, of course."

"You know what I think?" John asked. "I think it's possible that Eddie was down there, and Drake almost caught him."

"That would make sense," Clark agreed.

"Of course, Eddie claims all of his actions were about trying to solve the case," John said. "Yeah, whatever. If you ask me, the whole thing boils down to an insane case of jealousy. He just couldn't stand the thought of Drake solving another case, especially from the grave.

"Plus, the unique circumstances gave him a rare opportunity to impress Sherry," he added.

"Complicated dude," Clark said. "And he seemed like a pretty good guy."

"I know," John agreed. "Academy Award performance. As far as he goes, they still have a lot of details to unravel."

"Well, at least there's a happy ending for the Sweet family," Clark said.

"Yep, for sure," John declared. "We can feel good about that! And the captain will sort out the rest."

"Right," Clark said. "Was it out of character for Captain Riley to plan that sting?"

"Yeah, but I've got to say, he delivered," praised John. "I actually think he was jazzed about the whole thing. He hadn't been on an assignment like that in a long time."

"Yeah, I get it," Clark said. "Being right in the middle of things is way different than planning."

"Maybe it brought back the glory of his early days," kidded John.

Clark gave him an impish grin, and they both laughed.

"Well, it's been a wild ride, my friend," John said.

"That it has," Clark agreed. "But, in all seriousness, so worth it. Being part of the rescue and the reunion will stay with me forever."

John smiled. "Hey, before we head out, I wanted to run something by you. Remember when we were talking about looking into the cold case on Dr. Brill's husband?"

"Yeah," Clark brightened. "I've been thinking about that."

"Well, I've been doing some digging," John said. "And check this out. I found a starred photo in the evidence files. It's a missing leather journal, and for some reason, I remembered you saying there was a journal in one of your flashes."

"Yeah," Clark nodded. "I can still picture it."

"Well, humor me and take a look at this," John said, offering his phone. "This missing diary belongs to Tony Brill and might contain key information in the case."

Clark shook his head. "No! John . . . it's the same journal."

"I had a feeling," John said. "Ready to go again?"

THE END

www.ingramcontent.com/pod-product-compliance
Lightning Source LLC
Chambersburg PA
CBHW060415030726
47495CB00003B/596